Lost in the Never Woods

AIDEN THOMAS

LOST IN THE NEVER WOODS

Swoon READS

New York

A Swoon Reads Book

An imprint of Feiwel and Friends and Macmillan Publishing Group, LLC

120 Broadway, New York, NY 10271

Our books may be purchased in bulk for promotional, educational, or business use. Please contact your local bookseller or the Macmillan Corporate and Premium Sales Department at (800) 221-7945 ext. 5442 or by email at MacmillanSpecialMarkets@macmillan.com.

Library of Congress Cataloging-in-Publication Data
Names: Thomas, Aiden, author.
Title: Lost in the Never Woods / Aiden Thomas.
Description: First edition. | New York: Swoon Reads, 2021. | Summary: When children start to go missing in the local woods, eighteen-year-old Wendy Darling must face her fears and a past she cannot remember to rescue them in this novel based on Peter Pan.
Identifiers: LCCN 2019018603 | ISBN 9781250313973 (hardcover) | ISBN 9781250313980 (ebook)
Subjects: | CYAC: Missing children—Fiction. | Memory—Fiction. | Forests and forestry—Fiction. | Characters in literature—Fiction. | Mystery and detective stories.
Classification: LCC PZ7.1.T4479 Los 2020 | DDC [Fic]—dc23
LC record available at https://lccn.loc.gov/2019018603
Book design by Mike Burroughs

First edition, 2021

10 9 8 7 6 5 4 3 2 1

swoonreads.com

For every heavy heart that
had to grow up too fast

CHAPTER 1

Falling Stars

As Wendy Darling pushed through the door, all conversation died and every eye focused on her. As she stood there, files stacked in her arms, the whispers started in hushed tones. The hairs on the back of Wendy's neck prickled. As a lowly volunteer at the only hospital in town, Wendy had spent her day in the basement copying files. That part of the job was boring, but Wendy wanted to become a nurse. It probably wasn't the ideal way for the average teenager to spend their eighteenth birthday, but Wendy wanted to lie low and avoid attention.

And she was failing spectacularly.

The nurses' station was packed with people in scrubs and officers in uniforms, and they all watched Wendy as she hesitated in the doorway, trying not to drop her stack of papers.

Her sweaty hands were making the plastic folders harder to hold on to, so, even though her nerves told her to get out of there, Wendy hurriedly crossed the room and dumped them behind the desk. Curious eyes and the incoherent crackling of police officers' radios followed her.

"Lord, did you finish already?" Wendy started at the sudden appearance of Nurse Judy at her elbow.

"Uh—yeah." Wendy took a quick step back and dragged her hands through her short, blunt haircut. Nurse Judy was a small woman with a large presence, dressed in Snoopy scrubs. She had a booming voice that was perfect for talking over the sound of busy waiting rooms and a loud, unabashed laugh that she often used while teasing doctors.

"Dang, girl! You're making the rest of us look bad!" She took no nonsense and usually spoke her mind, which was why her tight-lipped smile and fidgeting hands made Wendy's stomach twist.

Wendy forced a small laugh that quickly died in her throat. Standing behind Nurse Judy, on the other side of the *U*-shaped nursing desk, was Officer Smith. The pale fluorescent lights bounced off his bald head and he stood with his chest puffed out and his thumbs tucked into the straps of his Kevlar vest. He stared at Wendy, mouth in a straight line as his square jaw worked on a piece of gum. No matter what time of year it was, Officer Smith always had a sunglasses tan framing his sharp eyes. He had a way of looking at you that made you feel guilty, even if you hadn't done anything wrong. It was a look that Wendy had been on the receiving end of many times over the past five years.

"Wendy." Her name always sounded gruff coming from him, like he was annoyed at the mere mention of her.

Wendy's head bobbed in an uncomfortable greeting. She wanted to ask what was going on, but the way everyone kept looking at her—

"There you are!" A sharp yank on Wendy's arm had her spinning around to Jordan's beaming face. "I was looking everywhere for you!" she said. Jordan Arroyo had been Wendy's best friend since middle school. If Wendy did anything outside her comfort zone, it was because Jordan was there cheering—and sometimes pushing—her along. It was Jordan who had talked her into applying to big-name colleges, and rejoiced with screaming and dancing when they both got into the University of Oregon. When Wendy worried that it was too far from Astoria and her parents, Jordan promised they'd make the four-hour drive back home together whenever Wendy wanted.

Wendy felt a small bit of relief. "I—"

"Are you done for the day?" Jordan's dark eyes cut to the stack of files. She was tall with warm brown skin that never broke out and had dark hair that usually framed her face in tight curls but was currently tied back in a ponytail.

"Yeah—"

"Great!" Before Wendy could object, Jordan snatched up their bags with one hand and pulled Wendy down the hall with the other. "Let's go!" Wendy half expected one of the three police officers to stop her, but even though they watched the two as they left—especially Officer Smith—no one said anything.

When the door closed behind them and they were alone in the hall, Wendy sucked in a deep breath. "What was that all about?" she asked, glancing quickly over her shoulder to see if anyone was going to follow them.

"What was what?" said Jordan.

Wendy had to take quick steps to keep up with Jordan's long, determined strides. "The cops and everyone."

"Pft, who knows!" Jordan said with a jerky shrug as she punched the code on the door to the nurses' break room.

Wendy frowned. Jordan never missed a chance for gossip. Any time anything interesting happened in the hospital—like a local boy shooting off his friend's toe when they were illegally hunting in the woods or a doctor making one of the medical assistants cry—Jordan was all over it. She bounced from person to person, poking for details and prodding for information, before finding Wendy and divulging everything she found out.

She was hiding something.

"Hey, hold on," Wendy said as tension clawed into her shoulders.

"Sit!" Jordan pushed her into a seat at the lopsided round table littered with paper plates and leftover takeout utensils. "Okay, I know you don't like celebrating your birthday—" Jordan blew through the room, snatching a pair of plastic forks and grabbing a Tupperware container from the old fridge. "But you're turning *eighteen*! So, I had to do *something*."

"Jordan."

"I made your favorite!" Jordan didn't so much as look up as her hands fumbled to get the Tupperware lid off. "See?" The smile on Jordan's face was shaky at best as she busied herself with placing a yellow cupcake on a small plate in front of Wendy. The dollop of chocolate frosting was melting down the side of the paper. "It didn't come out quite right, but you know I suck at baking."

Wendy's heart drummed in her throat. Why wouldn't Jordan look at her? "Jordan."

"But my dad ate, like, three and hasn't showed up at the emergency room," Jordan mused as she stuck a purple candle into the cupcake and lit it with a yellow lighter. "So it can't be that bad!"

"*Jordan,*" Wendy pressed insistently.

Jordan pushed the cupcake at Wendy, her wide smile looking more like a grimace. "Make a wish!"

"JORDAN!" Jordan cringed and even Wendy jumped at the loudness of her own voice. Finally, Jordan glanced up, her eyebrows tipped and lips pressed between her teeth.

"What's going on?" Wendy repeated, her words much more uneven now as she leaned forward. The heat of the candle brushed her chin. "Why are there so many cops here? What happened?"

When Jordan spoke, her voice was gentle. "Ashley Ford went missing."

It was like a giant hand pressed all of the air from Wendy's lungs. "Missing?" Automatically, Wendy pulled out her phone. She hadn't received an AMBER Alert, but the file room was concrete and got no cell phone reception.

"Earlier today," Jordan continued. She watched Wendy carefully as she spoke.

The room tilted. Wendy gripped the edge of the table with sweaty palms to steady herself. "But I just saw her this morning."

"Apparently, she was playing in the front yard. Her mom walked inside to get something, and when she walked back out, Ashley was gone."

Wendy knew Ashley well. When she wasn't doing paperwork, Wendy spent most of her time at the hospital in the pediatric clinic reading to kids or leading arts and crafts. Mrs. Ford was a patient at the hospital who regularly needed dialysis treatment, and when she had appointments, she left Ashley in the children's room with Wendy. Ashley was only eight years old, but she was smart and had an encyclopedic knowledge of trees. Just that morning, Ashley had been sitting on an oversized bean bag chair that practically swallowed up her petite form, rattling off the names of the trees she could see from the large windows.

"They can't find her?" Wendy asked. Jordan shook her head. No wonder everyone had been staring at her. "And Benjamin Lane?"

"They haven't found him yet, either." Jordan chewed on her bottom lip as she watched Wendy. "That makes two missing kids in the past twenty-four hours, but they've got loads of people looking," Jordan rushed to add, but her voice was muffled, like Wendy was listening to her underwater. "That's why the cops are here—asking folks who saw her last if they noticed anything suspicious . . ." Jordan trailed off, but Wendy knew what she was thinking.

Wendy's head swam. Benjamin Lane was a local boy who had gone missing yesterday afternoon. He was only ten years old, but he had a rebellious streak. Benjamin had run away from home once before, and everyone seemed to assume he was hiding out at a friend's house. It was an easy explanation that everyone in town was quick to accept, tutting about bad parenting and "kids these days."

Because in Astoria, Oregon, crime was practically nonexistent. Especially the sinister sort. Especially missing children. Except, of course . . .

Wendy's shoulders sank. "My brothers." Wendy swallowed hard. "Do they think—?"

Jordan shook her head vigorously and squeezed Wendy's shoulder. "There's no way this has anything to do with you. She probably just wandered off to a friend's house or something. Or they'll find her perfectly fine at a playground," she said, trying to sound certain, but it wasn't working on Wendy.

Dread settled over her at the thought of being questioned by the police again. At the idea of Ashley being lost and alone, or something even worse.

Wendy dropped her forehead into her hands, but pain suddenly seared across her chin. She lurched back from the candle flame with a hiss.

Jordan quickly blew it out. Purple wax dripped over chocolate. Cursing under her breath, Jordan quickly ran a brown paper towel under water from the sink and handed it to Wendy. "Are you okay?"

Wendy pressed the cool paper towel to the small welt forming on her chin. "Yeah." She winced. "It's just a little burn."

"That's not what I meant," Jordan said.

Wendy avoided her gaze. "I want to go home."

Heads turned to follow them through the lobby and out the main door. Jordan filled Wendy's silence, recounting her harrowing adventures in baking the cupcakes and how the first batch had somehow come out even more liquidy than before she'd put them into the oven.

In the parking lot, the sun had just set below the jagged ridge of tree-lined hills to the west. Wendy eyed the lingering rays of sun drenching the distant woods in a deep shade of maroon as Jordan walked her to her truck. She hadn't meant to stay this late. Being in the windowless basement for so many hours made her lose track of time.

Wendy's truck was old and run-down. At one point, it had been robin's egg blue, but now it was mostly faded with splotches of orange rust coming through. It was older than she was, but still ran thanks to Jordan and her dad. Mr. Arroyo ran one of the two auto mechanic shops in town, and Jordan was his protégé. Jordan always seemed to be taking care of Wendy, one way or another.

Wendy moved to open the door, but Jordan leaned against it. "You okay to get home?" she asked, brown eyes squinting in the waning sunlight.

"Yeah, I'll be fine," Wendy said, both to Jordan and to herself.

"I wish I didn't have to work tonight," Jordan said, her perfectly symmetrical eyebrows furrowed.

"It's fine," Wendy said. Her eyes cut to the fading light.

"Y'know, I can totally blow my shift off," Jordan added, speaking faster in the way she did when she was talking herself into doing something. "We can meet up with Tyler? They're doing Loopers on the back roads—or we could go to the Gateway and see a movie?"

"No, it's fine, really." Wendy liked Jordan's boyfriend, Tyler, but she didn't feel like driving around with him and his friends. Tyler's car was a Toyota truck on huge wheels that Wendy always struggled to get into. He took the twisty roads through town too fast, and the loud voices and smell of beer made her carsick. When it came to movies, Jordan always wanted to see the latest horror flick, and even though Wendy knew Jordan would suffer through an indie documentary on Amazon rainforest crocodiles for Wendy, her nerves were worn raw to make herself reciprocate. "I don't really feel like celebrating, anyway."

Jordan didn't look satisfied with that answer, but, to Wendy's relief, she let it go. "Get home safe, then." Jordan pushed herself away from the truck and gave a lock of Wendy's dark blond hair an affectionate tug. "And text me if you need anything, all right?"

Wendy smoothed a hand through her hair as she opened the door and climbed in. "I will."

"And you better eat this and tell me how you like it!" Jordan ordered as she handed her the Tupperware, the uneaten cupcake squished inside. "Oh! I nearly forgot!" Jordan dug into her duffel bag and pulled out a rectangular present, sloppily wrapped in shiny navy paper. "Open it, open it!"

Wendy couldn't help but laugh at Jordan's excitement as she bounced on the spot. She peeled back the wrapping paper to reveal a sketchpad. The cover had a drawing of a bird mid-flight and Jordan had taped a box of art pencils to the front.

"A sketchpad?" Wendy said, surprised and a little confused.

"Yes, a sketchpad!" Jordan announced triumphantly. "I noticed how much you've been doodling lately," she said, tilting her chin to a proud angle as she crossed her arms.

"You've seen those?" Wendy asked.

"Uh, yeah, of course I have!" Jordan said with a huff before grinning. "I was just pretending like I didn't so you'd be extra surprised when I gave you your present. I figured a sketchpad would be better than random bits of paper, don't you think?"

Wendy let out an awkward laugh as she thumbed the thick pages. "Yeah, definitely."

"Lots of trees, right?" It was clear by the smile on her face that Jordan was trying to prove how much she *had* noticed. "And who's the boy?"

Wendy's eye went wide. "Boy?"

"Yeah, the boy you're always sketching—" Jordan reached over and plucked a piece of paper from the center console. "Yeah, this guy! See?" She held it out for Wendy to see. It was a drawing of a boy sitting in a tree, one leg draped over a branch in mid-swing, the small hint of dimples in his cheeks. His messy hair drooped over his eyes, obscuring some of his features. In the corner was an unfinished sketch of an old, twisted tree with gnarled roots and no leaves.

A rush of heat went to Wendy's cheeks. "It's no one!" She snatched the paper from Jordan's hand and crumpled it.

Jordan's face lit up. "Oh my *God*—Wendy Darling, are you *blushing*?"

"No!" Wendy balked. Now her face was on fire.

Jordan threw her head back with a laugh. "Okay, now you

have to tell me! Who's the boy, Wendy?" She held up a finger. "And don't you dare try to lie to me!"

Wendy's head fell back against the headrest and she let out a groan. If she lied, Jordan would know it and just keep hounding her. But the truth just felt so embarrassing.

Wendy looked at Jordan, who cocked an eyebrow expectantly.

"*Ugh!*" She sighed. "It's Peter Pan," she muttered under her breath.

"Peter Pan?" Jordan repeated with a frown. "Peter—wait, you mean the guy from your mom's stories?" she asked.

"Yes," Wendy admitted.

When Michael was born, John was three and Wendy was five. Their mother told them stories about Peter Pan every night before they went to bed, about his adventures with pirates, mermaids, and his gang of lost kids. Wendy, John, and Michael had spent their days in the woods behind their house, running around pretending to fight off bears and wolves alongside Peter Pan, and their nights huddled under a blanket with a flashlight while Wendy told stories about Peter and the fairies. He was a magical boy who lived on an island of make-believe in the sky and, most importantly, Peter Pan could fly and he never grew up.

When she got older, Wendy took over the role as storyteller at bedtime. She recycled her mother's tales, but also came up with her own Peter Pan adventures that she told her little brothers.

After what had happened to John and Michael, Wendy only spoke about Peter during story time at the hospital. When they volunteered with the kids, Jordan would usually play board games with the older children, but sometimes she would listen to Wendy's stories.

"I've been having dreams about him, too," Wendy added, straightening out the paper over the steering wheel to study the unfinished drawing. "Sort of, anyway. I always forget what happened when I wake up, but I remember small things like wet jungles, white beaches, and acorns." She shifted uneasily in her seat. "A few nights ago I started sketching what I thought he'd look like."

"And the trees?" Jordan asked. A quiet intensity had come over her as she listened to Wendy talk.

"I have no idea. Just trees, I guess."

Jordan was silent for a moment. Wendy hated when she did that. She felt like Jordan could always tell when she was hiding something. But then Jordan shrugged her shoulders. "Maybe you're feeling old and just want to stay young forever, like this Peter Pan guy," she suggested. "Maybe you wanna run away with him to Neverland?" A smile started to creep across her lips.

Wendy rolled her eyes. "Ha ha."

Jordan suddenly leaned into the truck and hooked her arm around Wendy in a tight hug. Before she could do more than tense in response, Jordan released her and stepped back. Wendy wasn't much of a hugger. They always felt awkward and forced. Sometime over the last five years, she'd forgotten how to do it. She got teased for it a lot. It was painfully obvious how uncomfortable physical touch made her, but Jordan never made fun of her. And if anyone was going to give her a hug, Wendy preferred it be her best friend.

Jordan thumped her hand on the roof of Wendy's truck. "Happy birthday, Legal Eagle!" she called before heading to her own car across the lot.

Wendy waited until Jordan drove away, giving her friend one last wave as she disappeared around the corner.

Slumping in her seat, Wendy let out a long breath. With the coast clear, she leaned over and placed the sketchbook on the passenger seat. Under it, the floor was littered with pieces of paper. Some folded, some crumpled up, some even torn into shreds. Yes, Wendy had started drawing pictures, but it was more than that.

She couldn't get herself to stop.

It had all started innocently enough. She would be spacing out at the hospital and look down to see a pair of eyes drawn on the corner of a file. Sometimes she and Jordan would be at lunch and when she'd get distracted talking about the latest gossip from their friends, suddenly Wendy would find she had drawn a tree on the receipt she was supposed to be signing. It was happening more often, and Wendy never knew she was doing it until she looked down and there was the boy's face looking up at her.

Peter's face. Or something close to it. She knew it was *supposed* to be him, but there was always something off. Something about the eyes that wasn't coming out right.

And they weren't just trees. It was *a* tree. A specific tree.

Wendy didn't know what it was. She didn't remember ever seeing anything like it before, and it almost looked otherworldly. While the sketches of Peter Pan were pretty realistic—much more so than Wendy had even known she was capable of doing—there was something off about the tree. Something wrong with how twisted and sharp it was. For some reason, it gave her goosebumps, but she didn't know why.

And she couldn't explain why she kept doing it, or how she never knew she was doing it until it was already done. And now there were heaps of drawings on napkins, receipts, and even junk mail. She didn't want anyone finding them, so she'd tossed them into her truck, but apparently Jordan had seen them.

Wendy's stomach twisted. She didn't like that her brain and hands were capable of conjuring things up without her noticing. Wendy grabbed her hoodie and threw it over the drawings so she didn't have to see them out of the corner of her eye. When she got home, she'd throw them into the trash can. The last thing she needed was another reason for people to think she was strange. That she was a bad omen, if not cursed.

Wendy was starting to think they might be right.

Astoria was just a small outcropping of land surrounded by water, and the woods were a large inkblot of green spilled on a map, cutting them off from neighboring towns. Williamsport Road—or Dump Road, as the locals called it—twisted right through the woods to the far edge of town, where Wendy lived. Nestled against the hills, it was a road that only locals took. Several tire-worn logging roads splintered off from the asphalt street. They crisscrossed through the trees and looped back on themselves, and some just ended in the middle of the woods. Tourists constantly got lost on them and parents were always warning their kids to stay away, but they never listened. While she hated driving through the woods, especially at night, it got her home faster than the main streets.

For as long as Wendy could remember, all the kids in Astoria had been warned to never go down those paths. They were told the woods were dangerous, and to stay out of them. Wendy's parents had forbidden her and her brothers to explore the logging roads even though they ran right through the woods behind their house.

After what happened, Wendy became a cautionary tale.

The truck's engine roared as Wendy pushed it as fast as she dared. The faster she went, the sooner she'd be out of the woods. The branches of overgrown trees and shrubs reached out, occasionally swiping the passenger window even though she hugged the yellow centerline. Her gray eyes, wide and alert, directed furtive glances at the trees. Her fingers, dry and cracked, flexed on the steering wheel with blanched knuckles. The keychain hanging from the ignition thumped rhythmically against the dashboard.

She just wanted to get home, maybe read a book for a while, and then go to bed so her birthday would be over. Wendy glanced over at her bag on the passenger seat as it bounced with the movement of the truck. It had a blue ink stain on the bottom corner from a pen that had leaked and the adjustable buckle had turned from its once-shiny brass to a dull gray. But she loved the thing because her brothers had hand-picked it for her and had used their own money. It was the first and last birthday present they had ever gotten her.

Stuffed inside the bag were more drawings of Peter Pan and the mysterious tree.

It was a hot night and the cab was stuffy, but the air conditioner in her beat-up truck hadn't worked since probably before she was born and Wendy didn't want to roll down the windows. A trickle of sweat ran down her back as she leaned forward. Music would be a nice distraction. She would even take the whiny drone of one of the several country stations if it meant keeping her mind from wandering. She turned on the radio and a voice cut through the crackling speakers.

"*An AMBER Alert has been issued in Clatsop County for eight-year-old Ashley Ford, who went missing from her home at twelve forty-five p.m. today—*"

Wendy fumbled with the radio to change the station. It wasn't that she didn't care—she cared a lot—but she just didn't think she could handle all of this. Not today, not now. Wendy could already feel the quaking in her chest and it was taking all of her concentration to keep it at bay.

She just wanted to get out of the woods and into her house. Wendy punched another preset on her radio but the same voice came through the speakers again.

"Ashley has blond hair and brown eyes. She was last seen in the front yard of her house wearing a white-and-yellow checkered shirt and blue pants. This comes in the wake of local boy Benjamin Lane being reported missing yesterday afternoon. Authorities haven't commented on whether the disappearances are related to—"

She spun the tuner dial again. The sound petered out before breaking into loud static. Wendy took a deep breath in an effort to steady herself and peered at the flickering backlight of the stereo.

She knew every twist and turn of the road and could drive it with her eyes shut, so she gripped the wheel tightly with her left hand. She banged her right fist against the radio. This usually fixed most of the truck's problems, but loud static continued to fill the cab.

Wendy clenched her jaw and glanced up. She knew the wide bend was coming, but the loud crackling was putting her teeth on edge. She looked back at the radio, fingers spinning the dial, but not a single station would come in. She was about to press the AM button when all noise coming from the radio cut off, leaving her with just the steady rumbling of the truck's engine.

A branch slapped the passenger window.

Wendy jolted so violently it hurt.

A shadow dropped onto the hood of her truck, blocking her view. It was inky black and solid. Dark, crooked things like fingers dragged across the windshield. A terrible screech cut through her ears.

Wendy screamed and the shadowy *thing* slipped off the hood just in time for her to see a mass in the middle of the road illuminated by her headlights. A shout ripped through Wendy's throat as she slammed on the brakes. She gripped the steering wheel and her body tensed as she swerved to the right.

The tires spun over loose dirt and the truck jerked to a stop between the road and the woods. Wendy stared out the front window into a tangle of branches. Her sharp breaths robbed the cab of fresh air. Adrenaline coursed through her veins. Her neck and temples pounded.

Wendy cursed under her breath.

She pulled her stiff fingers from where they'd cramped around the steering wheel. With trembling hands, she patted down her chest and thighs, making sure she was in one piece. Then she buried her face in them.

How could she be so stupid? She'd let her nerves get the better of her. She knew never to look away from the road while driving, especially at night. Her dad was going to lose it! And what if she'd totaled her truck? Wendy could've gotten herself killed—or worse, someone else.

Then she remembered the mass in the road.

Wendy's breath caught in her throat. It could be a dead animal, but she knew in her gut it wasn't. She twisted in her seat and tried to see out the back window, but the red glow of her taillights hardly lit up the outline of whatever she had almost run over.

Please don't be a dead body.

Wendy struggled to untangle herself from the seat belt. She tumbled out of her truck and immediately looked to the woods. She took a few steps back, watching them cautiously. But they were silent and unmoving in the heavy summer air. The only sounds were the faint breeze through the leaves and her own labored breaths.

Tentatively, she peered at the front of her truck. It was pulled over onto the dirt shoulder of the road, the front bumper dangerously close to a thick tree, but still running. There was a dent in the hood from whatever had landed on it. The windshield was cracked—or, no, not cracked.

Were those scratches?

Wendy brushed her fingers over the lines. There were four of them parallel to one another in a long swipe. What could've done that? It hadn't been a deer or a branch.

And what had she almost hit in the road? Her head snapped to look back over her shoulder to the mass in the middle of the road. It still hadn't moved.

Wendy jogged toward the figure, trying to balance on the balls of her feet, so as to make as little sound as possible as she crept closer. She took each step slowly, willing her eyes to open wider, to adjust so she could see in the dark. She stood on her tiptoes and craned her neck to get a better look just as a cloud above shifted and a silvery glow was cast over the boy lying on his side.

A shudder racked Wendy's body and she ran forward, falling to her knees beside him. Sharp gravel pressed through her jeans.

"Hello?" Her voice shook and her hands trembled, hovering over the boy, not knowing what to do. "Are you okay?"

Are you alive?

He let out a pained groan.

She snatched her hands back. "Oh my God." Wendy scrambled around to his other side to get a look at his face. She'd learned from her mom never to move someone you'd found unconscious.

He was lying on his side with his arms curled into his chest, as if he were sleeping. He was clothed in some sort of material that wrapped around his shoulders and torso, hanging down to his knees. She couldn't tell what it was in the dark, but it had rough, jagged edges and it smelled like the leaves she dug out of the gutters in spring.

Bracing one hand on the ground, Wendy leaned in closer. Slowly and carefully, she reached out and pushed his wet hair back from his face, brushing her thumb over his forehead. There was something about the way his freckles ran across his nose and under his closed eyes that was familiar . . .

Before she could work it out, a groan sounded deep in the boy's chest. He rolled onto his back as his eyes opened and focused on hers.

Wendy's natural inclination was to shrink back, but she couldn't move.

His eyes were astonishing. A deep shade of cobalt with crystalline blue starbursts exploding around his pupils.

She knew those eyes. They were the same ones she'd drawn over and over again but could never get right. But that was impossible. It couldn't be—

"Wendy?" the boy breathed, the smell of sweet grass brushing across her face.

Wendy scrambled back from him. At the same time, the boy's cosmos eyes rolled back and fell closed again.

Wendy clamped her hand over her mouth.

He was older than the boy from her drawings. His face

wasn't as round and his cheeks weren't as full as in the dozens of sketches that littered her car, but there was something about the slope of his nose and the curve of his chin that she recognized.

Breaths shook her shoulders and escaped through her nose. How did he know her name? Her heart thrashed against her ribs like a wild animal. She couldn't recognize him. There was no possible way that the boy she was looking at was the same boy from her drawings.

Peter Pan was not *real*. He was just a story her mother had made up. She was just freaking out and her mind was playing tricks on her. She couldn't possibly trust what her gut was telling her.

Even though every fiber of her being screamed to her that it was him.

It didn't make any sense. Her imagination was getting the better of her. She needed to get him help.

Wendy tried to focus and ignore her swimming head. She dug her hand into her pocket and pulled out her phone. The screen was blurry and, in the back of her mind, she realized her eyes were watering, but she was able to call 9-1-1.

As soon as the ringing stopped, before the dispatcher could say a word, Wendy choked out, "Help!"

CHAPTER 2

Peter

"What's your name, miss?"

"Wendy Darling," she said, leaning to the side, trying to see the still-unconscious boy as the other paramedics put him on a stretcher.

"Do you know where you are?"

"I'm a mile from my house, sitting here with *you*." She jerked her hand back as he tried to feel the pulse at her wrist.

"I'm Dallas. I'm a paramedic."

Wendy glanced at the shiny badge on his navy uniform, the embroidered patch on his sleeve that read ASTORIA, OREGON FIRE DEPARTMENT—PARAMEDIC. "I can see that."

"I'm just going to do a couple of tests to make sure you're all right," he continued. After she had called 9-1-1, the fire department arrived on scene, closely followed by an ambulance. They went right to the boy before taking her aside to ask questions.

"I'm fine, Dallas the Paramedic," she said, pushing the penlight he was holding out of her face. With all the volunteering she did at the hospital, not to mention her mom working in the ER, Wendy knew all of the emergency medical service workers in Astoria, Oregon. Dallas the Paramedic was new. Probably still doing his volunteer hours, if she had to guess, based on how textbook his questions were.

"Does anything hurt?"

"Just my butt from sitting on the side of the road," she told him, again craning her neck to watch the ambulance. The gurney made loud clacking noises as the paramedics loaded the boy in. Wendy wanted to yell at them to be more careful.

"Did you hit your head in the accident at all?"

"It wasn't an accident. I'm fine, my truck is fine." She sucked in a deep breath. "There was no accident."

"Okay, miss," he said, standing up and putting his stethoscope back into his bag. The doors to the ambulance slammed shut.

They were taking him away. Wendy felt a swell of panic. She needed to see him, needed to talk to him, needed to find out who he was. She needed to prove to herself that he wasn't Peter Pan, just a boy. A very lost boy who had somehow ended up in the middle of the road.

"I want to go to the hospital," Wendy blurted out.

Dallas blinked. "What?"

"The hospital. I want to go. Can I follow? Like I said, my truck is fine, it's just on the side of the road." The tugging need to follow him only grew more persistent as the ambulance started to pull away.

Dallas frowned. "I don't think it's a good idea for you to drive if you think you need to go to the hospital to get checked out—"

Frustration flared. "No—my mom works there. I want to see my mom; she's a nurse," she told him. The lights of the ambulance disappeared around the bend.

"Oh." He blinked again. "All right." He hesitated and looked back to his sergeant, who was at the fire engine, talking on the radio. "Hey, Marshall," Dallas called. "Tell the officers to meet EMS at the hospital."

Officers. Great. She'd have to talk to the police. The hairs on her arms stood on end and she could feel sweat seeping through her shirt.

Dallas looked back at Wendy, expression pinched. "Are you sure you're okay to drive?"

Wendy looked him straight in the eye. "I have all of my mental faculties and am refusing care and transport," she recited.

His eyebrows drew together, but after a moment, he sighed and pulled out his metal clipboard. "Sign here acknowledging that you—" Wendy whipped it out of his hand and quickly scrawled her name on the line before shoving it back at him. He fumbled to grab hold of it again.

Dallas squinted at her license before holding it out to her. "Happy birthday, by the way."

"Yeah, thanks." Wendy jogged back to her truck. She revved up the engine, backed out of the tangle of branches, and headed for town. The woods disappeared behind her, fading into the night.

Wendy punched in the code to slip into the emergency room through the side door in the waiting room. The ER was small and outdated in shades of blue and green. The plastic covers on the terrible fluorescent lights were painted blue with clouds, as if that somehow softened the harsh glow. The nurses' station was placed in the middle, and the six emergency rooms surrounded it in a *U*-shaped ring. Drapes and sliding glass doors pulled closed around them. She walked straight up to one of the hand sanitizer dispensers attached to a wall, put exactly three pumps into her hands, and rubbed them together vigorously. It made the cracks in her fingers sting.

No one paid her much attention. The ER was cramped and chronically understaffed. There wasn't enough storage space, so the walls were lined with shelves on wheels, stacked full of medical supplies that could be carted from room to room.

At least here, everyone was too busy to notice Wendy. She only caught a glimpse of the boy lying on a gurney in the far alcove before a nurse tugged the curtain shut.

Wendy sat in a plastic cushioned seat along the wall, watching the feet of the nurses and doctors crowding around the bed. She kept telling herself that he was just a boy who had gotten himself lost in the middle of the woods. It had been dark on the road, she hadn't been able to see him properly. She was tired and stressed, and her mind was piecing together wild ideas. Once she could prove to herself he was just a stranger, she could go home and get some sleep.

But she wasn't going to leave without seeing him.

"Back already?" Nurse Judy's familiar voice snapped Wendy to attention. She stood behind the nurses' desk, holding a tray of syringes as she peered at Wendy over the top of her glasses. Nurse Judy provided Wendy with an excuse before she had to make one up. "Oh, waiting for your mom?" Her expression relaxed. "She's in the break room, should be out in a few."

"Thanks." That seemed to satisfy Nurse Judy enough and she went back to her work. Sometimes Wendy and her mom would drive home together, when they worked the same shift.

Wendy knotted her fingers into the hem of her tank top. She just needed to see the boy one more time. Then she could get out of there before anyone thought better of it, before anyone noticed her and started asking questions.

But, of course, that was too much to ask.

The ER doors swung open, and in walked Dallas, Marshall, Officer Smith, and another cop she didn't recognize. Wendy's stomach dropped and she pulled her feet up onto the chair and hugged her knees to her chest. Maybe they wouldn't see her.

Dallas handed Officer Smith some papers and nodded in Wendy's direction. Officer Smith fixed her with a harsh look, and Wendy's eyes darted back to the closed drapes.

Great.

Wendy didn't like cops. After what had happened to her in the woods, she didn't trust them anymore. They had done nothing but scare her and ask her the same questions over and over. They never believed her when she said she couldn't remember anything.

And they failed to get her brothers back.

Officer Smith had been one of those cops.

Wendy heard the clacking of their loaded belts and the squeak of their boots on the speckled linoleum. They came to a stop in front of her. Wendy tried to relax the muscles in her face and conjure up an expression of boredom as she continued to stare straight ahead. Her heart fluttered traitorously in her chest.

The officer she didn't recognize spoke first. "Miss Darling?" His voice was too gentle. He was in the wrong profession.

Wendy hummed in acknowledgment.

"We just have a few questions for you," he said. There was a rustling of paper as he pulled out a notepad.

"I already talked to the paramedics," Wendy said flatly.

Officer Smith stepped forward. His handcuffs glinted from his belt. "Yeah, well, we have a few more questions."

Angry defiance sparked in Wendy. "Shouldn't you guys be out looking for those missing kids instead of bugging me?" She regretted saying it almost as soon as it left her lips.

"Yes, we should, Wendy." She glanced up at his rough tone. Officer Smith scowled deeply, his fists propped on his hips. The other cop—young, with even, short-cropped hair—looked uneasy.

The name on his uniform read CECCO. Wendy knew it. She went to high school with a girl whose last name was Cecco. This must be her older brother.

Officer Cecco's eyes shifted between Wendy and Smith.

"Which is why you should cooperate with us so we can determine if this boy was a victim," Officer Smith added.

Wendy swallowed hard but raised an eyebrow expectantly. "Well?"

Cecco cleared his throat. "You said something fell onto the hood of your car?"

"Yes."

"Like a tree branch?" he prompted.

"No—not a tree branch, it was like . . ." Wendy thought about the strange black thing she had seen. It hadn't been solid enough to be a branch. It was murky and whatever it was made of swirled and shifted, like if you tried to touch it, it would just slip through your fingers.

But how on earth could she describe that to the police? "It dented my hood and scratched my windshield."

"Like a tree branch," Smith insisted, shifting moodily.

Wendy lifted her chin and tried to sound firm. "No." Of

course he didn't believe her. "I don't know what it was, but it wasn't a branch."

"The medics said there were no signs that the victim"—Wendy grimaced at the word—"was hit by a car," Cecco continued. "And you said he talked to you. Did he say what had happened?"

"No."

"You said he knew your name." His voice went all soft again. "Do you know him?"

She opened her mouth to say no, but the word lodged in her throat. She hesitated.

Wendy's eyes shifted to the nurse's desk.

Nurse Judy was watching the two officers talk to Wendy, startled. Her face was splotchy red, and for a moment, Wendy thought she was going to stomp over and tell the officers off. Instead, she marched quickly in the direction of the break room.

Wendy's grip around her legs tightened. Her breathing quickened. She hoped Smith and Cecco didn't notice. "No." But she didn't sound nearly as confident as before. She couldn't tell them that she thought she had almost run her truck over a boy she only knew from make-believe stories.

Wendy's head gave a painful throb.

"Are you sure?"

"Yes."

Smith's cold gray eyes narrowed. "How did he end up in the middle of the street?" he asked. "Did he come from the logging roads?"

Wendy finally looked directly at the faces of the two officers. She smiled, squinting her eyes. "Maybe he fell out of the sky?"

Smith's lips pressed into a hard line, the muscle in his jaw clenching. It gave Wendy a small feeling of satisfaction. Cecco uselessly rubbed at the back of his neck. After cutting Smith a nervous glance, he pinned his attention back to Wendy. "How does he know your—?"

"What's going on here?" The voice was quiet but stern.

"Mom," Wendy breathed.

Her mother appeared, standing between the two officers.

Mary Darling was in a pair of faded blue scrubs, her light brown hair done up in a messy bun. Her hands were at her sides, fidgeting, as her sharp brown eyes looked back and forth between the officers. The stern authority she'd once had was belied by sagging shoulders and dark circles under her eyes.

Wendy stood up, pushing past Smith and Cecco to get to her mother's side.

"Are you all right?" Mrs. Darling asked, giving Wendy a sidelong glance. "What happened? Your father—?"

"No, I'm fine," Wendy said quickly. Her mom could sort this all out, she could make sense of all this. "There was this boy—"

"Mrs. Darling, we need to talk to your daughter," Smith cut in.

"And why is that, Officer Smith?"

He took off his hat, clearly ready to launch into an explanation.

"Wendy!"

Everyone turned. The blue drapes around the boy's bed rustled. Nurses ran behind the curtains.

"WENDY!"

She couldn't make out what the doctors were saying over the frenzied shouts of her name. There were two loud bangs as metal trays were knocked to the floor.

Everyone was staring at her. The nurses, the doctors, the officers, her mom.

"WENDY!"

Her head spun. All other sound became muffled and garbled, except for his piercing yells.

This felt like a nightmare. Her chest heaved up and down and her hands curled into fists. She walked toward the curtained bed.

"Wendy." This time it was her mother, lightly placing a hand on her shoulder, but Wendy shrugged it off. She passed nurses who openly stared at her and moved out of her way.

"WENDY!"

She was close enough now to reach out and grab the cotton drape. She hesitated, noticing how hard her hand was shaking. Wendy yanked it back.

Nurses darted around. Men in blue scrubs on either side of the boy tried to grab hold of his arms. His legs thrashed under the waffle-knit blanket. There was a doctor with a needle and a small glass bottle.

But then everything stopped and it was Wendy looking at him, and him looking back. She could see now that his hair was a dark auburn, glints of red showing even in the dull hospital light. The color of late-autumn leaves. He was dressed in a blue hospital gown. They'd apparently cut him out of what he had been wearing.

"Wendy?" He wasn't yelling anymore. His head tipped to the side as he squinted at her with those brilliant blue eyes.

Wendy couldn't find her voice. She had no idea what to say. Her mouth was open, but nothing came out.

A wide smile cut across his face, revealing a small chip in his front tooth, and deep dimples. Those starry eyes of his lit up—the ones she'd never been able to capture in her dozens of drawings. But that wasn't possible . . .

"I found you," he said triumphantly. He continued to struggle against the two men holding him back, the smile never leaving his face. That look made heat bloom in Wendy's cheeks and sent her stomach flipping.

The doctor stuck the needle into his arm and depressed the plunger.

"No, don't!" The words flew from her mouth, but it was too late. The boy flinched but couldn't pull away. Almost immediately, those brilliant eyes went glassy.

His head swayed, and he sank back into the hospital bed. "I knew I'd find you." His speech was slurred and his eyes began to wander around the room in a daze, but he was so happy—so relieved.

Wendy slipped past a nurse and stood next to him. "Who are you?" she asked, gripping the bed rail.

The boy frowned and his eyebrows pulled upward, trying to stay awake. "You forgot about me?" His eyes swept back and forth in search of her face.

Wendy's heart raced. She didn't know what to do, and she was acutely aware of everyone watching. She had so many questions, but the sedative was quickly pulling him under. "What's your name?" she asked urgently.

His drowsy eyes finally found hers. "Peter." He blinked slowly and his head dropped back onto the pillows. He let out a small, drunk-sounding laugh. "You're so old . . ." His eyes slid shut and he went still, except for the slow rise and fall of his chest.

Peter.

The movement around her started again. People were asking her questions, but she couldn't hear them. She was swept up by people in scrubs, gently pulled away from Peter's side. Wendy suddenly felt like she was going to vomit. Saliva pooled in her mouth as the room swayed around her.

You forgot about me?

Wendy buried her face in her hands. Her heart pounded. She could still smell the soil and wet grass of his skin. She squeezed her eyes shut and images of trees and twilight between leaves flashed through her vision.

Hands rubbed her back and guided her into a seat where she put her head between her knees, clasped her hands behind her sweaty neck, and pressed her forearms against her ears.

How did he know her? Why had he been looking for her? And who was he? He couldn't be Peter Pan, *her* Peter. He wasn't real, he was just a made-up story. Wasn't he?

You forgot about me?

There was so much that she had forgotten—huge gaps of time just missing from her memory. What if he was one of them? What if he knew what happened?

Suddenly, the thought of him waking up terrified her.

All of the bodies around her backed away and she felt the light pressure of what could only be her mother's touch on the crown of her head. Wendy looked up at her mom from between her arms.

"I'm going to take you home, okay?" The nurses behind Mrs. Darling were still staring, but Mrs. Darling was looking at Wendy's hair, looping a finger around a lock of it and gently pulling it through.

Wendy nodded.

"Mrs. Darling." Smith was still there. "We have more questions we need to ask your daughter." The suspicion he had shown earlier was now replaced with a look of wary apprehension as he peered down at Wendy.

Mrs. Darling crossed her arms. "None of that will be happening tonight. My daughter has been through quite enough already, but we'll be happy to speak with you tomorrow."

Officer Cecco stood back and spoke quickly into his radio.

"I'm sorry, ma'am, but—"

Wendy stopped listening.

She leaned her cheek against her knee and looked back at Peter's bed.

The spilled tray had been picked up, and she could just make out one of his hands, the wrist bound in a padded leather cuff. They'd shackled him to the bed.

She remembered what those cuffs had felt like around her own wrists after they found her in the woods on her thirteenth birthday.

At first, she was just at the hospital to get her minor injuries checked out, but when the crying wouldn't stop and Wendy kept waking up in the middle of the night screaming and thrashing, they started buckling down her wrists and ankles. To protect her, they'd said. She couldn't remember much after that except for the steady ebb and flow of doctors, social workers, and psychologists.

Her brothers were still missing, and it was all her fault.

A nurse stood next to Peter, reading his vitals. Her mother and Officer Smith were deep in conversation. His face had turned a plum red, and her mother's chin was tilted stubbornly. The other officer was now talking into a cell phone, his back toward them all.

When the nurse left, Wendy slipped out of her seat.

She walked to the bedside again. Her eyes roved over the contours of his jaw, his ears, his hair. She searched for some sign to prove that he wasn't Peter Pan. He was definitely older than the boy from her stories and drawings. The Peter Pan she knew was a child who never aged. The boy in the hospital bed was definitely a teenager. It was a silly thing to grasp at, the idea that this couldn't be Peter Pan because Peter Pan could never grow up, but it was something.

The boy had defined cheekbones and, even in the pale fluorescent light, his skin was sun-warmed and tan. His freckles stood out like flecks of cracked autumn leaves among the smudges of dirt.

There was a small crease between his eyebrows. Wendy leaned in closer. He was frowning in his sleep, like he was having a bad dream.

Wendy gently brushed her thumb across the crease, over and over, until his brow relaxed and his face was nothing but smooth slopes and planes.

She looked down at his banded wrist again, her eyes following along the back of his palm to his long, lean fingers. His fingernails were bitten down, almost to nubs, and the nail beds were caked in dirt.

The image of her own fingernails when she had been found came flooding back. Dirty, broken, with bits of red stuck underneath.

Wendy lurched back, a tremor rolling up her spine. She squeezed sanitizer into her palm from the pump attached to the wall and rubbed it vigorously into her hands. The sharp, acidic smell stung her nose.

"Wendy."

She jumped and spun to see her mother down the hall, waving for her to come back.

"We're leaving now," her mom said, her hands tightly gripping her purse. Wendy thought her mother suddenly looked much older. As though something were pressing down on her shoulders, bowing her head and curving her back.

Wendy wiped the back of her hand across her sweaty brow. "What about my truck?"

"You can pick it up in the morning," her mother said, digging into her purse for her keys.

Wendy nodded. "Okay."

Mrs. Darling walked away at a brisk pace, and Wendy followed. As they passed through the sliding glass doors, two people in suits walked in.

As the doors slid shut, Wendy thought about Peter lying in bed and that smile playing across his lips.

CHAPTER 3

Closed Doors

On the drive home, Wendy sat in the back seat behind her mother. She curled up and pressed her forehead to the cool glass of the window, keeping her back to the woods. In an effort to keep her mind from wandering, she closed her eyes and repeated the lyrics to her favorite song over and over again in her head.

Tires rolling over gravel let her know they were home. Wendy sat up and pushed the door open, careful not to bump into the side of her father's car.

"I have to head back and finish my shift," her mom said.

"Okay."

"I'll talk to you in the morning."

"Okay." Wendy hesitated. Something like curiosity, or maybe just guilt, kept her in the car. "Mom, are you okay?"

Mrs. Darling sighed. Wendy tried to catch her mother's eye in the rearview mirror, but she continued to stare at the steering wheel. "I'm fine. Everything is fine."

Wendy couldn't tell who she was trying to convince.

Her mom drove away before Wendy could pull out her keys. Her father had forgotten to turn on the porch light again. She fumbled for a moment before she could get the front door unlocked.

The living room was dark except for the strip of light visible under the door of her father's study. She walked over, pressed her ear to the doorjamb, and listened. Everything was silent except for the sound of her father's deep, heavy snores.

Good. At least she wouldn't have to deal with getting questioned by him. For now, anyway.

Wendy's mind and body buzzed with anxious energy. She needed to distract herself with something, to put her restless hands to work, so she straightened up the kitchen. She emptied the dishwasher, which she had filled the night before. She broke down the small pile of beer cases and stacked them with the rest of the recycling. At the sink, she scrubbed at her hands again, the skin red and cracked from the compulsive habit.

The busywork kept her distracted for the most part until she sat down to write a grocery list. She stared at the small notepad, the tip of the blue pen poised, but she couldn't concentrate on what she needed to buy for groceries that week, one of the many chores she took up around the house. Now that she was sitting still, her mind raced. She contemplated turning on the TV to drown out her thoughts, but she didn't want to see the faces of Benjamin Lane and Ashley Ford staring back at her.

And she didn't want to wake up her dad.

Wendy closed her eyes and forced herself to take a deep breath. Her temples throbbed. She was not looking forward to him finding out about what happened tonight. Hell, *she* wasn't even sure what had happened herself, so how was she supposed to explain it to anyone else? The only things she knew for sure were that something had landed on the hood of her car and she found a boy lying in the middle of the road. And his name was Peter.

But that still didn't mean he was *her* Peter.

Wendy gave her head a small shake.

She needed to focus.

Groceries. She could make baked ziti. It was quick and easy to pack up for her mom and dad.

Wendy looked down at the notepad, about to write down *marinara*, but stopped short. She sucked in a sharp breath. Goosebumps raced down her arms.

She'd done it again.

The notepad was covered in blue ink. Scratchy lines etched out the gnarled tree. The trunk was thick, jagged. The roots twisted and curled at its base. The drawing had gone off the paper, leaving branches that hooked at sharp angles across the wooden table.

"*Shit.*" Wendy grabbed cleaner from under the sink and a handful of paper towels. She scrubbed vigorously at the table, but even though the blue ink vanished, she'd pressed the pen so hard that it'd left gashes in the soft wood. She cursed again and scrubbed harder.

Still, the ghostly outlines of the branches remained. Wendy yanked open the drawer where they kept the nice linens for holidays and pulled out the set of green placemats. She arranged them on the table to cover up the lines.

Wendy dug the heels of her hands into her eyes. What was happening to her? Was she totally losing it? She needed to get a grip on reality. The boy she'd found was not Peter Pan. The missing kids had nothing to do with her or her brothers. She was exhausted and just needed a good night's rest.

Wendy went upstairs, pausing for a moment at the top.

To the right was a door. It led into the room she used to share with her two brothers, John and Michael. Now, it was just a door that had remained closed for the last five years. After what happened, Wendy refused to go back inside, so her parents had immediately moved her into the playroom.

They had bought her all new clothes and furniture. A shopping trip like that should have been a fun mother-daughter adventure, but Wendy had spent most of the first few weeks in the hospital, seeing various doctors and not doing much talking. So her mom had done most of the shopping herself—and by the mix of styles and colors of wood, Wendy assumed that she had just pointed to the first things she saw and had them delivered to the house.

Turning her back to the door, Wendy ran her fingers through her short hair and walked into her room to the left. Just seeing her bed with piled-up pillows and a plush down comforter covered in a smooth, light blue duvet made her feel exhausted.

The bed was centered in front of the window at the far wall. There was a small trash can tucked under the end table next to it, overflowing with more crumpled-up drawings of Peter and the crooked tree.

In her small bathroom, Wendy splashed water on her face and the back of her neck. She held on to the edge of the sink and stared at her reflection in the medicine cabinet. Other than being a bit pale, she looked the same as usual. Eyes that were too big, hair that was too ashy to hold any luster, and shoulders that were too broad thanks to swimming. Plain and uninspiring, which suited her just fine.

Wendy changed into a white sleep shirt. The air hitting her damp skin gave her a small reprieve from the heat.

The top of her dresser was the only thing about Wendy's

room someone could say was untidy. It was scattered with little treasures she had collected through the years. There was a line of her favorite books, a stuffed seal her grandmother had gotten her from San Francisco, a royal purple swim cap with her school's mascot—the Fighting Fisherman—on the side, and her silver and bronze swimming medals placed at the corner.

Wendy picked up the swim cap to toss it into her duffel, only to reveal the small wooden jewelry box that had been hidden under it. She paused.

It was a simple box made of old wood. She had found it at one of the little shops on the coast several summers before her brothers were lost. She mostly used it to keep her books propped up, but there were a few little trinkets inside.

Wendy reached down and carefully opened the lid. There was an old necklace made out of cheap metal that had become tarnished and smelled like copper. There were a couple of coins, a small piece of purple quartz, and, tucked in the corner, an acorn.

She pulled it out and let the lid fall shut with a quiet snap. She held it carefully, turning it in her fingertips. The acorn was dark with age and had a polished sheen to it from all the times she had run her fingers over its surface. The cup of the acorn—or its little hat, as she used to think of it—was dried out and had pieces missing.

The acorn had been in her hand when the park ranger found her in the woods five years ago. According to the police report, she had been gripping it so tightly that the small point had bruised her palm.

She hadn't taken it out of its hiding spot in a long time. Wendy used to turn it over in her hand every night before bed, looking for a secret message or maybe an invisible latch that would open it up, reveal some secret, tell her something about those six months. It was the only thing from that day she had kept. Everything else—her long blond hair, her clothes—had been thrown out for good, but she'd held on to the acorn.

Carefully cupping it in her hands, Wendy walked over to her bed and collapsed onto her back. She sank into the comforter, which gently enveloped her like a cloud. Wendy reached back and turned on the strand of fairy lights that framed the window above the head of her bed, casting a warm glow over her and her shiny acorn.

What a disaster today had been.

No one liked her birthday. Her parents didn't like it because it reminded them that their two sons were missing. Wendy didn't like it for the same reason. The only good thing about this birthday was that now she was eighteen, it was summer, and in a few months she would be off to college. Away from the ghosts that followed her.

She couldn't stop thinking about Benjamin Lane and Ashley Ford. Wendy wondered if the police would start sending search parties into the woods like they did when she and her brothers had gone missing . . . Could the disappearances happening now be related to what had happened to her and her brothers?

She hoped not. She dreaded it, in fact. Wendy had spent the last five years trying to escape that looming shadow just to be swallowed up by it again.

And then there was Peter.

Was it just an odd coincidence that a boy had turned up next to the woods, unconscious in the middle of the road? Was this somehow all related? Had he been kidnapped? Had he escaped someone just before she found him?

Tilting her head back, she gazed at the small lights. When

she was little, her mother had always told her that fairy lights watched over children as they slept and kept them safe. It seemed like a ridiculous idea now as she rolled onto her side, still fiddling with the acorn.

Yet she still slept with the string of lights on every night. She wouldn't sleep with the lights off—or rather she couldn't. Jordan had tried inviting her to a sleepover once, a few months after she was released from the hospital, but when it was time to turn off the lights, Wendy had such a bad panic attack, it scarred both of them enough that they never tried again.

Wendy nuzzled her cheek into her pillows and curled her legs up under her night shirt. Maybe she would go back to the hospital and try to talk to Peter again. Maybe after a good night's rest, her head would be clearer and she'd be able to see that he was just a random, run-of-the-mill boy. She held the acorn between her thumb and forefinger.

Where did you come from? she wondered. Wendy placed it on her bedside table and stared at it for a moment longer before finally drifting off to sleep.

The next morning, Wendy put the acorn back in its hiding place, washed her hands, brushed her hair, and went downstairs. Her mother was in the kitchen, sitting at the small dining table. Her hands were cupped around a white mug filled with hot water, lemon, and honey. It sat on top of the green placemat hiding the carved lines. Her mom's head was lowered and her eyes were shut. It reminded Wendy of the quiet, huddled bodies of people in waiting rooms.

"Morning," Wendy said, the tile of the kitchen floor cool against her bare feet.

Mrs. Darling sighed and lifted her head. "Good morning." She gently stirred the contents of her mug with a teaspoon.

Wendy leaned on the kitchen counter. "Did you just get home?"

"Yes." Her mother pinched the bridge of her nose.

Wendy wanted to ask her about Peter, if he had woken up, if he had said anything, but Mrs. Darling didn't need prompting.

"They lost the boy," she said.

The world dropped right out from under her. "He's dead?!" Wendy spluttered.

"No! He disappeared," Mrs. Darling quickly corrected. "He must've run away during the night." She closed her eyes and rubbed her temples. "Nobody knows how he managed it. One moment he was there, and the next—" She rolled her wrist, fingers curling through the air.

Run away. Disappeared. Lost.

Wendy found herself dismayed, almost panicked at this information. But a part of her, a very cowardly part, was relieved.

"Had he been kidnapped? Was that why he was in the middle of the road? Are we sure someone didn't take him from the hospital?" Wendy asked, the words spilling from her lips. Various horrifying scenarios cycled through her head.

"No, no, nothing like that," her mother said gently. "The strange part is no one saw anyone go in or out. They even checked the surveillance tapes, but there was nothing. It's like he just vanished." She frowned at her cup.

That was odd. The hospital didn't have the most high-tech setup, but at least one of the cameras should've showed him leaving. "Did—did he say anything?" Wendy ventured, bracing herself for the answer.

"He woke up a couple of hours after he got the sedative," her mom explained as she squeezed another wedge of lemon into her mug. "I never saw him, but the other nurses kept saying he was talking gibberish, maybe an aftereffect of the sedative . . . He kept talking about a shadow?" She frowned in a way that made her look much older than she was. "I don't know. Maybe he was just lost in the logging roads and dehydrated, delirious . . . They had a social worker there but she couldn't get anything clearer out of him, either."

She was quiet for a moment before she finally looked up at Wendy. Those keen brown eyes bore into Wendy's with inquisitive intensity. "He also kept asking for you."

"That doesn't make any sense," she said, because it didn't. Wendy crossed her arms, uncrossed them, and then crossed them again.

Mrs. Darling ran the tip of her finger over her bottom lip as she watched Wendy for a quiet moment. "Do you know him?" she finally asked.

"No, of course not!" she said, a little too forcefully. Frustration started to crawl under her skin. This mystery boy was making it look like they knew each other when they *didn't*, but more importantly, he was making her look like a liar. Now she even *felt* like a liar, like she was hiding something, but how could she when she'd never seen him before?

And no, her imagination of what a make-believe boy could *maybe* look like did *not* count!

"He's some random kid that came out of the woods, how would I know him?" Wendy insisted, desperation starting to claw up her throat. She didn't need her mom, of all people, to doubt her, too.

"How—"

Knock. Knock.

Wendy jumped and they both turned to the front door. Mrs. Darling frowned but rose from the table and answered the door. Standing on the porch were a man and a woman, both dressed in suits and ties.

"Mary Darling?" The man spoke first as he dug in the pocket of his jacket. He was tall and broad shouldered.

Mrs. Darling's fingers flexed on the doorknob. Wendy slipped into a seat at the table, leaning over to peer around her mom. "I told the officers we would be at the police station later. I need to—"

"I'm Detective James, and this is my partner, Detective Rowan," the man said. Wendy tensed. He held out a badge, as did the woman behind him. Her black hair was shaved to a shadow, revealing every inch of her angular face: sharp cheekbones, dark eyes, and deep brown skin. She looked past Mrs. Darling to Wendy, her expression unchanging.

"Detective?" Mrs. Darling repeated, sounding confused.

"Yes, ma'am. We're with the Clatsop County sheriff's office. Do you mind if we come in?" His hazel eyes cut to Wendy. "We have some questions for your daughter."

Wendy mentally urged her mother to just say no and turn them away. She could tell her mother didn't want to let them in, but did you have much choice with detectives?

To Wendy's dismay, her mother stepped aside and let them in. Mrs. Darling walked over to Wendy and stood next to her, arms crossed over her chest.

"Wendy?" asked Detective James.

She didn't know why he was asking when he obviously knew.

"Yes." Sitting there, Wendy suddenly felt very small. Detective Rowan stood with her hands clasped in front of her while Detective James went into his pocket again and pulled out a notepad and pen.

"We just have a few questions for you and then we'll be

out of your hair." He smiled at her, but it was the fake kind that didn't wrinkle the skin around his eyes. His hair was dark and he had stubble and a scar running through his left eyebrow. Wendy wondered how he'd gotten it.

"Right." She knew it was never as simple as that.

"We already got the paramedic and police report," he said, flipping through at least five pages of notes. "So we don't need to go over that again. However, what we do need to know is if you knew the boy, Peter?"

So much for no repetitive questions.

"No, I don't know him." Or didn't know him? Should she talk about him in past or present tense?

"Are you sure?" he pressed, pen poised, waiting.

"Yes, I'm sure."

"Did he seem at all familiar to you?" Detective Rowan was the one to talk this time.

Wendy blinked. No one had asked it that way before.

"No," Wendy said, a little too late. Was the boy familiar? Yes, but she couldn't explain to them why. No one would believe her. It sounded impossible—it *was* impossible.

"You don't have any memory of him? He didn't look like someone you've met before?" Detective Rowan continued, slowly and even-toned. Wendy felt trapped under her stare.

"No." That time she said it too fast. "I—" She squeezed her eyes shut for a moment. "No, I don't know who he is."

Detective James looked over at Detective Rowan. Wendy couldn't read what they were thinking, but this sort of non-verbal communication was the result of years of closeness. Wendy understood, because she and Jordan could exchange looks across a classroom and she'd know exactly what her best friend was thinking.

Detective James turned back to Wendy and her mother. He clasped his hands in front of him, holding the small notepad and pen. Now the two detectives were mirrors of each other. Towering sentinels staring down at her.

"It was about five years ago that you and your brothers went missing, is that correct, Wendy?" Detective James asked.

Mrs. Darling inhaled a sharp breath.

The hairs on Wendy's arms prickled.

He said it so nonchalantly, as if Wendy didn't go through life carrying the burden of what had happened each and every day. As if it weren't a stain on her childhood, a family curse that they never spoke a word of.

As if it were nothing.

"Y-yes," Wendy croaked.

"According to the original police reports, you, your brothers—John and Michael—and your pet dog went missing from your backyard on the night of December twenty-third." Detective James spoke slowly as he watched her. "I believe you were twelve, John was ten, and Michael was seven?" He said it like a question, but it was clear he knew all of the details by heart. Not once did he glance at his notes. "Only your dog returned from the woods that day, and they found blood on her fur."

Michael's blood.

Wendy's stomach gave a nauseated lurch.

Her mother was still as a statue, her face nearly as pale.

"Officer Smith told us they had search parties combing through the logging roads and the woods, but nothing showed up. That is, until six months later when a park ranger found you in the woods. He said you were standing under a tree, looking up and not moving." She felt frozen under his steady gaze. "He tried to get you to move but you didn't respond, so he carried you out and called the police." Detective James finally looked down at his notebook.

Wendy felt like she was watching a movie. One of the British procedurals her mother liked to watch. What did this have to do with Peter?

She wasn't brave enough to simply ask.

"You had some minor cuts and bruises, but no major injuries," Detective James went on, thumbing lazily through pages of his notes, not actually reading them. "The most pertinent things of note were that you had no recollection of what had happened during those six months, that parts of your clothing had been patched with natural materials native to tropical climates but nowhere in Oregon"—he paused for a moment—"and that there were traces of your brothers' blood found under your fingernails."

Wendy's vision blurred. She barely registered that hot tears were trailing down her cheeks.

"Miss Darling," Detective James said in a low, serious tone. "I'm sorry, but I have to ask you again: Do you remember anything that happened to you in those woods?"

A choked breath stuck in Wendy's throat. She couldn't remember, but whatever happened still lived in her bones. It hid tucked between her ribs and nestled in her spine, stirring on occasion. Her body remembered what her mind couldn't.

Wendy's chin wobbled, a sour mix of embarrassment and fear twisting in her stomach. She pressed her lips between her teeth and tasted salt. She wanted to make some smart reply, to shut them down and get them to leave her alone, but she couldn't come up with anything clever.

It was her mother who took a step forward. "What exactly is this all about, detectives?" She raised her voice, but the hand she held against her chest trembled. Her face was pinched, almost in a grimace, like she was bracing herself for impact. Like she already knew what they were going to tell her.

Detective James spoke in a rehearsed tone. "After the police officers you spoke to reported to the main department, they noted some connections between your daughter, the location of the incident, and the dates. They pulled some dead files, and we got called in."

Dead files. Wendy shuddered. Mrs. Darling didn't say anything.

"Mrs. Darling." His tone was quieter now. "The material the boy was wearing matched the evidence collected from Wendy's clothing five years ago."

CHAPTER 4

Thunder

Wendy felt a stirring deep inside her bones. It had first started when they found her in the woods. An uncontrollable shaking. Not the kind she would get after swimming too hard for too long, or the shiver she got from playing in the icy water at the coast. It wasn't even the sort of terrified quiver you got in your hands or knees. This was at the very core of her body, like a small creature living deep in her chest, shaking her ribs like the bars of a cage in a wild frenzy. It was an immobilizing tremor.

It was her fault. It was all her fault. Wendy was the eldest—she was supposed to look after John and Michael. She was supposed to take care of them, and she'd failed. She was the only one to return.

Her brothers were still missing, and it was her fault. Everyone knew it—Wendy, her parents, everyone in town.

There must've been some way she could have brought them back with her. Why hadn't she? And why couldn't she just *remember*?

Wendy's fingers flexed against her sides. She couldn't let the shaking start, because she was afraid she wouldn't be able to make it stop.

"Do you understand, Mrs. Darling?" Detective James watched Wendy's mother, but she just stood there, fingers pressed to the base of her throat, staring at him.

Detective Rowan watched Wendy. Wendy's shoulders shuddered.

"We think that this boy, Peter, might somehow be involved with Wendy's disappearance," Detective James continued.

Wendy couldn't look at them. She focused her eyes on the ghost of a water ring on the table.

"There's a possibility he escaped from wherever your children were taken. There's a possibility that if he knows Wendy, maybe he knew John and Michael as well."

Knew.

She didn't like the sound of her brothers' names coming from this stranger's mouth.

"We also believe he might somehow be related to the string of disappearances in town, since they all occurred near the woods."

The trembling in her chest started to wind its way up Wendy's spine. She wanted to cry out, scream, run away, maybe just explode.

"Mrs. Darling?" As Detective James took a step toward her mother, the door to the study swung open.

Wendy's father stood in the doorway, filling the frame. He had salt-and-pepper hair, but a dyed mustache. His nose was large and bulbous, and his forehead had deep-set wrinkles even when he wasn't frowning, which, to be fair, wasn't often. He was in the same suit he'd worn to work at the bank yesterday. The dull black material was rumpled. The pinstripe shirt underneath was wrinkled, and his tie was missing.

Mr. Darling's face was red. His small eyes under thick brows darted back and forth between the two detectives before sweeping over to his silent wife and, finally, landing on Wendy at the table. His fingers gripped the wooden doorframe so hard it surrendered a small creak.

"Who are you?" He had a booming voice. "And what are you doing in my house?"

While Detective Rowan squared her shoulders and watched Mr. Darling placidly, Detective James quickly flipped through his notebook. "Um—George Darling?" Wendy's father did not reply. "I'm Detective James, this is Detective—"

"Detectives?" The lines in her father's face deepened. "What're two detectives doing in my house?" His eyes shifted to Wendy, full of accusation.

Wendy's shoulders hunched up and she shrank lower in her chair. Already she was in trouble. This didn't bode well.

"There was an incident last night—"

"What incident?"

Detective James started to recite the story again, but Wendy didn't pay attention. She didn't need to hear what she had been through last night. Instead, she watched her mother, who seemed to have come out of her trance a bit.

Mrs. Darling pulled out a chair and sat down. Without sparing Wendy a glance, she leaned forward, elbows on the table, and pressed her face into her palms.

Wendy's body gave another shudder. Maybe they were both thinking the same thing.

That no one had hope of finding John and Michael.

The detectives didn't mention it as a possibility. Her mom hadn't shown any sign of relief.

Wendy looked down at her hands, remembering the blood caked under her nails.

No. No one else would expect to find them alive, but

Wendy held out hope. There was something in her that *knew* they weren't dead. It was a gut instinct. Wendy didn't believe in much, but she believed in that, and she held tight to the feeling—the faith that they were out there, somewhere, even if no one else agreed.

Right now, she couldn't stand listening any longer. She needed to get out of there. To get some fresh air and clear her head.

Wendy pushed back from the table and stood up. She made for the front door, but her father's arm shot out, a finger pointing at her. "Where are you going?" he demanded.

Everyone was staring at her again.

She crossed her arms, trying to hide her shaking hands. "Jordan's," Wendy croaked.

His eyes bored into hers. "Don't go anywhere else." Wendy nodded and sprinted out the door.

She wanted to get away and get to Jordan. She was the only one Wendy could go to. Jordan never doubted or questioned her. She listened to what Wendy said and believed her, unlike everyone else in town.

"Wendy, you okay?"

The sudden voice made her jump. She turned to see her neighbor, Donald Davies, picking up his newspaper from his front porch in a dark red robe. He was a tall and slender man who only wore flannel shirts in various shades of red plaid when he wasn't in a business suit. He had curly brown hair and a thick, dark beard. Mr. Davies and her dad worked at the same bank. Wendy had been babysitting his boys—ten-year-old Joel and seven-year-old Matthew—for years. He always gave her a big tip, and whenever she tried to give it back, Mr. Davies insisted she use it for her college fund.

"Mr. Davies, hi," Wendy said, trying to keep her voice from shaking. She glanced down at the newspaper in his hand. Ashley Ford's picture smiled at her from the front page.

"Is everything okay?" Mr. Davies repeated, stepping down from his porch. Wendy could only imagine how she looked. Probably like she had just seen a ghost. Mr. Davies looked pale and his eyes kept cutting over to the police car parked in front of their house. He squeezed the newspaper in his hands.

Wendy forced a smile. "Yeah, I'm fine," she said, already starting toward the Arroyos' house again. "I've gotta go, though—I'm late to meet Jordan."

Mr. Davies blinked. Wendy was usually very neighborly and would stop and chat with him if she had the time, but right now she didn't have the energy for it.

Her mind buzzed. She needed everything to slow down so her head could catch up. Her own skin felt suffocating. She wanted out. She wanted to run away. She didn't want to be met with more stares and whispers when she went into town. She didn't want to pretend she was fine.

But Wendy refused to let herself cry. It had taken so long to board everything up the last time. Wendy didn't think she could manage it again.

The six months between running off into the woods and being found were just a black void in her mind. When she was in the hospital, the doctors had tried to get her to press against it, to poke and prod and see if she could remember anything, but she couldn't.

Of course she *wanted* to remember. If she could just remember what had happened, then she could find her brothers. Those lost memories held the secrets to finding them.

All that she had been left with were horrible dreams that made her wake up in the hospital screaming and left ghosts of images in their wake. Trees, Michael's smile, John's shoes, screams of laughter, and a pair of eyes like stars.

CHAPTER 5

The Arroyos

The garage door at the Arroyos' house was open, revealing shelves of tools and car parts. There were two cars in the garage. One belonged to Jordan—a beat-up sedan with a rusting hood that fit in well with the greasy car parts surrounding it. And then there was Mr. Arroyo's sleek, silver crown and glory next to it. Any time Wendy had problems with her truck, Jordan and her dad were the ones to help her out. She would need to enlist their services for her dented hood and scratched windshield, but right now, there were more earthshaking matters at hand.

Wendy half ran up to the porch and rang the doorbell. A large knot lodged in her throat.

Jordan opened the door. She stood, shoeless, in a pair of gray sweatpants. One arm stretched above her head, scratching her back and pulling up the hem of her beat-up Red Cross shirt. While Wendy always got up early—both every day during the summer and on the weekends during the school year—Jordan had the sleep habits of a very lazy house cat. Jordan had a piece of toast sticking out of her mouth, a sleepy smile playing on her lips. Her brown hair was a pile of springy ringlets framing her heart-shaped face.

"Hey, you—" Jordan cut herself off, brows furrowing as soon as she got a proper look at Wendy.

Wendy rocked forward onto the balls of her feet, wringing her hands.

Jordan's arm fell to her side. "What's wrong?" she demanded through a mouthful of toast.

Wendy opened her mouth, but nothing came out. She felt her lower lip wobble.

In one fluid motion, Jordan pulled her inside. They quickly started down the hall, passing the kitchen on the way. Jordan tossed the rest of her toast onto the counter and Wendy heard Mr. Arroyo say, "¡Ay, Jordan! ¿Qué haces?" She caught a glimpse of Jordan's dad, frowning as he picked up the piece of soggy toast and threw it in the trash.

"My bad!" Jordan maneuvered herself to block Wendy from her father's view. "Wendy just got here. We'll be in my room," she said casually.

"Oh, okay, fine— Hi, Wendy," Mr. Arroyo said distractedly as he wiped up the melted butter with a dish towel.

Jordan ushered Wendy down the hallway before she could attempt a reply. It was lined with pictures of Jordan and her dad at varying ages, all smiling and doing things like fishing, camping, or going to soccer games. There were even a couple of Mrs. Arroyo from when Jordan was a baby, before she passed away.

Wendy's house didn't have any family photos like that. The walls were mostly bare, except for a few Monet prints her mother had bought ages ago. Time had faded the vibrant colors to mostly pale shades of blue.

Wendy stepped into Jordan's room and Jordan shut the door behind them. The four walls were covered in black, red, and purple—a complete eyesore. There were pennants and posters of the Portland Thorns—Jordan's beloved soccer team—covering the walls, all clad in crimson and black. Jordan's medals hung on the wall from purple ribbons. The rest of her room was an absolute mess, as always. There was a heap of clothes in the corner and every surface was littered with a combination of magazines, trophies, and actual garbage.

But Jordan's room also had a window that cast the best light and a watery blue comforter. She had pictures of herself and her friends taped all over her headboard. Several included Wendy. Most were of her grimacing while Jordan, arm hooked around her, beamed widely at the camera.

Wendy sat down on the edge of the bed. Jordan tugged out her desk chair, pushed off the pile of shoes, and sat in front of her. "What happened?" Jordan asked, leaning forward and placing a hand on her upper arm.

Wendy could feel panic starting to reach its way up her throat again. She licked her lips and took a deep breath before telling Jordan everything that had happened the night before.

Jordan sat and listened intently, the corners of her mouth pulled down in a frown. Her eyebrows flickered upward now and then, but she never cut Wendy off to ask questions.

When she started to tell Jordan about that morning, words failed her.

"And the detectives said . . . they said maybe he had been with us—wherever we were—so he might know something?" Wendy rubbed her arms, trying to fight off the goosebumps. "Maybe he knows where my brothers are?"

There was silence. Jordan sat back and let out a puff of air. Wendy tried to steady her breathing, but that just made it even more difficult.

"How old is he?" Jordan asked.

"I don't know. He looked about my height, younger than us, though . . . Maybe a freshman?" Wendy pressed her thumbnail into her palm as she watched Jordan nod. It occurred to Wendy that if this boy was around her and her brothers' ages when they went missing, maybe that could provide some kind of connection.

"And you don't recognize him?"

Again, the question made her heart beat faster. She couldn't tell Jordan she thought he could be Peter Pan. Jordan, who had been the only one at school to really believe her when she said she couldn't remember what had happened to her and her brothers, had never pressed or doubted her, but even her best friend would never believe something like this. No, Wendy couldn't do that, not when it was just so entirely impossible.

Wendy shook her head.

"And they haven't found him?" Jordan asked, running a hand through her curls.

"Not that I know of . . . But I—I don't—"

"You don't want them to?" she guessed.

"No!" Wendy shook her head. "It's not that. If he does know, then of course I want the police to know so they can find my brothers." She was having a hard time meeting Jordan's watchful gaze. "This is the first time in five years we've had *any* new information, any hope of finding them," she went on. "But, it's—it's still . . ."

"Terrifying," Jordan finished quietly.

Wendy nodded.

Jordan stared past Wendy, frowning at the opposite wall.

Jordan had been there before, during, and after the disappearance. When Wendy was finally allowed to go back home, Jordan was the only person from school who stopped by to see her. She acted like nothing had happened, and, while they refused to go into the backyard for several years, they did play board games and put puzzles together in the living room.

Sometimes Mr. Arroyo even let them play catch in the house, as long as it was with a Nerf ball that couldn't cause too much damage.

A couple of times, when Wendy was in the hospital, Mr. Arroyo and Jordan had tried to visit her, but the doctors always explained the "delicate" state she was in and that she shouldn't see anyone who might trigger emotional distress.

Ever since, Wendy had felt overwhelming gratitude to Jordan and her dad. She felt so lucky to have them and indebted for her friendship. But it also meant she was very scared of losing it.

"I can't go through it all over again," she blurted out.

Jordan squeezed her arm. "You won't."

"What if—?"

"You can't think about that, Wendy."

"But—"

"It won't happen." Her voice was firm. Not the ground-shaking tone of her father's, but the solidness of stone. Her hands steadied Wendy. "No one is going to take you anywhere. Everything is going to be okay. Nothing is—"

"Different?" Wendy asked, angry but having nothing to take it out on. "How can things not change after this? How am I supposed to move on? I just—" Wendy clenched her hands into fists. "I just want to run away. I want to get out of here!"

"I know." Jordan stayed calm. "Off to Neverland, right?" she teased gently.

An exasperated laugh shot out of Wendy. Jordan had no idea.

"The good news is you get to run away—*both* of us do," Jordan went on, slapping her thighs. "To college! It's not a magical island in the stars, but there is gross dorm food, Olympic-sized pools, and lots of hot college guys." Jordan smiled, but Wendy could only manage a small tip of her lips. "We'll get to decorate our dorm rooms, stay up way too late, and drink *heaps* of coffee as we get ready for med school—"

"Nursing school," Wendy corrected her. Jordan had been trying to talk her into medical school for the last two years, but Wendy wanted to be a nurse. She wanted to help people, but the idea of being a doctor and saving people's lives was way more than she could handle.

Jordan ignored the rebuttal. "The point is, we can do whatever we want. We get to start over. We just need to get through the next few months." She squeezed Wendy's arms tight. "Okay?"

College. She kept reminding herself that it was the beacon, the light at the end of the tunnel. She just needed to get through it—get through this—and she could be free of everything. But what about now?

"None of this stuff happening is going to change that," Jordan reassured her, as if reading Wendy's mind.

"People like me don't get to live normal lives, Jordan." It was a mantra that repeated itself in Wendy's mind all the time, cycling over and over again. But this was the first time she had actually said it out loud. She knew she was generalizing and not being fair, but this town made her feel like there was something wrong with her. And, whatever it was, it was contagious.

Wendy looked away from Jordan as pity threatened to overtake her best friend's features. Jordan was usually so good at hiding it.

"Everything is going to be okay." She was so sure of herself.

Wendy shrugged. She didn't believe it, but this was the best she had felt since careening her truck off the road last night.

"Are you hungry? There's some cold, half-eaten toast I would be willing to share with you," Jordan offered with fake sincerity.

Wendy rolled her eyes, trying to laugh even though she felt weighed down. Smiling just took too much energy. "You're disgusting," she said, shoving Jordan's shoulder.

Jordan laughed and affectionately tugged a lock of Wendy's hair. "The sky's the limit for you, Wendy, okay?"

"Right."

CHAPTER 6

Dreams

They managed to kill most of the day at Jordan's house. Jordan was good at filling empty spaces and providing distractions. They talked about college and summer plans. When Wendy got quiet and stuck in her own head, Jordan coaxed her back. They'd even made muffins with fresh marionberries from Jordan's backyard. Later, Jordan gave Wendy a ride to the hospital after texting her dad for permission, since Wendy needed to pick up her truck.

Now home, Wendy slipped her sandals off by the door. The threadbare brown carpet was a disappointing contrast to the plush beige one at Jordan's house.

Her father sat at the dining table, his back to her. The news was on the television in the living room. A reporter was speaking off to the side, but the volume was too low for her to make out.

Ashley Ford's and Benjamin Lane's faces were front and center. Wendy got nauseated looking at their smiling pictures. She vividly remembered the school photos they'd used for her and her brothers when they went missing. Wendy was in a white blouse with blue flowers. John had on a white collared shirt, his hair perfectly swept to the side, his glasses making his eyes look huge. Michael, on the other hand, was a rumpled mess. His shirt was untucked and he'd missed a button.

Even after she had been found, they continued to run her picture along with John's and Michael's, explaining the details, what they did and didn't know. At thirteen she hadn't been able to handle seeing her brothers like that. After the first couple of times she had broken down in uncontrollable tears, her parents banned news from the television. Sometimes, though, her mother wouldn't hear her come downstairs and Wendy caught a glimpse of the news before she quickly changed the channel.

Wendy tore her eyes from the screen.

She turned to her father and inwardly sighed. She really didn't want to get yelled at, or lectured, or whatever else the hard set of his shoulders foretold. Well, the sooner she got it over with, the sooner she could go to her room. She steeled herself and walked up to his side.

Mr. Darling sat clutching a mug. It had a faded blue logo of his bank on the side, and it was half full of black coffee.

"Where's Mom?" Wendy ventured.

"Gone to bed." He didn't look up, but Wendy nodded anyway. Wendy imagined her mom especially needed sleep after last night and this morning.

She, herself, could have used about five years' worth of good nights' sleep.

"Do you know that boy?" Her father's sharp eyes locked onto her. The question jolted Wendy, but of course she had seen it coming.

"No."

"You just found him on the road?" One of his thick eyebrows lifted.

"I just found him on the road," she echoed through a sigh.

"Hmm." Her father made a gruff sound as he took a swig from his mug. When Wendy had been younger, he had made his coffee so sweet with hazelnut creamer that she and her brothers fought over who'd get a sip.

Wendy shifted her weight between her feet.

"If you see him again—" He raised his hand, pointing a finger at her. He was very good at making her feel small, even when he was sitting down. "You call the police and tell me immediately, do you understand?" His voice reverberated against the walls.

Wendy nodded. "Okay."

He dropped his hand. "Day after tomorrow I'm going into work late so I can take you down to talk to those detectives," he told her.

She knew better than to argue and that she didn't have a choice, anyway, so Wendy nodded again.

Mr. Darling pushed himself up from his chair, and went into his study. The door closed, and a moment later, Wendy heard the light clinking of glass.

Wendy dragged herself upstairs, dreading what tomorrow would bring.

At the top of the landing, she came face-to-face with the door to her old room.

There was nothing new about it. She walked by it every day, but now something made her stop. She didn't know what she was waiting for, yet her eyes were fixed on the doorknob. She extended a hand and rested her fingertips lightly on the cold, aged brass.

She wondered if her brothers' bunk bed was still pressed up against the right wall. John's bunk on the bottom was always properly made—it was the second thing he did every morning, after putting on his glasses. Wendy remembered how his hair stuck up in the back, his eyes barely open as he crawled along his bed, tucking in the corners.

Michael, on the other hand, always left his bed unmade, which irritated John to no end. He always slept with his socks on, just in case one of his feet slipped out from under his comforter at night. Everyone knew an uncovered limb was just asking to be chomped off by a monster.

That fear had actually been Wendy's fault—the premise of a story she had told her brothers one night before bed. The fact that Michael always woke up with one sock missing only seemed to perpetuate the story. It got so bad, in fact, that even in the summer, when heat hung thick in the room and Wendy and John slept on top of their sheets in little more than their underclothes, Michael still huddled under his comforter, socks safely in place.

Wendy wasn't sure how long she had stood there when a small noise broke her from her trance. She withdrew her hand and tripped back a step. She hadn't noticed she'd been perched on the balls of her feet like a bird ready to take flight. Wendy pressed both hands to her chest, feeling it rise and fall with a deep, steadying breath.

She heard the sound again, but it wasn't coming from the door in front of her.

This time she knew it was the quiet whisper of a voice.

Wendy's heart clenched painfully. She leaned forward to peer around the corner, down the hallway that led to her parents' room. All the lights were off and the small strip of space at the bottom of her parents' door was black.

Wendy's hand brushed the wall as she crept down the hallway where it was less likely she would step on a squeaky floorboard. She'd done this enough times to know how to linger outside her parents' room without being seen.

With her hands gripping the doorjamb, Wendy huddled against the wall and pressed her ear against the door. She closed her eyes and tried to slow her breathing, ears straining to catch any sound coming from inside the room.

Wendy pressed closer to the door, hoping with every fiber of her being that it had just been the wind, even though it was a humid, breeze-less day in the middle of June.

"My sweet boys . . ."

Wendy squeezed her eyes shut.

Her mother's voice had a light ring to it. A melody that Wendy never got to hear anymore. One that was lost in the woods, along with her brothers, and that now only passed her mother's lips when she was asleep.

"I miss you so much . . ."

One night, not more than a week after Wendy had been moved into her new room, she went downstairs to get a glass of milk. On the way back to her room, she thought she heard Michael's voice coming from her parents' bedroom. At the sound, Wendy dropped her glass with a quiet thud on the carpet and sprinted on tiptoe to her parents' door. She pressed her ear against it and heard her mother say, "My sweet boys."

And then she heard John's voice. She couldn't make out what he was saying, but it was him. It was John and Michael, just inside the door.

Wendy had shoved the door open only to find the room dark. Moonlight from the open window spilled over her mother's sleeping form. She was lying on her side, light brown hair gathered in loops on her pillow, one hand resting above her head. Her delicate fingers looked like they were reaching for something.

Confused, Wendy looked around. She'd heard her brothers, but they weren't there. She checked behind the door, but there was no one. Wendy carefully walked up to her mother's side.

Her eyes were closed, her lashes splayed across the dark circles under her eyes. Her lips parted and she said, the ring in her voice already starting to ebb, "Please come back . . ."

That was when Wendy discovered her mom was talking to her missing brothers in her sleep. She must have imagined her brothers' voices. It was nothing but the murmuring of her mother, in some state between sleep and wakefulness, speaking to people who weren't there, and who might never come back.

When Mr. Darling came home, he had found Wendy at the top of the stairs. She was crying, the neck of her nightshirt dark and damp with tears, as she tried to soak up the spilled milk with a rag.

Without a word, her father gently took the rag from her hand, picked her up, and carried her to her new bed. He flicked on the string of fairy lights and rubbed her back until the hiccups went away and, from sheer exhaustion, she fell asleep.

Now, Wendy let herself slide to the floor. Her cheeks were wet and her nose ran onto the hand she pressed over her mouth.

Eventually, her mother had stopped talking in her sleep. She hadn't done it in years, but now it was happening again. Wendy let herself take a gasp of air before she pulled her knees in and tucked her head down.

"Sleep, my darlings," her mother's gentle voice came from

the other side of the door. And then everything was silent, except for Wendy, who remained huddled on the floor, trying to force down the lump in her throat.

Wendy was sweating profusely and her head throbbed. She needed fresh air. She needed to get out of the house, away from her mother's words and the clawing feeling of being trapped.

Wendy pushed herself up from the floor, ran down the stairs and through the kitchen. She jerked back the sliding glass door and flew into the backyard.

Adrenaline coursed through her veins and pounded in her chest. Chains rattled as she shoved aside the swings and ducked under the abandoned swing set. She felt like she was trapped in a nightmare. All of the secrets and haunted memories she'd tried to outrun were catching up to her.

Wendy ran, and her feet were ready to carry her away, to take her anywhere else, to escape, but she had led herself to a dead end.

Her scrambling only took her a short distance until the faded, dilapidated fence corralled her in and she found herself face-to-face with the woods. The sun had just set, giving everything, even the bright green trees, an orange glow.

If she were braver, she would jump the small fence and keep running. But she couldn't bring herself to step into those woods.

Wendy doubled over, bracing her elbows on her thighs as she stared down at her dirty bare feet, gasping for breath. The smell of pine trees and heavy summer air filled her lungs.

Maybe she should go back to Jordan's house. Leave her parents a note and just stay the night there. Maybe being near Jordan would settle her nerves and keep back all the memories creeping out of the woods.

Maybe, if she could just suck it up and get herself together, her thoughts wouldn't spiral out of control. She could feel herself deteriorating under that sense of impending doom, inescapable fear, and a tiredness no amount of sleep could fix.

Maybe—

"Wendy?"

Her head shot up.

There he stood as if he'd just materialized from the fallen leaves on the ground.

Peter.

His eyes were impossible to evade and trapped her immediately. They were such an impossible shade of blue. The bright, cosmic flecks were no trick of the fluorescent lights in the hospital. She could see them clear as day now.

He perched on the fence, one leg extended down. His bare foot hovered just above the ground. It was the stance of someone trying not to scare off a bird.

"Wendy, why are you crying?" he asked gently. That voice was so familiar, like she'd known it her entire life.

She wanted to believe it was him, but her body reacted like he was dangerous. A wild animal, something that belonged in the woods she was so afraid of.

Wendy blinked away her blurry vision. A scream for help welled up in her lungs but couldn't escape. Her arms were heavy and useless at her sides.

Peter jumped to the ground, a landing so light that she didn't even hear it, though a loud roar was rising in her ears. He held out his hands at his sides, palms forward in surrender.

Wendy took a step back. "No, stop," was all she could muster.

"What's wrong?" he asked, his brilliant eyes searching her face. That crease between his eyebrows was back.

Wendy made a strangled noise that was something between a laugh and a cry. This wasn't happening. She had to get out of here. He couldn't be Peter Pan. He was a stranger with too many connections to her nightmares.

What if the detectives were right? What if he had been with her during those missing six months?

He stepped closer.

"Please, don't." Her feet tripped over each other as she tried to take another step back. He was right in front of her now. Wendy turned to run, only to collide with something hard. The last thing she remembered before it all went black was the clanking of swings and arms catching her.

CHAPTER 7

Crickets

The first thing Wendy noticed was the sound of snapping wood. It cut through her ears and dragged her back to consciousness. The air smelled like damp wood and musty earth. Smoke stung her nose. She was warm and there was something hard poking into the middle of her back. Wendy shifted and groaned as a pain in her temple throbbed. She rolled onto her side, eliciting a symphony of metallic squeaks from under her.

This wasn't her bed.

Wendy opened her eyes to find a blue pair watching her from less than a foot above. Images of the woods, the hospital, her parents, and the detectives flashed through her mind.

Peter's lips tipped into a grin, pressing dimples into his cheeks. His eyes sparked with amusement. "Hi."

Wendy punched him square in the face.

Peter let out a shout and stumbled back. He careened into a table, knocking an empty mason jar to the floor.

Wendy tried to scramble away, but the limp mattress slipped out from under her, throwing her back against the wall. Her right leg fell through the metal coils of the cot. She tugged, but the springs tangled painfully around her ankle.

"Don't touch me!" Wendy snarled, trying her best to be intimidating even as terror gripped her.

It seemed to do the trick, because Peter stood far back, looking downright shocked and even a little frightened. "*You* hit *me*!" he spluttered, rubbing his jaw.

She tried to shake her leg free so she could escape, but the springs only tightened, causing her to hiss in pain. "Where did you take me?" she demanded. "Where am I?" Her mind went wild with endless scenarios, each more terrible than the last, in the seconds it took him to respond.

"I didn't *take* you, you knocked yourself out on that swing set, so I brought you here!" He poked along the side of his face, one eye closed in a grimace.

Wendy's eyes darted around the small room, trying to take in her surroundings while keeping an eye on him.

It was only lit by a dented oil lantern hanging from a hook. Her eyes swung to the crooked window carved out of the wall. Through the grime-covered glass, she could see it was completely dark outside.

Nighttime.

She was in a small structure made of mud-chinked logs. It had a drooping roof and another dirty cot across the room like the one she was currently trapped in. Dust-covered beer bottles spilled across the wood plank floor. A deteriorating buck head was mounted above an old, empty gun rack.

"Hunting shack," Wendy suddenly realized with a groan. Kidnapped. She had been kidnapped and taken to a hunting shack in the middle of the woods. Was he—

"You really got better at fighting," Peter told her matter-of-factly, fists on his hips. "Who taught you to hit like that?"

Standing in the middle of a scene straight from a horror novel, Peter looked oddly . . . normal.

She'd half expected him to be flying and brandishing a pirate sword when she saw him next. It made her feel all the more ridiculous now, seeing him again. Of course he wasn't Peter Pan. He was just a normal boy, not some magical being from a bedtime story.

The fact that he was wearing cargo shorts and a faded blue T-shirt wasn't strange, but the shorts were way too big and they were held up by a knotted length of rope. The shirt hung loosely from his shoulders, the neckline frayed and unraveling. They were both covered in dirt.

Wendy gave her head a shake. She refused to be lured into a false sense of security by this boy who had taken her to a hunting shack in the middle of the woods.

"Are you going to kill me?" Wendy blurted out.

He blinked. "What?"

"Are you going to kill me?" she repeated. Hot, sticky blood trickled down her calf. She'd seen this same scene play out in at least a dozen different movies. She would go missing, her face would be plastered all over the news, her parents would have to go through the same torture all over again—

Peter laughed, but his eyebrows were still drawn in confusion. "I— What— Wendy, why would I want to kill you?" he asked, taking a step forward.

"STOP!" Her hand shot out, fingers splayed as if she could hold him back while she was stuck in a decrepit old cot. Wendy was surprised when he did actually stop, looking all the more confused.

He didn't look particularly large, but ropes of muscle still wound their way around his lithe build. Wendy's free hand went to her forehead, trying to steady herself. "Please, just stop."

"Stop *what*?" Peter's hand went up to touch his cheek again. "I'm not doing anything! Wendy—"

"Stop—stop calling me Wendy!" Her eyes darted around the room again. The only way out was through the door, and on the other side of it was the woods. Who knew how deep he had taken her or how far she was from home.

Peter cocked an eyebrow at her. "You . . . don't want me calling you your name?" he said slowly.

"No." He shouldn't even know her name to begin with!

Peter frowned and scratched the back of his neck. "That doesn't make sense," he said, his hand dropping to his side in defeat.

"Did you kidnap Benjamin Lane and Ashley Ford?" Wendy demanded.

"Kidnap?" He gave her a bewildered look, blue eyes going wide. "What—"

Frustration growled in the back of her throat. "Who are you? What do you want with me?"

He leaned closer to her and pointed to himself. "I'm Peter," he said slowly, as if he were trying to explain something very simple to a small child. She couldn't tell if he was being serious or making fun of her.

Either way, Wendy glared. "No. I mean, who *are* you?"

Peter scratched the back of his head again. There were pine needles stuck in his messy auburn hair. "You're acting really weird. Is this some kind of game I'm not getting?"

A manic laugh shotgunned out of her. "*I'm* weird?" Wendy demanded. "You kidnapped me and are holding me hostage in a hunting shack in the middle of the woods!"

"Kidnapped? I didn't kidnap you, you fainted—"

"I got *knocked out* because you—"

"Fainted," he corrected. Wendy spluttered—was he serious?—but he continued on. "You fainted, I brought you here so you weren't just lying out on the grass all night"—he paused in counting on his fingers to slant her a look—"you're welcome, by the way. And you're only being held 'hostage' by that mess of springs *you* got yourself caught in," Peter added, pointing at her leg.

Wendy teetered on her good foot. She didn't have a leg to stand on, metaphorically—or literally—speaking. This all sounded semi-rational, but Wendy still didn't trust him. She squinted at him.

The fact that he stood there, looking both triumphant and amused, didn't help her mood.

It was maddening because she *did* recognize him, but for reasons that didn't make any logical sense. It was all things she had imagined about Peter Pan. The small chip in the corner of his front tooth. The confidence in his voice. That damn charming smile. And those eyes that felt like she was looking at stars.

Wendy forced herself to focus, to think practically. She needed to get somewhere safe because being with him felt dangerous. It was the sort of danger you felt before jumping off a cliff into water: a low rush in the pit of her stomach that made her fingers tingle.

"Why didn't you just take me into my house instead of dragging me out here?" Wendy ventured.

She could see him chew on the inside of his cheek. The muscles in his jaw flexed and relaxed, accentuating the curve of his freckle-peppered cheekbones. "I didn't want to run into your parents," he said, scuffing the floor with his bare heel. "I mean, it'd look pretty weird if I just showed up at your house with you unconscious."

Wendy tried to judge whether or not he was lying. She still didn't know how he knew her name.

"You look pale," Peter cut in, giving her a worried look. He moved to take a step closer, but seemed to think better of it and stopped.

Maybe he was some sort of stalker, but that didn't feel right, either. She was terrified of him, but Peter also looked very wary of her. It was hard to keep up this idea that he was a threat when he kept dipping his chin and peering at her carefully. He squinted slightly.

Was he trying to study her face, too?

Wendy licked her lips. She wanted to ask him how he knew her, to get a real answer, but she couldn't work up the courage.

"So . . ." Peter rocked back and forth on the balls of his feet, his hands stuffed into his pockets. "Do you want me to help you out of there?" he asked. His mouth twitched with a suppressed grin.

Wendy's jeans were ruined. The metal springs had pushed them up her leg and the denim was torn. The cuts weren't deep, but they stung like hell. A thin red line of blood trailed down her ankle and into her shoe. She glanced back up at Peter. She didn't trust him, not by a long shot. But standing there, barefoot and apprehensive, he didn't seem like much of a threat. And the sooner she got out of here—and out of the woods—the better.

"Yes," she finally agreed, but not without shame.

Peter took a cautious step forward. "Do you promise not to punch me again?"

Wendy shot him a seething glare. "No."

Peter's lips broke into a smile. Dimples cut deep into his cheeks. Peter shrugged. "Fair enough."

He knelt down next to the cot. Lingering fear made Wendy lean away from him, pressing herself against the wall. The metal tugged at her leg. "You need to stop fighting against it or you won't be able to get out," Peter said, looking up at her.

His nearness was overwhelming. She couldn't tell if she wanted to shove him away again or reach out and touch him, just to see if he was real.

Wendy let out a half-irritated, half-pained growl. "Fine," she said through clenched teeth.

He was still watching her with those startling blue eyes.

"Stop looking at me like that," she told him. He quickly looked down, but she could just see the corner of his smile.

Carefully, she shifted her weight to her good leg, letting the other drop a bit and relax. Peter worked his fingers between the knots of spirals and gave them a quick tug, and suddenly her leg was free. Wendy's foot dropped to the wooden floor and she let out a surprised yelp.

As she toppled forward, she snatched Peter's hand to brace herself. His palm was rough but very warm. Wendy quickly retreated, causing her to lose balance again. She did an odd dance on one foot until she limped free of the ruined cot.

Peter stood and there was a wide grin on his face.

Wendy scowled. "What?"

"That looked funny," he said with a shrug.

"Shut up."

He made no effort to hide his amusement. "Does it feel okay?"

"It feels like I got my leg caught in a bear trap," she said tersely as she put her foot down and tried resting her weight on it. The cuts stung, but there didn't seem to be any other damage.

But at least she could move now, even if she was seconds away from falling through the half-rotted floorboards. "What are you doing here?" she asked him. She heard the harshness in her own voice begin to slip away.

"Well, I just got you unstuck from the bed springs—"

"No, I mean what are you doing *here*?"

Peter groaned and tipped his head back. "Not this again."

Wendy closed her eyes for a moment to rein in her frustration. "I *mean*," she started again, "why are you in this old hunting shack?"

Peter glanced around and shrugged his shoulders. "'Cause I'm staying here?" he said slowly, as if to judge whether or not he was answering her question right.

It didn't make sense. Why on earth would someone willingly decide to stay in a place like this? The woods had at least a dozen hunting shacks tucked into the logging roads. There was no sign of anyone other than Peter being here in the last several years.

"Where are your parents?" she asked. There was no way he was of legal age. He was much older than the magical boy, Peter Pan, that Wendy knew from her stories, but he definitely wasn't eighteen.

"Haven't got any." He said it so simply, and with such lack of importance, that it took a moment for it to register.

He didn't have any parents? So he was an orphan? Was he homeless?

"Are—are there other people in the woods?"

He shrugged. "Not that I've seen."

"So what are you doing in the woods?" Wendy swallowed past a lump in her throat. A question was bubbling up that she needed to ask, but she was frightened of the answer. "Did someone . . . bring you here? Were you kidnapped?"

But Peter laughed. "What? No! Jeez, what is it with you and kidnapping?"

And the frustration was back.

"If that's not it, then what are you doing here?" Wendy snapped. "Why were you in the middle of the road? Why did you come to my *house*?"

"Because . . ." His eyes dropped to the floor. "I need your help."

"What do you need my help with?" Wendy asked slowly. A chill ran across her skin. The flame of the oil lantern flickered behind the dirty glass.

Peter frowned. "I need you to help me find my shadow."

Wendy stared at him.

Again, he had said it so simply, as if this weren't a completely bizarre thing to say to her. She forced a laugh, not knowing how else to respond.

Seriously? Was he messing with her? "Uh, did you try looking on the floor?"

Peter tipped his head to the side, an eyebrow cocked like that was a ridiculous question. "You're kidding, right?"

Wendy let out a huff and rolled her eyes. "It's right th—"

She pointed to the floor where his shadow was. Or rather, where his shadow was supposed to be.

The ground below him had no shadow. It was just his feet—his very dirty, bare feet—and then the weather-worn planks. It was such a small thing to be so very *wrong* to the point that it was unsettling. It was like a Photoshop fail, but in person.

"That's not—" Wendy glanced up and Peter looked expectant. Her eyes went to the walls around them, searching for some indication, some smudge in the firelight that indicated Peter's shadow, but there was nothing.

Wendy examined her own shadow. It flickered and shifted below her, mimicking her movement across the wall.

Her shadow was there, but where was his?

"That doesn't make any sense." Wendy fixed Peter with a glare. Surely, this was some kind of weird trick. "That's not *possible*."

"I told you so," Peter said. He just stood there, looking infuriatingly placid.

"How did you do that?" she demanded. "You have to have a shadow—*everything* has a shadow!" Not in the dark, of course, but there was enough firelight in the shack for her to have one, and the cots, and the small pile of firewood in the corner.

"It must be a trick of the light or something," Wendy tried to reason with herself. She could probably search shadow magic tricks on YouTube and find an explanation. Wendy stepped closer to him, thinking maybe he was just standing in the perfect spot for all the light to bounce off him and not create a shadow—she wasn't entirely sure how that worked.

But when she moved next to him, her shadow followed, and his was still nowhere to be found. "I— What the—" Wendy stammered unintelligibly as she stared at him, bewildered.

"It got away somehow," Peter told her. All traces of a smile quickly fell from his face.

Wendy felt like she was in a very strange dream. One time, she'd had a dream where everything was normal, except there were three suns. This felt exactly like that.

But she was awake, not dreaming. She could feel the

stinging of the scrapes on her leg, and she could see Peter in front of her, clear as day. Not an apparition, not a daydream, not make-believe.

And yet Peter himself radiated the fantastical. A boy plucked from her dreams and her mother's stories, and set before her. He was something else altogether. He was stardust and the smell of summer.

"I get glimpses of it now and then," Peter continued to explain as if Wendy weren't about to have an existential crisis. "In corners, under beds." He glanced at the cot and his shoulders crept up to his ears. "But I haven't been able to catch it. The longer it's gone, the worse it gets." The firelight caught the worry lines on his forehead. He looked so tired. "I figured since you helped me find it before, you would be able to help me find it again." Peter chewed on his bottom lip, his eyes large and hopeful.

Wendy pushed back. "What do you mean, 'before'?" she asked, feeling all the more frustrated. "We'd never met before last night!"

Peter frowned as he inched a step closer. "Do you really not remember?"

She felt the urge to shout at him. To tell him no, there was no way she could remember him, because this was all impossible and Peter Pan wasn't real. But then, he was standing in front of her, as if he'd leapt from the pages and pages of drawings hidden in her truck. A few years older than she'd imagined, but still. He was flesh and bone, and he didn't have a shadow.

When she didn't respond, Peter pressed on. "I used to visit and listen to you tell stories about me, just outside your window." Wendy's eyes bulged and Peter was quick to continue. "I know, I know! That sounds weird, but—" He shrugged his shoulders, sheepish and at a loss for words and unable explain himself. "We didn't officially meet until one night, when I'd come to listen, but you guys were asleep already." Peter twisted his fingers together. "But before I could take off, somehow my shadow got loose in your room, and I had to chase it around—"

The slightest spark of a memory flickered in Wendy's mind.

"You woke me up," she heard herself say before she could stop herself. It felt more like a dream than a memory, but Wendy could perfectly picture it—waking up in her bed to a strange sound and finding Peter Pan, the young boy, probably about eleven years old, just like her, wrestling on the floor with something dark but translucent.

Peter looked just as surprised, but his face, instead of echoing the dread that Wendy felt, lit up with excitement. "Yes! I caught it, but I couldn't get it to stick back on—"

"So I sewed it . . ." she murmured to herself. Like with most dreams, she couldn't remember the details, just faded, splotchy images.

The large smile splitting Peter's face did little to make her feel better. "That's right! You helped me get it back on!" A relieved laugh shook his shoulders. "John and Michael slept right through it somehow—"

A sharp pang struck Wendy. She sucked in a breath.

Peter didn't notice and continued on. "But they're always heavy sleepers."

He knew Wendy. He remembered things she couldn't— things she'd thought were just dreams, because they were *impossible*, weren't they? But so was not having a shadow. And he did know her brothers. What else did he know? What else did he remember that Wendy didn't?

Wendy felt like she'd been dropped into freezing-cold water. Her skin tingled and she was dangerously lightheaded.

"Wendy?" Peter's voice called her back and she forced herself to focus on it, to ground herself back in reality. At some point, he'd moved closer. Peter watched her warily, his eyebrows pulled together and hands held out like he was readying himself to catch her. "Are you okay? You don't look so good . . ."

Wendy dragged her hand across her sweaty forehead. The shack suddenly felt uncomfortably hot, suffocating. This was too much to process at once. "Please take me home now."

"But—"

"*Please?*" She hated how pathetic she sounded and how her eyes were starting to prickle. She needed to get out of the woods. She needed to go home. "We can sort all this out—this shadow stuff or whatever—but I really need to go home first." Wendy knew she wasn't being very truthful, but right now she'd have said anything to get out of that shack.

Peter paused and for a second she feared he would object. She could see him thinking and watched as the muscle in his jaw worked anxiously. But then he nodded. "Yeah, okay." He crossed the room and opened the warped wooden door.

Outside, Wendy saw a small clearing in the light that spilled from the shack. Beyond that, everything was swallowed up by the darkness of the woods.

Wendy's body stiffened in the doorway.

"Are you all right?" Peter asked.

She could feel him just behind her shoulder.

Wendy wrung her sweaty hands together and nodded. "Y-yes, I'm fine. Just a little afraid of the . . . dark." It was only half a lie. She was afraid of the woods, but especially afraid of them at night.

Peter laughed. It came so easily to him.

"That's a strange thing to be scared of." He grabbed the lantern from a hook on the wall and pressed it into her hand. "There," he said, chin tilted proudly. "Problem solved."

Wendy gripped the metal handle. "Right."

Peter hopped through the doorway and leisurely strolled toward the woods.

Begrudgingly, Wendy followed.

"Since when are you afraid of the dark, anyway?" Peter asked, glancing back at her over his shoulder.

Wendy almost stopped, wanting to pull back from the familiar way he kept talking to her. He stared at her, so open and unabashed. Meanwhile, her own cheeks felt hot under his gaze.

Wendy's hands shook so fiercely that the metal handle of the lantern clattered. Peter frowned at it. She gripped it tighter in an attempt to stop the shaking. The strain made the dry, cracked skin of her knuckles sting.

Peter continued leading the way through the woods. His bare feet easily traversed rocks and tree roots. "I mean, lions, quicksand, nasty-tasting medicine: Those are all valid things to be afraid of," he said, leaping onto a fallen tree, his arms out at his sides as he walked along it. He seemed perfectly at home. "But the dark?" he asked. Peter jumped down and fell back into step next to Wendy. "Really?" There was a teasing note in his voice as he ducked to avoid a low-hanging branch.

Wendy only needed to dip her head a bit to clear the same branch.

She scowled at him. Her sense of pride tried to bubble its way to the surface through the sour fear in her belly. "I'm not afraid of the *dark*," Wendy said, correcting her previous statement. "I'm cautious of what's *in* the dark that I can't see." She lifted the lantern a bit higher in an attempt to get a better view of the woods ahead. Her shadow caught her eye as it walked along the tree to their right, unaccompanied. Peter's shadow was still nowhere in sight. It was just so . . . odd. "Something that could hurt me," she mumbled, more to herself than Peter. The cut on her leg ached, and it was hard to keep branches and leaves in the underbrush from slapping it.

Peter stopped walking and stared at her for a moment, his head tilted to the side. It reminded her of her old dog, Nana, when Wendy used to speak to her—confused and trying to understand. It was an innocent and kind of stupid expression. Despite present circumstances, Wendy felt a laugh rise in her throat.

But then Peter started walking again. "I think people are more frightening than the dark," he said. "A person can stand right in front of you and be dangerous without you even knowing it."

His back continued to retreat into the darkness, but Wendy remained where she stood. That was . . . surprisingly insightful.

Jogging a bit to catch up, Wendy fell into step next to Peter. Against all logic, she felt better being in the woods with him by her side. It was almost like he emitted his own light that kept the darkness of the woods at bay.

"So that's what you're afraid of?" Wendy asked. "People?"

"What?" Peter snorted and gave a fierce shake of his head. "No. I'm not afraid of anything."

Wendy rolled her eyes. What a childish response. "Every-one's afraid of *something*," she insisted.

"Everyone but me," Peter corrected.

She fought the urge to give him a shove.

Wendy concentrated on his face, trying to read his

expression as the light danced across his features. She wetted her lips, tasting the questions that were demanding to be asked.

"How old are you?" she finally asked.

"How old are *you*?" he countered evasively, lifting an eyebrow.

Wendy had to bite back a petulant reply of *I asked you first.*

"I'm eighteen," Wendy told him.

Peter looked like he'd just been slapped. He jerked back with a blink before scrunching up his face. "You're eighteen?"

Wendy felt very exposed as he blatantly looked her up and down. Indignant, even. She knew she was short, but she thought she at least looked her age.

Wendy smoothed a hand through her short hair and cleared her throat. "It was actually my birthday when we— when . . ." *When I almost hit you with my car? When you freaked me and half the hospital out? When you came crashing into my life?* "Yesterday. My birthday was yesterday."

"Oh." His stare was unfocused as he looked ahead, lost in thought. Still, he walked through the woods with ease while Wendy tripped along behind him. "I'm nineteen," Peter said, coming out of his daze and tilting his chin up. Even the smallest grin pulled deep dimples into his cheeks.

Wendy was starting to get a headache from frowning so much. "Nineteen? There's no way you're nineteen," she said flatly. "You look like you're fifteen."

His face still had a childlike roundness to it—his nose turned up at the end and was a little too small for his face. Even though he had muscles, they were still lean and sinewy. He could easily fit in with the crowds of lanky freshmen at her school.

He was looking smug now, his hands clasped behind his back as he grinned at her. "I'm taller than you," Peter pointed out, as if that was cold hard evidence for his case.

Okay, he was a tall fifteen-year-old, but still a fifteen-year-old.

"Barely!" she shot back. "And that doesn't mean anything, anyway."

Snap.

A twig cracked in the distance.

The lantern clanked loudly as a violent jump ripped through her. Wendy tripped, her back colliding with Peter's shoulder. He stumbled but caught her upper arms, steadying them both.

"What was that?" Wendy asked, the words tumbling from her lips. Was there something hiding in the trees? A person? Were they being watched? Wendy swallowed hard. She just wanted to get out of these damn woods.

"I was going to ask you the same thing." He loosened his hold on her, but Wendy backed up again, pressing into him.

"I heard something in the trees." Even though her whole body shook, she could feel his warmth radiating through his shirt.

"It's okay," Peter said. His tone was gentle. She wanted to believe him. "Here." He took the lantern from her and she automatically wrapped her arms around her middle. Peter raised the light above her head to get a better look. "There's nothing there," he told her. "Probably just an owl or something."

As if on cue, a faint hoot echoed from the trees.

Wendy let out a heavy sigh of relief.

But then a much louder hooting came from just behind her and Wendy jumped away from Peter. She whirled around to see his lips pressed into a small *O*. The owl in the woods hooted again and Peter responded.

Wendy pressed her fingers to her chest and felt her heart fluttering under them. "How did you do that?" she asked. He matched the owl's call perfectly. Jordan could whistle pretty decently to match the pitch and tune of a bird, but Peter sounded exactly like a real owl.

Peter grinned and rolled his shoulders in a shrug. "Practice, I guess." He started to walk again and Wendy stayed close to his side. Her arm brushed against his with each step.

"You must've had a lot of practice, then," Wendy said, lacking her usual sarcastic tone.

"I'm just good at imitating things," Peter said. "Animals. People."

"People?" Did he imitate their voices like stand-up comedians did sometimes, or walk around pretending to be a pirate? She was about to ask when Peter knocked the lantern into a branch, producing a clatter of glass and metal. Wendy jumped again, wincing at the sound.

"Oops. Sorry," said Peter.

She didn't know how much more of this she could take. "Are we almost to my house?" she asked, squeezing her eyes shut for a moment. Every nerve in her body was on edge, rippling anxiously under her skin.

"I think so."

"You *think* so?" Wendy groaned. "If we—"

"Want to hear what else I can do?" he asked.

No, she didn't. She wanted to get out of here and back to her house.

But before Wendy could say anything, Peter handed back the lantern and cupped his hands around his mouth, producing a light, warbling tune. It was another birdcall. Wendy knew she'd heard it before, but she couldn't place it. A swallow? Or maybe a nightingale? She didn't really know anything about birds.

Peter dropped his hands, tucked his bottom lip under his front teeth, and produced the quiet thrum of cricket chirps.

It sounded just like the crickets that lived outside her window. Wendy fell asleep to that sound every night during the summer. The edges of his lips quirked up and the lantern's light sparked in his eyes. Peter continued to make the gentle chirps. The sound melted the knotted muscles in her shoulders.

Memories of catching crickets at night with her brothers danced in the back of her mind. John quietly waiting in one spot with a paper cup in his hand, listening hard to find one of the musical insects. Michael careening through the bushes when he caught one, scaring the rest off. John always threw a fit. They were never able to catch more than one at a time. They would put it in a jar, turn off the lights in their bedroom, and sit in silence—after Wendy told Michael to shut up at least three times—until the cricket felt safe enough to start singing for them. Even in the dark, she could always tell that John and Michael were smiling just as much as she was.

It was one of her favorite sounds.

"You're really good at that," she said softly as she stared up at Peter. They weren't walking anymore.

He gazed down at her, no longer chirping. The way his eyes searched hers made her want to look away, but it seemed impossible to manage right now.

"You really don't remember me?" he asked quietly, tension caught in the lines of his face.

"How could I remember you? We just met . . ." She lied

because the truth just didn't make any sense, no matter how much she wanted to believe it.

"What about your dreams? Do you not dream about me anymore?" he pressed.

Wendy squinted. "My dreams?"

Sadness, almost a sort of hurt, fell across his face.

"You can't dream about someone you don't know . . ." Could you? The sound of the crickets floated back to her even though Peter's lips were completely still.

Peter's chest rose and fell in a sigh. "It's me, Wendy. Peter. Peter Pan." His blue eyes bored earnestly into hers. He closed his hands around both of hers. "I know you remember me, you have to . . ."

Wendy felt like she wanted to cry, laugh, and run away all at the same time. She shook her head quickly. "That's not possible. Peter Pan isn't real," she told him. Even as she said it, she felt herself doubting her own words. A part of her wanted to believe, as silly as it felt.

One thing was certain: He knew who Peter Pan was. So, even though she fought against it, the truth was that he'd heard the stories before. At some point, she had told him.

"Wendy Moira Angela Darling!"

Her father's voice cut through the night. Wendy looked around. They were at the edge of the woods. The crooked white fence of her backyard was no more than twenty feet ahead.

She could see the back door to her house through the sparse trees. The kitchen lit up her father's bulky silhouette.

"Where have you been? It's the middle of the night! I've been calling you for hours!"

Wendy knew her phone was in her pocket and on silent,

as always. The ringer always made her jump, and she found the vibration setting just as jarring.

"I—" Wendy turned, but Peter was gone, leaving her to stand alone at the edge of the woods, her hands cold, the lantern gone with him. "Peter?" she hissed into the darkness. She stood on her tiptoes and tried to peer deeper into the trees. "Where are you?"

But no one was there.

Wendy swallowed and faced the house. Behind her, the breeze through the woods tickled the back of her neck. They were only slightly more terrifying than her father waiting for her at the door.

She half ran to the fence, clumsily climbed over, and steeled herself against her father's angry glares and shouts as she crossed the backyard.

He stood there, red-faced, his large fingers gripping the doorframe. Wendy wouldn't have been surprised if he ripped it right off. "Were you in the woods?!" he demanded. Spittle flew from his lips as he yelled.

Wendy tried to think up some reasonable excuse, but her mind was back in the woods with Peter. "No, I thought I saw something, so I was just looking—"

"Don't you *dare* lie to me, Wendy!" he said.

Wendy's face turned red. She didn't know what to say. She couldn't tell him the truth. If he knew she had been in the woods with the boy from the hospital—who the police thought might be connected to her and her brothers' disappearance—well, Wendy had no idea what he would do, but it wouldn't be good.

She felt guilty and, to her surprise, scared for Peter. He was out there alone with only the hunting shack as shelter.

For the second time in the past twenty-four hours, she wondered if she would ever see him again.

"I—"

"And what happened to you?" His chest swelled and his face darkened from red to purple.

Wendy looked down at her torn pant leg, felt the throb of her head. Luckily, the pain had subsided to a dull ache. "I was sitting on the fence and fell off by accident," she said.

"I *forbid* you from going into those woods." His eyes glared into hers, but they had a glassy sheen. "I thought you were smart enough to know better after what happened!"

Wendy winced.

No, she couldn't tell him the truth. Not until she figured out what to do about Peter. But this also wasn't a situation she could lie her way out of.

"I'm sorry, Dad," she said quietly.

Her father breathed heavily through flared nostrils. Wendy braced herself for more shouting, but his shoulders sank. "Just go to bed," he told her, his voice now a low rumble. She almost preferred the yelling. The defeated tone just made her feel worse.

He moved out of the doorway to let her pass. As she did, he lifted his hand. Wendy thought he was going to place it on her shoulder, but he hesitated and let it drop back to his side. "Stay out of there," he repeated.

Wendy nodded and crossed her arms over her chest. "I will." She didn't blame him for being mad at her.

She wasn't the only one who'd lost something in those woods.

CHAPTER 8

Memories

Wendy listened at her bedroom door to the sounds of her father's frustration. She noticed that he only did chores when he was using them to announce his anger, even in the middle of the night. Wendy knew too well what it was like to have someone furiously fold a sock at you, or resentfully wash a dish in your direction.

When things grew quiet and she was pretty sure her father wouldn't come barging in to say, *And another thing!* Wendy went into her bathroom. She turned on the bathtub faucet and peeled off her jeans. They had two jagged tears, but it wasn't a big deal since they were old anyway. She sat on the edge of the tub and scooped up handfuls of water to pour over the cuts in her leg. They weren't very deep and stung only a little now. She'd gotten far worse scrapes from the edge of the pool during swim practice.

She dipped a facecloth into the water and watched her shadow mirror her movements against the wall. As Wendy let her leg soak, she dabbed at the dried blood caked to the angry bump on her head. She was a mess. The last twenty-four hours had been a mess. Everything was a mess!

As her leg soaked in the warm water, Wendy stretched

for the cabinet under the sink and dug out her sewing kit. She did her best to mend the pant leg. To save money, she'd spent many afternoons patching holes and resewing the hems on her parents' clothes. Her father's suits weren't cheap, so it made more sense for her to reattach a button or fix a pleat than to buy a new jacket. Her mother was petite, which meant standard scrub pants were always too long. The bottom hems wore out too fast from dragging on the ground, so Wendy would hem them whenever they got too worn. Wendy inspected her work, giving a tug to see if her stitches held up. They were a little askew, but the jeans were perfectly fine as junk pants if she only wore them around the house.

With a sigh, she tossed them in the hamper.

What was she supposed to do now? How was she supposed to explain any of this—Peter, his shadow—to anyone?

Oh, yes, I almost ran a boy over with my truck last night. Turns out, he claims to be a character from stories my mom made up! Did I mention he doesn't have a shadow? Like, literally. And he needs my help to find it!

Wendy scowled. Logically, it didn't make any sense, but she had seen with her own eyes that his shadow was missing. There was no denying who he was any longer.

Wendy tried to organize her thoughts. What did she *know?*

She knew he was the boy she had been subconsciously drawing. He was her daydreams come to life, even if he was a bit older than the Peter in her mother's stories. He'd definitely heard her tell stories before, but more important, he knew her brothers. In the middle of all the wild coincidences and impossible things like missing shadows, Peter knowing John and Michael was the most unsettling.

Wendy dried off and changed into an oversized sleep shirt. She crept to her dresser and pulled out of the small jewelry box the one thing she had always associated with her lost memory: the acorn. She sat in the middle of her bed and stared at the acorn, balancing it in the center of her palm.

Peter knew things that she couldn't remember. He was the key. If he could fill in the chunks of memories that had been ripped from her mind, then she could figure out what happened. She could find her brothers and get them back. It felt like an invasion of privacy—the idea that Peter knew something about what had happened to her. That he held the secret to those missing months. That this could mean Wendy finding the answer to the questions that had been eating her alive for years.

And at the center of all this was the question: Was he really Peter Pan?

Wendy dug into her small trash can and uncrumpled one of the many drawings she'd made of Peter Pan's face. She lay on top of the blankets because it was still too hot to sleep under them, then sighed and tried to force herself to calm down. Counting the fairy lights around her window and rolling the acorn between her thumb and index finger, Wendy drifted off to sleep.

Wendy sat on a fallen log in the middle of a mass of trees, but not like the woods behind her house back home. The log was covered in vines as thick as rope. The bark under her hands was wet and smooth. Dark green giants with shiny leaves shot up into the sky. Sunlight filtered through a covering of palm fronds. Palm trees rose from white sand, bowed with coconuts. She was under a lush canopy of gleaming leaves.

Even though Wendy had never been away from the Pacific

Northwest, she knew this had to be a jungle. Colorful parrots with vibrant red, blue, and yellow feathers called from nearby branches. In the distance, there was a soft thump of overripe fruit dropping to the ground. There must have been a beach nearby. Wendy could recognize the rhythmic song of waves crashing on the shore as it filtered through the jungle. The air was warm and heavy. Her skin felt sticky and she could taste salt on her lips.

Wendy looked down at herself. She wasn't in the same bulky swimmer's body she'd grown into over the last several years. This one was small, skinny, that of a child. She wore a pair of white leggings with lace hems and a white buttoned blouse with flowy sleeves. Even though they were smudged with dirt, she instantly recognized them as the clothes she had gone missing in.

Wendy's heart pounded in her chest, but she couldn't do anything. She couldn't make herself get up or move. She had no control over her body. The sound of an owl drew her attention. That was when her head turned and she saw a young boy sitting next to her, his hands cupped around his mouth. He had a shock of wild auburn hair and dazzling eyes, all the more radiant in the sunshine.

A giggle escaped her own lips. The boy dropped his hands to his side and grinned at her. He had that same small chip in his front tooth.

Wendy's throat felt tight, but she heard herself say, "You're so good at that, Peter! Will you teach me how to do it?"

Of course it was Peter. This was the Peter she always pictured in her head. Much younger than he had been last night, but unquestionably him. Undoubtedly the same.

"Sure!" His voice was higher and it squeaked with his enthusiasm, but the self-assured tone was still there. "I can do this, too." Peter pursed his lips and made a medley of cricket chirps. The same sounds he had made last night in the woods.

The sense that she had lived this scene before was painfully strong. It was more than déjà vu, it was a memory.

"Oh, I love crickets!" said her much younger voice again.

Peter grinned and scooted a bit closer, dangling his skinny legs over the log next to hers. "I know," he said, knocking his bare foot into hers.

"Wendy! Peter!"

The breath she sucked in ripped her chest open.

"Wendy, where are you!"

She would have recognized those voices anywhere.

Peter scrambled away from Wendy. She heard herself giggle again, but she strained to hear the voices of John and Michael calling for her.

"We're over here!" Peter called back.

She could hear both sets of their feet thumping through sand. The slap of lush undergrowth as they ran through it. She could hear John laugh while Michael whined, "Wait for me!"

They were right there, just behind that set of trees. At any moment, they would come into view and she would see her brothers again.

"Wendy?"

She woke with a jolt. Cold sweat covered her body and her hair stuck to her damp forehead.

Wendy was alone in her room again. She opened her hand. She'd fallen asleep holding the acorn. Maybe it was nerves, but Wendy swore she could almost feel the acorn thrum with some kind of energy. Her hand shook so hard that the acorn rolled off and onto the bed. She hugged her legs and pressed her forehead into her knees as she took deep, shuddering breaths.

It was real, it had to be. It wasn't a dream, it was a memory.

She didn't know when or where, but her brothers and Peter had been there.

Peter.

A delirious laugh bubbled in her throat. Her Peter. Peter Pan. He was real.

And she needed to find him.

CHAPTER 9

Stories

Unfortunately, responsibilities and volunteer shifts kept Wendy from immediately searching for Peter. She was already late for her shift, and rushing around to get dressed and out the door did little to ease her raw nerves.

Wendy was already halfway across the yard and digging her keys out of her bag when she saw the cop car. She froze, keys dangling from her finger. Her head whipped around, searching for someone in uniform. Right now was really not a good time for them to come poking around again! She needed to find Peter and—

"I don't understand why I'm being *questioned*." The frazzled voice came from next door. Mr. Davies stood on his front porch. He fidgeted with a rolled-up newspaper in his hands, the knuckles white. Next to him, his wife clutched the robe she wore. Detective Rowan was on the step. Detective James stood just behind her and to the right.

"We're just talking to people in the area, Mr. Davies," Rowan said in a mild, even tone. Her hands were clasped behind her back, her expression impassive. Her badge glinted on her hip.

Mr. Davies was still in his pajamas. His face was ghostly pale. Wendy imagined her face looked very similar when she had to talk to the police.

"We think one of the missing kids was taken from their home, so we want to remind people—especially those with children—to lock their doors and windows at night, and to make sure any weapons have been properly locked up." Detective Rowan paused. "Do you have any firearms in the house, Mr. Davies?"

Mr. Davies quickly shook his head no.

"Donald used to hunt, but he hasn't done that in years," Mrs. Davies explained tersely, as if Detective Rowan was a huge inconvenience to her.

"I got rid of all my guns a long time ago," Mr. Davies confirmed. He looked past Detectives James and Rowan, and his eyes snagged on Wendy standing in her yard. He quickly turned away, but Detective James followed his gaze and was now watching her.

Guilt made her cheeks burn red. She ducked her head, jogged the rest of the way to her truck, and quickly got inside. As she drove down the street, Wendy forced herself not to stare.

The police thought someone kidnapped Ben and Ashley? Mr. Davies was right to look so scared. All the parents in town would be terrified for their kids. And now they were going door to door to talk to people?

Wendy knew she hadn't seen the last of Detectives James and Rowan. Not by a long shot.

Arriving at the hospital, Wendy fished around for her lanyard and badge as she headed for the elevator to the third floor. She crinkled her nose at the photo. Her smile looked painfully forced, her blue eyes were too wide from the shock of the flash, and her shirt was wrinkled.

A handmade quilt hung on the wall behind the information desk. Artwork the kids had made lined the walls between doorways. Nearly all the nurses wore brightly patterned scrubs. The sharp sting of chemicals hung in the air, but so did that light, sweet smell that seemed to follow little kids around wherever they went.

The last place she wanted to be right now was the hospital, but she would only draw more attention if she didn't show up for her volunteer shifts. That, and she actually liked hanging out with the kids—even though, right now, every fiber of her being ached to go find Peter.

With a deep breath, Wendy tucked the loose strands of her hair behind her ears and headed to the recreation room. She did her best to avoid making eye contact with the two nurses watching her from behind the front desk, whispering to each other quietly. Her attempt to avoid their prying eyes meant she wasn't paying attention to where she was going, which was why she ran right into someone wearing Snoopy scrubs.

"Whoa!" A pair of hands caught her shoulders. "Don't trip, Skip!"

"I'm so sorry!" To her relief, it was Nurse Judy.

The head nurse chuckled and waved the apology aside as she picked up the stethoscope Wendy had knocked from her hands. "Not a big deal. Don't worry about it!" Nurse Judy looked up and immediately frowned. "Wendy? What are you doing here?" she demanded. She had a way of talking that sounded like she was yelling at you, but Wendy had learned that scolding was her way of showing affection.

"I—I have volunteer hours today," she stammered. If one more thing startled her this week, she was going to have a damn heart attack.

Nurse Judy's frown deepened. "You didn't have to come in today," she said. "You can stay home, you must be—"

"I'm fine," Wendy cut in. She really didn't want to have this conversation, especially out in the open with everyone watching. "I want to be here, really. It's a nice distraction." Wendy tossed a nervous glance back over her shoulder.

Nurse Judy followed her gaze. Her lips set in a firm line. "Well, go on then. And you let me know if anyone gives you any trouble, okay?" Wendy nodded in reply. She slinked off to the recreation room as Nurse Judy barked at the other nurses, "You two must be bored if you're just standing around! I've got some bedpans you can clean!"

Wendy ducked around a corner and pushed open the door to the recreation room. A wave of noise rushed over her as she walked in. Building blocks were stacked in a heap in one corner of the room. There were tables in the back with a flurry of construction paper and markers. Bean bags were piled up by the books and kids bounced around everywhere. In the far corner were two outdated desktop computers that the older kids sometimes ventured in to use. There was always at least one nurse there overseeing the chaos, but right now she was trying to wrestle a glue stick out of Cindy-Who-Puts-Everything-Up-Her-Nose's hands.

Something crashed into Wendy's knees. She let out a strangled yelp and stumbled back. Luckily, she was able to catch herself before toppling over.

"Miss Wendy!" the little girl squeaked as she attached herself to Wendy's legs.

"Rachel." Wendy breathed a sigh of relief. She did her best to give her a smile even though her skeleton had nearly leapt out of her skin. "You scared me!"

"Are you going to tell us a story?" Rachel asked, giving her a big smile. There was a large gap where her two front teeth should have been. Rachel had beautiful brown curls that her mother tried to force into ponytails, but they were always crooked and tufts fell out at the nape of her neck. Rachel liked to color and had a knack for getting rogue marker lines all over her cheeks. Her wild gesturing must have made her parents a nervous wreck, since Rachel had been in and out of the hospital getting procedures done to her eye.

"Of course I am," Wendy said. She led the way to the corner of the room that housed a couple of short bookshelves. They were crammed with a rainbow of book spines.

Finding Peter would have to wait. Right now, she just needed to focus and get through her shift.

"Yes!" Rachel clapped her hands together before launching herself onto a beanbag chair.

Wendy sat down in the red plastic chair. "So," Wendy began, "what do you—" She stopped. A boy was planted face-first in the beanbag next to Rachel, arms and legs splayed out around him. "Uh, Tristan, are you okay?" she asked. He was only seven but had a knack for dramatics.

"I'm a starfish," was his muffled grumble of a response.

Yup, there it was. "Starfish?" Wendy repeated, only somewhat hiding her amusement.

Rachel crossed her arms and huffed. "We were playing Under the Sea and Tristan wanted to be the shark, but we decided to let Alex be the shark because he's new and all, but then Tristan got mad when we told him he had to be the starfish, and now he won't talk to nobody."

Tristan gave a *hmph* in reply.

Wendy nodded solemnly. "Oh, I see," she said in the most serious tone she could muster.

Rachel wasn't satisfied. "Tristan, if you keep being mean like that, we won't play with you no more!"

"I don't *care.*"

Rachel glared and turned away with a flourish. "Alex! Come sit next to *me*," she said, waving her hand—which was smudged with blue ink—at a little boy Wendy hadn't noticed before who was standing away from the others. He had a mop of dark hair and big, brown, very concerned-looking eyes. He was small, but the fact that his blue hoodie was about two sizes too big exaggerated that fact.

"Hi, Alex. I'm Wendy," she greeted him with a smile. A few other kids came to join them.

Alex's cheeks turned bright red and he scurried over to a chair. He propped his chin on the table and peered at Wendy from between the sleeves of his hoodie.

"Alex is shy," said Lucy, who took the seat next to Rachel instead. Lucy had been born with fused bones in her wrist and was going through a series of corrective surgeries. Wendy had discovered early on that Lucy was one of those kids who had constantly sticky hands for no apparent reason. Lucy whispered loudly, "He's not a very good shark."

Rachel shoved Lucy and Alex hid his entire face.

"That's why I shoulda been the shark!" Tristan declared as he flopped over onto his back. They all—except for Alex—started talking at once.

"Okay, okay!" Wendy piped up. Sharks were clearly a touchy subject. "What book did you want me to read today?" she asked, running a finger along the books on the shelf.

"Peter!" Lucy shouted. The name made Wendy stop. "Tell us a story about Peter Pan!" Lucy continued. The other kids enthusiastically agreed.

Wendy bit down on her lip. Seriously? This shift was supposed to help take her mind off things, but apparently she wouldn't be able to escape thoughts of Peter.

She almost wanted to laugh, but not a funny ha-ha laugh, more of an I'm-losing-my-mind laugh.

"But, Miss Wendy, Alex don't know who Peter Pan is!" Rachel said, very concerned.

"So what?" mumbled Tristan.

Wendy tried to push her thoughts aside. "Well, that's okay. I'll just have to fill Alex in," she said. Even though Alex was currently rubbing a piece of blue construction paper between his thumb and finger, he kept stealing glances at her. Wendy leaned forward and propped her elbows on her knees, and her small audience grew quiet. Even Tristan the Forlorn Starfish sat up.

"As most of you know, Peter Pan is a magical boy," Wendy began. "He never grows up and has been a boy for as long as the stars have existed. With help from his fairy friends, Peter uses pixie dust to fly to Earth and finds Lost Ones—boys and girls who join him in Neverland, where they get to stay and go on adventures with him. You can reach Neverland by following—"

"The second star to the right!" the group cheered.

Wendy smiled. The familiarity of the story was a comfort. "That's right. The second star to the right, and straight on till morning." The line was well rehearsed—the same one her mother had told her, the same one she told her brothers, and now told the children at the hospital. "Peter and the Lost

Ones go on treasure hunts, build tree houses, fly with fairies, fight pirates—"

"And meet mermaids!" Rachel added.

Wendy nodded. "Yes, and meet mermaids! One day, Peter Pan was exploring rocks in the mermaid lagoon and collecting shells from tide pools when he heard someone calling for help." Wendy lowered her voice to an ominous tone. "The voice was coming from the mouth of a deep, dark cave surrounded by jagged rocks. But, since Peter Pan is very brave, he went into the cave to help whoever was in danger. Inside, he saw a mermaid trapped on a rock, held captive by a—"

"A pirate!"

"No, a bear!"

"Bears can't swim, dummy. How could it—"

"Yes they can. I saw one swim on TV once—"

"A shark!" Wendy continued. The kids all gasped. "The mermaid was crying, and she told Peter the shark wouldn't let her go until she gave him her pearl necklace. But the mermaid had spent years finding all the perfect pearls on the shores of Neverland to make the necklace, and it would break her heart to give it up.

"So Peter chucked a seashell at the shark and hit him square in the nose!" The kids laughed. "Peter yelled at the shark, 'Hey, leave that mermaid alone! Just because you're big and scary doesn't mean you can boss other people around!' But the shark swished his big pointy tail and splashed Peter with seawater.

"'I want those pearls to give my wife!' the shark said. 'I forgot it was her birthday, so I need to get her an extra special gift so she won't be mad at me anymore, and I want those pearls!' Peter could tell the shark wouldn't listen, and while Peter was an excellent fighter, he knew he couldn't take on a shark. And even though he knew how to fly, the mermaid would be too heavy to carry. But Peter Pan was a very clever boy.

"'Hey, shark!' Peter said. 'If I can find you a pearl necklace, will you leave her alone?' The shark thought about it and swam back and forth for a moment. 'If you can find me another pearl necklace, I'll take it and let her go. But you need to get me one soon! It's almost dinnertime and I need to get back to my wife!' So Peter promised the mermaid that he would be right back and took off to the beach.

"He found the whitest sand and used his spit to roll it into teeny tiny balls the size of pearls and strung them together with a thin piece of seaweed. Peter quickly flew back to the cave and waved the fake pearls in the air. 'Hey, Mr. Shark! I found you a necklace of pearls!'

"The shark swished his tail in excitement. 'Good! Give it to me now!' Peter Pan knew that sharks have terrible eyesight, so before he gave the shark the fake pearl necklace, Peter said, 'First let her go, then I'll give you the necklace and you can take it to your wife!'

"The shark was irritated but agreed. The mermaid leapt into the water and escaped the cave. 'Now give me those pearls!' the shark said.

"Peter tossed the necklace into the air and it splashed into the water. The shark grabbed it in his teeth, but the fake pearls made of sand dissolved as soon as they hit the water. When he brought them to his wife, there was nothing left but a string of seaweed. Mrs. Shark, now only having a piece of seaweed for a birthday present instead of a beautiful pearl necklace, was so mad at Mr. Shark that she chased him around the ocean, nipping at his tail!

"Peter and the mermaid watched from the shore and laughed at how silly the shark looked. Even now, there's still a shark that wades through the waters of Neverland with a big bite missing from his tail fin."

The end of the story threw the kids into fits of laughter.

"Stupid shark!" said Tristan.

"Don't say 'stupid,' it's a bad word!" Lucy said. "'Sides, you're the one who wanted to be a shark!"

"Not anymore!"

Wendy laughed and shook her head while an intense debate began about whether Joel should be a shark or a star-fish. The kids at the hospital all loved her Peter Pan stories. Whether they had already heard a dozen of them before or it was their very first time, they all seemed to love the character of Peter Pan. And who wouldn't? He was magical and amazing. He never had to grow up and he could do whatever he wanted. Wendy envied him.

She stood up from her storytelling chair and stretched. Wendy wondered if Alex had liked the story. He seemed so shy. She hoped Rachel and Tristan hadn't scared him off from the recreation room.

As she turned to the table where Alex was sitting, Wendy saw that he wasn't alone anymore.

Peter sat next to Alex, who was perched on the edge of his seat, peering into Peter's cupped hands. He was in a pair of nurse scrubs and had a satisfied grin plastered across his face. Alex's jaw was slack, those big brown eyes of his wide.

Wendy stumbled over beanbags and dodged running kids.

"What are you doing here?" she snapped, jerking her head back and forth to see if anyone had noticed him. There were a couple of parents and a nurse in the room, but, for some reason, no one even glanced in their direction. Which was odd, considering all the stares Wendy had been earning. Her pulse thudded with panic. If someone recognized him, she was going to be in *so* much trouble. How the hell would she even begin explaining herself? And Peter?

Alex jumped, but Peter looked up at her with a smile, as if all of this were completely normal and he broke into hospitals regularly. Cupped in Peter's hands was a simple but delicate shark folded out of blue construction paper. "Hi," he greeted cheerily.

"Where did you get those?" she asked, gesturing at the blue scrubs.

"I found them," he replied, vaguely waving his hand.

"What are you doing here?" Wendy repeated, annoyed at how calm and nonchalant he was. She had thought it was going to be impossible to find him again, but here he was, sitting and making origami.

"I came to listen to you tell stories," he said simply before turning back to Alex. The small boy was now staring intently at the paper shark as he poked it with a finger. "That was a pretty good one, but mermaids are usually the ones bugging the sharks," Peter continued.

Wendy scoffed. Now was not the time for him to critique her storytelling.

"They can be really mean. Don't you remember the mermaid who tried to drown you?" Peter asked, finally sparing her a glance.

"What?" Wendy asked, incredulous. "No—"

"Hmm, well, that's probably for the best," he agreed, nodding.

She wanted to shove him out of his chair. "Alex, why don't you go play with the others for a bit?" Wendy suggested.

She needed to get Peter out of here unseen. Or, unseen by anyone else.

"It was swimming!" Alex exclaimed, pointing at the paper shark.

Wendy frowned. "Swimming?"

"Yeah, he made it swim!" Alex insisted.

Peter smirked, looking quite pleased with himself as he leaned back in his chair. "You can keep it if you'd like," he told Alex. He placed his creation into the little boy's hand.

Alex put it on the table and stared at it so intently, Wendy thought the strain might damage his eyes.

"What does he mean, you 'made it swim'? Wait, no." Wendy held up her palm, cutting off Peter before he could answer. She would not let him distract her from the matter at hand. "How did you get in here? Where did you get those?" Wendy demanded through gritted teeth, pointing at the blue scrubs he wore.

Peter shrugged. "I found a stack of them in the hallway," he said, tugging at the collar of the shirt.

Wendy rubbed her palm against her forehead, letting out a small growl. She had spent all morning wondering how she was going to track down Peter. Now that he'd just apparently *waltzed* into the hospital, she had no idea what to do with him. What she did know, however, was that if someone recognized him, and saw her *with* him, they were screwed.

"I need to talk to you," she said, casting a nervous look around the room. "We need to get out of here before someone notices you." It seemed wrong to hide him from the people at the hospital, or the police who were looking for him, but she had her own questions that needed answers before anyone else got hold of him.

Rachel collided into Wendy again and tugged on the

hem of her shirt. "Miss Wendy!" she whined. "Tell us another story!"

"Not right now, Rachel," Wendy said. She tried to get herself free of the little girl's vicelike grip. "Me and my *friend* here need to go talk." She gave Peter a pointed look and jerked her head toward the door.

Rachel whirled around to look at Peter, apparently just having noticed him. "Hello," he said to her with a smile.

Wendy had never witnessed Rachel being as quiet as she was in the following moments.

Rachel studied Peter carefully, her eyebrows pulled together in concentration. Peter seemed completely unfazed. Wendy just stood there as the silence stretched out, long and awkward.

Wendy was about to ask Rachel if she was feeling all right when a big, gap-toothed smile broke across her face. "PETER!" she all but squealed, launching herself onto him.

"Rachel, no!" Wendy tried to pull her off, but Rachel kept wiggling free and grabbing hold of Peter's shirt in her little hands.

Peter laughed, loud and bright.

"Wendy, it's Peter Pan! You're friends with Peter Pan?" She looked back and forth between the two of them. "Ooh, I knew you were real!" she told him as she yanked on his arm.

"See? Rachel here knows who I am," Peter said with a smug look.

Wendy had to fight the urge to drag him out of there by his ear. She pointed a finger at him. "*Not* helping!" They were going to draw someone's attention. "Rachel, that's not Peter Pan. Peter Pan isn't real—he's just make-believe." Though, she wasn't convinced of that anymore.

The wounded look on his face almost made her regret saying it, but they really didn't have time for this right now!

Regardless, Rachel wasn't buying it. "Of course he's real!" she said. She jerked her arm free from Wendy and squished Peter's cheeks between her small hands. "See?"

Yes, she did see it. It was hard to not laugh at his smooshed face, but she did see it. The eyes, the chipped tooth, and the auburn hair. It was all there, whether she would openly admit it or not.

"He's a bit old," Rachel went on, as if this were a count against him. "But it's still him. You can see it right there in his eyes!" she said, pointing. "And his mouth." She poked his bottom lip. "And see, that's the scar he got from fighting Captain Crash McCreevy!" She pointed to a *V*-shaped scar on his upper arm. The mention of Captain Crash McCreevy reminded Wendy of the Peter Pan story she'd told at least a dozen times. It was about a crazy old pirate captain who wanted to steal all the tiger cubs to make a blanket, until Peter challenged him to a harrowing duel. In the story, Captain Crash McCreevy fought Peter Pan with the nose of a sword-fish that left a *V*-shaped cut in Peter's arm.

The evidence sent Rachel into another bout of wiggly excitement. "It's Peter Pan!"

"She makes valid points," Peter confirmed, nodding his head.

"But, Peter, why are you so old?" Rachel asked, the smile on her face dimming with concern.

"Well, that's something I've been trying to talk to Wendy about, but she seems to be having trouble believing me," he told her.

Rachel gave Wendy an accusatory look.

Wendy scowled. The last thing she needed was Rachel telling everyone she'd met Peter Pan. But, apparently, Peter was already two steps ahead of her.

"Can you do me a favor, Rachel?" Peter asked as he leaned closer to her. Rachel nodded vigorously. "You can't tell any adults I'm here, or I might get in trouble, okay? It needs to be a secret between the three of us—oh, and Alex here," he added, nodding to Alex, who was still staring unblinkingly at the paper shark.

Rachel nodded solemnly. "I won't. I promise. Will you come back and visit us again soon?"

"Yes—"

"No!" Wendy cut in, finally pulling Rachel away from Peter. "We need to talk now, Rachel. Go play with Alex."

Peter stood up and mussed the top of Rachel's already frizzy hair.

"Bye, Peter!" Rachel said, throwing her arms around him and giving him a hug before sliding into the seat next to Alex.

Wendy glared at Peter. "Let's go," she growled.

As she led Peter to the door, she overheard Alex tell Rachel, "He made it float!"

"Well, yeah, he's Peter Pan!" Rachel replied.

Wendy walked as fast as she could down the hallway, dragging Peter along behind her, her hand clasped around his wrist. She kept looking around, paranoid that someone would spot them and Wendy would somehow get in trouble. She pulled him down the stairway and crossed the lobby to a glass door that opened up into an empty courtyard.

When she spun to face him, he had a very amused look on his face. Both of his eyebrows were raised and the right side of his lips twitched as he suppressed a grin.

It did nothing to improve her mood.

"How the hell did you even get in here without anyone stopping you?" she asked. There was a front desk on every floor of the hospital and every visitor was required to check in and wear a visitor's pass, even if he *was* in scrubs. "How come no one noticed you?" He didn't exactly blend in. There was something about Peter that was decidedly . . . otherworldly, for lack of a better term. She couldn't pinpoint it, but it was a sort of aura he gave off.

Aura? Wendy pinched the bridge of her nose. What was she even thinking?

"Because I didn't *want* them to notice me," Peter said, as if this were a very obvious answer to a very dumb question. "I can get past adults easy—they don't pay much attention to begin with, anyway. But I can get by anyone without them seeing me, you know that," Peter added with a laugh.

"No I don't. I don't even know you!" Wendy shot back, her eyes darting back to the door. She said it, but she could hear her own doubt in her words.

Peter groaned and threw his head back. "Are we really still playing this game?" he asked. He stepped closer, his brow furrowed. "It's me, Peter—you know me, Wendy! I'm real, Neverland is real. You just forgot about me—that's what happens when you grow up!"

His tone surprised her—it was nearly pleading.

"You've got to remember *something*," he pressed, catching hold of her elbow.

"I *can't* remember!" Wendy shot back, wrenching her arm free. She was sick of people saying that to her over and over again. "I can't remember *anything*!"

Peter's shoulders slumped.

Though, that wasn't entirely true, was it?

"I mean . . ." Wendy swallowed hard. "I had a dream last night. Maybe—maybe a memory." Lord help her, was she really admitting this?

Peter perked up. "You did?"

Wendy nodded. "About you." She felt breathless. "And me. And Neverland."

A smile broke across Peter's face, bright and immediate and all-consuming. It hit her in the chest. "Then you *do* remember!"

But Wendy wasn't so ready to accept it. "If you're really Peter Pan, you should be able to fly, and you're supposed to be a child," she added. "The whole point of Peter Pan's existence is that he never grows up, right?" Wendy couldn't believe that she was actually arguing the logistics.

"Yeah, well." Peter scuffed his foot against the ground. "Those things are sort of part of the problem. For some reason I'm getting older—and *fast*." He looked genuinely worried. Ever since Wendy had first met him the other night, she had only seen him as grinning and cocky, if a bit delusional. But now he couldn't stand still and kept fidgeting with his hands. "My flying has gotten all messed up since my shadow left," Peter added, gesturing to his feet.

Sure enough, while Wendy's shadow pooled on the cement below her, there was still nothing beneath Peter, just like last night. Wendy exhaled a laugh. "This is ridiculous."

"If we don't find my shadow, more kids are going to go missing," Peter blurted out impatiently.

"What?" she asked incredulously. "What are you talking about?" The pieces of the puzzle began to click into place. "Wait—do you know what happened to those missing kids?" Her hand pointed in the general direction of the rec room where, presumably, the news coverage was still rolling.

"That's what I've been trying to tell you!" Peter said, throwing his hands up in frustration. "I'm the one who is supposed to find and help lost kids, like in the stories, right?"

Wendy nodded. "But ever since I found you and your brothers in the woods—"

Wendy felt like she had just been slapped across her face. The casual mention of her brothers was violent and jarring. The hair on the back of her neck stood on end and her heart leapt into her throat.

Apparently Peter didn't notice, because he continued on.

"Everything has been so messed up."

Wendy felt like she was drowning in his words. It was too much, too fast. She didn't feel very brave anymore, and she couldn't maintain her look of skepticism. The wave of nausea washing over her was the same one she felt every time someone mentioned her brothers. "What?" she breathed.

Peter's face became very serious. "That day, you, John, and Michael came with me to Neverland. When everyone thought you went missing, you were with me."

"I— How—" Wendy struggled to find words. Under the panic and confusion, she couldn't help feeling a flicker of hope about John and Michael. "You know about John and Michael?" she asked urgently.

Peter winced and looked at the ground.

She stepped toward him, pressing him for further explanation. "Have you seen them? Do you know where they are?" Peter's few words sparked hope, a fleeting, dangerous thing.

Just a moment ago Peter's words had been coming out in a rush, but now he paused. "It's a long story . . . It's complicated. It would be easier if you could just remember—"

"You have to tell me," Wendy ordered, grabbing hold of his hand. She needed answers, and she needed them now.

Peter's ears tinged red. He took a deep breath. "Like I told you, I used to come by your house to listen to you tell stories about me. I would travel from Neverland looking for lost kids who needed my help," he explained. "And I heard you telling my stories to your brothers once, so I listened in from outside the window—"

"Right, the super-creepy window thing," Wendy interrupted, dropping his hand.

"I mean, yeah, but—" Peter scratched the back of his head, red blooming in his cheeks. "It was just to hear you tell stories about me! I would go back and retell them to the lost ones back at Neverland—it sounds a lot creepier than it was, I promise."

Wendy narrowed her eyes at him.

"Anyway, we actually talked one night, when my shadow went missing for the first time." He said it so casually. "And then, well . . . when you guys got lost in the woods."

Wendy's heart hammered, demanding to be felt. For the past five years she had been wondering what had happened to her and her brothers. For years she'd had nothing and now the answers she had been looking for had fallen out of the sky. She didn't know if it was out of desperation, but right now she wasn't even questioning whether or not he was telling the truth. "Do you know what happened to us?" she choked out.

Peter gave her that look. That same look everyone always gave her whenever her brothers were brought up: tipped eyebrows and a frown. The universal look of pity. She hated that look.

"Maybe we should go somewhere else and talk about this," he said quietly.

"No, you have to tell me now!" Wendy said, grabbing hold of his hand once again. She didn't know if she could go another second without losing her mind, let alone wait long enough to relocate.

"Okay, okay," Peter said, motioning with his free hand

for her to keep her voice down. "When I found you, you were in the middle of the woods. I—I don't know what happened before that." He hesitated for a moment. "But it was almost dark and you were scared, so I took you back with me to Neverland."

"Neverland, as in the magical island in the sky, from the stories?" Wendy asked. She was still struggling to accept all of this, but, more importantly, she wanted him to tell her the rest.

Peter squinted. "I guess that's the easiest way to describe it, yeah."

"Why didn't you take us home?"

Another long pause. "I . . . You didn't want to go home, you wanted to go with me," Peter said with a small shrug.

If it weren't so impossible, it would almost make sense. One of the last things Wendy remembered before the gaping hole in her memory was how, right before she and her brothers went missing, she had gotten into a fight with her father. He'd wanted her to move out of her shared room with her brothers and into her own room. He had told her that it was time for her to grow up and that she couldn't keep playing make-believe with her brothers all the time.

Wendy remembered being so mad at her father. She knew he thought that was why they'd gone missing, that they had run away because he was splitting them up.

But what about Nana? She had run off into the woods and they had chased her. Wendy remembered that part.

"Having you come to Neverland was great," Peter continued, quieter. Wendy was very aware of how close he was, the warmth of his hand wrapped around hers. "We went on adventures, you guys got to meet the other Lost Ones, and I got to listen to you tell stories all the time." He gave her a weak smile, but it quickly faded. "But then a bunch of weird stuff started happening. First, it was just little things. The fairies started getting spooked—they wouldn't come out and play with us at night anymore. They all hid in the trees. I tried to talk to them, but they wouldn't tell me what was wrong, like they were too scared to or something."

Wendy found herself nodding along.

"After you guys came to the island, all of a sudden it started to get harder for me to fly, which had never happened before. The longer you were there, the worse it got. It was like I couldn't control it anymore. Then, one night, I woke up and my shadow was gone."

He stopped. Clearly he was expecting some sort of big reaction from her, but Wendy didn't say a word. She was too busy trying to comprehend it—the magic, the fairies, and Neverland.

When she didn't respond, Peter sighed heavily. "There's a *reason* shadows are supposed to be attached to people. They're dark, wicked things," he explained. "Not like fairies, who cause trouble because it's fun. Shadows are made up of all the dark and bad parts of yourself. They feed off of bad thoughts— fear, worry, sadness, and guilt." Peter dragged his teeth over his bottom lip. "When you start getting consumed by those feelings, it gives the shadow power over you. If it gets strong enough, it can run off and do terrible things. Especially my shadow," he said. "And when mine got away, it started stealing lost kids."

"But how can a shadow *steal* someone?" Wendy asked. "It's just an absence of light!" Or something. Now that she thought about it, Wendy didn't think she could concisely define what a shadow was. She'd never given it real thought.

"Well, yeah, *your* shadow couldn't," Peter told her. "All

of you who live here, in this world, are lucky. Magic left this place so long ago that your shadows are weak and can't escape. They *can* take over a normal person, though. Those dark thoughts can devour a person and take all of their happiness away. They want you to feel isolated and alone. It's like they suck the energy out of you and leave you with nothing."

Wendy thought of the years she spent crying at night, riddled with guilt and missing her brothers so much it was a physical ache. She thought of her father falling asleep at his desk with a bottle in his hand. Of her mother talking in her sleep.

"But my shadow?" Peter shook his head. "My whole existence is filled with magic. Neverland has kept it awake."

"But what happened to me and my brothers?"

"When lost kids started disappearing, I realized it wasn't safe for you to be in Neverland anymore, so I brought you back to your world." Peter shifted back and forth. "I left you in the woods."

"Just me?" said Wendy. "But what about my brothers? What happened to them?"

Peter spoke slowly, clearly thinking carefully about what words he spoke. "They couldn't come back . . ." He trailed off.

"What—why?" If all this was true, and Peter had taken her back to protect her, then why hadn't he brought her brothers back, too? A thought hit her. "The shadow? Did it kidnap them, like the other lost kids?" she asked.

Peter nodded silently.

"Then we have to get them back!" It wasn't good news, but at least it was something she could work with. "Where did it take them?"

"I don't know—I thought I would find them after I took

you back," Peter said, dismayed. "I thought if you returned to your world, maybe things would go back to normal, but it only got worse. I started growing up." He visibly shivered. "I could feel the magic in me starting to drain away. I knew I needed to find my shadow—to stop it from taking kids and to get my magic back. I finally tracked it here. I think it was looking for you, since this all started happening when you came to Neverland." Peter fixed her with a stare. "It's the shadow that's been kidnapping the kids in town," Peter explained. "And I think it's keeping them in the woods."

The woods.

Even if it defied all logic—and physics, for that matter—it was still more of an answer to what had happened to her brothers than anyone else had given her.

"When you found me in the middle of the road, I had chased down my shadow. I almost caught it, but I couldn't keep hold of it and I fell," Peter told her.

Then he really had fallen out of the sky.

Wendy suddenly remembered what had made her veer off the road in the first place: the black mass. "I . . ." Wendy frowned, trying to make sense of everything. "Before I found you, something crashed onto the roof of my truck," she explained slowly. "It was a black thing . . . It kind of looked like the shape of a person, but it was dark, and sort of . . . see-through."

"You saw it?" Peter asked, suddenly lighting up. "You saw my shadow?"

"I don't know what I saw," Wendy said quickly. "It could've been a bunch of things, really. But . . . if it is your shadow—and if all of this is real—then it still has John and Michael?" she asked.

Peter said nothing for a moment, but then he nodded.

Wendy let out a strained laugh and finally pulled away from Peter's grasp. She ran her fingers through her hair and squeezed her eyes shut. "This can't be real!"

"Wendy." Something caught his eye behind her and he spoke quickly. "You *have* to believe me," he said, catching her wrists in his hands.

"But how can I believe anything you're saying? Everything you've told me is impossible!" Wendy told him. Her head swam with overwhelming desperation. She wanted to believe him, to believe that all of this was possible and real, that he knew where her brothers were. That she could get them back.

Peter let out a frustrated growl. He leaned closer and looked into her eyes. Wendy held her breath. "You've gotta help me, or else kids are just going to keep going missing," Peter said.

"Wendy?"

She whirled around as Jordan stepped through the door to the courtyard.

Jordan had a Dutch Bros coffee cup in her hand and she was chewing on the bright green straw. She gave Wendy a strange look. "You okay?" she asked as she crossed the pavement.

"What?" Wendy looked back to where Peter had been standing, but he was gone. She twisted to look around.

"I said," Jordan repeated with an apprehensive laugh, "are you okay? You look like you've just seen a ghost or something." She was dressed in scrubs and had her lanyard around her neck. Jordan always got coffee before volunteering and had the disgusting habit of drinking one cup over the entire day until it was cold. Her shift must've just ended.

"Yeah, I'm—I'm fine," Wendy stammered. Where had he

gone? There was only one door in and out of the courtyard, and Jordan was blocking it.

"Who was that guy you were talking to?" Jordan asked.

Wendy had to stop herself from saying, *You saw him?* "Um . . . what guy? I wasn't talking to anyone," she said.

"I thought I saw a guy out here with you," Jordan said as she looked around. "Wait—" Jordan sucked in a dramatic gasp. Her lips quirked into a devilish smile. "You weren't having a secret *rendezvous,* were you?"

"I—uh . . ."

"Wendy Darling, you are turning RED!" She laughed.

"What!" Wendy squeaked. "No—I—*no*, I wasn't talking to anyone. I just needed some fresh air." Wendy tugged on the neck of her shirt, her skin quickly getting hot and sweaty.

"Uh-huh, suuuure." Jordan slurped down the last of her coffee through the twisted straw. "Whatever, I'll get it out of you eventually." She gave Wendy a pointed look. "You're a terrible liar."

The best option was to distract. "Wait, what are you doing here?"

Jordan's eyebrow arched. "Looking for you so we can go to dinner! Like we do *every* Wednesday after our volunteer hours."

"Oh, right." Wendy's brain was completely jumbled. She could barely focus on anything other than what Peter had told her.

"Hey, are you sure you're all right?" Jordan's tone was serious now. She placed a hand on Wendy's shoulder. "You don't look so good. Maybe we should have one of the doctors check you out?"

"No, no, I'm fine." Wendy wiped the sweat off her forehead with the back of her hand and stepped away from Jordan's hand. "I just didn't get enough sleep last night," she said. "You know, after everything that happened . . ." Wendy trailed off.

Jordan gave her a little smile, the *poor Wendy* smile. Luckily, Jordan knew when to take a step back and not push. "Let's get you out of here, then," she said. "We can stop at Coffee Girl and grab some food." She held the door open.

Before she walked through, Wendy looked up. She half expected to see Peter there, maybe hovering beneath the clouds. But all she saw was a white bird flying across the blue sky.

CHAPTER 10

The Shadow

They spent a couple of hours at Coffee Girl. It was a cozy café out on a tiny pier from the main Astoria River-walk. When she wasn't volunteering at the hospital, Jordan spent most of her time working at the café. She was determined to save up as much money as possible before they started at the University of Oregon in the fall.

Inside the café, the walls were painted orange and the tables and chairs were all mismatched. A small teapot with a succulent inside propped up the menu on their table. They sat in the back at one of the many windows that looked out over the river. String lights adorned the walls and windows all year round. Wendy could hear the faint barking of seals in the distance.

She'd only taken a few bites of her sandwich, and her cup of tea was doing little to settle the twisty feeling in her stomach. Wendy was exhausted and not up for making small talk and pretending everything was okay when it *wasn't* okay, and *she* wasn't okay.

Luckily, Jordan spent most of the time talking through mouthfuls of turkey panini about an intramural swim team she was on for the summer, her mental shopping list for moving into the dorms, and the latest horror movie she and Tyler had seen. Wendy traced her finger along the Coffee Girl logo on her mug—a profile of a woman sipping from a cup—and stared out the large window facing the Columbia River.

"Are you sure you're okay?" Jordan asked again when they were in her car, driving back toward the hospital so Wendy could pick up her truck. Wendy had been watching the shipping liners travel down the river, when Jordan's question pulled her out of her thoughts.

"Yeah, I'm fine," she said, rubbing her temples. She was tired and it made her prickle with fatigue and annoyance.

But Jordan was well trained in the art of reading Wendy Moira Angela Darling. "Well, you haven't actually made eye contact with me since we left the hospital earlier," she started to count off on one hand, guiding the steering wheel with the other. "All you've said to me is a variety of *yeah*s, *hmm*s, and *oh*s." Her eyebrows set in a hard line.

Wendy wasn't used to seeing Jordan get upset like this. Usually when she closed up, Jordan was gentle and didn't push her too far. Jordan was frustrated with her.

"You hardly ate anything, and you keep pulling on your hair, which you only do when you're upset."

Wendy's fingers were halfway through her hair. She stopped and dropped her hands in her lap.

Wendy looked over. Jordan's eyebrows were raised expectantly.

Jordan was the one person who she felt she could really trust in the world. She had never judged Wendy or believed the gossip when it spread through town. Jordan was Wendy's first line of defense, the only one who stood up for her when even her parents backed away.

Jordan was the only one Wendy felt she could talk to about the things that haunted her: her brothers, the woods, and her parents. But the events of the last two days were in a whole other realm. How was she supposed to tell Jordan about Peter? If she said that he had showed up in her backyard and then at the children's wing of the hospital, Jordan would probably freak out. Any sane person would. Jordan would just see him as some guy who'd escaped from the hospital and who the cops were looking for.

And the crappy part was that when she thought of it that way, those were perfectly logical reasons to be scared of Peter. Or at the very least wary.

And what about everything else Peter had said? What would Jordan say if Wendy told her Peter claimed to be *the* Peter Pan? Or that his shadow had gone missing and was kidnapping kids? Or what about the fact that she was actually starting to believe him? Wendy almost laughed.

There was no way Jordan would believe her. Wendy was alone in this.

"Wendy?" Jordan looked genuinely concerned now as she tried to get a proper look at Wendy while still keeping an eye on the road. Wendy knew if she didn't reassure her soon, Jordan might crash the car. Or worse, say something to her parents.

"Do you ever . . ." Wendy cleared her throat to find her voice. "Do you ever wonder if there's . . . more to the world than we know?"

Jordan pulled up into the hospital parking lot near her truck and put the car in park. She twisted in her seat to face Wendy and canted her head to the side. "Like what? Aliens?"

"No, not aliens—"

"'Cause I definitely believe in aliens."

Wendy fixed her with a withering look.

"All that space and unexplored planets up there?" Jordan went on, waving her hand through the air. "You can't tell me there's no other life out there—"

"No, not like aliens," Wendy cut her off, feeling frustrated.

Jordan's laugh died off.

"Like magic," she finally said, fiddling with the strap of her bag.

Jordan's expression pinched in confusion. "Like . . . ?"

"Like fairy tales and stuff," Wendy said, saying the words before she could chicken out.

"Like Peter Pan?" Jordan guessed.

Wendy sat up straight. "Yes!"

Jordan's eyebrows shot toward her hairline.

Wendy cleared her throat. "I've just been thinking about it a lot, I guess," she confessed, raking her fingers through her hair. "I've been drawing pictures of him, and other weird stuff—without even realizing I'm doing it," Wendy tried to explain.

Jordan nodded along, but she looked far from understanding.

"And I've been having weird dreams, too." Wendy's cheeks burned as she stared down at her hands. "It's just been making me wonder if magic is real, if Neverland *could* exist." She licked her lips. "If Peter Pan could be real."

For a moment, they both said nothing. Somewhere down the street, a dog barked.

"Wow." Jordan let out a small, awkward laugh. "It sounds like your imagination is really running rampant, huh?" She smiled, but it was forced. "Giving you these wild dreams and . . ."

Disappointment slumped Wendy's shoulders.

"Hey." Jordan gently touched Wendy's arm. Worry was written across her best friend's face. "What's going on with you?"

Of course Jordan wouldn't believe something that sounded so impossible. Wendy wouldn't, either, if the roles were reversed.

"It's nothing, really," Wendy said. "All these kids going missing is starting to get to me." That was true enough. "And I'm not getting enough sleep." She tried to force her lips up into a smile. "Like I said, I'm just really tired."

Jordan didn't look very convinced, but her expression softened. The way she chewed on her bottom lip made Wendy think she was going to press further, but after a moment she just let out a heavy sigh. "Okay . . ." Then more resolutely, "Okay."

Jordan cut the engine. Without the air conditioner running, the car quickly grew hot under the afternoon sun. Sweat immediately prickled on the small of Wendy's back.

"Go home and go to bed early tonight," Jordan said. She gave Wendy a small smile and crinkled her nose. "Drink some of that nasty chamomile tea you like so much."

"Okay, *Mom*," Wendy said, trying to follow suit and ease the tension. She slung her bag over her shoulder and got out of the car.

"You're not funny," Jordan called after her. It lacked her usual ring of humor. Jordan didn't leave until Wendy was in her truck and the engine had roared to life.

Wendy gripped the steering wheel, the leather hot and sticky under her palms. She was parked at just the right angle so the sun glinted in the scratches left on her windshield.

Wendy took the long way home.

The front door was unlocked. Wendy's mom's car was

gone, but her father's waited in the driveway. She walked into the living room and found him sitting on the couch. His head was tilted back and snores rumbled from under his bushy mustache. The local news was on the television. Benjamin Lane and Ashley Ford smiled at her from the screen.

Wendy turned away and went into the kitchen. The guilt and fear were starting to harden into anger. If what Peter had said was true, then they needed to do something.

She tossed her bag on the counter, turned on the faucet, and rinsed off the dishes in the sink. There were mostly coffee mugs, one with a tea bag still in it from her mom's usual pre-work cup.

As she scrubbed at a dirty pot, Wendy tried to figure out how she would even find Peter. Yes, he was hiding out at a hunting shack in the woods, but where? Even if she did know the location, there was no way in hell she could force herself to go searching through the woods on her own, even in broad daylight. Her heart pounded erratically just thinking about it.

Luckily, Peter seemed to pop up out of nowhere, so maybe she didn't need to go find him—maybe he'd just show up. Wendy turned off the faucet and gazed at the glass doors that led to the backyard, half expecting to see him standing there. She tried not to think about how creepy it was that he could find her so easily in the first place.

Although, he'd given no *real* reason to be afraid of him, had he? He certainly wasn't intimidating. There was no way someone with that much happy energy was dangerous. Someone who smiled like that—with complete abandon and not an ounce of self-consciousness—couldn't be insidious.

Frowning, Wendy dried her hands on a dish towel. What now? It was dark out but too early to try to go to sleep, even with Jordan's orders. She couldn't watch something on TV because she wanted to leave her father undisturbed. There was no way she could concentrate enough to read a book. Maybe more chores were the solution.

There was her swim bag that needed to be cleaned out, still shoved under the passenger seat of her truck. She wasn't part of a summer team like Jordan, so it had been abandoned. The only use it'd gotten this summer was as a trash receptacle for the dozens of crumpled-up drawings Wendy had hidden. She really needed to practice and get some laps in at the aquatic center so she'd be ready to try out for the college swim team in the fall. Maybe having a fresh towel and clean suit would give her the motivation.

Careful not to wake up her father, Wendy snuck out the front door to where her truck was parked in the driveway. She opened the passenger-side door and leaned down to pick up her purple duffel bag when the streetlight in front of her house went out soundlessly. Wendy yanked her bag out of the truck and stood up. Everything plunged into darkness. Even the streetlight from across the road didn't seem to reach very far.

Almost immediately, her heartbeat thudded in her veins. Wendy mentally chided herself—was she really that afraid of the dark?

But it was more than just that. Something was . . . off.

The air felt heavy and her chest felt tight. Something sharp dragged up her spine, like a nail ghosting over her skin. A violent shudder ran through her. The air shifted, as if someone was standing right behind her. Wendy sucked in a breath and turned to rush back inside.

"Hello."

The sudden greeting caused all the nerves in her body to jump. Wendy swung around, clutching her duffel bag.

A boy who looked about her age stood just a couple of

yards away. Wendy squinted at him. In the dark, she could make out his outline and vague features, but she couldn't see the details of his face.

"Hi?" she said warily.

"You're Wendy Darling, right?" he asked. As Wendy inched toward the front door, he took a step closer.

There was something strange about his voice. It was pleasant and almost lazy. The low, deep timbre of someone who had just woken up. Whatever clothes he was wearing must have been black. He had his hands tucked into his pockets. His stance and tone were so casual—too casual, for the way her heart hammered in her chest, thudding out a warning in her pulse.

Wendy hesitated. "I—yes."

Peter?

"What are you doing out here at this time of night?" he asked. She could just make out the shape of his eyebrows as they arched with curiosity. Wendy had seen Peter do that same head tilt, but no, it definitely wasn't Peter. This guy's hair was jet black, far darker than the rest of his face, which was still bathed in shadows.

"I live here," she said curtly.

He laughed, and, for the first time, she could make out a distinct feature: his white teeth and sharp smile. Too white, too sharp, like a caricature.

Wendy squinted again. "Do I know you?" she asked. The hair on the back of her neck prickled, like it knew something she didn't.

He grinned, and it stretched unnaturally across his face. "No, you don't know me," he told her. "I've seen you around, though." Something about his eyes was unnerving. Black like a shark's, but it must've been a trick of the darkness.

"I was going for a nice walk in the woods. Maybe you could join me? We could get to know each other," he offered, extending a hand.

His fingers were long, the joints angular.

Wendy backed up. "No," she said firmly, tilting her chin up. "I need to go back inside now. Please leave."

The boy laughed again. "That's probably for the best. You shouldn't wander, not with all those kids going missing." A far-off streetlight glinted in his eyes. "Wouldn't want to get lost in the woods again, would you?"

For a moment, she was so scared she couldn't breathe, but fast on the heels of fear was white-hot anger. "What did you say?" Rage-induced bravery swelled inside her. "I don't know who you think you are, but—"

A child's scream cut through the air. She jumped and swung around toward the wail. It sounded like it had come from her backyard.

The stranger laughed again, but when Wendy turned back to face him, he was gone.

Another cry rang out, and this time it continued without stopping. It *was* a child.

And it was definitely coming from behind the backyard.

Without another thought, Wendy dropped her bag and ran for the gate. She raced along the side of the house, feet pounding on the cement. She tripped over the handle of a rake and sprinted into the backyard. It stretched out before her. The old swings waved in the breeze, and standing just past that on the other side of the small fence was a little boy. He continued to cry, and Wendy slowed her pace, taking cautious steps.

Closer now, she recognized the back of the little boy's head, and his oversized blue hoodie.

"Alex?" Wendy said. The crying cut off abruptly. He remained still, facing the woods with his back to her. Wendy's own breaths roared in her ears. "Alex, what are you doing here?" She slowly stepped closer to him.

Alex finally turned.

Small twigs and leaves were stuck in his mess of brown hair. His eyes were huge. Black pupils devoured any trace of his brown irises. Tears rolled down his dirt-stained cheeks.

"Alex, what happened?" she asked gently, extending a hand out for him to take. It quivered.

Something was very wrong. Not just the fact that he shouldn't be here, in her backyard, but the stricken look on his face, the earthy smell in the breeze, even the deadly quiet that hung in the air.

Wendy's eyes kept darting to the woods behind him. The dark trees loomed over Alex's tiny form. She couldn't see into them, but the feeling of something waiting there in the dark made her skin crawl.

"*Alex*." Urgency leapt in her throat. "Take my hand—" Wendy lunged forward to grab him, hips slamming into the short fence, but before she could reach, Alex's mouth opened wide.

He screamed with his whole body.

Wendy cringed as the sound's sharpness split through her. She stumbled forward, nearly toppling over the fence as she tried to reach him. With a violent gust of cold wind, something like large, crooked fingers made of tar lashed out from the trees and ensnared Alex's legs, knocking him to the ground. He scrabbled at the dirt, trying to claw his way toward Wendy, but the fingers dragged him to the trees.

"*Alex!*" Wendy screamed.

His eyes found hers. For a moment, she could clearly see his face—terrified and chalky, his fingers digging into the dirt—before the woods swallowed him whole.

Without pause, Wendy jumped the fence and ran straight into the forest.

The woods were alive.

It was hard to see a path through the brambles and gnarled roots. Wendy kept tripping, her forward momentum the only thing keeping her upright. The tree branches reached out at her like thorny arms, trying to pull her into a painful embrace. They slapped her cheeks, tangled in her hair, and bit her legs, but Wendy urged herself forward. Each footfall on the uneven ground jarred, ankle to knee, ankle to knee. She had to get to Alex. She wouldn't let him be taken by the woods or whatever that *thing* was.

Wendy ran as fast as she could after Alex, straining her ears to guide her to his voice. She couldn't see him, but she could hear his cries up ahead.

She threw herself forward, forcing herself to go faster, to keep up, not to lose him in the woods. "ALEX!" she tried to call out to him, but her lungs burned.

Wendy didn't notice the voices at first.

They were quiet, just whispers coming from the woods around her. They could've been the hiss of passing branches. Then came the sound of light footfalls, like people—or things—ran in the woods around her. All she could make out were low-hanging branches and dark figures darting between the endless rows of trees. Voices snaked through the ivy-covered giants. They whispered against her neck, but Wendy couldn't understand what they were saying. Each breath brought a new swell of fear.

It was disorienting. Everything was off-kilter. Wendy was lost. Was she running to Alex, or was she being chased?

"Wendy, help!" Alex's wail broke through the murmuring.

A choked cry forced its way into her throat. Wendy threw herself forward with even greater abandon.

She latched on to his voice like a lifeline and ran after it. Her brain screamed at her to turn around and go back, but she couldn't abandon Alex. She wouldn't.

Suddenly, something caught around her ankle and she tumbled forward. Wendy pitched head over heels before slamming to the ground. The force sent her skidding onto her side. Leaves and rocks scraped against her shoulder.

Wendy groaned. Dirt and the coppery taste of blood were on her tongue. With effort, she pushed herself up onto her knees. Her body protested, but she couldn't stop. She had to get up, she had to keep running, she had to find Alex.

Wendy staggered to her feet.

She had collapsed in a clearing. Tall trees stood around her in a circle. Their bodies towered over her, their branches reaching high above their heads. Thick leaves blotted out any view of the night sky. Sucking down air, Wendy tried to regain her bearings. She was completely turned around.

Which way had she come from? And where was Alex? She couldn't hear his voice anymore. In fact, she couldn't hear anything—no crickets, no wind, no owls. The silence pressed in around her, broken only by her labored breaths.

Then Wendy heard a faint noise, something she couldn't quite make out, but it was growing steadily louder. Fingernails dug into her palms as she clenched her fists.

The sounds of breathing filled the air around her. It was like standing in a room packed with people she couldn't see. She could only hear their breathing, could only feel it exhaled against her skin. Some breathed slowly, others erratically, all toppling over one another and only getting louder.

Wendy's head jerked from side to side, desperately looking for where the noise was coming from, but no one was there. The breathing turned into indecipherable whispers.

Wendy grimaced against the sound. What was happening to her?

"ALEX!" Wendy shouted, trying to find his voice among the murmurs. Maybe if he heard her, he would call back. "ALEX, WHERE ARE YOU?!"

Something cold and wet slid across Wendy's ankle.

When she looked down, something pitch black had seeped out of the ring of trees. Wendy stumbled back, but her feet sank into the muck, nearly knocking her off-balance. The whispers grew urgent and called out to her. Wendy tried to run, but her feet were stuck. Tendrils reached out and wrapped around her legs, ice cold as they traveled up. She was slowly sinking, being pulled down into the earth.

"No, no, no!" Panic seized Wendy. She tried to pull her leg free, but the shadows snatched her wrists. Sticky claws wound up her arms to her neck. Wendy thrashed as she sank to her waist. Hot tears streamed down her cheeks as she tried to pull it off her face, but it just stretched and oozed over her hands as it continued to make its way to her mouth.

As it started to curl over her lips, Wendy jerked her head back, sucked in a deep breath, and screamed for the only person she could think of.

"PETER!"

The blackness closed over her mouth. As it engulfed her,

she had only one thought through her panic and searing fear: Was this what had happened to her brothers?

Just as the shadows slid over her eyes, there was an explosion of light. Suddenly, Wendy could see again. Gold sparks sizzled on contact with the blackness. A screech filled the clearing as the substance shriveled and fell away from Wendy in clumps of ash. The sparks disintegrated the blackness but didn't hurt her.

A strong arm hooked across Wendy's chest and pulled her free. She thrashed and fell to her knees. She scrambled back, frantically kicking away the last of the falling ash.

Ash, and a carpet of golden sparks that lit up the clearing. They danced and flickered around her. Was she dreaming?

Peter stood in the center. The sparks winked beneath his bare feet. He held his right hand at his side, palm forward in caution. In his left hand was a sword, but not a normal sword—not that Wendy had ever actually seen a sword in person. But this one was made of the same golden sparks that surrounded him. It looked solid and weighty in his hand, a shelled hilt that curved into a long blade. It sparked and glittered in his grip. The light caught in the deep lines of worry on Peter's face. His eyes were intense as they searched Wendy's. The light reflected and danced in them.

"Wendy, are you okay?" Peter took a step forward and Wendy flinched back. His gaze followed hers, which remained locked on the weapon in his hand. He cursed under his breath and, with a twist of his wrist, the sword disappeared in a shower of sparks.

It only made her feel a little better. She was in a daze, chest heaving up and down. All traces of that thing were gone.

"What *was* that?" Wendy croaked. She could see from the lights that whatever had attacked her was gone, but they were starting to fade. She didn't want to be left alone in the dark again. Wendy scrambled to her feet, but her legs were shaky and fatigued. She stumbled, and this time she let Peter reach out and help her.

"Peter, please, we need to get out of here. There's something in the woods," Wendy pleaded, her voice hoarse and cracking. She tugged on his arm with her quivering hands. Her eyes dashed around wildly. They weren't alone. Something was in there. It was going to take her. Tears blurred Wendy's vision.

"Shh, it's okay, it's gone now," Peter said, gently cupping her cheek in his warm hand, but his soft voice did nothing to reassure her.

Wendy shook her head violently. Her knees buckled under her. Their only source of light was fading rapidly.

She pulled harder on Peter's arm. "We have to get out of here—we can't stay here! I can't!" She felt the woods pressing in around her. Any moment, fingers would reach out and snatch her up. She would be trapped and lost among the trees forever.

They needed to leave, they needed to escape—

It came crashing back with violent weight: the reason she was in the woods to begin with. "Alex," Wendy choked out. "It took Alex!" She spun, looking in all directions. "ALEX!" she shouted, throat raw. Her head whipped around. Her hair stuck to her lips as she called out for him.

Which way had he gone? Where had it taken him? "We have to get him back," Wendy said. She made for the woods, but Peter caught her by the elbow.

"We need to get you home," Peter said. His voice was steady, which only angered Wendy.

Peter was calm, and she was furious with him for it.

"No, we need to find Alex," Wendy insisted. "We can't just abandon him here!" She tried to jerk her arm away, but Peter held on.

"They're already gone," he said. His expression was defeated but certain. "It's dark, we don't know which way it went, we need to go back—"

"*No!*" Wendy shouted at him. Wrenching her arm free from his grasp, she shoved him away. "He's alone!" She squeezed her hands into fists. "You don't know what it's like, being in these woods! We can't just leave him!"

Wendy's eyes stung and her vision blurred. She rubbed at them angrily. Couldn't he see that? Didn't he understand?

Peter's arms fell to his sides. His eyebrows tipped and the look of pity on his face made her want to slap him.

"Wendy," he said gently.

But gentleness was not what Wendy needed. She needed to rage and scream against the night.

"We have to find him!" Wendy imagined Alex's terrified cries. She pictured him lost and alone. It was her fault he was gone. She should've rescued him. She should've kept him safe. Wendy imagined her brothers.

"WE CAN'T LEAVE THEM!" she shouted before sobs overcame her. Collapsing on her knees, she ducked and twisted her arms over the top of her head, trying to shield herself. Her fingers tangled themselves in her hair. She was terrified and exhausted. She wanted to find Alex. She wanted to find her brothers.

She wanted to go home.

Wendy felt Peter kneel down next to her. Through her elbows, she could see him hold a closed fist out in front of her.

Just as the last of the lights died out on the forest floor, right before they were plunged into darkness, Peter opened his hand and sparks jumped to life in his palm. The clearing was silent for a moment before, slowly, crickets began to sing from deep in the woods.

Wendy stared at the glittering lights. They were bright and danced around his fingertips. They gave off no heat and didn't seem to burn him.

It was mesmerizing. Wendy stared and wiped her nose on her shoulder. "W-what is that?" She hiccupped into the fabric of her shirt.

Peter gave her a weak smile. "Would you believe me if I said pixie dust?"

CHAPTER 11

Old Friends

B y the light of the pixie dust sparking in his hand, Peter navigated them through the woods. He told her they couldn't stay any longer, in case the shadow came back. Wendy would've fought him, but he made a good point—they would be blindly searching the woods. Wendy's body was so heavy and stiff with grief and exhaustion, she simply didn't have enough fight left to object further. It took every ounce of energy she had left to walk back to her house.

Peter led the way, and, though it bruised her pride, Wendy held on to his arm as they wove between trees and ducked under branches. She had a hard time looking at where she was going. Her eyes kept getting drawn to the pixie dust in Peter's hand.

The small flecks of light leapt and bounced on his skin. They looked like they were dancing, or shaking with welled-up excitement. It reminded her of how Michael often looked, sitting in bed and squirming with glee when she began telling a story before bed.

The light danced on Peter's face, casting a warm glow across his cheekbones and the tip of his nose and sparkling in his already bright eyes. Some shot up higher into the air, making corkscrew swirls before fizzling out, like embers popping in a bonfire, but with more life. Wendy wondered if they tickled his hand.

The woods no longer whispered, but Wendy still felt like they were being watched. After what seemed like ages, they hopped the fence into her backyard. Just as she was wondering what he would do with the pixie dust, Peter simply clapped his hands and the lights went out.

Wendy didn't want to be near the woods any longer. The crushing sense of loss threatened to pull her down a path she tried hard to stay away from.

With some coaxing, she was able to talk Peter into coming inside.

Mr. Darling wasn't sleeping in the living room anymore, and, after checking that his car was gone, Wendy assumed her dad had gone to the store or something. He never left notes about where he went, so she could only guess when he'd be back. Either way, she knew she would be in trouble when he did. She'd told him she wouldn't be out past dark.

But there were more pressing matters at hand.

"Pixie dust," Wendy repeated, wiping her nose off on the back of her hand.

Peter nodded, drumming his fingers on the counter. "Yup."

Standing in her kitchen, leaning against the counter, it struck her how weird this all was. She believed him now, that he was Peter Pan—her Peter—because how else could she explain what had just happened? She kept catching herself openly staring at him.

Peter Pan was in her kitchen. To her annoyance, she felt more nervous now, like she was meeting her favorite singer.

Under the fluorescent lights, she could see how much of a mess Peter was.

He'd found a new set of clothes again. This time, it was a pair of faded jeans with a hole in the left knee and a dark green T-shirt. She wondered where he had gotten them. Maybe he'd stolen them from someone's backyard or nicked them from a lost and found.

Peter's face was flushed and had a couple of small cuts. His hair stuck out in disheveled tufts and dirt was smeared across his cheek. Wendy was certain she didn't look much better. Her own hands were filthy.

She quickly walked to the sink and ran her hands under hot water.

"As in the stuff that makes you fly?" she continued. In the stories her mom had passed down, Peter used pixie dust from the fairies in Neverland to help himself and the lost kids fly.

"It's supposed to, yeah," he said, lightly touching a cut on his temple that was caked in dried blood. He winced. A branch must have scratched him. "Usually, I don't even need it, but ever since I brought you to Neverland . . ." Peter glanced away and toyed with the lighthouse-shaped pepper shaker by the stove. "I have to use a bunch of it just to get off the ground." His brow furrowed, his expression pinched, as he ran his finger around the spiral base of the shaker.

Wendy squeezed the dish towel she was using to dry her hands and ran a corner of it under warm water. "So, what, do you just keep pixie dust in your pocket?" she asked.

Peter moved to the fridge and began rearranging the magnets. "What? No!" He chuckled as he examined a Fort

Stevens State Park one. "I don't need pixie dust—or, I mean, pixie dust is a part of me. I'm made up of it, I guess?" Peter frowned and scratched his chin.

Apparently he hadn't put much thought into it, either.

He tried again. "It's like—it's like it's already in my veins, you know?"

Wendy nodded slightly when he turned to her for confirmation. "And the sword?"

"I can conjure it up with pixie dust," Peter said. "It's a way to focus my magic and defend myself and the lost kids."

Wendy frowned. "From what?"

Peter shrugged and snatched a red apple from the bowl on the counter. "I don't know . . . stuff."

"Stuff?" Wendy repeated, annoyed.

Seeing that she wasn't going to let it go without some kind of answer, Peter huffed. "Like keeping bad stuff away— like bad thoughts," he said, eyes following the apple as he tossed it between his hands. "Lost kids' bad thoughts can manifest as dark things on the island, like huge spiders, or killer hippos, or—"

"Pirates?" She said the word without even thinking.

Peter caught the apple out of the air and stared at Wendy. The intense look in his eyes made Wendy shift uncomfortably.

After being found in the woods, Wendy remembered, she'd had nightmares for months about being chased by a pirate captain, cloaked in bright red with a black beard, who always wielded a silver pistol. She would wake up in the middle of the night sobbing until her mother could coax her down.

Had that pirate been the bad thought that had chased her in Neverland?

Finally, Peter cleared his throat. "Yeah, like pirates." He slowly turned the apple over and over in his hands as he spoke. "The sword is how I protect the lost kids and keep those manifestations of their bad thoughts at bay."

"Can you turn it into something else?" Wendy wondered, picturing the glowing sword again. "Like a net?"

"I mean, I *could*." Peter's lips curled into a grin. "But a sword is just so much cooler."

A surprised laugh bubbled in Wendy's throat.

"And way more fun," he added.

Wendy rolled her eyes but couldn't help smiling. "Yeah, okay."

"Pixie dust is my magic," Peter continued, getting back on point. "It's how I fly, how I take care of the lost kids, how I stay young—" Peter looked down at himself. "Or *used* to, anyway." His shoulders slumped. "I can feel myself getting weaker, like my magic is just draining out of me, you know?" Peter set down the apple and approached Wendy. "Getting rid of that *stuff* that was trying to take you used up a lot. If we don't get my shadow back soon, I have no idea what will happen, but it won't be good."

Wendy exhaled a deep sigh. She knew this was a problem, but she had no idea how to fix it.

Peter stared at her with his big eyes, as if waiting for her to come up with a solution to fix all their problems, but how could she do that? She could barely understand what he was telling her to begin with and she could barely take care of herself. She couldn't help her brothers, so how was she supposed to help him?

Wendy stepped forward, closing the distance between them. "Here, let me clean that," she said, holding up the damp cloth. At least the cut was something she could fix.

Peter squinted at her and leaned away.

"It's not going to hurt, you big baby," she said with mild exasperation.

"I'm *not* a baby," Peter grumbled petulantly, but he remained still.

Wendy did her best to ignore the flutter of nerves through her entire body, being this close to him. Was there anyone else in the world who'd found out their imaginary friend was real?

Wendy pressed the cloth to his temple and Peter winced. He sucked in a sharp breath. "That *stings*!" he hissed, his jaw muscles flexing.

"Don't be so dramatic," she grumbled. Peter's face scrunched up, but he let her gently pat the cut until the blood was gone, only leaving a small red line. "There," Wendy said before retreating back to the other side of the kitchen. She yanked open the junk drawer and sifted through old scissors, expired coupons, and chip clips before she found a small red sewing kit.

"What's that for?" Peter balked as if she were brandishing some sort of weapon.

"For the hole in your jeans," Wendy said, gesturing to his torn knee.

He only looked slightly less worried.

"Just sit, would you?" she said, placing a hand on the counter.

Peter gave her a dubious look before perching himself on the edge of the cool tile. "Okay, but be careful; don't stab me," he instructed.

"Then don't fidget," Wendy told him. His knee stopped bouncing, and Wendy got to work cinching the frayed material back together with deft fingers as well as she could.

Peter probed the cut on his temple, flinching. "I need to save my energy and not use my magic for stuff like flying, you know? I need it to fight off the shadow. Pixie dust is its opposite." Peter gestured, as if weighing two things in his hands.

"Shadows are made up of darkness. They feed off of sadness and despair. They manifest what you're most scared of and use it as a weapon to feed off your fear. That's why it's stealing all those kids." He dropped his hands and they hung heavy at his sides. "It's collecting them and using their fear as a source of energy. They're making it stronger."

"That's . . . terrifying," Wendy breathed. Her eyes flickered away from her work toward the back door. Somewhere, deep in the woods, there were kids who were scared and alone, being tormented by the shadow.

"That's why we need pixie dust to fight the shadow," Peter continued. "It's made from light and laughter and joy. That's why when you use pixie dust and think of good things—happy things—it makes you light enough to fly. That's why I'm the only one who can fight it. I can use my light against my shadow and weaken it enough to capture it, and you can reattach it like you did before."

"That was your shadow, then?" Wendy looped the end of the thread, tying it off securely. "That took Alex and attacked me?" She couldn't explain with logic what had happened to her in the woods just now, and that in and of itself was terrifying to realize.

"Yes." Peter rubbed his eyes. "The stronger it gets, the weaker I get. I can feel the magic bleeding out of me." He looked so tired and defeated. It only made her more worried.

As she tugged the seam to test her work—it was good enough to hold together for now—a thought occurred to her. "The woods." Heat clawed up her neck. Wendy put the needle and thread away and left the kit on the counter. "Is that why it's keeping them there—the missing kids and my brothers? Because of me?"

Wendy was terrified of the woods and the shadow was using it against her. It had lured her in there to taunt her with Alex, with the promise of finding her brothers, just to feed off her fear. It was her fault. It was all her fault. Wendy raked her fingers through her hair. "But *why*? Why my brothers? Why me?"

"I don't know," Peter murmured quietly, thumbing the stitches on the knee of his jeans. "All I know is you're the only one who can help me catch my shadow and put it back." He looked . . . not good. His tan skin was paler than normal. Puffy bags were starting to form under his eyes. He was missing his usual spark. The change was unsettling.

Wendy wondered when was the last time he'd gotten some rest and something to eat.

"If we can't stop it, what will happen?" she asked. "To the kids? My brothers?"

Peter shrugged and stared at the floor. It pained her to see him like this. It pulled at something in her chest. At the same time, she was frustrated with him. If she was going to help him, she needed more guidance and answers. She couldn't just magically solve this mystery on her own. Those kids needed her and Peter—they *had* to find and rescue them. She needed to see her brothers again, to bring them back.

"Peter . . ." Wendy hesitated, scared of the answer she might get. "What will happen if you keep getting weaker, and it keeps getting stronger?"

Peter looked up and watched her for a moment. She could see him thinking. Physically, he was so young, even if he was growing older. But his intense eyes felt like they held the age of the galaxies swirling behind them. He was a star locked inside a boy's body.

Peter shrugged again. "Nothing good." He tried to conjure up a smile, but it was nothing compared to its brilliance when he really meant it. "So we can't let that happen."

Wendy pressed her fingers to her mouth and tried to think.

"We need to call the police. We need their help," Wendy finally said. She couldn't believe she was even considering it, but where else could they turn for help?

Peter arched an eyebrow, shaking his head. "Wendy, *you* barely believe me, do you really think a bunch of grown-ups are going to believe a word of this?" he asked. "They'll lock me up and throw away the key!" He scowled. She had hit a nerve. "They can't help us."

"Then we need to at least tell them about Alex!" Wendy pulled her phone out of her back pocket. Her mind raced, thoughts tumbling over one another. She needed to do something. She needed to come up with some immediate solutions to these daunting and insurmountable tasks.

"They need to know he's missing—his parents need to know! At least then people can be on the lookout for him," she insisted. Wendy paced back and forth, tightly gripping the phone. "I—I don't know what I'll say, *how* I know he's gone missing," she mused. "I can just make something up—"

Wendy's cell phone lit up. An AMBER alert with Alex's name filled the screen.

"Too late," Wendy said. Peter leaned over to give it a look. "They already know." Wendy snatched the remote from the counter and turned on the TV. Sure enough, it was on the news, too. Alex's face smiled at her from the corner of the screen. In the center, Detective James stood in the middle of a street. Bright lights from news cameras lit up his face, causing him to squint.

"Mrs. Forestay witnessed Alex being taken from their backyard this evening, but didn't get a good enough look at the abductor to provide a description," Detective James said.

Guilt swarmed inside Wendy.

"I heard voices when I was in the woods," Wendy said, turning back to Peter. "I couldn't hear what they were saying, but they were definitely kids. I couldn't see them but it felt like they were *right* there, just out of sight." Her skin crawled as she thought about the voices, the breathing, the footsteps. "That's gotta be where it's hiding."

"That's where I had tracked it to, when you found me in the road," Peter said, walking to stand next to her. His shoulder lightly brushed against hers. "After what you saw, I think that's a pretty safe bet."

"Do the police know that?" Wendy wondered as she watched Detective James talk about a special hotline the police department had set up for anyone who had any information about the missing children. "Should we tell them?" she asked, looking up at Peter.

His jaw was tight. "Grown-ups can be slow at figuring stuff out," Peter said flatly. There was that disdainful tone that always crept into his voice when he talked about adults. "But they're bound to put it together sooner or later."

Wendy chewed on her bottom lip. She felt compelled to call the police about the woods, but how would she explain herself? The detectives were already looking at her for answers—they suspected her of lying or holding back *some-*

thing. That was why they showed up at her house to begin with. If she talked to them and they started investigating her more, if they started searching the woods, would they find Peter? And how would they explain him and his connection to all of this?

"They're going to search the woods," Wendy said, because of course they would. "They'll find the hunting shack you're staying in. They could find you, Peter."

Peter, who had been scuffing the toe of his shoe on the floor, froze. Apparently he hadn't considered that, either. He tipped his head back and let out a halfhearted laugh. "I guess we better hurry then," he said, looking down at her with a sad grin.

Wendy pressed her hands against her abdomen. She felt like she was going to be sick.

In the living room, the view of Detective James changed on the television, catching her attention. It was a drawing of another missing person.

"Oh no," Wendy groaned.

Detective James spoke: "We have also been alerted to another child who went missing from the hospital the day before yesterday. The boy was originally found unconscious on Williamsport Road but went missing shortly after being brought to the hospital for treatment. His name and whereabouts are unknown, but we have reason to believe he is connected to the string of local disappearances," he went on.

Wendy's eyes grew wide. *Reason to believe he is connected to the string of local disappearances?*

"What's wrong?" Peter asked. He stepped closer, peering at her carefully. "You look like you're going to barf."

"If they think *you* have something to do with the missing kids," Wendy said, the panic rising in her throat pushing the words out rapidly, "and they think you have something to do with what happened to me and my brothers, then that means that they think *I* have something to do with it, too!"

Peter blinked, but then everything seemed to click into place. "Oh," Peter said with a cringe. "Oops . . ."

What could she possibly tell the police? *Yes, detective, my brothers and I actually ran off to a magical island in the sky called Neverland. They were kidnapped by an evil shadow, but a magical boy saved me and brought me back home! Oh, and all those kids that have gone missing? Yes, well, the shadow got them, too, and now it's up to me and the magical boy to get them back!*

"You're right," Wendy said, staring unblinkingly at the TV. "I might barf."

Peter stepped back.

A composite sketch took over the screen.

It was a drawing of Peter. Not a very good one, but definitely him nonetheless. His nose was pretty accurate, and they got his ears right, including the way they pointed and sort of stuck out. But his cheeks and jaw in the picture were too round and young looking. It was a sketch of how Peter had looked when she'd found him in the street—but, looking at him now, as he leaned across the counter and intently stared at the TV, it was clear to Wendy that he was still aging quickly.

And the eyes, of course, didn't do his real ones any justice.

Detective James continued on in the background: "He has been described as having brown hair, blue eyes, and standing at about five foot five. He's guessed to be between the ages of twelve and fourteen and may be confused or disoriented. If seen, please call—"

Wendy inspected Peter. She was five foot five and, standing next to Peter in the kitchen, he was definitely a good few inches taller than her. She looked at the screen again. Wendy remembered how he had looked when she first found him in the middle of the road. But now? He was definitely taller, and his cheeks weren't round anymore. Still covered in freckles, they sloped over more defined cheekbones and blended into his more defined jawline. Had he really aged that much in just a couple of days?

"Why are you staring at me like that?" Peter asked, squinting as he frowned at her.

"I'm not *staring* at you," Wendy said, cheeks growing hot as she gave his shoulder a shove. "I guess if anything, losing your magic is useful, since the aging will make it harder for people to recognize you from the ER," she said in an attempt to find a silver lining.

"Yeah, but *not* useful in getting my shadow back." Peter scowled. "The weaker my magic gets, the more I age. I'm not supposed to grow up, Wendy. If we can't fix me soon . . ." Peter looked lost for words. "I don't know what'll happen, but those kids will be lost for good."

"And so will my brothers," Wendy said.

Peter dug the palms of his hands into his eyes.

The sound of a key sliding into the front door lock made Wendy nearly jump out of her skin.

"Crap!" she hissed, immediately grabbing Peter's arm and giving it a yank.

"Ouch! What?!"

"Shh! Someone's home! My dad will freak out if he sees you!" Wendy pulled Peter to the sliding glass doors that led to the backyard.

Oh, God, oh no, she needed to get Peter out of the house. If her dad found them, she wouldn't be the only one in trouble. The lock clicked and the front door began to creak open. "You need to leave, now, out the back door!" She pushed against him, but Peter didn't budge.

"Wendy?" Her mother's tired voice drifted in from the living room. "Is that you?"

"Go!" Wendy pleaded as quietly as she could, but Peter wasn't even looking at her anymore.

All of his focus had turned to the sound of her mother's voice, his face suddenly very alert. Wendy squeezed his arm in a silent plea, but it was no use. He balanced on the balls of his feet, peering in the direction of the living room like a fox trying to spot a bird. There was something in his eyes, an intensity in his face, but Wendy couldn't place it. What was he doing? If he didn't move, she—

Mrs. Darling rounded the corner and stepped into the kitchen.

"Uh, hey, Mom!" Wendy chirped, trying to sound casual, but the truth was that she never had company over, except for Jordan.

Peter retreated a few quick steps back to Wendy's side. He clasped his hands behind his back.

Wendy looked up at him, surprised by his sudden strange behavior.

Mrs. Darling was in her usual blue scrubs, her hair tied up in a messy bun on top of her head. She was wearing her glasses, but Wendy could still see the dark circles under her eyes.

"Oh, you have company," she said, a pleasant but tired smile on her face as she turned to Peter. However, when she saw him, she faltered.

Mrs. Darling's brown eyes were suddenly wider and more alert than Wendy had seen them in ages. Her hand moved to the base of her throat. Her mouth formed a small *O* in silent—what was it? Surprise?

Peter stood still, his head cocked to the side curiously.

"Er, Mom?" Wendy asked quietly. Had her mom seen Peter in the hospital? Was that why she was looking at him like that? Why was Peter acting so weird all of a sudden? The quiet intensity of the situation made her feel as if she were interrupting a private moment. "Are you okay?"

"Hmm? Oh, yes—I'm fine," Mrs. Darling said. That seemed to break her out of her trance, but she still continued to stare at Peter. Wendy could feel an odd energy hanging in the air between them. Mrs. Darling squinted, delicate wrinkles forming at the corners of her eyes as she peered at him through her glasses. "I'm sorry, have we met before?" Mrs. Darling asked Peter.

Before he could open his mouth, Wendy cut in. "No!" she practically shouted. She cleared her throat and lowered her voice. "I mean, no. This is—uh—Barry," she lied.

"Do you go to school with Wendy?" Mrs. Darling pressed. "You look so familiar—"

"Nope!" Wendy answered again. "He's new—from out of town—visiting family—just for the summer!" She was talking way too fast. And way too loud. "We just kinda ran into each other downtown, so I thought I'd show him around," Wendy finished, twisting her hands in the air as she tried to come up with a logical explanation.

Wendy wasn't very good at making up lies on the spot, but she hoped it was convincing enough. Either way, her mom didn't seem to be paying enough attention to notice.

"It's nice to meet you, Mrs. Darling," Peter finally said. He leaned forward in a strange little half bow, one hand pressed to his chest, before straightening back up again. He smiled at her, deep dimples cutting into his cheeks. That smile of his was dazzling. It made you feel like it was meant only for you, and he gave it to her mother.

A laugh bubbled past Mrs. Darling's lips. "It's nice to meet you too, Barry," she replied, patting at her messy hair.

It was strange seeing her mother interact with Peter. It made something in her ache. She hadn't seen her mom smile or laugh like that in ages. Five years ago, when Wendy was finally able to go home, she'd spent all day trying to come up with ways to cheer her mom up with drawings, beaded necklaces she made from magazine scraps, and jokes. Wendy kept a tally of how many times she could get her mother to smile. When Wendy had told her therapist about the tallies, coincidentally, Mrs. Darling started smiling more. But it was always a forced one that didn't reach her eyes.

Wendy couldn't help feeling a bit jealous at how Peter had so easily gotten something she coveted. At the same time, Peter also felt like *her* secret, her own piece of magic, but there was obviously something shared between the two of them.

"Do you want to stay for dinner?" Mrs. Darling asked as she pushed some stray hair out of her face. "I'm not sure what we have in the house, but I could order some takeout—"

"Nooo, no, that's okay," Wendy interrupted, waving a hand and laughing nervously. "Barry has to go home, don't you, Barry?"

"Uh," Peter replied unintelligibly.

Wendy took hold of his bicep and gave it a squeeze.

"Yeah, I guess I do," he finished. He looked disappointed, but Wendy didn't care. She needed to get him out of there. She didn't have enough of her wits about her to keep up the charade, and Peter was proving to be entirely useless.

"Oh." Mrs. Darling's face fell. "Well, would you at least

like a ride home? It's dangerous to be out by yourself this time of night, what with everything that's going on."

Peter looked at Wendy—his eyebrows arched expectantly, waiting for her to provide him with his answer.

"That's okay, Mom. He lives super close, don't you, Barry?" Wendy said.

Peter nodded vigorously. "Yes, super close."

Now, Wendy could see he was trying not to laugh at her. She wanted to shove him but refrained.

"Okay, well, if you're sure," Mrs. Darling said, but Wendy was already pushing Peter toward the front door.

"Just going to walk him to the porch!" Wendy called over her shoulder. She pulled open the front door. As Peter turned to wave good-bye to her mom, Wendy placed both of her hands against his back and pushed him out.

Outside, everything was quiet except for the sound of traffic filtering down from the main road.

Wendy shut the door behind her and let out a long sigh of relief. "That was close," she said, pressing her palm against her forehead as she willed her heartbeat to slow down. They were lucky it hadn't been her father, but still, running into her mother was bad enough. Peter needed to keep a low profile—the fewer people to see him, the better.

Peter didn't say anything. He stared at the closed door, just above her shoulder. His eyebrows pinched together and his jaw moved like he was chewing on the inside of his cheek.

Wendy's thoughts immediately went to Peter's interaction with her mother. How curious Peter was, how lost in memory her mother seemed to be. It was like overhearing a private conversation. Wendy folded her arms and leaned back against the door. "Did you know my mom? When she was younger?" she asked quietly as she watched him.

Peter nodded. "Yeah, those stories she used to tell you weren't just stories. Better sword fighter than you, in fact," Peter added with a short laugh, stuffing his hands into his pockets. "I mean, she doesn't remember it now, obviously." He shrugged his shoulders like it was nothing, but there was a clear tone of hurt in his voice. "But that's what happens when you grow up—you forget about the magic you've seen."

Wendy idly wondered what it was like to be Peter, to meet people when they were young and could still believe in magic. To take them on adventures, to places they could never imagine in their wildest dreams, only to be forgotten with time and age. It must be a lonely existence . . .

Peter nodded at Wendy. "That's probably why you forgot. When you turned thirteen, you weren't a kid anymore, so when I rescued you and brought you back to the woods, you forgot about Neverland . . . and me."

Wendy bit her lip. Did that explain why she couldn't remember what had happened to her during those six months?

"Do you think that's why things started going wrong in Neverland?" Wendy asked.

Peter frowned and shook his head slightly, not understanding the question.

"I turned thirteen the day you brought me back, right? What if all the weird things that started to happen on the island were because I was too old? If getting older means losing magic, maybe me being there was what started all the problems?"

"It might have," Peter considered hesitantly. "But that still doesn't explain me and my shadow. You being too old and defying the rules of Neverland could've caused the animals and the fairies to start acting strangely, sure, but why would *I* start getting older and losing my magic?" he asked.

Wendy sighed and shrugged. "I don't know," she told him. "But it's a start." She shivered. A breeze was starting to pick up. "Are you okay to get back to the hunting shack?" she asked.

Now, more than ever, she was completely terrified by the prospect of being in the woods, especially alone at night. She didn't like the idea of Peter being in them, either. What if something happened and the shadow tried to go after him next? She wanted to ask him to stay, but the words caught in her throat.

Peter laughed and cocked an eyebrow at her. "Uh, yeah. Thanks, Mom, but I can take care of myself."

Wendy scowled and nudged her elbow into his side. "Oh, shut up. When can I see you tomorrow? We need to come up with a game plan. Should we meet up somewhere?" she asked. This would be a lot easier if he were a normal teenager and had a cell phone.

"Don't worry," Peter replied. He wiggled his eyebrows and dropped his voice to an ominous tone. "I'll find you when the time comes."

Wendy narrowed her eyes at him. "Wait, seriously?"

Peter laughed, a large grin cracking across his face, showing off the small chip in his tooth. It was the first genuine smile she'd seen on him today that wasn't edged with worry or apprehension. It was a welcome relief.

"Uh, no, actually," he said, rocking on the balls of his feet, satisfied with himself for being so clever. "You should probably tell me when and where to meet you."

Wendy rolled her eyes but couldn't hide the smile tugging at her lips. "Just meet me at the corner of my street by the orange house at noon tomorrow, okay?"

"Aye aye, captain," Peter replied with a sweeping salute. He jumped off the porch and started walking across the yard.

As she watched his retreating back, Wendy couldn't help herself. "Be careful going into the woods, okay?" she called after him as quietly as possible.

Peter turned around and gave her an amused smirk. "You know, if you keep worrying like that you're going to give yourself wrinkles," he said, walking backward as he reached the driveway. "Just there." He tapped his finger on the middle of his forehead.

Wendy shook her head, conjuring up her best look of disdain. "Good night, Peter," she told him.

"Sweet dreams, Wendy."

She watched as he turned back around and walked down the street. The sound of crickets drifted in his wake.

When she went back inside, Mrs. Darling was standing in front of the fridge. "How do leftovers sound?" her mother asked. Mrs. Darling pulled out a Tupperware full of cheesy chicken and rice Wendy had made for dinner a couple of nights before.

"Sounds good to me," Wendy said as she took a seat at the table. Her shins already ached from running through the woods. She felt like she was still covered in dirt and ashes. She really needed to get into the shower and scrub herself clean, but at the moment, walking up the stairs seemed daunting and the promise of melted cheese made her stomach growl.

She realized her mother was watching her, but Mrs. Darling's eyes flitted away when Wendy looked up and she busied herself with pulling out a pair of forks.

Wendy thought about what Peter had said. How, once upon a time, her mother had known Peter, had even been a swordfighter. The idea seemed preposterous now, with her messy hair, medical scrubs, and perpetually tired smile.

Even before Wendy and her brothers had gone missing, her mother had always seemed like the perfect lady to Wendy. Her hair had always been long and fell down her back in waves. Wendy had been in love with those silky locks and used to run her fingers through them over and over when she was upset and being held. She used to have such a graceful walk, too, like a ballerina. And when she had told them stories, her mother's voice was a gentle tune, like she was singing.

Those were the only two versions of her mother Wendy knew. The idea of her being a little girl, running around with Peter Pan and brandishing a sword, seemed impossible.

But a lot of things that seemed impossible were turning out to be very real lately.

"So, Barry seems nice?" Her mother's question brought Wendy out of her thoughts.

"Hmm? Oh, yeah, he's nice," Wendy said, caught off guard.

"You've never brought a boy over before. Are you two . . ." Mrs. Darling started slowly, casting Wendy a furtive glance, "dating?"

"What?" Wendy almost shouted. "No—we—NO, definitely not," she stammered, completely flustered. "I only just met him the other day!" She could feel her cheeks turn red.

Oh, God, they weren't going to have *that* conversation, were they?

"Okay, okay." Mrs. Darling held her hands up in surrender. "I was only asking," she said, an amused look on her face. As she started the microwave, Wendy tried to melt into her chair. "You just seemed nervous when I walked in on you two—"

Wendy slapped her hand on her forehead. "You didn't *walk in* on us. We weren't doing anything—"

"And you kept touching his arm and giving him this

look," Mrs. Darling continued. She was nearly smiling—it was almost there, hiding in the right-hand corner of her mouth.

Wendy groaned and buried her face in her hands. She had only been touching him because she had been trying to get him out of the house! And what look on her face was her mother even talking about? The only look she could have possibly been making was of a girl on the brink of panic! Wendy dropped her hands to the table. "Trust me, there is nothing going on with me and P—between the two of us."

Mrs. Darling walked over and set a paper plate of chicken and rice in front of Wendy, along with a glass of water. "Well, he seems very nice either way," Mrs. Darling said as she walked back to the kitchen.

Wendy made a huffing noise as she stabbed her fork into a piece of chicken and popped it into her mouth. She wasn't the best cook—nothing compared to what her mother used to make when she was little—but the chicken was seasoned with just enough spice, and the rice was gooey with cheese.

"He just seems so familiar, though," Mrs. Darling continued. She frowned at her plate as she scooped up a portion. "Maybe I used to go to school with his father? Do they look very much alike?"

Wendy took another bite and shook her head. "No, like I said, they just moved here," she said through a mouthful of food, "from Florida." Wendy hated lying, mostly because she was terrible at it. "He just has one of those faces, I guess . . ."

Mrs. Darling nodded slowly, lost in thought.

It was then that Wendy noticed the TV was still on. "I guess you heard about Alex?" she ventured, staring down at her plate as she picked at her rice.

This refocused Mrs. Darling's attention. Her delicate brows furrowed and a heavy sigh pulled down on her shoulders. "Yes," she said. "The police were at the hospital all night, checking sign-in sheets and getting security camera footage."

Wendy coughed. It felt like a piece of chicken had lodged itself in her throat. "Security cameras?" she repeated.

"Yes," Mrs. Darling went on, not noticing Wendy's sudden change in mood. "But they're only positioned at the entrances, so I'm not sure what good they'll do for the search." She sighed and closed her eyes for a moment. "I guess they want to look for anyone suspicious, maybe anyone who might've followed him and his parents out of the hospital this afternoon."

That probably should've relieved Wendy—at least there would be no footage of Peter interacting with her or Alex—but would the security cameras have caught him coming in or leaving? She'd never asked him how, exactly, he got in and out without anyone noticing. Would someone recognize him?

Mrs. Darling put the empty Tupperware into the sink but paused instead of joining Wendy at the table. "They're looking for the boy from the hospital, too, who you found in the road," she started hesitantly.

Oh no . . .

"They seem to think that this is all related somehow," Mrs. Darling continued. "You haven't seen him, have you?"

Wendy shook her head.

"Well, just keep an eye out. If you do, you call the police straightaway, okay?" Mrs. Darling twisted her wedding ring around her finger, something she did when she was anxious.

Wendy nodded. "Have they—the police, I mean—have they . . . told you and Dad anything new?"

Wendy watched as her mother's eyes slid across the room to the door of her father's study. "I'm not sure . . ." she said.

"Where is Dad?" Wendy asked.

Mrs. Darling sighed again. "After I was questioned at the hospital, they asked me about the night you went missing, too." Wendy cringed at her mom's avoidance of mentioning her brothers. "Then they called your father down to the station, too. He's there now." Maybe she could see the alarm in Wendy's face because she quickly added, "But there shouldn't be anything to worry about, they're just trying to get as many details of that night as possible."

She picked up her plate and sat down next to Wendy. "They'll probably want to talk to you again," she said, gently placing her hand on Wendy's arm. "Who knows." She stared down into her bowl of soup. "Maybe we'll finally find out what happened . . ."

Wendy pushed her food away. "I think I'm going to head to bed now," she said quietly as she stood up from her seat.

It was possible Wendy saw a flicker of disappointment cross her mother's face, but she just gave her a small smile and nodded.

"Night, Mom," Wendy said. She wanted to reach out and give her mother a hug, but she felt like she had forgotten what hugging looked like, or even where to put her arms. She picked up her plate with her half-eaten chicken instead.

"Good night, Wendy."

Wendy walked up to the second floor and at the top, as always, she was met with the door to her old room. She stood there for a moment, plate in hand, and stared at the handle. Even though John and Michael weren't here, it still felt like she could open the door and there they would be, sitting on her bed, riffling through her art supplies so they could make a treasure map or draw pictures of make-believe beasts.

She rested her hand on the doorknob. It felt like cold electricity under her fingertips.

If Peter was right, and they were able to stop his shadow, she would finally get her brothers back.

A surge of energy ran from her core and down her arm to her hand. For the first time in five years, Wendy gripped the doorknob and gave it a turn.

But it was locked.

Deflated, Wendy's hand fell back to her side. Of course it was locked. How had she not predicted that? Her father had probably locked it up after she refused to go inside. It had probably stayed locked ever since.

Wendy rubbed her stinging eyes. Even though she was alone, she felt silly and embarrassed. Without a second glance at the door, Wendy turned and went to her bedroom. She left her dinner on her dresser, having lost her appetite completely. She needed to clean up, so she went into the bathroom and scrubbed away at her skin in the shower until the smell of dirt and ash was replaced with jasmine and green tea.

She changed into her oversized sleep shirt and turned on the fairy lights that twinkled around her window. But before she lay down in bed, Wendy paused. Ever since she had entered the woods earlier that night, she'd felt a heavy weight. Not only of the anxiety around keeping Peter a secret, or the responsibility of needing to stop the shadow so she could save her brothers, but something else. Something dark. She couldn't shake the feeling of being watched.

Wendy looked out her window. The lights from the main part of town blinked lazily in the distance. For the first time all summer, she crawled up onto her bed, pulled her window shut, and locked it tight. It was still hot and humid, but she was willing to sleep uncomfortably warm if it meant not being worried that something would crawl in through her window while she slept.

She jerked her curtains shut and shoved the comforter off her bed, leaving only the white cotton sheets.

The acorn was still on her nightstand from where she had left it that morning. Taking it into her hand, Wendy leaned back against her pillows and gently rolled it between her fingers.

Even with the window shut and locked, and her curtains preventing anyone from possibly being able to look in, Wendy didn't feel any better. It was like whatever was in the woods had attached itself to her back and was clawing its way into her skin, no matter how hard she tried to scrub it clean. Wendy shuddered and squeezed the acorn tight in her hand.

If she was going to get any sleep tonight, she needed a distraction.

Keeping the acorn in her fist, Wendy pulled out the notebook from her bedside drawer, a red Sharpie, and a stack of pamphlets. The university had sent her a large manila envelope full of information on housing and academics.

Jordan had convinced Wendy to sign up for the health sciences housing. Jordan knew what she wanted to do and was already reaching out to premed students with questions.

Wendy wished she had that confidence.

Chewing on the cap of the red marker, Wendy flipped to the page of her bullet journal saved with a ribbon. Across the top center of the page she had written *Nursing*, and on the next several pages were bulleted lists, dates, and calendars. After poring over the university website's academics section, she had mocked up an entire four years' worth of classes to graduate with a nursing degree. Wendy had used her collection of fine-tip Sharpies to meticulously map out potential schedules, all color coded with their respective credits. It had taken her weeks.

Everything was carefully laid out for her. If she followed these steps, she would have her nursing degree and be ready to enter the real world after graduation. She would have a steady job in a high-demand field.

But . . .

Wendy turned to a blank page. At the top in small, red letters she wrote *Premed.*

It was a crazy idea. Becoming a doctor took *ages*—four years of undergrad, four years of med school, and then a three-to-seven-year residency? That was a lot of time and a lot of money. She was relying mostly on grants and scholarships for college. How would she be able to afford going to med school?

Nursing was perfectly respectable. She'd earn a degree faster and make a decent living. Sometimes, she entertained the idea of becoming a doctor, specifically a pediatrician, but she was just toying with the idea. Realistically, it was too much of a risk and too big of a cost if she failed.

Being a pediatrician meant the wellness of children—their *lives*—would be in her hands. It made Wendy start to sweat just thinking about making the wrong decision, or messing up so colossally that she'd lose a patient. There was no way she could handle that sort of responsibility. She couldn't even keep her brothers safe—how could anyone trust her with their children?

She pulled out the athletics brochure and busied her mind reading about the state-of-the-art training facilities on campus.

The acorn remained tight in her hand. *I wish Peter were here*, she found herself thinking as sleep began to lull her eyes closed. She would never admit it out loud, but he emitted a warmth that Wendy couldn't help being drawn to, and she felt it when she was holding the acorn.

CHAPTER 12

Warning

endy shivered in the middle of the woods. The fading light of dusk tinged the trees a cold blue-gray. They were dense here, like they only got in the heart of the woods. There was a light layer of snow covering the trees and frosting the ground beneath her feet. Her wet clothes clung to her skin. The smell of moist dirt filled her nose. Wendy tried to remember how she had gotten there, but her head was in a fog.

It felt like she was supposed to be looking for someone. Or was someone looking for her?

Wendy wanted to call out for help, but something told her she needed to be quiet, to not break the dead silence that hung thick in the air, pressing against her ears. Craning her head back, Wendy searched the trees above, noting the silvery sky as it peeked through the boughs. She slowly turned in a circle, naked branches turning above her. When she stopped, Wendy found herself facing an old tree.

Its trunk dwarfed the others that encircled her. Its bark was an oily brown, and its branches twisted and curved above her, completely devoid of any leaves or needles. Its roots were thick and gnarled, knotting and tangling with one another before plunging into the frozen earth.

It was the tree. *The* tree. The one she had sketched a hundred times, just as crooked and eerie in person as it had been on paper.

Wendy's heart thudded violently in her throat. Cold sweat beaded on her skin. Her nails bit into her palms. Harsh, ragged breaths billowed white before her. The trembling in her spine began to awake.

At the base of the great tree, the roots formed a small opening, like an entrance to a dark cage. Rotten leaves brushed past the gaping mouth and, just below the sound of their ruffling, Wendy heard quiet voices murmur.

She knew this place.

Everything in her screamed for her to run. Wendy needed to get out of there. She needed to get away from this tree. But it was like she had no control of her body, because suddenly she was moving toward it. The hushed whispers became steadily louder as she stepped closer, one foot after another.

They were children's voices. Wendy could only watch as her own hand reached out toward the opening of the roots.

The voices grew harsh and urgent. The whispers turned to soft cries, then gut-wrenching wails, the kind that howled with unhinged fear. Wendy wanted to scream and drown them out, but her lips remained closed as she leaned in.

"I'd be careful if I were you," a voice behind her said.

Wendy whirled around. There stood the guy who had talked to her when she was getting her bag out of her truck. She had almost forgotten about him.

"Who are you?" she asked. Her voice sounded far off and distant.

She still couldn't make out his face. The light continued to fade and she couldn't see his features clearly.

They seemed to shift and change the more she tried to

focus on them. Black eyes. White teeth. An unnaturally wide grin. His features twisted and morphed.

"You never know what you might find in dark places," he continued, ignoring her question as he moved closer to her.

The shadows of the trees behind him started to sway and converge. Wendy took a step back, but he pursued. The black shapes behind him became towering figures, bowing down in the darkness.

"If you insist on poking around, Wendy . . ." His hand lashed out and snatched her wrist. His sharp fingers dug into her skin.

Wendy cried out in pain and tried to twist her arm free of him. He pulled her roughly toward him, and his face came into focus.

Peter's face. But wrong, very wrong, with pale skin and inky pits for eyes.

"You won't like what you find," he breathed. It smelled like rotten leaves and wet dirt.

The shadows behind him gathered, piling up high then forming long, sharp fingers. He laughed and it shook Wendy's bones. She tried to struggle but he held tight. The shadows lashed out and crashed down over her.

Wendy thrashed and jerked herself upright. She was home, in her own bed and drenched in sweat. Her clothes stuck to her skin and her hair was matted to her forehead. Shuddering gasps wracked Wendy's body as she gripped her sheets. *It was just a dream*, she told herself, squeezing her eyes shut as she tried to steady herself. But it felt so *real*.

Wendy gulped a deep breath, but when she looked down, a strangled shout caught in her throat.

She scrambled back so quickly, she slammed the back of her head against the headboard.

Everything was covered in red.

At first, Wendy thought the ink was blood, but after the initial terror cut through her, she realized that she still held the red marker she had fallen asleep with.

They were drawings of the tree, over and over again, in haphazard lines that crossed and dragged over everything—her nightshirt, her legs, and all over her sheets. Pages of her bullet journal were also covered in red, ruined and ripped from the notebook. Gnarled branches and tangled roots buried her carefully written notes.

Clutched in her other hand was the acorn.

Wendy threw the marker and clutched the acorn tight to her chest as she tried to steady her rapid breathing. Had she done all of this in her sleep?

Wendy squeezed her eyes shut.

What was happening to her?

Surrounded by torn pages and red ink, she felt trapped. The shadows, the drawings, the murmurings—everything was creeping in.

Wendy dropped the acorn into her bedside drawer. She leapt out of bed and yanked the fitted sheet free. Some of the red had bled through and stained the mattress. She bundled everything up into a heap and ran into the bathroom, where she shoved it to the bottom of her hamper and out of sight, along with her ruined nightshirt.

She couldn't have her parents seeing what she'd done. Wendy was the only one who did laundry around the house. This was the perfect place to hide it until she could sneak it out into the trash.

As she shoved the bundle of sheets and torn pages under her dirty clothes, Wendy caught a glimpse of her hands. They were smeared with red. Some had even gotten under her fingernails.

At the sink, Wendy turned the hot water faucet on full blast. With shaky hands, she scrubbed furiously at her hands with soap and a facecloth.

That tree. It had been so familiar to her when she had seen it in her drawings. There was something there, some sort of connection she couldn't place, but after seeing it with her own eyes, she couldn't deny it anymore. She knew that tree. She had seen that tree in person. Been next to it.

To call what she'd experienced a dream just wasn't true. It was more than a dream. She could smell the earth and feel the cold of the snow. The forest looked just as it had that winter when Wendy and her brothers had gone missing in the woods. It wasn't a dream; it was a memory.

A shudder ripped through her from head to toe, her hands jolting so hard that she dropped the bar of soap. She scrambled to grab it out of the sink and began working on the red slashes of marker up and down her legs.

A memory. She'd spent years with a gaping hole in her mind where those six months had been ripped out. Wendy had been dropped into a flashback, however brief.

And the boy in her dream—there was no doubt in Wendy's mind it was the same person who had approached her in her driveway right before Alex went missing.

It was Peter, but it also *wasn't* Peter.

It had his face, but a horrible, nightmarish version.

Was that Peter's shadow? Wendy had assumed that his shadow was just that—a black, amorphous thing. Could it take a solid human form? Did Peter know?

She needed to find him and tell him. If Peter's shadow could walk and talk, and knew where she lived—

Wendy shut off the water and gripped the edge of the sink. Her hands were bright red, the knuckles blanched. Pin drops of blood spread through the dry cracks. The hot water had burned, and her skin stung, but she'd gotten rid of the ink. Even her legs only had bright streaks left from being scrubbed raw.

A shaky breath filled Wendy's lungs, an attempt to steady herself. She looked at her reflection in the mirror. The hair at her temples and the back of her neck was damp with sweat. Her gray eyes stared back at her, puffy and bloodshot.

She needed to find Peter and tell him what had happened. He was the only one who could make sense of it.

The clock on Wendy's counter read 11:32 a.m.

"Shit!" she cursed. She had told Peter to meet her at noon.

Wendy jumped into the shower to wash the sticky, stale sweat off her skin. Drying her hair would take too long, so cold drips hit the back of her neck as she rushed around her room. She pulled on a pair of green shorts and a navy tank top before sliding on her tennis shoes. Grabbing her bag, she bounded down the stairs and nearly tripped on her laces.

Wendy was halfway across the living room when her father's voice rang out. "Where are you off to in such a rush?"

She whirled around to find her father standing in the doorway of his study. He wore a dark blue suit that was a little too tight across his barrel chest. He had somehow managed to wrangle his hair with gel into an uneven comb-over. Even his bushy mustache was trimmed.

Wendy frowned. He never dressed this nice for work. And why was he home in the middle of a weekday?

"Why aren't you at work?" Wendy asked, momentarily distracted from her mission by his odd appearance.

"I'm not at work because I need to take you down to the police station, remember?" Mr. Darling grumbled as he hooked a sausage-like finger over the knot of his tie, trying to wiggle it loose. "I'm taking a half day to deal with this."

"What?" Wendy said, starting. Her mind went into a panic with visions of handcuffs and mugshots and dark interrogation rooms.

Mr. Darling furrowed his thick eyebrows. "Those detectives still want to talk to you."

"Oh, right." A wave of relief washed over her. Wendy rocked onto the balls of her feet so she could read the clock next to the TV: 11:54 a.m. She was supposed to meet Peter any minute now, and she had so much to tell him. "Can we go a bit later?" Wendy tried, wincing in anticipation of his answer.

Mr. Darling scowled. "No, we can't go later," he barked, waving his hand in the air. "Where do you have to get to that's so important?"

"Nowhere," Wendy answered quickly, smoothing her hands through her wet hair. "I just made plans to meet up with Jordan at the hospital, you know, after her shift." Another lie. The more she told, the easier it got.

"This is more important," he told her. He waved his hand dismissively. "Text her and tell her you're going to be late. I can drop you off at the hospital after." Mr. Darling snatched his keys from the kitchen table and started for the door. "Let's go."

Wendy gave a nod and pulled out her phone, pretending to text Jordan as she followed him out the door. She'd lied herself into a corner. She wanted to see Peter, and she especially didn't want to leave him waiting for her, but what choice did she have? This wasn't really something she could talk her way out of.

In the car, Wendy tried to look for Peter as they drove down the street, but there was no sign of him. How was she going to find him when she got back? She'd have to wait at the hospital until her mom got off work to get a ride home. It wasn't like he had a cell phone she could call him on, and there was no way she was going to just wander around the woods calling his name.

But for now she had more pressing matters to deal with. Like what Detective James wanted to ask her. Were they going to accuse her of having something to do with Alex's disappearance? Was she a suspect? Was Peter?

Her mind grew frantic. She tried to distract herself by focusing on the quiet rhythm of music flowing out of the speakers. Her dad only ever listened to classic rock.

The police station was located on a main road that paralleled the shore. The ocean funneled into a large bay that eventually turned into the Columbia River. With her window rolled down, the ocean breeze felt cool in the heat of the mid-day sun. The air smelled like salt water. Large ships laden with crates trudged along, and behind them she could make out the blue mountains of Washington across the river.

Her father didn't say anything, so Wendy didn't, either. The awkward silence stretched on until they pulled up to the old brick building.

"Let's go," Mr. Darling said, trying to loosen his tie again as he got out of the car. Wendy followed.

As they walked into the lobby, Wendy tried to shrink behind her father. She shivered and fidgeted with the strap of her bag. She didn't like being back here. It felt like walking into a cemetery crowded with ghosts.

The police department was all but devoid of color. Everyone was either wearing gray or black suits, or else they were dressed in police uniforms. Desks were placed in rows and detectives and officers walked around, speaking to one another, talking on the phone and handing off documents. Usually, the police didn't have much to worry about in their small town, but the string of missing kids appeared to be keeping everyone busy.

Wendy stood in the middle of the lobby, arms wrapped around her middle as her father went to ask for Detective James. On the wall behind the front desk was a bulletin board. Tacked to it were the missing posters of Benjamin Lane, Ashley Ford, and now Alex Forestay. There was also the poorly done police sketch of Peter.

Quickly, Wendy cut her gaze away. She tried to avoid making eye contact, but she'd already spotted Officer Smith. When he saw Wendy, he stopped talking to a female officer. He stared at her for a moment before nudging his fellow officer's arm and nodding in her direction. Wendy stared at the floor. Her cheeks burned with embarrassment and anger.

"Ah, Mr. Darling, Wendy." Detective James rounded a corner and approached them. He looked exactly the same as he had in her living room, in a perfectly pressed suit with his black hair parted to the side and a forced smile on his face. He held a thick file under his arm. Wendy noticed a silver ring on his middle finger. "Thanks for coming in. This shouldn't take long," he said.

Mr. Darling grunted in response.

Wendy kept quiet, but Detective James turned to her. "Wendy, if you'd follow me, we'll head back to my office." Wendy nodded and began to walk, but when Mr. Darling started to follow close behind, Detective James held out a hand. "Sorry, Mr. Darling, you'll need to wait here until we're finished."

Wendy wasn't used to people telling her dad what to do. Her eyes cut back and forth between the two.

Clearly Mr. Darling wasn't used to it, either, because he puffed out his chest.

"She's my daughter—you can't talk to her without me being there," Mr. Darling all but growled. Now even more people were starting to watch. Mr. Darling was very big compared to Detective James. An angry bear lumbering in front of a guy in a fancy suit.

To his credit, Detective James remained placid and unaffected by this show. "Actually, as of four days ago, Wendy is no longer a minor, so I need to speak with her alone," he said plainly.

Wendy watched as her father's face flushed, starting at his bulbous nose and spreading across his cheeks. His bushy mustache ruffled and Wendy knew he was going to argue with the detective.

"It's okay, Dad," she cut in, trying to defuse the situation before it turned into a real mess.

In all honesty, she almost wanted her dad to stay with her, if only to make her feel less frightened. But she also didn't want him there to listen to any accusations or evidence that might be in that big file Detective James held.

"I'll let you know if I need you," she added. She tried to give her father a reassuring look, even though she was quite certain she probably looked like a pale, haggard, nervous wreck.

Mr. Darling's small, dark eyes darted between Wendy and Detective James. "Fine," he said tersely after a moment.

"Like I said, shouldn't take us too long," Detective James said. "Mr. Darling, please have a seat. Help yourself to some coffee if you'd like."

Mr. Darling didn't move. Instead, he crossed his arms over his chest, showing the detective that he had no intention of doing either.

Detective James said nothing for a moment. His scarred eyebrow flicked upward momentarily, but then he turned to Wendy and said, "This way."

Detective James's office was small but not cramped. There was one window through which she caught a glimpse of the river between buildings, and sun filtered in through a set of blinds. All the shelves were filled with books, papers, and files, and there were a couple of boxes on the floor next to his desk. The desk itself was tidy, with one very old computer and a name plate. Hanging on the wall behind his desk was an elaborate drawing of an old ship with full sails. Small, delicate handwriting labeled the parts of the boat on old yellowing paper.

Detective James sat down in a wooden chair with cracked black leather cushions behind his desk. "Please, have a seat," he said, gesturing.

Wendy sat down in the only other chair in the room. It was metal, cold and uncomfortable. Wendy fidgeted with her hands in her lap.

Detective James set a pad of paper and a pen on his desk, but then leaned back casually in his chair. "So," he began, giving her that smile again. Wendy gripped the edge of her seat. "Let's get right to it. I assume by now you know that Alex Forestay went missing last night?"

Wendy nodded. "I saw you on the news talking about it." It was true enough.

"You saw him yesterday before he went missing, is that correct?"

"Yes, I read to the kids in the children's clinic," Wendy said. She wondered if he could hear the guilt hammering in her chest from across the desk.

"How often do you do that?" He began writing on his pad of paper, giving her a reprieve from his icy blue stare.

"Once a week." Should she give longer answers? Were short ones suspicious? Or would she sound guilty if she rattled off information?

"Had you seen Alex prior to that day?"

Wendy shook her head. "No, that was the first time he'd ever come to story time," she answered. "I think that was his first visit for treatment?" Shouldn't he already know that? Was this a tactic for catching people in lies?

Detective James nodded. "Did you talk to him?"

"Yes."

"What about?"

"Sharks."

"Ah, sharks." Detective James's eyebrows arched in amusement, but he continued to write. "Was he acting strange? Did he seem at all scared?"

"Scared?" Memories of Alex's cries and the look of sheer terror on his face as he got dragged into the woods flooded her vision. "No, not scared," Wendy said, swallowing past the dryness in her throat. "He was shy, definitely shy . . ." Her fingers itched.

"When you were at the hospital, did you notice anyone suspicious in the children's ward? Anyone who looked like they didn't belong there?" Wendy could tell he was trying to keep his voice casual and light, but there was a distinct severity to his eyes as he watched her.

Wendy shook her head. "No, I pretty much know everyone that works in the children's department," Wendy said.

Detective James hummed to himself. "Small town. Everyone knows everyone else, right?"

"Right . . ." Wendy cleared her throat. "It was just nurses and doctors, some of the kids' parents, too."

"So, there wasn't anyone in the room with you who was a stranger? No one you thought didn't belong?" he asked, watching her.

Wendy's palms were sweaty and her hands shook.

Did they know about Peter? Did they know he had been in the room? Peter said adults didn't notice him, but was that right? What if someone had seen him talking to Alex? And then talking to her? Wendy didn't know how to answer that question, but she was taking too long. She had to say something.

So she shook her head again. "No, I didn't notice anyone like that." Technically that wasn't a lie. She knew who Peter was now, so he wasn't a stranger. But he definitely shouldn't have been in the hospital to begin with . . .

Detective James took a long moment to jot down some more notes. Did he know she was lying? He must.

Wendy straightened her back, bracing herself against impending doom. For Detective James to reveal his hand.

After what seemed like an eternity, he put down his pen and sat back in his seat. "I have to say, Miss Darling, I find it very curious how, after what happened with the mystery boy you found in the road—Peter, I believe he told you his name was?—and now Alex's disappearance, things seem to keep coming around back to you." His expression was serious. He didn't even try to put on that plastic smile.

Wendy didn't know what to say, so she said nothing.

He continued on, "Have you seen anyone strange around town, Wendy? Has anyone been following you? Bothering you at all?"

She could feel the tremor starting, barely a quiver in the center of her chest. "No, no, nothing like that," Wendy said. A rough shudder jolted her shoulders.

Detective James leaned forward in his seat. "Are you sure?" he asked, snagging her in his gaze. "Wendy—" His eyes flicked to the edge of his desk. His brows drew together.

Wendy looked down. She held a pen, poised as if about to write something down. Her hand shook furiously, the tip a mere inch from the desk, bobbing through the air as if writing on its own.

Or drawing.

Wendy slammed the pen down.

She shoved her hands under her thighs.

Detective James watched her, expression unreadable.

Wendy made herself stare back. She took slow, deliberate breaths.

After a long pause, Detective James asked, "Have you seen Peter since he went missing from the hospital?"

"No." She hesitated. "Do you think he had something to do with this?" she couldn't stop herself from asking.

He considered her question before responding. "Right now, all we know is that kids are going missing—disappearing from their homes—and that this boy, Peter, also went missing. While, currently, I can't say that we've recovered enough evidence to make any connections . . ." He said it in a way that sounded very rehearsed. "What we can say is that you and Peter were, at one point, in the same place. We don't know in what capacity, but we can't deny that all of these disappearances could be connected, because the two of you are connected. It's possible that he's being held captive with the other children who have gone missing."

Wendy chewed on her bottom lip. So, they still weren't sure what to make of Peter. That was reassuring. Hell, she still didn't know quite what to make of him, either. Peter wasn't being accused of anything yet, which was good. They were even considering that maybe he was a victim.

One way or another, everything kept leading back to her. Back to her brothers. Back to what happened in the woods.

Detective James's expression hardened. He braced his elbows on the desk. "There is a very real possibility that whoever took those missing kids also took Peter, and could have taken you and your brothers. You need to be careful, Wendy," he said in a low and even tone. "This isn't a game, and this isn't just about you anymore."

Wendy wanted to snap at him, to remind him it had never been just about her. It had been about her *and* John *and* Michael. It angered her, the way people kept talking about them as if they were gone for good.

He pulled out a card from his pocket and handed it to Wendy. "If you think of anything that could help, see anyone suspicious, see Alex or Peter, or need help, call me."

Wendy took his card. The corner was sharp and poked into her finger. She took a deep breath and nodded. "I will."

CHAPTER 13

Bubblegum

The police station was only a few blocks from the hospital, but Wendy's dad still insisted on driving her there. He kept looking over but didn't say anything until they pulled up to the entrance.

He turned to face her, expression stern. "No more leaving the house alone," he told her.

Wendy nodded. She knew it was best not to try arguing with him, especially about this. All the missing kids, cops, detectives, and mentions of her brothers were making him even more intense than usual, and she couldn't blame him. Honestly, she thought he would be drinking more, but she'd noticed that the recycling bin was noticeably less full.

"No more staying out past dark, lock the house up when your mom and I aren't there, and keep your phone on you at all times. If we call, I expect you to pick up immediately," her father ordered. He held up a finger and pointed it at her. "Do you understand me?"

Wendy nodded and wiped her sweaty palms on her shorts. "Yeah, Dad," she said, not wanting to say anything to anger him further.

Great. Now she would need to be more careful sneaking

around with Peter. Her father would be on alert, noticing more and asking questions. She was surrounded by interrogators. Her parents had only her best interests at heart, but still, there were things she needed to do without them.

For a moment, her father stared at her, his face still etched with a deep frown. Wendy thought he was going to say something more, but then he let out a huff of air, sat back, and gave her a curt nod.

Taking that as her cue to leave, Wendy climbed out of the car. She walked to the glass doors of the back entrance, as if she were going to go inside. She turned and waved to her dad.

Satisfied, he gave her another nod and drove off.

What a *day*. She hadn't even been awake for two hours and she was already exhausted. She felt guilty for not telling Detective James everything that she knew, but how could she? There was no way he would believe her. He would probably think she was having a mental breakdown, reliving the trauma of losing her memory and her brothers. They would probably lock her up and throw away the key if she started talking about magic boys, evil shadows, and other worlds.

She just needed to keep it together and help Peter. Knowing that she had the chance to see her brothers again was what mattered. And the sooner they figured out how to stop the shadow, the sooner she would get John and Michael back.

The sooner they could move on.

Right now, she needed to find Peter.

Wendy checked the time on her phone. It read 1:00 p.m., above a list of unread texts from Jordan. She would text back later. Right now she was stuck downtown and needed to find a way home. Wendy pulled up the ride share app.

Her backyard seemed like a good place to start looking for him, since that was closest to the woods. She was waiting for the app to load nearby drivers when a high-pitched whistle from across the street, followed by a series of giggles, caught her attention.

Across the street was a row of houses nestled right up against the woods. A minty-blue house was set back in the shade of the towering trees.

There, just sitting in the middle of the yard, was Peter and a little girl Wendy recognized.

What the hell was he doing? Wendy rushed over, practically running across the street.

"Now you try," Peter was saying.

The pair sat cross-legged and facing each other. They were focused on a piece of grass that Peter held in his palm. The little girl wore a purple sundress, with a pile of grass and small flowers across her lap.

A flower crown of wilting, small yellow buds sat lopsided on the top of Peter's head. He grinned lazily and gave the girl a nod of encouragement.

She took the blade of grass, squeezed it between the sides of her thumbs, and blew against it, eliciting a high-pitched squeak. She broke into a fit of laughter.

Peter chuckled along, looking quite pleased with himself.

"Peter! What are you doing here?" Wendy cut in, absolutely bewildered.

He cast her a fleeting glance. "Oh, hey," Peter said. "You are very late." He sent Wendy a stern look before nodding at the little girl across from him. "You weren't home, so I thought maybe you were at the hospital," he explained casually. "But then I ran into Cassidy, here." Peter fixed Wendy with a wide smile. "We're making grass whistles."

"Grass whistles," Wendy repeated. She fought the urge to shove him over.

Cassidy beamed up at her. "I made Peter a crown," she said in a small, shy voice. Her dad was an X-ray technician who worked with her mom. Wendy used to babysit Cassidy and her older sister, Rebecca, when they were younger.

Peter looked up at Wendy with a lopsided grin. It crinkled the freckles on his nose.

Wendy cleared her throat and tucked her hair behind her ears. He needed to stop looking at her like that. "You look ridiculous," she told him.

"You're just jealous she didn't make *you* one," he said with a dismissive shrug of his shoulders.

Cassidy giggled behind her hands.

Wendy shook her head. He looked so pleased with himself! "Cass, you really shouldn't be talking to strangers, and you especially shouldn't tell them your name!" she chided. Cassidy had just started elementary school, hadn't they taught her about stranger danger yet?

Cassidy tried to wrestle the blade of grass back between her thumbs. "I know, but I didn't. He already knew!" she said, face screwed up in concentration.

Wendy gave Peter a confused look.

He leaned back on one hand and made a wide sweeping gesture to himself with the other. "Peter Pan, remember?" he asked with a conspiratorial wink. "It's kind of my job."

Wendy let out a huff. "You're impossible," she muttered before turning back to Cassidy. "Well, where are your parents, Cass? They should be watching you."

"They're at work. *Rebecca* is supposed to be watching me," she said, glaring in the direction of her house. Sure enough, Rebecca sat in a lounge chair on the porch. She seemed deeply engrossed in a book, a set of headphones covering her ears.

Wendy's frustration boiled. How did Rebecca not notice her sister talking to a random guy?

As if he could hear her thoughts, Peter said, "Sometimes teenagers are just as bad as adults when it comes to noticing magic." He raised an eyebrow, giving Wendy a pointed look, which she pointedly ignored.

Wendy glared at Rebecca, feeling a surge of protectiveness for Cassidy. "Well, this teenager has a lot of things she needs to talk to you about," she told Peter. "Let's go, Flower Prince."

"Only if you promise to call me prince," he said, helping Cassidy readjust her thumbs.

"Peter."

"Your Highness is also acceptable."

"Peter."

Finally noticing her tone, Peter looked up. He gave her a quizzical look, cocking his head to the side. He took the flower crown off his head and held it out to Cassidy in both of his hands. "I think you should hold on to this," he told her. Cassidy reached a hand out to take it, but before she could, Peter added, "But I think it needs to be a bit more fitting for a princess."

Slowly, the small, wilting buds began to glow a faint gold. Cassidy gasped and Wendy's heart fluttered.

The flowers swelled into huge blooms, the stems growing thick and knotted together. Rotating slowly, the circlet rose into mid-air. Eyes wide, Cassidy watched as it came down to rest around her neck, too large to perch on the top of her head.

"There!" Peter said, wiping his hands off on his worn jeans, looking pleased with his handiwork.

Pixie dust.

Cassidy let out a squeal of excitement and clapped her

hands together. "Are you a magician?" she asked, bubbling over, her tiny body literally bouncing with glee.

"Actually—" Peter started, but Wendy quickly cut him off.

"Yes!" she said. "But you can't tell anyone. It's a secret, okay?"

Peter huffed.

Wendy narrowed her eyes at him.

Peter sighed.

He turned and gave Cassidy a look of mock seriousness and nodded solemnly.

"I won't tell. I won't!" Cassidy insisted.

Wendy doubted she could actually keep that promise, which meant they needed to get the hell out of there.

"Let's go, Peter," Wendy said, tugging on his arm. Before leaving, Wendy shouted across the yard, "HEY, REBECCA!"

Cassidy's older sister jumped and yanked the headphones off. She looked startled, clearly having just now noticed Wendy and Peter with her sister.

Wendy waved enthusiastically, giving Rebecca the biggest, fakest smile she could. At least now she was paying attention.

Wendy stomped off and Peter followed. He looked back over his shoulder and waved good-bye to Cassidy, who cheerily waved back.

"Cassidy, get back on the porch!" Wendy heard Rebecca say.

Once they were out of earshot, Wendy threw her elbow into Peter's side. "You can't just go around hanging out with little girls in the middle of the street!" she hissed at him.

Peter laughed, rubbing at his ribs and furrowing his brow. "What do you mean?" he asked, as if he wasn't sure if she was serious or not.

Wendy groaned. Did he really not get it? "Because!" she snapped, squeezing the bridge of her nose with her thumb and forefinger. Clearly, living in Neverland didn't leave him with a lot of knowledge of social etiquette in the real world. "People will think you're up to something, maybe that you might hurt her," she told him. "You could get into a lot of trouble—you could get *us* into a lot of trouble."

Now he looked genuinely confused. "What? But I would never do that." The hurt in his voice made her feel bad for chastising him.

"I know, but people—other people, grown-ups—they wouldn't know that. They would just assume the worst," she explained, trying to be more gentle. "Especially with every-thing going on. If an adult saw you talking to random kids, they'd probably think *you* were the kidnapper."

They were at the end of the street now. Peter stopped and turned to face her. "Why do I have the feeling you're not telling me something?"

Wendy bit her bottom lip. "The detectives think you have something to do with the missing kids."

Peter's arms fell to his sides. "What do you mean?" he asked, shifting his weight between his feet.

Wendy took a deep breath. "I was late because I had to go down to the police station. Detective James—from the news, remember?—he questioned me about Alex, the missing kids." She added hesitantly, "You."

Peter groaned like a kid who had just been found while playing hide-and-seek. "Did you tell them anything?" he asked.

"No, of course not! How could I?" she spluttered, throw-ing her hands in the air. "It's not like they would believe me. We already ruled them out from being any use," she muttered.

If the police couldn't find her brothers when they'd first gone missing, how could she expect them to help now? This was up to her and Peter.

Wendy cast a wary glance down both sides of the street. "Let's keep walking," she said.

Peter fell into step beside her. Fewer and fewer places felt safe anymore, and the last thing she needed was to be overheard talking to Peter by Jordan or the cops or, even worse, her parents.

"They *do* think you have something to do with the missing kids," she continued.

"We already knew that from the news," Peter pointed out.

"It doesn't seem like you're a suspect"—Peter winced—"I think they think that you were kidnapped, too," she added quickly. "And since they connected you to *my* disappearance, they think that the person who is taking the kids *now* is the person who took me and my brothers."

Peter only nodded. It was hard to read his expression as he stared down at his feet, deep in thought.

Wendy sighed and rubbed her palm against her forehead. "I guess, technically, they're right?" she thought out loud. "Your shadow took my brothers and now it's taking more kids."

Again, Peter said nothing.

Wendy wrung her hands together. "It's not hurting them, is it?" she asked, nervous to hear the answer.

Peter shook his head. "No, they need to be alive," he told her, looking dismayed.

Wendy didn't like how that sounded.

"In order for the shadow to feed off them, they have to be awake."

"Awake and terrified," Wendy finished.

Peter nodded again.

He'd told her before how shadows got stronger by feeding off of a person's fear. Their terror and sadness, their sense of hopelessness. John and Michael had been trapped by the shadow for years. What was it like for them? What kind of existence was it, to be consumed by fear and unable to escape it?

Wendy's chest ached. She couldn't stand the thought of them suffering, especially for so long. She and Peter needed to rescue them.

"Do you know where they are?" Wendy asked.

"No—well, in the woods," Peter corrected himself. "Definitely in the woods, but it could be hiding them anywhere with magic."

They crossed the street and started walking down the road that led into town. It was the road that hugged the woods. The same one where Wendy had found Peter. They walked along the shoulder but, even in daylight, it made the hair on the back of her neck prickle. Her steps became slower and more hesitant. The overgrown trees and hanging branches loomed above them.

Peter put himself between her and the woods, pushing rogue branches out of the way as they walked. His presence made her feel . . . better. Less scared, like she had someone who finally knew what she was going through. Someone to go through it with. But then there was also this undeniable warmth that she could feel radiating through her body when she was close to him.

She took a quick couple of steps to catch up to Peter and fall into stride next to him, far away enough to not be touching him, but close enough that she could reach out and brush her knuckles against his if she wanted to.

Wendy glanced over and took in his profile: his nose that

turned up just a little at the tip, the hard line of his jaw, the small points to his ears. He wore the jeans Wendy had patched and a dusty rose T-shirt that was sun bleached but made his eyes all the more disarming.

Wendy wondered if the heat she felt was part of Peter's magic. Or was it just . . . him?

It was comforting, but she could still feel the woods pressing against her mind. They buzzed like the pressure in her ears when she dove into the deep end of the pool at swim practice. She still felt like she was being watched, just as she had last night in her driveway. The memory came flooding back to her.

"There's something I forgot to tell you about last night, before you found me in the woods," Wendy said slowly.

Peter turned to look at her. "What happened?" he asked, face scrunched up like he was bracing himself to get hit.

"I went to get my swim bag out of my truck last night," she began. "It was dark out and while I was digging around for it, I could—" Wendy paused, trying to put the experience into words. "Feel something behind me. I turned around and out of nowhere there was this guy. He started talking to me." Wendy watched him for his reaction, absently rubbing her arm as she remembered how her skin had crawled.

"Didn't you just get done telling Cassidy not to talk to strangers?" Peter asked, cocking an eyebrow at her.

Wendy felt a flare of annoyance. This wasn't a time for jokes.

"He knew who I was, Peter," she snapped. "He knew my name, he said he had seen me at the hospital before, he actually asked me if I wanted to go for a walk with him in the woods." Wendy shuddered.

Now Peter looked concerned.

"And he said something about how I had to be careful because I didn't want to 'go missing' again," she said, doing her best to remember exactly what happened.

Deep frown lines creased Peter's forehead. "Maybe he just recognized you from the news?" he offered. "It's a small town, maybe he just remembered you going missing . . ." It was like he was trying to convince himself.

Wendy shook her head. "No, like you said, it's a small town, and I had never seen him before," she explained. "Not only that, but there was something really weird about him. He was *creepy*. He felt . . ." She paused, trying to think of a way to describe him. "Dangerous. I couldn't see what he looked like, either," Wendy continued. "It was dark, sure, but it was more than that. He was standing right in front of me, but I couldn't make out his face. It was like I couldn't focus on a feature because they kept . . . moving around, like I was looking at him through water, you know? But dark."

He shook his head, not understanding her train of thought.

Wendy swallowed. Her mouth felt dry. "It was like he was made of shadows."

Peter stopped walking. "Shadows?" he repeated, suddenly very alert. Wendy nodded and Peter stared off into the woods, deep in thought.

"Yeah." Wendy shifted her weight between her feet. She didn't like that look on his face. She wanted to keep walking. She was scared to hear the answer to the question she needed to ask. "Peter, your shadow can't . . ." How could she put it into words? "It can't . . . take a human form, can it?"

Peter shook his head. He looked dazed. "That's never happened before," he said. "It's never even become a solid being before."

Wendy felt hopeless. "Why is this happening, Peter?"

He looked like he was holding himself back from saying something as he sucked on his bottom lip. But then he just sighed and shrugged. "I have no idea." That was not what she wanted to hear.

"Well, when I heard Alex's voice, he—it—disappeared, or maybe he was still there? I don't remember. I just took off running into the woods," Wendy continued. "Then another thing happened after you left and I went to bed . . ."

Peter groaned. "Another thing?" he asked dejectedly.

"I . . . think it was in my dream last night," she began, glancing up at him apprehensively. Peter looked at her intently, waiting for her to go on, so she did. "When I fell asleep, I dreamed that I was in the woods," Wendy told him. "There was snow, so it must have been winter, and it was starting to get dark. I was standing in front of this huge tree—"

"A tree?" Peter asked abruptly. His shoulders went rigid, his blue eyes intense.

She nodded. For some reason, his reaction unsettled her. "Yeah, it didn't look like any of the other trees in the woods," she explained. She could almost smell the dead leaves from her dream. "It was huge and its branches bent at weird angles. They were completely bare and it almost looked like it was dead. It had a huge tangle of roots."

Peter was standing so still, Wendy wondered if he was even breathing.

"And I could hear something coming from the tree. Like the voices in the woods last night, did you hear them?" Wendy asked.

Peter only responded with a short nod.

"Before I could get closer to the tree, the shadow appeared, but this time I could see him."

"What did he look like?" Peter asked, but his voice was laced with dread, like he already knew the answer.

"Like . . . well, like you," she said, shifting uncomfortably. "But not you. His hair was dark, his skin was pale, and his eyes were like looking into a pitch-black room," Wendy tried to explain. She searched the cloudless sky for the right words. "He was a twisted version of you that only a nightmare could conjure up, but it wasn't just a bad dream."

"What do you mean?" Peter asked cautiously.

"I mean, I don't think it was a dream at all." Wendy swallowed and wet her lips. "I think I got a memory back, from when I was in the woods."

All the color drained from Peter's face.

"And when I woke up, I had drawn the tree everywhere in my sleep—on my blankets, all over my legs, my hands." Wendy gestured at herself. She held up her hands for him to see. They were less red, but still dry and irritated from all the scrubbing.

Peter stepped closer to her, staring at the marks in disbelief.

"I've been drawing that same tree for weeks now," Wendy murmured, unable to find her voice with Peter standing so close. "But not on purpose." Peter gave her a confused look. "Like, I wouldn't notice I was doing it. I would be writing a grocery list and then I'd space out for a second, and the next thing I knew there would be drawings all over it."

Peter took her arm carefully with one hand and gently brushed his fingers along the faded red marks. There was a deep crease between his freckled brows. The sudden closeness made warmth swell in Wendy's chest.

"I think there's a part of me that remembers what happened, and it's trying to lead me in the right direction. I think that's why I keep drawing that tree . . ." She paused, collecting her bravery before adding, "And you."

Peter's eyes snagged hers, still worried but with a touch of curiosity. "Me?"

Wendy could only nod. Heat flamed in her cheeks.

She was acutely aware that she hadn't been this close to him since she found him on the road. The light flecks in his deep blue eyes sparked in the sunlight.

She couldn't think clearly with him this close. Wendy cleared her throat and took a step back, pulling her arm away from him.

Peter seemed unfazed by it and let his hands fall back to his sides, still stuck in his own head.

Wendy knew the feeling. She started walking down the road again and Peter followed.

"This is bad," he said, stuffing his hands into his pockets. "It's never been this strong before. With all of the kids it's taken, it's getting too powerful," Peter tried to explain. "Every day I'm getting weaker, and it's getting stronger. We need to stop it, Wendy. And soon. If we don't, who knows what it'll be able to do."

Wendy thought for a moment. They still needed more answers, and there was really only one way of doing that, right? She shook her head and rubbed her collarbone. "I can't believe I'm saying this," she mumbled to herself, "but I think we need to go into the woods and find that tree."

Peter reeled back. "*What?*"

"If what I saw was a memory, then there's obviously something important about that tree," she told him. "And all those drawings? They have to be some sort of clue. I mean, I saw your shadow there, too—maybe that's where it's hiding? Maybe that's where they are—those missing kids and my brothers?" She hated herself for even suggesting it, but if it meant getting her brothers back, then she had no choice.

"It might just be an imaginary tree," Peter pressed. "It might not mean anything at all. Or what if it's a trap being set up by my shadow?" He gestured toward the woods.

"I can't say that it's not a trap," Wendy confessed. "But we have to try."

Peter glanced over his shoulder into the trees. "I don't know, Wendy," he said uneasily.

"What other option do we have?" Wendy asked. Peter didn't seem to have an answer. "We should try to find it. Maybe today? We still have enough daylight to at least start looking."

He still seemed unconvinced.

"Look, you're the one who said you needed my help to stop your shadow, remember?" Wendy pointed out. "And since when is Peter Pan afraid of danger?"

Peter scowled at her. "I'm not afraid of anything."

Wendy couldn't help but grin.

They stopped at the corner of the street. They had made it to a small shopping area between Wendy's house and downtown. There was a convenience store, a gas station, and a couple of mom-and-pop shops. A pair of women were out, walking their kids in strollers, but a majority of the people meandering about were other teenagers enjoying their summer break.

"Should we head back and start looking now?" Wendy asked, turning to Peter. "I think we're going to have to go pretty deep into the woods because of how old that tree looked . . ."

Peter didn't seem to be listening. He was craning his neck around, looking down the different streets.

"Should we look for clues somewhere?" She had no idea how to go about solving a mystery. She felt like she had been dropped into the middle of a Scooby Doo episode. "How do you even go about *looking* for clues that'll lead you to a supernatural shadow? This is all new to me," she said.

And Peter was entirely useless.

"Peter, focus," she snapped, jabbing a finger into his arm.

"Hmm, yeah, I know what we should do," Peter said, nodding firmly, looking at something off in the distance.

"What?" Wendy asked, getting annoyed.

"Get ice cream," he said, beaming at her with a wide grin.

Wendy stared at him. He couldn't be serious. "Come again?"

Peter pointed across the street and Wendy turned to see that the Frite & Scoop across the street had captured his attention. The front window displayed a picture of an ice cream cone and fries wrapped in paper.

"Peter, no," Wendy objected. How could he be thinking about ice cream at a time like this? Even if it did sound nice, especially with the summer sun beating down on her bare shoulders.

"Wendy, yes," Peter said, nodding fervently.

She placed her hands stubbornly on her hips. "We can't just go get ice cream and sit in the grass making daisy chains all day!" she snapped.

"Sure we can!" He took her hand in his and started walking backward, pulling her along with him. A huge, mischievous smile was plastered across his face. "It'll only take a few minutes!" he coaxed.

Wendy reluctantly let him pull her along. "No!" she whispered harshly, glancing around at the people carrying on with their perfectly normal days and errands. "We need to figure out how to stop *your* shadow from *stealing kids*." She tugged back on his hand.

"It's not going to take that long," Peter said dismissively. He quickly stepped behind her and placed his hands on her shoulders, guiding her toward the door. "I promise," he said into her ear. His breath tickled her neck.

She could hear the smile in his voice.

"You're a nuisance, Peter Pan," Wendy told him.

He pushed open the door to the café and steered her inside. He was a pain in the ass, but she still had to purse her lips together to hold back a smile.

The shop was pretty small but quaint, lined with warm wood paneling. There was a bar along the windows that overlooked the pier and rivers, lined with teal stools. The flavors of the day were written on a chalkboard behind the counter. A cooler to the side had an array of old-school soda bottles. The walls were filled with art from local artists, along with local awards the ice cream shop had won. The patio area was right on the pier, with some weather-worn picnic tables to sit at and silver dog bowls filled with water. The air smelled of sweet cream and greasy fries.

As they stood in the entrance, the cool air-conditioning washed over them. Peter closed his eyes for a moment, reveling in the chilly breeze, a small grin curling his lips.

Wendy couldn't help letting out a pleased sigh. She tilted her head down to let it cool the back of her neck. Sweat trickled down the middle of her back from their walk. She didn't even want to look at what kind of sweat spots were forming under the arms of her tank top.

When she looked up, Peter was giving her a sidelong glance, an eyebrow arched. "You sure you don't want to stay for a bit?" he asked, looking far too smug for Wendy's liking.

She scowled at him. "I really hate it when you do that," she told him.

"Do what?" he asked, feigning innocence.

"You know *exactly* what." Wendy's stomach growled loudly. She hadn't eaten since dinner with her mom the night before. "Fine," she said. "But only because I need to eat something."

Peter walked up to the counter and stared down at the huge tubs of ice cream, his nose practically pressed against the glass while his fingertips tapped out an erratic rhythm.

"What kind of ice cream do you like?" Peter asked, his breath streaking across the glass, not peeling his eyes away from the brightly colored tubs.

"I'm not a huge fan of ice cream," Wendy said, stepping forward to stand next to him.

Peter balked, looking downright insulted. "What kind of person doesn't like ice cream?" he asked incredulously.

"Not everyone likes ice cream!"

He gave her an intensely disapproving look. "Okay, well, when you *do* eat ice cream, what kind do you have?"

"Vanilla."

"Vanilla?"

"What!"

"Vanilla is the most *boring* flavor of all the ice creams!" he argued, dramatically throwing his arms in the air. "Jeez, you sound like an old lady," he said, giving her a bump with his shoulder.

"Vanilla is classic!" Wendy shot back, returning his bump with a nudge.

Peter threw his head back and let out a loud, forlorn sound of disgust.

Patrons sitting at the bar turned their heads.

Wendy's cheeks flared with heat. She shoved Peter's side. "Shh!" she hissed.

Unperturbed, Peter shook his head slowly. "You really need to branch out—broaden your horizons," he told her.

"There's nothing wrong with vanilla," she muttered darkly.

"Whatever you say, Wendy."

Wendy huffed, doing her best to ignore his stupid face and that damn smile. "What's *your* favorite ice cream, then?" she asked, rolling her eyes.

"Bubblegum."

Wendy scoffed. "What are you, eight?"

Peter shrugged his shoulders as his eyes drifted to the handwritten menu. "Sometimes."

Wendy narrowed her eyes, unsure whether or not he was joking.

"Whoa," Peter said, suddenly pointing at something behind the counter. "I want *that*."

He was pointing at a picture of what looked like three scoops of chocolate ice cream with swirls of dark chunks, topped with caramel drizzle, whipped cream, and a cherry. The lettering below it read, TRY OUR NEW TRIPLE CHOCOLATE MOCHA ICE CREAM! MADE WITH REAL STUMPTOWN ESPRESSO BEANS!

Wendy snorted. "The last thing you need is sugar *and* caffeine," she told him.

"I'm getting it." Peter turned to the cashier. "Can I order one of those things, please?" he asked.

Wendy recognized the girl behind the counter from school, but she didn't know her name. Her light brown hair was pulled up into a messy bun on top of her head, loose strands framing her face. She had on dramatic eyeliner that accentuated her brown eyes. A purple rhinestone nose ring sparkled in her nostril.

Wendy pushed her hands through her own short, blunt hair, suddenly feeling very plain.

Not unlike vanilla ice cream.

"Sure," the girl said. She leaned on the counter and flashed Peter a smile. "How many scoops?" she asked.

"THREE!" was Peter's enthused reply.

"*Two*," Wendy cut in. When Peter jutted out his bottom lip, she added, "I'm the one who's paying, remember?" She turned back to the girl. "And I'll take an order of fries and a cup of ice water." Wendy glanced at the ice cream again. "And one scoop of London Fog," she added.

Peter's smirk was knowing and triumphant.

Wendy rolled her eyes. "I happen to like Earl Grey."

The smile the cashier gave Wendy was markedly less warm.

Wendy slid her debit card across the counter to the cashier. When she looked down, she saw Benjamin Lane, Ashley Ford, and Alex Forestay smiling up at her. They had taped the missing posters to the countertop. HAVE YOU SEEN ME? was written in big, bold letters at the top of all three.

Guilt cramped Wendy's empty stomach.

When they got their order, they sat down at one of the picnic tables outside, where a cool breeze rolled in from the Columbia River. In the distance, sea lions crooned from the piers. She sucked down large gulps of ice water. The cold in her throat was refreshing.

As soon as he sat down, Peter swept a finger through the whipped cream and popped it into his mouth. "Mmm," he hummed, eyes rolling back and lids fluttering in euphoria. He held out the paper bowl to Wendy. Waggling his eyebrows, he asked, "Wanna try?"

"When was the last time you washed your hands?" Wendy asked, eyeing him suspiciously.

"You don't want to know," Peter told her, grinning around the stem of the cherry he'd popped into his mouth.

Wendy shook her head at him, but she loved whipped cream. Leaning onto her elbow, she got a dab of the whipped cream on the tip of her finger and licked it off. It was real whipped cream, the thick, heavy stuff. Not the kind that came out of a can and tasted like an oil slick.

Peter dug in with his plastic spoon. He hummed to himself and Wendy wondered if he always did that when he ate.

Wendy went for her fries first. They were fresh and piping hot. She had to blow on a golden brown fry before taking a bite. The outside was crispy, the inside soft and fluffy. It was perfectly salty. They were the best fries in town by far. She cooled off her tongue with a taste of ice cream. The cool sweetness of the London Fog, with a nice balance of bergamot and vanilla bean, was the perfect mix.

"How is it?" Wendy asked as she bit into another fry.

Peter's lips pressed together but his smile was still big enough to crinkle the corners of his eyes. "*So* good," Peter said through a mouthful of chocolate and espresso beans.

Wendy laughed and shook her head. "Gross." He clearly was no ace at table manners. She ate another scoop of her own light gray ice cream.

"Did you come here with John and Michael?"

The question jarred Wendy, causing her hand to hover mid-air, ice cream dripping from her spoon.

No one ever asked her about her brothers, especially in public, especially something so . . . normal. When John's and Michael's names came up, it was in hushed tones and whispers, usually when people thought Wendy couldn't hear them. Or, like the past couple of days, in reference to something terrible happening.

But Peter asked it so casually. He patiently waited for her reply, his tongue chasing melted chocolate down the side of his hand.

Wendy cleared her tight throat and put her spoon back into the bowl. "Yeah, actually . . . All of us used to go along the Riverwalk during the summer." She gestured to the path that went along the edge of the river, lined with piers. "We'd get fries and ice cream." Wendy toyed with the straw in her ice water. "You know, bubblegum is Michael's favorite flavor, too," she told Peter.

He paused from scraping his spoon along the bottom of his bowl. "Michael's got *excellent* taste." Peter's soft smile encouraged her to keep talking. He was the only person who didn't give her that look of pity, like she was some wounded dog, whenever her brothers came up.

Wendy smiled and shook her head. "Whenever we came here, he picked out all the gumballs as he ate and saved them in a little paper cup," she explained. "After he finished all the actual ice cream, he'd shove this pile of slobbery gumballs into his mouth all at once." Wendy crinkled her nose. "It was disgusting." She let out a small laugh. "He would crash so hard from all the sugar, my dad would have to carry him back to the car."

Wendy remembered Michael's small body draped across her father's strong arms, brown curls bobbing with every step, completely knocked out. She and John would follow behind, holding their mother's hands and dancing along dusk's shadows as the sun set behind the hills.

Peter laughed. "That seems like something he would do," he mused. "Michael was always sucking all the nectar out of the honeysuckles in Neverland. Really pissed off the hum-mingbirds."

Wendy put her spoon down and listened intently, eager to hear stories about being on the magical island with John and Michael.

"You gathered up all the flowers and strung them into a canopy over your bed," he explained. "You said you liked how the light shone through the pink petals. Do you remember that?"

Wendy gave her head a small shake. "No. Not really, any-way," she confessed. "All I ever get are flashes of Neverland, short glimpses of it in my dreams sometimes. I remember you, though you were a lot younger looking."

Peter made a sound of acknowledgment. Clearly, the fact that his body was aging was weighing heavily on both their minds.

"The jungle," she continued. "And a beach?"

"John really liked the beaches," Peter told her. "We had to beat some sea lions at a game of tug-of-war to get dibs on the nicest one." He said this like it was a completely normal, run-of-the-mill, everyday occurrence.

Wendy's brows furrowed. "I'm still having a hard time with all this," she confessed, dropping her voice low so no one could overhear. "It still sounds like a children's book or something. A story." And it had been. Several stories, ones her mother had told her, and Wendy had told her brothers, and now the kids at the hospital. "Like it's all make-believe."

"That's the point, though, isn't it?" Peter said. "Whatever you can imagine, you can do." His tone sounded nostalgic as he stared off toward the river, the ghost of a smile playing across his lips.

Wendy wondered if he ever got homesick.

"I wish I could remember it," she said, picking at her paper cone of fries. "Maybe, after we get your shadow back and save John and Michael, and the other kids, I'll get my memories back?"

Peter's smile faltered. "Probably," he said with a small shrug as he toyed with his cherry stem.

Wendy looked down at her dry, cracked hands. Thinking about the missing kids being held hostage by that shadow made her insides twist. She couldn't stand the thought of them being afraid and lost. Hopefully, they at least had each other, someone to lean on in a situation that seemed hopeless and terrifying.

Wendy hadn't given up yet, and she still wouldn't. She was determined to bring her brothers home.

When she and Peter finally rescued them, would they still look the same as when they'd disappeared? Or had they continued to age, too? The thought of John now being sixteen and Michael being thirteen was jarring. Would she even recognize them? Would they recognize her?

Wendy pressed a finger to one of the red lines on her hand and winced.

Peter's shoulders sank and his auburn hair fell into his eyes. He squinted, a small grimace playing across his face. "Does it hurt?" Peter asked.

She shrugged. "A bit. It's mostly sore." Wendy sat up straighter. Her dry, cracked hands were a constant reminder. She couldn't keep herself from scrubbing away at them. People stared at them and sometimes the kids asked how she'd gotten hurt. It was embarrassing and she felt like they outed her as being odd, but the feeling of her hands being dirty made her skin scrawl. She bit her nails down to nubs, but things still caught under them sometimes. The Burt's Bees hand salve she kept in her bag did little to help the irritated skin.

Wendy exhaled a deep breath and splayed her fingers on the table. "It's not a big deal."

"Here." Peter leaned forward, picked up the plastic cup of water, and reached out for Wendy's arm. Gently, he pressed the side of the icy cold cup to the cracks in her knuckles. Trickles of condensation ran down her wrist, making her shiver. "Does that help?" he asked, glancing up at her with those big blue eyes. His breath smelled like chocolate.

"Yeah, actually . . ."

Peter rested his elbow on the table, propping up his chin in the palm of his free hand. His smile peeked around the corner of his fist, and she couldn't help smiling back.

She hadn't laughed or smiled this much in a long time. Her cheeks were starting to ache.

"Wendy?"

The voice came from behind her. Wendy looked over her shoulder to see Jordan standing in the entrance to the patio, her boyfriend, Tyler, at her side. Jordan wore a maroon tank top and khaki board shorts. Over it she wore a black apron with the silhouette of a girl sipping from a cup, circled by the words COFFEE GIRL. Her brown curls were tied back in a knot. Jordan's mouth was agape, her eyes wide with surprise as they bounced back and forth between Wendy and Peter.

Tyler thumbed through his phone with one hand, and the other held the leash to his husky, Bucky, who panted merrily at his side. Bucky was half blind, the fur around his snout a pale gray.

"Jordan, Tyler—hey!"

Tyler nodded in greeting, barely sparing her a glance.

Meanwhile, Jordan's eyes immediately snagged on her out-stretched arm in Peter's hand.

Wendy jerked it back and jumped to her feet. Peter also stood, giving Jordan a curious look. Wendy pushed her fingers through her hair, uncomfortable laughter clogging her throat. "What are you doing here?" she asked.

"I'm on my way to work," Jordan said with an awkward laugh of her own, gesturing down at her apron.

"Right—obviously!" Dumb question, Wendy.

"We grabbed lunch at the brewery before I had to start my shift. Tyler and Bucky are walking me down to the pier." Jordan's eyes went right back to Peter.

Suddenly, he stepped forward. Wendy nearly grabbed him, anticipating that he might say or do something incriminating.

"Hey, can I pet your dog?" Peter asked Tyler, looking hopeful.

"Mm?" Tyler spared him a quick glance from his phone. "Yeah, go for it, man."

Peter sank on his heels and buried his fingers in Bucky's golden scruff, his face splitting into a wide smile.

Bucky, in kind, sat back on his rump, his tail sweeping back and forth as his tongue lolled to the side.

As soon as Peter ducked out of sight, Jordan's eye bulged as she emphatically pointed down at him and mouthed in silent exaggeration, *WHO IS THAT?*

"Oh, uh, this is Barry," Wendy said. "He's from out of town, just visiting his relatives for the summer." The lie was simple enough, as long as Jordan didn't ask too many questions. She hated lying to Jordan. It didn't feel right at all, but Wendy couldn't just tell her the truth, especially in front of

Tyler. "I've been showing him around town. Being neighborly and all that."

Wendy hoped Peter wouldn't say anything strange, but, apparently, she didn't need to worry.

Peter sat cross-legged on the ground, distracted and chuckling as Bucky licked at his face.

Jordan gave Wendy a knowing look. "Uh-huh, *neighborly*." The smirk on her best friend's face let Wendy know exactly what she was thinking. But, just to be sure, Jordan mouthed, *He is SO cute.*

Heat rushed to Wendy's cheeks. "*Jordan*," she hissed. She felt silly and embarrassed under Jordan's not-so-subtle interest.

Jordan's smirk only grew, but she kept her thoughts to herself. However, when she spoke again, her tone shifted. "My dad told me he saw you in town earlier," she said, drawing her attention away from Peter to look at Wendy. A delicate crease appeared between her manicured eyebrows.

Wendy knew—without Jordan outright saying so—that meant Mr. Arroyo had either seen her going into, or coming out of, the police department. "I tried to go by your house before work, but no one answered. I also tried texting you, like, a million times," she added, her smile beginning to fade.

"Oh, yeah, sorry," Wendy mumbled. Normally, Jordan would have been the first person she ran to, especially about something as major as being called to the police station. Wendy didn't blame her for being suspicious or worried, or whatever she was right now. "I meant to text you back, but I've been kind of . . . distracted." It wasn't like Wendy, and she owed Jordan more than that.

Jordan quirked an eyebrow. "I can see that," she said. More heat flooded Wendy's face. Luckily for Wendy, Jordan glanced at her watch. "Ugh, I have to get to work," she grumbled.

"Yeah, we were about to leave, too," Wendy said, taking the out.

Jordan fixed her with a stern look. "Now, you." Jordan took a step closer and dropped her voice to a quieter tone. "Will you please call me later? Or stop by? I'm off at five o'clock," she said, eyes searching Wendy's—for what, Wendy wasn't sure.

She could feel Peter watching her, too.

Wendy nodded. "Yeah, of course," she said, her voice small. She knew Jordan was worried about her. She had been so distracted by Peter and everything else she had suddenly found herself thrown into, that she was forgetting about the person who was always there for her.

Jordan gave a curt nod. "Good." She tugged on Tyler's arm, breaking him from the trance of his iPhone. "It was nice to meet you, Barry!"

Peter continued to scratch behind Bucky's ears, murmuring happily to the dog.

Wendy nudged him with the toe of her shoe. "*Barry.*"

"Oh yeah," he said, glancing up to flash Jordan a smile. "Nice to meet you, too." Bucky climbed out of Peter's lap and waddled off after Jordan and Tyler. Peter stood, let out a wistful sigh, and gave a small wave. "Bye, Bucky."

Jordan waved at them over her shoulder. "Later, *Wendy Lou Who!*" she sang before disappearing around the building.

Wendy rolled her eyes. It was a terrible nickname Jordan had picked up, in reference to Wendy's *least* favorite live-action Christmas movie.

Peter was grinning at her.

"What?" Wendy asked.

"*Later, Wendy Lou Who!*" Peter said, imitating what Jordan had said, except in Jordan's voice.

Exactly her voice. Hearing it come out of Peter's mouth startled Wendy so much that she actually jumped. "How did you do that?" she demanded.

Peter looked at her as if that were a very strange question to ask. "What? I told you, I'm good at mimicking things. Like the crickets, remember?"

"Well yeah, but I didn't realize you could do people's voices that well, too!" She frowned at him. "That was dead-on! And kind of creepy," she added.

"Want me to do you?" he asked, lips hooking into a grin.

"*God*, no."

At the table, what was left of Wendy's ice cream was a melted puddle, so she dumped it and the rest of their trash. Wendy squared her shoulders, summoning her nerve. She plucked at the hem of Peter's shirt. "Come on," she said, leading the way across the street to the road that wound back to her house. "We've got a shadow to find."

CHAPTER 14

Into the Woods

Peter and Wendy stood side by side at the small white fence that separated her backyard from the woods. A breeze snaked its way through the trees, lightly brushing against her cheeks, her neck, her wrists. She took three slow, deep breaths, eyes stinging as they stared, unblinkingly, into the depths of the forest. Peter was watching her out of the corner of his eye. She could feel his apprehension, but she lifted her chin and blew out one last breath between pursed lips.

They needed to do this. *She* needed to do this. John and Michael were depending on her, and she wouldn't fail them again.

Wendy pulled out her phone to check the time. The screen was filled with unread text messages and missed calls from Jordan. It felt wrong, but she closed them and cleared her throat.

"It's three o'clock now," she said to Peter, finally glancing over at him. "We just need to make sure we're back before my parents get home, or else my father will kill me. It's not much time, but it's enough to get started."

"Are you sure you want to go looking for this tree?" Peter asked. He kept massaging his right thumb into his left palm, shifting his weight between his feet like he couldn't stand still. "For all we know, this could just be a wild goose chase or a trap." But even Wendy could tell by the way his jaw clenched that he knew she wasn't going to change her mind.

"Yes, I'm sure," Wendy said. He wished he would be less reluctant, because it wasn't soothing her nerves. "It means something, I *know* it," she told him. Even though the tightness in her chest and the thrumming of her heart told her to be afraid of the tree—something primal and instinctual— Wendy would push past it to find her brothers and the other missing kids. To put a stop to the shadow. "Besides, it's the only clue we've got to go on."

Peter looked at her like he was trying to decide if he wanted to keep arguing with her about it.

Wendy crossed her arms and fixed him with a stern look.

Peter groaned, craning his head back and closing his eyes for a moment. "Ugh, fine," he muttered before straightening up. He hopped the small white fence and Wendy followed. "I've been getting to know my way around the woods," he told her as they wound their way through the trees. "At least, what's between my hunting shack and your house." Peter gestured east. "I can get us to where you followed Alex and where I found you with the shadow," he offered. "Maybe that's a good place to start?"

"It's the only plan we've got," she conceded, jogging a few quick steps to close the distance between them.

The woods looked different in the daytime, but no less unsettling. Instead of only being able to make out things in her immediate vicinity, now she could see the vast expanse of trees stretching out in every direction, as far as she could see. It made her feel small and outnumbered.

The trees formed an erratic pattern of different shapes,

sizes, and colors. Some trees were thick, with reddish-brown bark and patches of emerald moss. Others were tall, skinny, and pale with perfectly round leaves that rustled in the breeze. A sea of ivy spilled through the woods, puddling around the bases of the trees and climbing up into the canopy. Fallen trees leaned drunkenly against one another. Sun-dappled leaves flickered shadows on the sun-heated earth. Lights danced across fern fronds and thick brambles. Pinecones littered the forest floor like lost trinkets.

Wendy walked as close to Peter as she could but, as she kept throwing furtive glances over her shoulder, she kept treading on the heels of his shoes and bumping into his back.

"Ouch!"

"Sorry!" Wendy said as she caught her balance.

"Would you be more comfortable *on* my back?" Peter asked, hopping on one foot as he tugged his shoe back onto his foot. "Maybe a nice piggyback ride would save us both some trouble?" He grinned at her, but Wendy couldn't manage to return it.

"I'm just a bit jumpy, okay?" she said, rubbing her sweaty palms on her thighs.

"A bit?" Peter repeated, arching his eyebrow.

"The woods and I aren't exactly on good terms." She squeezed her eyes shut and sucked in a deep breath through her nose. Every muscle in her body was tense. She could feel herself starting to shake.

Peter's grin faded, lips twisting into a guilty smile. "At least walk next to me, then," he said, no longer teasing. He stepped to the side and, as Wendy caught up to him, closed the space between them. Their arms were close enough that Wendy could practically feel the warmth radiating off his skin. The brush of his shoulder against hers was a grounding rhythm as they walked.

They walked farther in silence. Wendy was jealous of how he avoided tripping on roots or running into low-hanging branches, his feet moving deftly and with ease. Meanwhile, she kept stumbling at his side over uneven ground pitted with rocks and roots. To Peter's credit, he did pause and wait every time she faltered.

When they walked into a clearing, Peter slowed to a stop. The towering trees around them formed an almost perfect circle. Tilting his head back, he looked around, blue eyes squinting in the sun. "This is where I found you last night," he said, nodding to himself.

Wendy nodded along as she followed his gaze around. "I recognize the clearing . . . sort of," she said. "The woods pretty much all look the same to me . . . but I definitely remember the clearing looking like this and being surrounded by trees and shadows." She looked at the ground, curious whether there was still ash from the pixie dust's destruction of the shadows, but there was only the spongy crunch of layers of dead pine needles and twigs underfoot.

Wind shuddered through the branches. In the distance, trees creaked and groaned.

"My shack is that way," Peter said, pointing into the distance. "There's a creek up ahead. Maybe we can follow that to go deeper into the woods?" he suggested.

Sure enough, Wendy could hear babbling water off in the distance if she held her breath.

"That way, we can retrace our steps." He was looking at her—staring, really—a bit too closely. It made her feel like he was carefully gauging her reaction. Peter could push things too far and get distracted, but she was also starting to see that he was a Noticer. And the worst thing about Noticers is that it was hard to hide from them.

"Good idea." Wendy nodded. She followed Peter another few yards until they came upon the creek. It was a few feet wide, with water tumbling over rocks and fallen branches. They started to follow it downstream, the ground sloping gradually through a ravine.

"How did you even find me, anyway?" Wendy asked, still thinking about the night before. It had been bugging her, sort of nagging at the back of her mind. There was still so much about him she didn't know or understand. His ability to find her when she was lost in the middle of the woods was a big one. "I feel like as soon as I called your name, you just magically appeared." Hearing herself, she frowned. Was that it? "Can you still fly?"

Peter laughed, though his smile wasn't easy. "No, I don't have enough magic left in me to fly anymore." He looked down at his hands and Wendy did, too. Was she expecting to see them spark with light again? For the sword made of pixie dust to appear?

"I need to save it to use against my shadow," he went on. "I could hear you yelling for Alex like a mile away." He leapt to the top of a fallen tree covered in moss. He followed it down the river, feet easily stepping over knots and through vines without getting tangled. Peter held his arms out at his sides for balance, moving slowly so Wendy could keep up beside him as she tripped over wet rocks.

"So, I ran after you. It was pretty easy to hear your crashing through the woods." He frowned, glancing over at Wendy. "They've been unnaturally quiet at night. No owls, no crickets. I haven't even heard any animals scurrying around. Anyway, when I caught up to you at the clearing, I saw that the shadows were trying to take you, so I used the only thing I could think of to try to stop it: pixie dust. But if we have to rely on that in order to stop my shadow, I think we're in trouble." Peter's hands went back to his sides as he hopped to the next rotting tree.

"Like I said, my magic is still getting weaker. The longer I'm here, the faster it fades. These shoes could barely stay on my feet yesterday morning," he said, balancing on one foot and raising the other as evidence. "Now my toes are crammed into them."

Wendy tried to look at him more closely as he stood perched on the fallen tree. It was hard to tell exactly how much he was changing day by day.

No one could possibly mistake him for a middle school–aged boy now. Indeed, he looked like he could be one of the senior guys on her swim team: tall, toned, and tanned. This was good news, really. It meant it was far less likely that someone from the emergency room or one of the police officers would recognize him.

But the far more dire reality was that they were running out of time. Wendy didn't want to think about what might happen to Peter if he lost all of his magic. Would he turn into an old man? Disappear? Turn to dust? Something worse?

"Peter, what if that was all part of the shadow's plan?" she asked.

He jumped down from the tree, landing lightly beside her. "What do you mean?" he asked, eyebrows knitting together as he looked down at her, head canting to the side.

"What if it used Alex to lure me into the woods because it knew you'd come after me and use more of your magic?" Wendy said. "What if it's just buying time, trying to wait you out until your pixie dust is gone and your magic has been drained out of you?" She didn't want to think it was possible. Peter gleamed with energy, from his quick smile to his easy laugh. Standing next to him was like being bathed in sunlight. Even now she could feel his warmth on her cheeks. Could the shadow really suck all of that brightness from him?

Peter said nothing for a moment. His eyes stared off into the distance, flickering with intensity and thought. When his face grew pale and his expression fell, Wendy wished she had never brought it up.

"Then I guess we better hurry up and put a stop to it," Peter said, trying to force a confident smile. He didn't do a very good job.

As they continued their trek, Peter's eyes stayed on the ground. Wendy wanted to reach out, to touch his arm and tell him that they would figure it out and find a way to get him back home. But what if the doubt she felt was thick in her voice? So she said nothing.

The trees were denser now. They stood close together, their branches reaching out and embracing one another. Peter suddenly stopped and looked around. "Does any of this look like where you were in your dream?" he asked before letting out a huff of air and dragging the back of his hand across his sweaty brow. "Do you remember hearing running water?"

"No," Wendy said. She rubbed her temple and tried to remember every detail, but the more time passed, the more they slipped away from her. She was irritated with herself for not writing it all down when she woke up. "The sun was setting, and everything was covered in snow," she told Peter. "I couldn't hear anything at first. Then, when I noticed the tree, I started to hear whispers, just like the ones I heard when I was chasing Alex and your shadow . . ." The intense heat wasn't making her focus any better. She sighed and shook her head, and her hand fell back to her side. "But no running water."

Peter turned in a slow circle, looking at their surroundings. The filtered light caught the copper in his hair. "If the tree was really that old, and the other trees around it were really that dense, then we need to go right into the heart of the woods," he explained. He stopped and turned to Wendy. "And that is going to take longer than just a few hours."

As much as she hated the idea of going even farther into the woods, Wendy knew he was right. She wrapped her arms tightly around her middle. "You're right," she said. Thick defeat settled inside her. There would be no outsmarting the forest. "But we haven't got enough time to do it now. We should probably head back for the day."

Peter nodded.

Wendy closed her eyes for a moment, trying to fight off a sense of impending doom crawling under her skin.

There was a crunch of leaves and then the light pressure of Peter's hand against her arm.

"Hey." She opened her eyes to find his, brilliant and blue, watching her. "I've got an idea. Let's go this way," he told her with a quiet smile, tilting his head down the slope.

Seeing as she had no idea where they were, let alone how to get back home, Wendy nodded in agreement.

Instead of going back the way they'd come, Peter led her farther down the ravine. She did her best to navigate the flat rocks and boulders.

Peter was an entirely different creature. Instead of moving slow and lazy, taking his time teetering across the terrain, now he was alert. He leapt from rock to log, pausing every so often to listen before setting off again.

Wendy panted, doing her best to keep up, but the farther they went into the woods, the quicker Peter moved. Her hair clung to her sweaty forehead and stuck to her lips. "Is this the way back home?" she asked through huffs of air. "Where are we going?"

"You'll see!" Peter said, flashing her a smile over his shoulder.

Wendy scowled in reply. She was too hot and winded to argue. Gradually, she noticed slight changes in the scenery. The foliage was a darker green in this part of the woods. The earth was damp, and Wendy nearly broke her butt sliding on a patch of mushrooms. Gradually, she could hear a steady sound, like thunder, growing louder over her own heavy breathing. Was it passing traffic?

"Peter, where are we going?" she finally demanded, fatigued and annoyed.

He was up ahead, standing on a large boulder. Peter's posture straightened and he let out a whoop. "Found it!" he cheered, beaming at Wendy before bounding out of sight.

"Ugh, *Peter*!" Wendy scrambled after him.

When she found him, he was standing on a flat rock at an outcropping, his back to her.

A frothy cascade of water tumbled from a cliff tucked into the back of the ravine. It spilled into a pool at its base before flowing over rocks and boulders down a stream and deeper into the woods. Wendy's jaw went slack. It wasn't a huge waterfall, maybe only thirty feet high, but the pool was a glistening blue-green. Mist ghosted over Wendy's cheeks, cool and welcoming.

Peter turned to face her, his arms spread out wide. His excited, cheek-dimpling smile was infectious. Wendy couldn't help returning it with one of her own. "How *awesome* is this?" he said, his words garbled with laughter.

"I had no idea this was even here!" Wendy called back.

"Me either!"

Wendy's eyes went wide. "You just *blindly* led us deeper into the woods?"

Peter smirked. "Not *blindly*," he denied with a nonchalant roll of his shoulders. "I followed the sound of the water, obviously."

"Obviously," Wendy echoed flatly, watching Peter as he edged around the pool. Wendy carefully navigated the slippery rocks and shifting, multicolored pebbles.

Meanwhile, Peter had found an old length of rope, sun faded and fraying, tied to an overhanging branch. He gave it a tug. Some leaves floated to the rippling water below. The branch creaked but held true.

Wendy didn't like the mischievous grin on Peter's face.

"What are you doing?" she demanded, but he was already tugging the faded pink shirt over his head.

Peter laughed and tossed his shirt to the side. "What does it *look* like I'm doing?" he asked. He stood there, fists on his hips, cocking an eyebrow.

Wendy glanced at his bare chest. It was tanned and toned, with more freckles splayed across his collarbone. A small trail of copper hair led down his flat stomach.

She forced her eyes back to Peter's. "H-How do you know the water's deep enough?" she stammered out, cutting a glance to the pool of water. Ripples from the waterfall made it impossible to see down.

Peter shrugged and turned back to the rope. "I don't!"

"But what if the rope breaks?"

"Then I'll fall *into* the water." Peter laughed, gripping the rope with both hands.

He backed up a few steps and Wendy's heart leapt into her throat. "But—"

"Peter Pan, remember?" he said, cutting her off and hooking a thumb at himself. "Not afraid of anything!"

Before Wendy could think of another objection, he took a running start off the rock. Hands gripping the rope and knees pulled up, Peter soared out over the water. He crowed loudly and it echoed against the rocky side of the cliff before he plummeted into the water.

Wendy scrambled to the edge of the rock. Below, the water bubbled where he had disappeared. She counted to three in her head, and the seconds dragged by. "*Peter!*" she shouted. Panic ripped through her. She shot to her feet, ready to jump in after him. She was on the swim team and had taken lifeguard lessons as an elective in the spring. If she dove out far enough, she could—

With a spray of water, Peter's auburn head popped out of the water. He spluttered and howled, arms viciously cutting through the water. "*Argh!*" he shouted, voice tight.

"*Peter!*" Wendy's heart pounded erratically. "*Are you okay?*" She frantically searched for any sign of blood or a broken limb.

And Peter was—laughing.

Peter was laughing.

"Holy *crap*, it's *cold!*" he shouted, head bobbing above the surface as he laughed and treaded water.

Relief crashed over her, quickly followed by anger. "You scared me half to death!" she fumed.

Peter smiled up at her, lazily floating on his back. "Come on!" He beckoned for her. "The water feels amazing! After the initial freezing cold, anyway—"

"Peter Pan, I am going to kill you myself!" Wendy barked.

"You'll have to get in and catch me first!"

Wendy gave him an unimpressed look. "You think you're so clever, don't you?"

Peter's head bobbed, his wet hair sticking out at odd angles. "I do, yes."

Wendy glowered.

"Oh, come on, live a little, Wendy!" he coaxed. "It's not even that far! And it's *plenty* deep!" He flicked water up at her and it landed on her arm.

She had to admit, it did feel nice.

Wendy groaned and raked a hand over her face. "I can't believe I'm doing this," she said, more to herself than Peter. Wendy slipped her sneakers off and left them next to Peter's abandoned shirt. There was no way she was going to take off her clothes. If she was going to do this, then she would just have to walk back a sopping-wet mess.

"*Yes!*" Peter cheered triumphantly from the water.

Her grip on the rope was vicelike. She tried to gauge the safest way to swing and gave the rope a hard tug, just to check.

"*Yesssss!*"

Wendy couldn't believe she was actually going to do this. She took two steps back and then ran to the edge of the rock before jumping off. She held tight to the rope and tucked in her knees. When she swung out as far as she could, Wendy squeezed her eyes shut and let go.

The sensation of falling through empty air sent a thrill up Wendy's spine. A strangled shout caught in her throat, but it was quickly swallowed up by water as she plummeted through the surface. The icy water shot through her like electricity, robbing her of the breath she'd held. She kicked her legs and broke the surface of the water, gasping for air and flailing.

Peter's crow echoed loudly.

"Holy sh—"

"Told you it was cold!" Peter said, swimming to Wendy's side. There was a wild, excited look in his eyes. "See! That wasn't so bad, was it?" he teased.

No, it wasn't so bad. It was thrilling. Wendy couldn't remember the last time she'd felt a surge of adrenaline like that—the *good* kind that made your stomach flip and your heart flutter.

Water lapped at Peter's grin as he watched her expectantly. Maybe she could.

"Well?" Peter asked.

Wendy reached out and held Peter's shoulders. Confusion flickered across his face, then quickly jumped to surprise when Wendy shoved him underwater.

He resurfaced, spluttering and wiping water from his face.

Wendy laughed, the loud sort that came right from the belly. "Come on, I'll race you to the top!" she called to him. Wendy dove forward, arms slicing through the water as she swam for shore.

"Hey, that's cheating!" Peter called after her.

The water tasted cold and sweet through her smile.

They raced each other over the edge of the rock and through the water. Sometimes with the rope, sometimes without. Wendy stuck to the safety of a pencil dive, but gradually she leapt with less trepidation and more speed. Peter tried different tricks, from backflipping off the edge of the rock to hanging from the rope upside down. About half the time, he either landed flat on his back or ended up belly flopping.

Wendy laughed hard and loud every time. After a while, she wondered if he was doing it on purpose.

Exhausted and content, Wendy floated on her back, staring up at the blue sky framed by the green canopy. White clouds drifted by. Her blue tank top billowed around her, tickling her waist and wrists. Under the water, the rhythmic thundering of the waterfall filled her ears. Wendy inhaled a deep breath, reveling in the sensations.

When she opened them again, Peter was there, a curious expression on his face. His lips moved, but she couldn't hear what he said.

Wendy shifted, lifting her head out of the water. "What?" she asked.

A strange little chuckle quaked Peter's shoulders as he shook his head. "Nothing."

Wendy flicked water in his face.

In return, Peter scooped her up, hooking his arms under the back of her knees and across her mid-back. He twisted, dragging Wendy through the water as he rotated.

Water rushed over Wendy's shoulders and tickled her neck. She let her fingers drag through the surface of the water. Laughs bubbled through her lips.

Peter laughed along with her, eyes crinkled, droplets clinging to his lashes. When he stopped, Wendy still felt like they were spinning. "Whoa," he chuckled, blinking his eyes hard. "Dizzy."

Wendy looked up into his face. He hadn't let go. "Yeah." Dizzy and lightheaded. "Me too," she said.

Peter grinned down at her, his soft chuckles gently reverberating in his chest pressed against her arm. Light sparkled in his wet auburn hair. A drip of water glinted from the tip of his nose. Peter wet his lips. She saw his Adam's apple bob. He opened his mouth as if to say something, but the words seemed to die in his throat, followed by a loud, uneven laugh.

Wendy felt like she was swinging out over the cliff again, weightless and short of breath. She couldn't even feel the water anymore.

Brow furrowed, Wendy glanced down. They weren't in the water anymore. Instead, they hovered in mid-air above it. Drops of water fell from their wet clothes into the pool several feet below.

Wendy gasped and latched on to Peter's shoulders. "*Peter!*"

"It's okay," he said, calm and steady. The words tickled her ear. His skin was warm and reassuring under her cold hands. Wendy tore her eyes away from the water below and looked at Peter. He grinned. "I've got you."

Sunlight lit up and sparked in his brilliant blue eyes as he stared into hers. Her arms looped around his neck, holding on tight. Wendy thought she wouldn't mind gazing into the cosmos of his eyes forever, searching for hidden answers in their stars and coming up with her own constellations like the ancient Greeks.

"Shouldn't you be saving your magic?" she asked, nearly whispering.

Peter's dimples came out to play. "Probably."

They were almost nose to nose. Water dripped from his hair onto Wendy's cheek.

Was he holding his breath, too?

In the distance, a shotgun boomed.

Wendy's chest bucked. A violent jolt ripped through her. She jerked back from Peter, knocking him off-balance and sending them both crashing back into the water.

When Wendy resurfaced, she gasped for air. Her heart clenched, her whole body rigid as she tried to stay afloat. She swore she could still hear the echo of the shotgun fading in the distance.

"What happened?" Peter swam to her, face etched with worry. "Are you okay?"

"Y-Yeah." Wendy's teeth clacked together. "It just s-s-startled me," she stuttered out.

Concern dug lines into Peter's face. He reached out, but Wendy pulled back. Hot shame swirled with ice water through her veins. "Come on, we should g-go," she said. Without looking back, she swam for shore.

The walk back was quiet. Peter seemed lost in thought and Wendy was trying to just focus on the back of his neck and not look around. Soaked to the bone, she shivered and trembled her way back through the woods. Peter offered her his dry shirt, but Wendy declined. The longer they were there, the more she felt like they were being watched again. She half expected to look up and see a figure standing among the trees. The trek back was uphill and went even slower than their hike in. Her canvas shoes rubbed raw blisters into her wet feet.

After what seemed like ages, the trees became sparser and Wendy could make out the fence that separated her yard from the woods. A sigh of relief heaved through her. "Finally," she breathed.

Peter stopped and turned to her. "You should see if you can find a map of the woods." He stuffed his hands into the pockets of his soaked shorts. "That would make it easier for us to find our way around and check off where we've already looked," he suggested.

Wendy nodded in agreement. "That's a good idea. I'll

see if I can dig one up around the house. I should probably head in now—my parents are going to be home soon," she explained. But she lingered, eyeing Peter.

He stood there, rubbing his arm and rocking onto the balls of his feet. Apparently he was quite interested in examining his shoes. "I'd invite you in, but I'm paranoid my mom might suddenly recognize you from that crappy police sketch," she said with an uneasy laugh. "And I don't think my dad would be too excited about me bringing a guy home while all of this is going on," she added.

Peter let out a short laugh and arched his eyebrows. "Yeah, I'm not too excited about the idea, either."

Wendy smoothed her hands through her wet hair, pulling out a twig as she did so. She didn't like the thought of Peter being in the woods alone. "Are you going to be okay out there by yourself tonight?" she asked.

"I'll be fine," Peter said, waving off her concern. "I'll just lie low and practice my origami." The smile was back, accompanied by a waggle of his eyebrows.

"You aren't afraid of your shadow?" she pressed, not comforted by his nonchalance.

"Me? Afraid?" Peter gave her a grin, ducking his head closer. "Never," he whispered.

Wendy bit down on her lip. "Well, if something does happen or you need me, just . . . throw a pebble at my window or something. It's the top one on the right, in the front of the house."

"I'll be sure to serenade you awake with a flower between my teeth," he said with a solemn nod.

Wendy rolled her eyes and nudged his shoulder with her own. "You're not funny," she told him. Her mouth started to twist into a smile.

Peter's smile grew wide again, his dimples coming back out to play. Just then, something caught his eye over her shoulder. The smile faltered.

Wendy turned to see Jordan coming through the gate at the side of the house. Even from across the yard, she could see her dark eyes locking onto Peter before frowning at Wendy.

A heavy weight dropped into her stomach. "You should probably leave," she told Peter quietly. He clearly didn't need to be told twice. Peter gave her a curt nod, but when he turned to the woods, Wendy caught his arm. "Go around the front of the house," she said in a harsh whisper. Seeing Peter walking off into the woods would only make Jordan ask more questions.

Wendy and Peter climbed back over the small fence. Wendy stopped in the middle of the yard, waiting for Jordan. She and Peter passed each other. She couldn't see Peter's face, but Jordan said, "Hey, Barry," in a tone that lacked her usual warmth.

Peter gave a small wave and slipped through the gate.

"I thought you were going to call me," Jordan said as she walked up to Wendy. It was more of an accusation than a question.

"Yeah, I was about to, actually," Wendy said. She tried to force the most innocent smile she could muster, but it felt all wrong. She never lied to Jordan like this. "Me and Barry were just . . ." She trailed off.

"Going for a stroll through the woods?" Jordan suggested with a lift of a skeptical eyebrow. She looked Wendy up and down. "You're soaking wet!" She pulled a leaf from Wendy's hair, then huffed. "What is going *on* with you, Wendy?" she asked. Jordan had her own brand of "angry" that lacked any real heat and was mostly a cover for concern.

"What do you mean?" Wendy didn't like feeling chastised.

"You're not acting like yourself at all! You're avoiding me—"

"I'm not avoiding you!" Now it was Wendy's turn to cross her arms.

Jordan ignored her and lifted her palms. "Listen, I'm all about you branching out and getting a secret boyfriend—"

"He's *not* my boyfriend!" Wendy spluttered. "He's—he's just—"

"Some *stranger* you're gallivanting off into the woods with?" Jordan pressed. "I don't get it, this isn't like you! You're not calling me back, or telling me when you get *called down to the police station?*"

"They just wanted to ask me questions about Alex."

"Yeah, Alex, from the hospital where we *both* volunteer," Jordan pointed out. Her arms fell to her sides. "How could you not come and talk to me as soon as you found out he went missing?" she asked. Her brown eyes searched Wendy's for an explanation.

Wendy didn't have one.

"I'm your *best friend*," Jordan continued, voice quivering. "You used to say that I was the only person you felt like you could rely on, remember? And now you're, what, going into the woods with some *guy* you just met? Wendy, you're terrified of the woods!"

The maddening part was that she knew Jordan was right.

Wendy groaned and pressed the heels of her palms against her eyes. What could she tell Jordan? She couldn't explain herself, there was no way. She didn't want to hurt Jordan, but she also couldn't tell the truth. Jordan would either think she was having another mental breakdown or that she was flat-out lying. "You wouldn't understand," was all she could say.

"Look, I *know* you're going through hell right now—the missing kids, your brothers—" Wendy's eyes burned. "Just the other day you came to my house practically in tears over those missing kids and the detectives showing up at your door. You've always been able to talk to me about what's going on!"

"I know, but this is different!" She didn't like being yelled at by Jordan, and she wanted to push back. They never got into shouting matches. It made her feel like she was talking to her father, not her best friend. "You say you know what I'm going through, but you have *no clue*, Jordan!" Wendy didn't want to yell, but she couldn't help it. She felt backed into a corner.

"We've always been able to talk to each other about anything," Jordan pressed on. "When we're stressing out together about college, when me and Tyler are having a fight." Jordan's brow furrowed and the anger in her voice broke when she said, "Or when I'm missing my mom—"

The tension in Wendy shattered. "This is bigger than that, Jordan!" she shouted. Jordan took a step back, as if Wendy had just slapped her across the face.

Wendy regretted it as soon as the words left her mouth, but she couldn't stop herself. Everything that had built up swiftly unraveled. "And I don't expect you to get it! Just because you listen to me doesn't mean you can understand because you *can't*, you just can't!"

Jordan reeled back another step. Her cheeks were flushed. Her brown eyes shone in the waning sunlight. "Don't shut me out, Wendy," she said. Her tone was quiet and resigned. "If you don't want to tell me what's really going on, I can't make you. But I'm worried about you." She glanced up at Wendy. "You need to be careful. Those missing kids haven't been found yet, and, for all we know, you might be in danger." Jordan turned around and started to walk away.

This was all wrong. Wendy needed to stop her and apologize. "Jordan—" She reached out to catch her elbow, but Jordan was too quick.

"Call me when you actually feel like being real with me," she said over her shoulder, rubbing at her eyes. She rounded the gate and then was gone.

Wendy was left alone in her backyard, feeling like someone had ripped a hole in her gut. She couldn't tell Jordan what was going on. She wouldn't believe Wendy, and even if she did, Wendy would just be dragging Jordan into danger. Who was to say the shadow wouldn't try to use Jordan against her? She hated herself for hurting her best friend like that, but she was also mad at Jordan for making her feel so guilty. Right now, the most important thing was to protect Jordan, and that included protecting her from herself.

Wendy stomped across the yard to the back door. She went inside and slammed the sliding glass door behind her. When she turned, she saw someone standing by the sink and jumped so hard that she stumbled back.

Mrs. Darling was standing there, dressed in her scrubs with two glasses in her hands.

"Mom, hi," Wendy said, breathing a heavy sigh. She paused. How long had she been there? Had she seen her and Peter coming out of the woods? Or her fight with Jordan? "When did you get home?"

Mrs. Darling gave her a small smile as she reached up to put the glasses away in the cupboard. "Just a few minutes ago. Your father is upstairs taking a shower," she said, drying her hands off on a tea towel. She looked past Wendy into the backyard. She smoothed her hands down the front of her shirt. "I saw that you and Jordan were talking, so I thought I shouldn't bother you." Her delicate eyebrows lifted. "It looked like a pretty heated discussion," she said. The inflection in her voice posed it as a question.

"We were fighting," Wendy said. Frustration dug its way back under her skin.

The corners of Mrs. Darling's lips pulled down into a frown. "You guys don't usually fight. That's not normal for you two . . ."

Wendy's mom was right, of course. The biggest arguments she and Jordan usually got into were about what movie they were going to watch on Friday nights. "A lot of things aren't *normal* these days," she muttered.

This was the closest Wendy had come to asking her mother for advice in what seemed like ages. She hardly knew how to ask anymore, and it was clear that Mrs. Darling wasn't sure how to give it. She fiddled with the tea towel, twisting a corner around her finger. "I'm sure it'll blow over. Maybe you two just need some time to cool off?"

Wendy sighed. "Probably." Though she wasn't sure she believed that. Maybe she just needed to keep Jordan at a distance until this was all over with. For Jordan's own sake.

Mrs. Darling pressed her lips together. Wendy thought maybe she had something else that she wanted to say. But she just sighed and tucked a lock of stray hair behind her ear. "I was going to make grilled cheese and tomato soup," she said. "How does that sound?"

Wendy blinked. "Really?"

Mrs. Darling nodded in reply.

Usually, Wendy did all of the cooking in the house. She couldn't remember the last time her mother had cooked anything, besides reheating leftovers. Even if it was grilled cheese made with processed yellow squares, white bread, and con-densed soup, it still felt . . . oddly domestic. "That sounds great, Mom."

"Great." Mrs. Darling turned to the cupboards and pulled out a can of tomato soup. "You should probably change into some dry clothes before we eat," she said, cutting a knowing look to Wendy.

She looked down at herself. She was still soaked. A small puddle of water had gathered beneath her shoes.

A couple hours later, Wendy headed up to her room for the night, smelling of soap and with a belly full of deliciously greasy cheese. Mr. Darling had taken his dinner in his study, claiming he had work to make up after starting late today. As she and Mrs. Darling ate at the dining room table, the sound of clinking glass came from behind the door.

Wendy's mother liked to read while she ate dinner, with her small, square-rimmed glasses perched on the end of her nose. Tonight's pick was *The Turn of the Screw*. She'd only looked up to say good night when Wendy announced she was going to bed early.

Once in her room, Wendy threw herself onto her bed. Lying on her back, she stared up at the fairy lights. She won-dered if Jordan had texted her. She dug her phone out of her pocket, but there was nothing.

What did she expect? An apology? It wasn't like Jordan had anything to apologize for. As much as Wendy hated to admit it, everything Jordan had accused her of was right. *She* was the one suddenly acting weird, and she was taking her frustrations out on Jordan. She tossed her phone onto the nightstand.

Wendy's mind wandered to Peter. She wondered if he was

okay, secluded in the woods with the shadow gaining power with each passing moment. She grew worried, thinking about him alone in that dingy hunting shack. Maybe she should have asked him to stay. The thought made her shift uneasily. That would be awkward. Where would he sleep without her parents knowing? In her truck? That didn't seem much better. Clearly the shadow had no problems with lurking around her driveway.

Either way, there was nothing she could do about it tonight. She and Peter hadn't had time to arrange a place and time to meet tomorrow because Jordan showed up, so, once again, she'd have to just wait and hope.

Wendy's mind kept cycling through worrying about Jordan, then Peter, then the shadow, then the missing kids, then back to Jordan, then over to Peter again.

She needed a distraction. She dug a book out of her backpack and tried to read, but every time she'd start a sentence, her mind would wander and she would forget what she had just read and have to start the sentence all over again. After reading the same sentence five times, Wendy gave up.

When she put the book on her nightstand, her fingers itched, twitching toward the drawer. She hesitated for a second before pulling it open and taking out the acorn. Lying back, she rolled the acorn in her palm. The longer she played with it, the warmer it seemed to get in her hand. It reminded her of how she felt when she was around Peter. It was comforting.

That gave her an idea.

Wendy went to her closet, got on her hands and knees, and started digging through the stack of boxes in the far corner behind her shoes. It took her a few minutes of opening lids and rifling through contents until she found what she was looking for.

She pulled out a yellow plastic pencil box. Inside were old jewelry-making supplies that Wendy had used to make necklaces and bracelets when she was younger, most of which she only ever gave her mom and Jordan. Inside were small beads and pieces of yarn in different colors. There were spare toggles and barrel clasps, and various jump rings. She took out a silver one and a long piece of leather cord.

Sitting cross-legged on her bed, Wendy used the supplies to fashion the acorn and leather cord into a necklace. When she put it around her neck, the acorn hung in the center of her chest, long enough to safely tuck under her shirt.

Wendy leaned back against her pillows. Exhaustion weighed her body down, from her sore feet to the prickle of a sunburn on her forehead. The weight of the acorn felt reassuring. The warmth from where it lay against her skin seemed to radiate through her. Wendy sighed and closed her eyes. What was it about the acorn that made her feel so much more at ease? At least now she would be able to carry it around with her, and that seemed to soothe her worries enough for her to fall asleep.

CHAPTER 15

The Acorn

Wendy was in Neverland. To her left, the trees at the edge of the jungle grew thick and lush. Tucked against them were a couple of crudely made huts, fashioned from branches and huge palm fronds nearly as big as she was. Above, craggy, pitched mountains reached into the clear blue sky. Waterfalls poured over cliffs, nothing but thin silver ribbons in the distance. To her left, white sandy beach kissed the vast, empty, crystal blue ocean. Small birds in vibrant neon shades chased the rolling waves in and out, digging up seashells and singing.

Wendy sat in the sand, back in the body of her twelve-year-old self. She wore the same white leggings and she was sewing a patch into the knee with thread and a needle. The patch itself was made from a strip of thick green leaf.

And there, just in front of her—

"John, you have to share the white!"

"I'm not done with it yet! 'Sides, you'll just spill it again."

"No I won't!"

Before her sat Michael and John. Just the way she remembered them, before they went missing in the woods.

Michael had the same curly mess of light brown hair.

Leaves were tangled in the downy locks. His face was round, his cheeks full. He had their father's upturned nose. Michael, wearing nothing but his khaki pants torn into shorts, struggled to grab a cup of white paint that John held out of his reach.

John sat cross-legged, with his usual carefully poised posture. He ignored Michael and continued painting with his index finger on a piece of burlap. His glasses perched on the very end of his nose as he made each stroke with careful deliberation. He still had his white button-down shirt on, though it was far worse for wear, and his dark hair was parted to the side.

Wendy wanted to cry out, to throw herself onto her brothers and hug them but, in this memory, she had no control of her body. She could feel sobs bucking in her chest, but no sound came out. In a frenzy, her eyes flew back and forth between their faces, trying to drink in every detail, willing them to just *look at her* so she could see their eyes again.

If this was a dream, it was a very cruel one.

"Stop fighting, you two," said Wendy's voice from her own mouth. "There's plenty of paint to go around. Michael, why don't you use blue from the berries you gathered?" There was an assortment of thick liquids in small bowls fashioned from coconuts in blue, green, white, yellow, and black.

"Because I want *white*!" With the last word, he lunged for John's arm, only to have his older brother pull it away at the last second.

Michael tumbled over.

Wendy heard herself sigh. "You guys are making a mess of yourselves." Indeed, there were splatters of different-colored paint on the burlap and surrounding sand. Wendy noticed a glob of red on Michael's chest that trickled down to his belly-button. As he laughed, John turned, and there was some on his neck, too, just below his ear. Wendy frowned.

The crashing of leaves in the branches above caused Wendy to look up. Peter was flying—actually flying. Well, sort of. He seemed to be losing his balance and was descending at a rapid speed. He hit the ground hard on his feet, causing him to stumble forward, kicking up sand, but he recovered before he could fall.

Wendy stood up and ran over to his side. "Peter! Are you okay?" she heard herself ask.

No! Go back to John and Michael! She wanted to see them—she *needed* to see them longer than just a fleeting glance.

"I'm fine," Peter said, but worry was etched into his young features. He glanced in the direction of Michael and John, who she could still hear bickering behind her, before turning back to Wendy. "I got you something," Peter said. He made a face, the one people do when they're trying to smile, trying to reassure, but it just doesn't sit right.

He took her hand and placed an acorn in her palm.

It had to be her acorn—the one that had been clasped in her hand when the park ranger discovered her in the woods, the one she hid in her jewelry box.

The one she had fallen asleep wearing around her neck.

Wendy cupped it gently in her small hands.

"The fairies helped me pick it out," Peter went on. Pink bloomed in his freckled cheeks. "It's so that you won't forget about me . . ."

"Forget about you?" Wendy laughed. "Why would I forget about you? I'm not going anywhere!"

Peter looked down at his bare feet.

"Wen-dyyy," Michael whined behind her. "I don't feel so good."

Wendy turned to look at her brothers, but before she could see their faces again, shadows crashed over Wendy, flooding her vision, and plunging everything into darkness.

Wendy sat bolt upright in bed. Morning sun streamed in through the window. Shuddering breaths shook her body as she tried to gulp down air. She buried her face in her palms and tried to calm herself down. Her cheeks were slick with tears. A miserable pain ached through her, a pit of longing that felt like it would swallow her whole.

John and Michael.

She'd seen her brothers—or, at least, a memory of them. A memory that had been taken from her years ago. That had been just a big, gaping hole in her memory. This was the second time she'd remembered something from their stay in Neverland together. It was so *vivid*. She could smell the ocean, taste the salty air, and feel the warm sand between her toes.

Why were her memories coming back now? Was it because of Peter? The shadow?

Her brothers were *right there*. She needed to see them again. She needed to get them back. The memories felt like they were taunting her, holding her brothers hostage, just out of reach.

If she and Peter could just find the shadow, find her brothers and the other missing kids, she could finally get John and Michael back. Everything would be okay.

Wendy's hand clutched the acorn hanging from her neck. It was warm to the touch. It almost felt like it was buzzing, like a hive full of bees, but very faint.

Peter had given it to her. That was why she had held on to

it so desperately, and that must have been why she had kept it for all those years. Somehow, something inside her remembered what it meant.

Wendy frowned and tried to replay everything that had happened in her dream. Peter had looked so guilty when Wendy said she wasn't going anywhere. Did he know, then, that something was wrong? That he would have to take her back? At what point did the shadow take her brothers, making it impossible for them to go with her?

It's so you won't forget about me.

Wendy pressed her hand to her mouth, the words repeating themselves in her head as she stared at the acorn.

The last time Wendy had gotten one of her memories back, she had fallen asleep with the acorn in her hand. She turned it between her fingers. Was this the key? Was the acorn the secret to getting her memories back?

She needed to find Peter and ask him.

After a quick shower, Wendy pulled on a pair of jean shorts and a loose-fitting white tank top to combat the heat. This time, she put on a pair of old running shoes in case she and Peter ventured back into the woods. If she was going to stumble around through trees, roots, and creeks, she needed to be in the right shoes for it. The trek yesterday had left blisters on her heels and toes.

Wendy threw her bag over her shoulder and leapt down the stairs two at a time. When she reached the ground floor, she walked into the living room and found her parents sitting on the couch next to each other, watching the TV.

"Morning," Wendy greeted them as she crossed the living room, trying to rub the exhaustion from her eyes.

Her mother jumped and turned to face Wendy. One of her delicate hands was pressed to her collarbone. Her eyes were bloodshot and glassy. Her father remained still, facing forward. He gripped a mug of coffee, his knuckles white.

There was a heaviness in the air that slowed her down. When she stepped closer, it felt like moving through quicksand. Her heartbeat thudded through her veins.

"Mom? Dad? What's wrong?" she asked.

Mrs. Darling said nothing but gestured toward the TV.

Wendy looked up and shock hurtled through her chest.

The news was on. The female anchor sat at her desk. A picture of two boys floated on the screen next to her. The older boy sat behind the younger. They were dressed in red, white, and blue. Small American flags were in their hands. Their smiles were wide and excited, sitting in their backyard for the annual Memorial Day BBQ. Wendy knew, because she had been there.

They were the spitting image of their father.

JOEL DAVIES, AGE 10 AND MATTHEW DAVIES, AGE 7, was written on the red marquee below their photo. The boys next door had gone missing.

Wendy thought of quiet Mr. Davies who always seemed to look out for her. She remembered him and his wife talking to the detectives just the other day. Mr. Davies had looked so worried and frightened, and now his sons had been taken from him.

A sudden wave of nausea made Wendy lightheaded. Everything around her swayed like she was on a boat. She gripped the back of the couch to keep her balance.

Again, the missing children were connected to Wendy. They were her neighbors, boys she watched regularly, especially over the summer.

The anchorwoman continued speaking: *"The boys' father, Donald Davies, said his sons were playing in their backyard yes-*

terday evening when he saw them picked up by a young man who then ran into the woods behind their house. Mr. Davies said he tried to pursue but was unable to keep up. Although he wasn't able to get a physical description of the kidnapper, police are setting up a special unit to—"

It was silent as all three continued to stare at the TV. But they really didn't need to. Wendy knew her parents were thinking the same thing she was: The Davies boys were the same exact ages as John and Michael when they went missing. Her brothers were friends with Joel and Matthew and had known Mr. and Mrs. Davies their entire lives. And they had gone missing in the woods behind their house, just like John and Michael had.

For her parents, it must have been like watching the news from five years ago all over again.

For Wendy, it was like waking up in a nightmare.

The shadow had done this on purpose. Peter was right. It was goading her, trying to hurt her, trying to make her angry. And it was working.

"Police have set up headquarters at the northern point of the woods. They will begin searching the woods for the Davies children, as well as the other missing children and signs of the kidnapper."

A map appeared on the screen with a dot indicating where the police were starting their search. It was almost directly on the other side of the woods from Wendy's house.

"The search-and-rescue units will be starting north and working their way south. The police have recommended that anyone living on the outskirts of the woods lock their doors and windows when they aren't home, and keep their children under constant supervision. Anyone willing to volunteer to help with search efforts is encouraged to call . . ."

They were running out of time. Wendy knew it wasn't safe for Peter to stay in the woods anymore. What if the cops started searching and found him hiding out in the hunting shack? He would probably get arrested and detained. Wendy doubted he would be able to break out of a holding cell, especially now that he was losing his magic at such an alarming rate. And if he was locked up, they wouldn't be able to stop the shadow and all those kids would be lost and Peter would—well, they still weren't sure what would happen to him, but it would be bad. Very bad. Wendy's heart clenched. She refused to take that risk. Had she made a mistake by letting him go off on his own last night?

They needed to find that tree before the woods were overrun with cops and volunteers. Now, more than ever, they were running out of time.

"I'm going to the hospital," Wendy said abruptly. She thought her parents would be so engrossed in the news that they might not even hear her, but they both swung around to face her.

"The hospital?" Mrs. Darling asked, confused. "But you don't volunteer on the weekends."

"Absolutely not!" Mr. Darling fumed, eyeing Wendy as if she were completely out of her mind. "I don't want you leaving this house, and certainly not on your own!" She could tell his jaw was clenched by the way his mustache ruffled.

They were on edge and worried.

She needed to come up with a solid excuse.

"I promised Nurse Judy I would help out," Wendy tried to explain. "They're short staffed in the playroom and need someone to be there all day to keep an eye on the kids."

"No," Mr. Darling said in a low growl.

"I'll be in the hospital surrounded by people," Wendy

reasoned. "Nothing is going to happen to me there. I'll even call you when I'm heading home." What would make him agree to her being gone all day? "Not to mention, Nurse Judy will be there looking after me the whole time."

Mr. Darling made a gruff sound through his nose but didn't object. Both her parents respected Nurse Judy, but it was more than just that.

There was a reason she was the head nurse, and why parents trusted her with their sick and injured kids. She was a hard-ass who didn't beat around the bush, but, most important, she protected her patients fiercely and fought tooth and nail to get the best treatment for them. Even when Wendy was hospitalized, she remembered being scared and crying alone in her room while, in the hallway, Nurse Judy's booming voice laid into doctors when she didn't agree with their treatment plan.

It had been under her insistence that they ease up on the sedatives and, when Wendy was overcome with fear and grief and entirely unable to pull herself out of it, it was Nurse Judy who came in and guided her through with gentle words and distractions.

When her mother and father were too deep in their own mourning—her mother spending daylight hours in bed, her father joining search parties in the woods until he could no longer stand upright—it had been Nurse Judy who stepped in to take care of Wendy.

It was a solid bond of trust, one that Wendy needed to abuse in order to see Peter and stop the shadow.

Wendy's mother glanced at her husband. For three heartbeats, she waited as they exchanged a silent look before Mrs. Darling turned back to Wendy. "Why don't you ask Jordan to go with you?" she suggested.

Wendy inwardly groaned. She knew her mom was trying to help her out, that her father would feel better if Jordan was with her. She was probably also suggesting it in an attempt to nudge Wendy into making up with Jordan.

Her mother's parenting was coming at a very inconvenient time.

Mr. Darling didn't say yes, but he also wasn't saying no.

"Fine, I'll ask Jordan if she'll go with me," Wendy conceded.

She could tell her father didn't want to agree to it. In all honesty, she didn't blame him. It also felt kind of nice—but mostly strange—to know that he was still being protective of her. Again, it was terrible timing. It also made lying to him harder.

"Keep the volume up on your phone," he finally said. "If I call it, you better answer, or I'll come down to the hospital and get you myself."

Wendy pulled out her cell phone and tilted the screen to face her parents as she turned the volume all the way up. "Done," she said with a nod.

"And call when you're on your way home!" he added. Mrs. Darling gently rested a hand on his shoulder.

"I will, promise," Wendy said. She bolted out of the house before he could change his mind.

Now that she was outside, she could go find Peter. She would have to figure out the details of lying about Jordan later. For now, she just had to hope that her parents didn't call the hospital to check her alibi. And, hopefully, Jordan was still mad enough at her to stay away and not blow her cover.

As soon as she stepped out onto the porch, Wendy froze. Two cop cars were parked outside of the Davieses' house next door, as well as a crime-scene van. Mr. Davies stood on the front lawn in his bright red robe, surrounded by police officers and talking to Detective James. One arm was across his chest, the other hand clamped over his mouth. His curly hair was tousled. Detective James was speaking in a low, even tone. Mr. Davies nodded or shook his head intermittently. Behind him, the door to his house stood wide open as police officers walked in and out. Wendy could hear Mrs. Davies wailing inside, an animalistic croon of mourning that made goosebumps race up her arms.

Wendy's chest ached for them, the scene all too familiar.

She walked to the driveway, barely paying attention to where she was going, eyes glued to the scene next door. Was this how her own house had looked? Had her mother and father had the same expressions on their faces? It was almost like déjà vu, the same terrible echo through the universe.

Before she could even start to worry about how she was going to find Peter, she caught a glimpse of someone standing by her truck. She jolted to a stop, far too wary of strangers hovering in her driveway, but then she saw the shock of auburn hair and realized it was Peter.

He stood leaning against the door of her car, out of sight of the police officers next door. He was hunched in a way that, at first, suggested he was hiding from view, but there was something wrong. His expression was strained, and he was curled around his stomach, his hands pressed into his side.

Wendy rounded the truck, her eyes immediately searching for him. "Peter, what's wrong?"

He looked sick, like he hadn't slept in days. There were dark purple circles under his eyes that looked more like bruises. His lids were puffy, his blue eyes bright, bloodshot and glassy. His hair was a mess, as if any effort to tame it was just too much.

Peter, who brimmed with light and was constantly flitting

around like a hummingbird, was changed. There was a small crease between his eyebrows and his shoulders were hitched up to his ears, his back curved as if he were trying to protect himself from a biting wind. His already full bottom lip was swollen and split down the center with a thin, wet line of crimson.

Wendy's heart fluttered. "Jesus, what happened to you?" she whispered, reaching out to tilt his chin. When he winced back, she saw a bloom of red on his jaw, promising a bruise.

"It's nothing. I'm okay," Peter said. He tried to conjure up a smile, but even that looked pained. As he pushed himself from the car door, he swayed on his feet. Wendy rushed forward and caught his sides, trying to help steady him, but Peter sucked in a harsh breath between his teeth. His face twisted in pain, his hands pressing gingerly to his stomach.

She quickly withdrew her hands. "What happened to you?" she repeated, her voice harsh with worry. Wendy glanced over her shoulder, stepping closer to Peter as she tried to shield him from the gathering next door. "Come on," she said, trying to make her voice sound gentler as she pulled him toward the side of the house, where no one could see them. "Tell me what happened." Her eyes darted from his shoulders, to his arms, to his face.

Peter's chin dipped, sending his hair splaying across his forehead, hiding his eyes from view. "I went after my shadow last night," he mumbled.

"*What?*" Wendy hissed. Her hand went straight to his arm, gripping him before she could realize what she was doing. "Sorry!" she said, withdrawing quickly. She growled and dragged her fingers through her hair. "Why would you do that, Peter?" she demanded.

He shrugged, looking miserable and chastised as he leaned

against a trash can. "I thought I could take it on my own. I thought . . ." He glanced furtively at Wendy. "I thought if I could just do it myself, then you wouldn't have to—"

"No!" Wendy cut him off. "We were supposed to go together so I could help you! You could've gotten hurt—you *did* get hurt!" Wendy gestured at him and Peter cringed. She wanted to scream and shout at him for doing something so incredibly *stupid* and *reckless*, but she couldn't with all those people next door.

"I thought I could do it," he repeated. "But it was just too powerful." Peter's breathing was uneven and short. He hesitated for a moment before he pulled up the bottom of his shirt. Cresting over the tanned skin, just above his hip, bloomed an array of bruises. Purple, blue, and bright red grouped together like galaxies.

Immediately, she felt like a complete asshole for yelling at him. "Oh, Peter . . ." Lightly, she touched the bruise with her fingers, but he flinched back. Wendy's skin crawled with a boiling mix of anger and fear. The shadow was capable of doing *this*? What else would it do? To her? To Peter? To the kids it had taken? To her brothers?

"It's getting stronger," Peter told her before tugging his shirt back down. "And I'm only getting weaker." A shudder rolled through him, as if it physically repulsed him to admit it. Peter's eyelids were half shut as he stared at the ground. "It just tossed me around like I was nothing." Peter rubbed the heel of his hand against his eye. "I can feel my magic draining out of me," he mumbled. "I feel like I haven't slept in weeks." He frowned and his eyes roved over her body. "Are you okay? It didn't come after you, did it?" A spark of intensity crossed his face.

"No," Wendy said quickly with a shake of her head. She'd

been safe and sound in her room last night, but that did little to comfort her. The thought of Peter, alone in the woods, being attacked by the shadow was enough to make her sick. She should've been there to protect him. She shouldn't have left him. She should've made him come home. Wendy swallowed down a lump in her throat. She hated herself for letting him go.

"We're in this together, okay?" Wendy insisted, stepping closer to Peter, making him look her in the eyes. "No more going off on your own. We beat it together, or not at all, just like you said, right?" Peter looked miserable and unconvinced. "You're not the only one with something to lose," she told him.

Peter held her gaze. She realized how close they were standing, Peter leaning against a trash can and she standing between his knees. There was a low rush in her belly. Warmth flooded her face.

Peter's eyes drifted from hers, down to her mouth, and then to her neck.

A tired grin curled the corners of his lips. "Hey, you found it," he murmured.

He was staring at the acorn she wore around her neck. "Yeah, I-I did," Wendy stammered, and she quickly came back to reality. "I mean, I've always had it," she corrected herself, holding it in the palm of her hand. "I just kept it in a jewelry box." Some of Peter's light seemed to slowly start returning. "I wore it around my neck last night when I fell asleep, and I had this dream—but it was a memory—about Neverland, and my brothers, and you." Wendy looked up into Peter's face. "I remembered you giving it to me. Do you remember that?"

Dimples pressed gently into Peter's cheeks as he took the

acorn between his thumb and forefinger. "Of course I do," he said. Their bowed heads and close bodies made a small alcove. "I gave it to you so you wouldn't forget me, you know, when you came back here. I mean, it clearly didn't work," he added with an airy laugh. He glanced up at her then, face close, eyes watching her so intently that she almost moved away. "But now that you've found it again, I guess it's helping you start to get your memories back . . ." Peter's smile was small and tight.

Wendy bit down on her bottom lip. Did that mean that all this time, she could've just used the acorn to get her memories back? She'd spent years without them, hating herself for not being able to remember when everyone asked her questions she didn't know the answers to, when they accused her of lying, when she became a social outcast. This could change everything. She could get more of her memories back now. For some reason Wendy's heart fluttered in her chest and her head swam.

"When you gave this to me," Wendy said, changing the subject and thinking back to how Peter had looked in her memory, "did you already know you were going to have to take us home?"

Peter nodded. "I could tell things were going wrong in Neverland—it wasn't safe for you to stay any longer," he said, watching her carefully.

"It was so weird to see them so clearly," Wendy told him. He gave her a sad smile. She sighed and stepped back. "There's a lot I need to tell you. Two more kids went missing last night, and the cops are starting to search the woods." Peter's smile faded. "We need to find that tree, and your shadow, fast." Wendy glanced toward the front of the house. With sudden determination, she tugged on Peter's arm. "Come on," Wendy said as she led him from the side of the house to the driveway.

Checking to make sure no one was looking in their direction, she guided him to her truck and opened the door.

Peter obediently slid into the passenger seat. He sat up straight, suddenly looking much more awake as he peered at the dashboard. "I've never been in a car before," he confessed, his fingers brushing over the knobs of the stereo.

"Technically, you were in an ambulance," Wendy pointed out.

Peter looked at her, unamused. "That doesn't count, I was unconscious."

Wendy's lips twisted as she suppressed a smirk. She turned the key and the old truck roared to life. Peter's hands latched on to the dashboard. If she weren't so worried about him, she would've laughed at the deeply concerned expression on his face. "Put on your seat belt," she told him as she pulled her own across her chest.

He took the seat belt in his hand and pulled it across, mimicking what Wendy did, but then his longer fingers fumbled with the buckle. She gently took it out of his hand and clicked it into position.

When she started to back out of the driveway, Peter's hands went right back to the dashboard. "Don't look so scared," she told him, shifting into drive and starting down the road. "I'm an excellent driver."

"You almost ran me over." Peter scowled, but when she got to the end of the street, he started to relax into his seat. "It's like flying, but a lot . . . bouncier," he mused, watching houses go by.

Her plan was to drive to one of the small side roads that bottomed out into the woods. That way, they could go into the woods without being seen, and no one would notice her truck.

Only a minute had passed before Peter figured out how to roll down the window. He leaned out as far as he could with the seat belt still restraining him. Peter squinted in the sunlight as his hair whipped in the air. His laughter caught in the wind and floated off. The sunbaked road stretched and curved before them, hugging the line of trees. White mile markers leaned on the shoulder, nearly lost in the overgrown weeds.

"So, what's going on with the latest missing kids and the police at your neighbor's house?" Peter asked, back inside the cab and rubbing his eyes.

"They were two boys," Wendy started. "Ten and seven, the same age as my brothers when we went missing. They were taken from their backyard, just like we were. Their dad even *saw* them being taken by someone, but he couldn't see what they looked like."

"My shadow," Peter stated.

She nodded. "It has to be taunting us, right?" Wendy asked. Anger heated her skin. "That's why he took those kids like that. It's too similar to my brothers to just be a coincidence, isn't it?"

"Probably. It knows that we've been in the forest, that we're looking for it. It knows you're afraid of the woods. It wants you to be frightened." Peter looked over at her. The worry aged his already pale face. "It might be drawing us into a trap, Wendy," he said. "Are you sure you want to go looking for this tree? What if that's exactly what it wants us to do? It can probably smell the fear on you as soon as you step into the woods." He shook his head. A frustrated growl sounded at the back of his throat. "Maybe I should just—"

"No way," Wendy said, sharp and succinct. "My brothers are being held captive by this thing. There's no way I'm going to let you fight it on your own."

Peter stared down at his lap.

She didn't want to point out that, in his condition, she was worried about him even being able to navigate the woods, let alone put up a fight against the shadow. He needed her help, and she needed to get her brothers back. "Besides, you said I'm the only one who's been able to reattach the two of you, remember?" she pointed out.

"It was worth a shot," Peter muttered. He sunk lower in his seat. With his head leaning against the cool glass of the window, Peter closed his eyes.

Wendy almost wanted to keep circling the tree-lined roads to let him rest, but finding his shadow was becoming all the more imperative.

She turned down one of the old logging roads. The grass was beaten down into a set of tire prints that faded into the trees. She parked her truck a little way down the road so it was out of sight from the main stretch.

Peter sat up as the springy seat jostled him when she put the truck in park.

"Did you get ahold of a map?" Peter asked, staring off into the woods ahead.

"I have one in here." She reached across Peter and gave the dashboard handle two hard yanks before it flew open. Peter tried to move out of the way as a pair of old swim goggles and a bottle of sunblock fell onto his feet. "Sorry," Wendy said. She dug into the glove compartment and pulled out a map of the town.

"My dad got me this when I first started driving," she told him. "He doesn't trust cell phone GPS"—it was very obvious by the look on his face that Peter didn't know what that meant—"so he got me a map so I could find my way around if I ever got lost." She unfolded it and smoothed her hands along the edges. "It has the woods." She pointed to a large patch of green in the center of the map. "But it doesn't have a whole lot of detail." It showed the outline of the woods, the creeks that snaked through it, and some logging roads. "It's old, so there's way more logging roads now, but it's better than nothing." She turned to Peter. "Do you think this will help? Do you know how to read a map?"

Peter snorted and took it in his hands. "Of course I know how to read a map," he said, puffing up his chest like a rooster. "I'm constantly using pirate maps back in Neverland. I've got a whole collection of them."

Wendy rolled her eyes. "Pirate maps," she said flatly. "Of course, how could I forget."

"We can use the creeks and these trails as points of reference," he said, trailing his finger along a blue line. "Shouldn't be too hard."

"Great." Wendy took out her phone and sent a quick text to her mom, letting her know she was with Jordan and would be home later. Wendy took a deep breath. "Are you ready?" she asked.

Peter sucked in his upper lip and gave her a look. A lot of things flickered in his eyes that she couldn't quite read. He forced a smile, though it was more like a grimace. "As ready as I'll ever be."

CHAPTER 16

The Tree

Plants and ferns flanked the tire-worn path. Wendy and Peter followed until it branched off and faded into the trees. "We just need to keep heading north," Peter said, his eyes sweeping back and forth. "We should cross one of these trails and then hit the creek."

"We also need to be on the lookout for the search parties," Wendy added, coming to a stop at Peter's side. "I don't know how long it'll take them to comb through the woods, but they're starting on the northern side and working south. It would be bad if we ran into them halfway," she said, tucking the map into her bag. "Especially if we haven't found the tree yet."

"We should be able to hear them from pretty far off," Peter said. He jerked his head and gave Wendy a small grin. "Come on."

Long grass gently slapped Wendy's legs as they moved deeper into the forest. She could feel the prickle of sunburn on her shoulders as the hot summer sun streamed through the trees. The air smelled of sweet cedar and tangy sap beading on bark. Black beetles bumbled over logs and the sharp cry of hunting birds sounded overhead. The sound of Peter and Wendy traversing the landscape joined the chorus.

Wendy frowned. She watched Peter navigate the fallen logs and underbrush and it occurred to her that he wasn't moving with the same ease as he had last time they were in the woods. Peter kept his eyes trained on the ground, his footfalls as heavy as hers. He used to be so at home in nature, but now he was as unbalanced as she was.

Maybe it was because of his drastic growth spurts? He was almost a head taller than her now. His arms and legs were noticeably longer, and his movements made it seem like he was still getting used to them. The way he walked reminded her of a newborn deer trying to find its balance.

Following him closely, Wendy watched as he moved through the woods. Tendons stretched up his forearms, swelling at his biceps before disappearing under the sleeves of his T-shirt. She could see the muscles of his back shift and flex under the material. The sunlight filtering through the trees caught the red streaks in his auburn hair. A small trickle of sweat ran down the nape of his neck and disappeared into the collar of his shirt. His full lips were parted, his breaths a steady rhythm.

Wendy's face grew unbearably hot and she cut her eyes away. She frowned at the ground. These changes Peter was going through were . . . distracting. And frustrating. Wendy was used to seeing guys in Speedos at swim practice. She was no stranger to the human anatomy of a teenage boy. Wendy was largely unaffected by it, and barely batted an eye when her teammates tried to flex and show off. Peter shouldn't be any different. She just needed to get a grip. She was irritated with herself for being so flustered. There were important matters at hand, things she needed to focus on.

It was while she was staring determinedly at the ground that she realized Peter wasn't wearing shoes.

"Peter, where are your shoes?" she asked.

"My feet got too big. They don't fit anymore," he told her with a shrug, as if walking through the woods barefoot was a perfectly reasonable solution.

"How does that not hurt?" she asked, face screwing up in confusion. She could hardly stand walking across the cement of her backyard to throw out the trash without flip-flops on.

"It's not a big deal. I didn't wear shoes in Neverland," he pointed out, glancing at her with a raised eyebrow. "I've got some pretty serious calluses." Peter's lips teased a grin.

"Okay, but you're here now," she said. "You'll call attention to yourself walking around without any shoes on." If people saw him, they'd probably think he was a transient, or maybe even a runaway.

Peter blinked. "Oh. I hadn't thought about that."

"Should we stop by the hunting shack and get you another pair?" she asked. "You won't be able to go back to it after today." Which was another distressing thought. Another problem on their ever-growing list that needed a solution.

"I don't have any more shoes that fit." Peter still didn't seem very worried. "I could try looking around the neighborhood for a pair," he considered.

"No," Wendy said firmly. "No stealing. The last thing we need is someone seeing you steal a pair of tennis shoes off their back porch." Wendy racked her brain, trying to come up with a solution. The idea of taking Peter to go shopping for new shoes felt ridiculous. She couldn't even picture him standing in the middle of a Fred Meyer. It'd be like seeing Bigfoot in a hipster café: wrong and laughable. "My dad has some old tennis shoes lying around you could try on?" They were probably too big, but at this rate, Peter would fit them fine in a matter of days. It gave her little comfort.

Peter nodded in agreement. His eyebrows pinched together. He looked bothered by something, but he didn't say anything, and Wendy thought it best not to ask. There was tension in the air and heaviness between them.

Maybe he knew what she was thinking already.

Wendy spent so much time thinking about how all of this was affecting her, she hadn't spent much time considering how Peter felt. It must be frightening, to be so far from his home, and alone. Except for Wendy, but she doubted that brought Peter much comfort. It must have been wearing on him to be holding the safety of all those kids on his shoulders. Not to mention, to be so unsure of his own fate. It made her chest ache to think about him going through that alone. How had she let herself get so caught up in her own nightmares that she didn't consider what this was doing to him? Looking at him now, the effects seemed clear on his face, in the dark circles under his eyes and the way the corners of his lips tugged down when he wasn't paying attention.

She wanted to reach out and touch him, to tell him that it would be okay and they would figure it out. But would he hear the doubt in her voice? Wendy chewed on her bottom lip. What did Peter have to keep the darkness away? After they got out of these woods, she would figure out how to keep him safe.

They crossed the first trail, which was just some gravel on hard dirt, pounded into place by logging trucks. The creek was a short hike past that, and they followed it downstream, sloping deeper into the woods. She started trailing closer to Peter again, but, this time, she was more careful not to step on him. The woods were vast. Even with a guided plan, it was a lot of ground to cover. Not to mention, the terrain became rough, which slowed Wendy and their progress.

The farther they went, the quieter the woods became. There were no more birds chirping or chipmunks scrabbling their claws against trees as they chased one another. The only sound left was the bubbling of water in the creek.

"Do you miss Neverland?" Wendy asked, wanting to break the eerie quiet.

Peter tilted his head back, looking up into the boughs of the trees as he considered her question. "Sort of. It's a lot nicer there," he said. "I miss the beaches, playing games with the lost kids, being able to spend all day just lounging in a hammock by the waterfall," he said in a far-off tone with a sigh.

"That definitely sounds better than trudging through the woods, looking for your shadow with me," Wendy agreed with an airy laugh. "How terribly dull Oregon must be in comparison to Neverland."

"It's not *that* bad. Being here has its perks." He nudged his shoulder into Wendy's. She pressed her lips together as they threatened to quirk into a smile. "What I really miss is being able to fly. This body"—he looked down at himself—"just feels weird."

Wendy trained her eyes on Peter's face, actively keeping herself from taking inventory. Again.

"What do you think started all of this in the first place?" she asked. "Losing your magic and growing up, I mean?"

"I don't really know," Peter confessed. "I just assume the shadow did it, but it *did* only start when you came to Neverland with me . . ." He squinted, giving Wendy a curious look. "This has something to do with you, but I'm not sure what."

"Do you have a plan?" Wendy asked. "For when we find it? How are we going to . . ." Wendy struggled to find the right word. "Stick it back on?"

"Well, we'll need to weaken it somehow. And then you can sew it back on!"

Wendy looked at him. That wasn't much of a plan. She was a decent seamstress. One of the doctors at the hospital had even showed her and Jordan how to do basic surgical stitches on an orange, but how would it work with a shadow?

Suddenly, Peter jerked to look over his shoulder. Wendy's gaze followed, but she didn't see anything in the mix of greens and browns.

A shiver ran from the top of her head to the tips of her toes. She edged closer to Peter and twisted her fingers into the back of his shirt. She looked between Peter's sharp expression and the unmoving trees. "What is it?" she asked.

The woods were getting darker as the trees grew closer together, blocking out the sunlight from above the canopy of branches. When had it become so cold? She moved still closer to him, her shoulder pressing into his warm back.

Peter kept staring into the distance, standing still as the silent trees. Fear swelled in Wendy's body and thrummed through her veins. She tugged on his shirt. "Peter?" Was he even breathing?

"I thought I heard something," Peter murmured. He tilted his head, listening to something Wendy couldn't hear over the pounding of her own heart. After a moment, he gave his head a small shake and sighed, though his shoulders remained tense. "It was nothing."

A nervous laugh escaped her tight throat. "I thought you weren't afraid of anything," she said in an attempt to ease the tension.

Peter only looked at her. When he started walking again, she let the material of his shirt slip through her fingers. "What'll happen if we can't do it?" Wendy asked, rooted to the spot, hands clenched into fists at her sides.

Peter turned. His hard expression softened. "My magic is supposed to keep me young forever so that I can help lost kids find their way," he said. "If I keep growing up, then I lose my magic, and I can't fly or find those kids or take them to Neverland with me. Without me, there'd be no one to guide them. They'd just . . ." His shoulder lifted in a shrug. "Stay lost."

Wendy wanted to ask what that meant, but the prickling on the back of her neck pulled her attention.

Peter must have felt it, too, because his body tensed and his blue eyes darted around them.

A long silence stretched. Wendy's skin crawled.

"Do the lost kids stay in Neverland forever?" Wendy asked. Maybe if she just kept talking, the feeling would go away.

Something breathed against her neck, like a quiet whisper. Wendy jumped and spun around.

Only motionless trees stood, flanked and waiting, as far as her eyes could see.

A dense and heavy silence hung in the air. It was like she was underwater. The air felt like it was pressing against her skin, and her ears needed to pop.

"Sometimes." The air shifted behind her. Peter's warmth pressed between her shoulder blades. "But most of them are able to find their way and move on," he said, his voice low.

Wendy's breaths came short and quick. The sleeping creature, nestled between her ribs and spine, began to wake and tremble.

Her hand went to the acorn around her neck. "I think we're close," she murmured, squeezing it tight in her palm. A sense of déjà vu, a ghost of a memory, teased at the edge of her mind.

Peter moved to her side. His bare arm pressed against hers for once provided no ease. His eyes were alert and sharp.

"Can you feel it, too?" Wendy breathed in barely a whisper.

Peter nodded slowly. "Maybe we should leave, Wendy," he said quietly, as if trying not to wake up the trees. His hand slipped into hers, warm and calloused.

Wendy heard the whisper again, this time louder but still indecipherable. She couldn't tell which direction it came from. Her heart thudded against her chest.

Wendy took a step back. Peter's hand gave hers a squeeze.

A soft sob above Wendy's head sent her neck snapping back. She stared up into the boughs trying to spot something, she didn't know what.

"Can you hear them?" she asked Peter. Quiet sniffles. A far-off cry. "They're getting louder. I think they're coming from over here . . ." She pulled on Peter's hand, taking a tentative step in the direction where the voices seemed to be louder.

When he didn't respond or move, Wendy tore her eyes away from the woods to look at him.

Peter was still as a statue. The color had drained from his face. His eyes were wide, staring at something behind her. His hand was limp in hers.

There was buzzing in the air, hanging over her shoulders. Every muscle in her body coiled in a burning sear. She let out a rattling breath. It billowed through her lips in a white cloud.

Peter's grip on her hand tightened again. "Wendy, get away from it," Peter said, his eyes still locked on the space behind her shoulder. He said it quietly, but it might as well have been a shout in the silent woods.

Wendy slowly turned.

Behind her stood the tree. Its thick trunk twisted upward and split off into jagged, bare branches. They loomed above, sharp fingers reaching out. The tree's bark stood out in stark contrast to the others: ghostly pale compared to their rich greens and browns. Gnarled roots knotted and churned through the underbrush. The air smelled of rotting leaves and dirt.

The woods hummed. The hair on her arms stood on end. She could hear the voices growing louder now. A swirl of whispers and gentle weeping. They were coming from the tree. No, from the roots that curled and sank into the earth, making small cages and gaping holes. A wind picked up and rustled the leaves. The voices grew louder, more frightened.

Wendy took a step closer, taking her hand from Peter's grasp and reaching for the tree. The whispers coaxed and warned her. Was there something there? Hidden under the roots, in the dirt?

The voices grew harsh.

"There's something there," Wendy mumbled. She leaned down but suddenly Peter stepped in front of her. His large hands gripped her arms.

"We need to get out of here." His expression was all taut muscles and hard lines. His eyes pleaded with her to listen.

"He's right, you know." The lazy voice floated down to them through the trees.

Wendy and Peter both craned their necks back.

Lounging on a thick branch, with its back against the tree, was the shadow.

She could clearly make out all its features. It was a haunted, distorted version of Peter. Instead of having his warm hair that shone in the sun, its hair was like shiny black oil. Its nose and chin were pointy and severe. Its skin was pale white, its eyes hollow and black. They seemed to suck in all the light from around them. Its thin lips twisted into a cruel smile, revealing unnaturally white teeth. It was made of sharp angles, cheekbones and a jawline she could cut herself on.

In every way that Peter was bright and warm, the shadow was dark and twisted.

It looked as solid and real as Peter now. "You should really be more careful—there's no telling what you'll find in these woods." It curled a dead leaf between its pale fingers.

Wendy's blood stuttered in her veins, but surging anger pushed her forward. "Let them go," Wendy demanded, trying to pull herself free of Peter's grasp.

The shadow laughed and dissolved, spilling down the tree like a heavy black fog. It was a deep, rumbling laugh that reverberated through her bones. The shadow pooled on the ground before her and materialized back into its human form.

"Let who go?" it drawled.

Peter stepped forward. "You need to stop this," he said, voice firm. "Let the kids go." Peter drew his hand through the air. With an explosion of light, the sword materialized in Peter's grasp. With his shoulders squared, Peter faced the shadow. The sword sparked and shone, a weapon made up of tiny golden particles. But then it started to flicker.

The shadow leaned its head back and let out a sharp, barklike laugh that echoed through the trees. "Oh, Peter," it purred. "Do you really think you can stop me?" it asked with a wide grin.

Peter gripped the hilt with both hands. The sword surged with energy and glowed bright, but only for a moment before it started to wane and fade out. Peter's knuckles blanched as he aimed the blade at the shadow. "I'm warning you," he growled through gritted teeth.

"Oh dear." The shadow's mouth split at an unnatural angle. "Are you having some difficulty performing?" it asked. "You've hardly any fight left in you, Peter." The shadow reached out and flicked the edge of the sword. Like a lightbulb, it blinked out of existence, dissolving into a quickly disappearing pile of sparks at Peter's feet.

Peter's shoulders went rigid. His hands clenched into fists at his side.

"Soon, all your magic will drain from your body, and not even you, the great Peter Pan, will be able to stop me," it said in a singsong tone, twirling its long fingers in the air.

Wendy shook and her eyes stung, but she wouldn't let herself run away. This was it. This was the thing that had taken her brothers from her and was keeping them captive. It was the thing keeping them apart. Wendy surged forward, trying to push past Peter. "Let them go!" she shouted.

The shadow's attention shifted to her. "Wendy," it breathed. "So nice of you to join us this time." The shadow sucked in a deep, rattling breath. Its eyes rolled into the back of its head, eyelids twitching. "Mmm," it hummed before looking at her with sharklike focus. "You are *delicious*, aren't you?" The shadow's smile split its face in half. "All that fear and guilt just streaming from you." It chuckled. "It's nearly overwhelming!"

She might have been afraid, but anger boiled through the ice in her veins. "Where are my brothers?" Wendy tried to move in, but Peter held an arm out, keeping her back. She wanted to rip and claw that grin off the shadow's face.

It let out deep, booming laughs. "They're here, of course!" It held its hands aloft, gesturing around them.

Wendy gritted her teeth together. What game was it trying to play?

"Don't you remember, Wendy?" it asked, observing her curiously, twisting its head this way and that. It started walking in a slow circle around Wendy and Peter.

"What are you talking about?" she demanded. She couldn't trust anything it said. It was probably just trying to manipulate her, to trick them. Wendy knew it fed off negative energy—she couldn't let it get the better of her.

The shadow feigned a look of surprise. "Why, this is where dear Peter found you and your brothers!"

An electric shock ran through Wendy's body. Caught off guard, she felt her resolve waver. Wendy glanced in Peter's direction, unwilling to let the shadow distract her. "Is that true?" she asked him.

Peter gave a curt nod, eyes still locked on the shadow. He was poised, ready to lunge, a smoldering glower on his face.

Was that why she kept drawing the tree? Why she had seen it the other night in her dream? Was it some sort of muscle memory that kept coming back to her, that had brought her here? This was where Peter had found her. It was where she and her brothers had gone missing. Where her living nightmare over the past five years had begun.

Wendy turned back to the shadow. "Where are my brothers?" she repeated, losing her patience and composure.

Its eyebrows arched high, wrinkling its forehead. "Hasn't Peter told you?" Its bright white teeth dragged over its bottom lip in amusement.

"He told me you have them, and all the other kids who have gone missing from town," Wendy seethed through gritted teeth.

The shadow broke into another round of rumbling laughter that Wendy felt in her bones. After a long moment, they died down and it looked at her. "You'll never see them again, Wendy," he told her quietly with a smile.

A sudden burst of rage and anguish cut through Wendy like a knife. She lunged for the shadow, but it collapsed into a pool of black and dissipated into the woods, leaving echoes of laughter in its wake.

"No!" Wendy shouted. She wouldn't let it get away, not now, they needed to stop it, she needed to get her brothers back. Wendy made to chase after it, but Peter grabbed her from behind.

"Wendy, stop!" Peter said, his breath harsh against the side of her neck. He locked his arms tightly around her middle, pulling her against him, lifting her off her feet.

Wendy struggled and thrashed. She kicked her feet out and tried to yank herself away from him, but he didn't budge.

"*Let me go!*" she screamed into the woods. She pushed at his arms and attempted to jerk herself from his grip. "I need to stop it!" she yelled. She pounded her fists against his arms. "I have to get them back. I have to get my brothers back!" She was shaking now. "John and Michael, I have to get them back!" Her voice cracked and wailed. She felt like she had been broken in two. Her body ached all over, the longing for her brothers coursing through her skin. There was a gaping hole in her stomach.

"It's gone, Wendy," Peter said in her ear.

Wendy wanted to shout at Peter, but when she sucked in a breath, a wobbly sob choked her. Wendy's legs gave out from under her, but Peter held her tight, keeping her close. She doubled over in Peter's arms. Uncontrollable wails ripped through her throat. Sobs wracked her body.

"Shh, it's okay," Peter said gently into her ear, trying to

coax her down, his cheek pressed against her hair. His words were as shaky as her hands.

She had failed them. Again.

The guilt and grief were all-consuming. She couldn't breathe, she couldn't pull herself out of it.

Under the cries of her mourning, Wendy could've sworn she could hear far-off chuckling.

Wendy twisted in Peter's arms, burying her face in his shoulder. She balled his shirt into her fists and bawled with abandon.

Peter's body tensed at first, but then his muscles relaxed. He placed one hand on the back of her neck and the other on the small of her back, pulling her closer. He tucked the top of her head under his chin.

The shadow had been right there in front of them. They should've stopped it. They should've done something. Wendy should've stopped it. That was why she was here, that was what she was supposed to do, but she hadn't. She couldn't— she didn't know how. The thing that was holding John and Michael captive had been right in front of her, but she was still no closer to saving them.

Wendy didn't know how long they stood there. She would start to calm down, but then she would think of her brothers scared in some dark room together, or Alex alone and crying in the woods, or the little girl, Ashley, being tormented by the shadow, and a new wave of guilt would consume her.

But Peter remained, holding on to her and occasionally speaking softly in her ear, "It's going to be okay. We'll find the missing kids. We'll figure this out. Wendy, it will be okay."

Eventually, the crying subsided into intermittent hiccups. Maybe she had finally cried out all the tears left in her, or her body just didn't have the strength to keep it up. Every sob and ache drained Wendy of her energy to fight. The very air seemed to be weighing on her shoulders. She was exhausted and defeated.

The only comfort was the radiating warmth of Peter as she huddled against him. When she finally pulled back, the front of his shirt was soaked with her tears and snot. She rubbed her nose off on the back of her hand and tried to wipe the wetness from her cheeks. Her eyes stung. Everything was blurry. Her whole body ached with grief.

"Let's get out of here," Peter said gently. He tucked some of her hair behind her ear. "It's getting late. We don't want to run into the search crews . . ."

Wendy could only nod in agreement as she wiped her nose on her arm. She started to follow Peter, fingers lacing with his, but as she left the clearing, Wendy couldn't help sparing one last look at the tree.

It stood there, silent and gray as stone. All trace of the whispers had vanished.

CHAPTER 17

Fairy Lights

When they got back to Wendy's truck, Wendy slid into her seat and leaned her forehead against the steering wheel. With her eyes closed, she took a deep breath to steady herself. The springs of the passenger seat groaned as Peter climbed in. "What now?" he asked quietly at her side.

Good question.

Wendy turned her head, her cheek pressed into the warmed leather as she looked at him. Red tinged his freckled cheeks. His shoulders slumped, hands clasped in his lap. The auburn hair at the nap of his neck was damp with sweat. There was a tilt to his eyebrows that made her want to reach out and touch his arm.

Peter couldn't stay in the woods. Soon enough, they would be overrun with police officers and volunteers. Even then, there was no way she was going to let Peter be by himself, not after what the shadow had done to him last night. Peter needed to be protected, too. She wanted to hide him away somewhere safe. The idea of something—or another thing—happening to him was out of the question.

There was the fleeting and outlandish desire to just run

away and disappear, but Wendy wouldn't abandon her brothers, not again.

She sighed and forced herself to sit upright. "Now, you come home with me," she said definitively. She glanced over at Peter, half expecting him to object.

Peter simply stared out the windshield and, after a pause, nodded. "Okay," he said. "I don't really have anywhere else to go." An airy laugh escaped his lips.

"Good, then let's go home." Wendy moved to put her key into the ignition when she caught sight of the sun sinking below the tree line. She swore under her breath.

"What?" Peter said, suddenly alert, wide eyes jumping to the direction of the woods.

"The sun is going down and I haven't called my dad yet," she said, frantically digging her cell phone out of her pocket.

"Oh." Peter sounded relieved. Wendy wished she felt the same.

She selected her father's number from her favorites list and held the phone up to her ear. She pressed her lips together. The last thing she needed was to further piss her father off, or make him even more suspicious, when she was about to try to sneak Peter into the house overnight. Hiding a person in her room was a lot different than trying to hide something like a pet mouse, which she had done when she was little.

No. Peter was a person. A boy-type person.

Oh, God, was she really going to be one of those girls who snuck boys into their rooms?

The line rang once before he answered. "Hello?"

"Dad, hey," Wendy said, tucking her hair behind her ear. "I'm leaving the hospital now and heading home."

"Did Jordan go with you?" Muffled voices in the background made it difficult for her to hear him.

"Er, no." She cringed. "I couldn't get ahold of her," she lied. Wendy sniffed and rubbed her nose against the back of her hand.

There was a pause. Mr. Darling's voice became gruff. "What's wrong?" he demanded.

Wendy cleared her throat. "Nothing, I'm fine. I'm just getting really bad allergies," she said. Out of the corner of her eye, Peter wrapped a stray thread from his shorts around his finger.

There was another pause. More muffled voices. Mr. Darling's exhale crackled against her ear. "Go straight home. Your mother should be there waiting for you."

"What do you mean?" Wendy asked. She frowned. "Wait, Dad, where are you?"

"I'm in the woods with the search parties," he said. Wendy sat bolt upright. Quickly, her head jerked around, half expecting her father to be standing right in front of them at the edge of the woods.

Peter frowned. His head tilted curiously to the side.

"I told Donald Davies that I would help."

Of course: Donald Davies, the father of the two boys who'd gone missing the night before. Wendy had completely forgotten that he worked with her father at the bank. They weren't just neighbors, they were coworkers.

"But, like I said," he went on, "your mom is home waiting for you, so hurry back. She's had a long day and needs some rest. I won't be home until late. Maybe in the morning."

"Okay."

"Night, Wendy."

"Bye, Dad."

Wendy put her phone away. Peter watched her, eyebrows raised expectantly. "So . . . what's going on?" he asked.

"My dad is out helping the search party. He won't be back until late tonight or early tomorrow." Wendy couldn't help being surprised. Her dad usually kept to himself. He didn't really hang out with anyone outside of work—not that Wendy knew of, anyway. He wasn't social or even all that friendly.

But it made sense, she supposed. Of course he would want to help. Mr. Davies had lost his sons, just like her father had lost John and Michael.

Wendy swallowed past the tightness in her throat. "One less parent to sneak you past, I guess." She tried to say it casually with a laugh, but it came out as a squeak.

Peter didn't say anything, just nodded. His jaw worked under his cheek, eyes trained on the thread again.

"You're being too quiet," Wendy told him. There wasn't enough room in the stuffy cab for them both to be awkward. Wendy jabbed a finger into his shoulder. "I don't like it."

Peter glanced up at her. A shadow of an amused smile played on his lips. "Sorry. I'm just picturing the spot above your TV where your dad is going to mount my head if he finds me."

Wendy let out a surprised laugh. It pushed some of the tension from her lungs. "Don't be ridiculous." She turned the key and the truck's engine roared to life. "If he finds you, there won't be enough left of you to mount."

When Wendy pulled into the driveway, she told Peter to meet her at the back door. It would be easier to sneak him upstairs from there.

As soon as she stepped inside, she saw her mother lying on the couch. The TV was still on, the volume down low. Wendy crept forward to see that her mother's eyes were closed behind her glasses, her chest rising and falling in a gentle rhythm.

Well, at least she was asleep. Wendy wondered if her mom had been trying to stay awake until she got home.

The evening news caught her attention. A reporter stood in the woods with a floodlight illuminating his face. Behind him was the hunting shack Peter had been staying in, blocked off with police tape. Washed with bright light, it looked tiny and unassuming compared to when she had seen it in person. Men and women in police uniforms carried out items in small plastic bags. Some of them examined something on the ground, others were dusting the doorframe for fingerprints. The volume was off, but a marquee scrolled the story of what she could already tell was happening:

. . . HASN'T BEEN IN ACTIVE USE FOR 6 MONTHS. CLOTHES, FOOD, AND TRACES OF RECENT INHABITANTS. WOOD-BURNING STOVE HAS BEEN RECENTLY USED. TWO SETS OF FOOTPRINTS INSIDE HUNTING SHACK AND AROUND EXTERIOR. POLICE TRYING TO FIND FINGERPRINTS OR DNA EVIDENCE. CURRENTLY, NO SIGN OF MISSING CHILDREN . . .

Wendy wondered if her dad had been part of the search party to discover the shack. She and Peter were lucky they had gotten out of there when they did.

Frustration worked its way through her. The police were getting distracted from the real culprit. They were losing valuable time tracing Peter's path when they should be on the hunt for the shadow. But how could they even do that? She and Peter were having a hard enough time tracking it down, and at least they knew what they were up against.

Quietly, Wendy crossed the kitchen to the back door.

Peter was there, waiting patiently.

She unlocked the sliding glass door and slowly pulled it

open, just wide enough for him to squeeze through. Wendy pressed her finger to her lips. She didn't want to risk making any noise that would wake her mom.

Peter's face was screwed up tight, his brow furrowed. He pinched his bottom lip between his thumb and forefinger. It struck Wendy how much he looked like Michael when he wanted to come inside after stomping in puddles, but knew he would get in trouble for tracking mud on the floor.

Wendy had to pluck impatiently at his sleeve before he finally slunk inside.

She pointed to the living room. "Try to be quiet, my mom is asleep on the couch," she whispered to him. He nodded in reply. His blue eyes were wide and alert. "Look," she said, nodding in the direction of the TV. "They found your hideout . . ."

Peter quietly stepped into the living room for a closer look. He squinted as his eyes scanned, reading the information scrolling by on the bottom of the screen. He sighed.

"Good timing on our part, I guess," he said, keeping his voice low. His eyes slid over to Mrs. Darling asleep on the couch. She had a pillow propped under her head. Her glasses were askew. Deep frown lines scrunched her brow and pulled down at the corners of her mouth.

Peter's shoulders sank.

Wendy gestured for him to come back and pointed toward the hallway that led to the stairs.

His eyes slid back to Mrs. Darling. He lingered for a moment before retreating. Peter had just entered the kitchen when Wendy pushed the sliding glass door shut. It let out a high-pitched squeal of rubber against glass.

Mrs. Darling stirred on the couch.

Wendy grabbed a bewildered Peter and shoved him into the hallway and out of sight.

"Wendy?" Mrs. Darling's voice, thick from sleep, mumbled from the living room.

"Yeah, Mom, it's me!" Wendy called back. "I just got home from the hospital."

Peter pressed his back against the wall, cringing.

Mrs. Darling sat up and readjusted her glasses on her face. "Just now?" She looked down at the plastic watch on her wrist and frowned.

"It was a really crazy day," Wendy said, nodding vigorously. "They needed all the help they could get! But I'm really exhausted, so I'm going to head up to bed."

"Oh . . . all right." Mrs. Darling sat back on the couch and gave Wendy a tired smile. "Sleep well, sweetheart."

The only thing that saved Wendy from her poorly constructed lies was the fact that she'd never lied to her parents before, so they had no real reason to doubt or question her. Especially about things like sneaking around with mysterious boys. Or any boys.

"You too, Mom."

Peter was waiting for Wendy in the hallway with his hands clasped behind his back. He looked like a child inside a museum who had been scolded not to touch anything. She tried not to smile.

Wendy pointed up the stairs and poked the middle of his back, urging him forward. Peter led the way up and, when they got to the second floor landing, he made to open the door to her and her brothers' old room.

"Not that one," Wendy said quietly, gently catching his elbow. She nodded her head to the right. "My room is over here now."

Realization shadowed Peter's features. His eyes went to the doorknob for a moment before he nodded.

Wendy opened her door and was immediately glad that she had cleaned it up last night. The fairy lights cast a warm glow over everything. Peter walked to the center of the room and turned in a slow circle. Wendy closed the door behind him and stood there, tucking her hair behind her ears, watching as he looked around.

Other than Jordan, she had never had anyone in her room after her brothers went missing. It was the singular place in this world that was hers. The only place she could hide and feel at home. And now, there Peter stood, in the middle of all her things. Somehow, he stood out and fit in at the same time.

Peter moved to her dresser, his long fingers brushing against the spines of her books. "Is your mom okay?" he suddenly asked.

"What do you mean?" Wendy said, distracted as she tried to remember if she had put her bra in the hamper last night, or was it still hanging on the towel rack?

"She looked . . ." He paused. "Sad."

"Oh." Wendy nudged a badly written romance novel under her bed with the toe of her shoe. "She's been working a lot," she told him. "And, obviously, the missing kids have been weighing on her. My dad, too. I don't think she's been sleeping very much . . ." Wendy thought back to when she had listened outside her mother's door and heard her talking in her sleep. "I think she's been having bad dreams." Wendy crossed her arms. Her thumb rubbed against her elbow. "Sometimes I can hear her talking to John and Michael in her sleep."

Peter stared down at his hands. His expression was . . . mournful.

Wendy wondered if he still pictured her mother as the little girl he'd gone on adventures with. She found herself wishing she'd known her back then.

"I don't like seeing people in pain," Peter finally said. There was a strange edge to his voice, almost an urgency, like he was trying to make her understand something very important.

But of course he didn't like seeing people in pain. She knew that. When children were lost and alone, Peter was the one to find them and take care of them. He was the one who took their fear away. The nature of him was to stop people's pain and suffering. So of course he couldn't stand seeing her mother like this. Maybe as much as Wendy.

Wendy didn't know what to say, and Peter didn't elaborate further. He just stood in the middle of the room, hands clasped behind his back again, shifting his weight between his feet. The time between leaving the clearing and now was the quietest she had ever seen him. It wasn't normal for him, but then again, nothing about any of this was particularly "normal."

"Do you want to take a shower or something?" Wendy suggested. "I have my own bathroom, and you're kind of a mess." Peter looked down at himself. His clothes were covered in dirt, as were his legs and arms. There was a dark smear on his cheek, debris from the woods stuck in his hair, and spots on his shirt from where her tears had landed. At least the swelling of his lip had gone down, but there was still that small cut. "I can throw your clothes in the laundry and give you an old shirt. I, uh, probably have a pair of gym shorts that would fit you?" she offered.

Peter narrowed his eyes at her. A grin twitched at the corners of his lips. "Are you trying to tell me I stink?" he asked, his humor starting to come back.

Wendy nodded, unable to keep herself from smiling. "A

bit, yes." Wendy cleared her throat and moved to her dresser. She dug out an oversized shirt along with a pair of gym shorts her mom had bought her that were too big to be practical. Wendy handed them to Peter and showed him into the bathroom. "Give me your dirty clothes when you've got them off," Wendy said through the door once he was inside.

She pressed her palm to her temple and huffed out a breath.

This was weird. This was very weird. She jumped when the door cracked open and Peter's arm reached through, dropping the ratty clothes into her arms.

Peter looked through the crack of the door. She could see his bare arm and chest. "Be careful with those," he told her in mock seriousness. "They're very delicate."

Wendy rolled her eyes. "You're not funny," she told him.

Peter laughed. His toothy grin peeked around the edge of the door before he closed it. She was about to walk away when he asked, "Wait, how do I turn this thing on?"

Wendy tried not to laugh. "Turn the knob," she told him. She heard the water turn on. "Oh, and don't—"

Peter yelped.

"—turn it all the way to hot," she finished. She pressed her hand to her mouth as laughter bubbled.

"Right, got it!"

She heard the shower curtains slide shut. Wendy was left by herself, standing in her room, holding Peter's clothes. And Peter was here, in her room. In her shower, using her spare towel, and she was holding his clothes.

Peter Pan was in her shower and was going to stay the night in her room.

And he was naked.

Wendy's face burned red hot. No, she would *not* start

thinking—absolutely not. She tried to will her face to cool down. Nope. Not okay.

Wendy hurried out of the room and went downstairs.

Her mother wasn't on the couch anymore. The TV was off and the room silent. It was a small comfort to know her mother must have gone to bed. She needed to sleep, not spend the night on the cramped couch with the news looming over her.

Wendy went into the kitchen and to the small side room where the washing machine and dryer were kept. She threw in Peter's clothes and added a generous amount of detergent. Next, she raided the fridge and loaded her arms up with whatever she could find: an array of leftover Chinese food, two apples, and an orange. She doubted Peter would mind. What had he even been eating in the woods, anyway? That was probably a question better left unanswered.

When she went back upstairs, she dropped the food and some paper towels onto her bed. Now that there was food in front of her, she realized how starved she was, so Wendy dove into the cold noodles. She ate so much so fast, she quickly gave herself a stomachache. Brushing off her hands, Wendy stood up, staring down at her bed for a moment.

Where was Peter going to sleep?

She blinked. It wasn't like he was going to sleep in her bed with her. No. Certainly not. The closet wasn't big enough, nor under her bed. She wouldn't make him sleep in the bathroom, even though it was less likely that her parents would walk in on him if he were curled up in the tub. He was too tall to fit, and her parents never barged into her room, anyway. Her mother always knocked lightly on the door, and her dad just yelled at her from downstairs if he wanted her.

The floor seemed like the best option—on the side of her bed farthest from the door, just in case.

The shower water turned off. Wendy angled herself away from the bathroom door and hurried over to the closet. She reached up to the shelf and took down her sleeping bag. It hadn't been used in a month, but it still smelled like campfire smoke. Wendy rolled it out on the floor and was smoothing out the slick material when the bathroom door opened.

"I set my sleeping bag up for you." She stood and turned to face Peter. "And I've got—" Wendy's hands flew up to cover her open mouth. "Oh my god."

Peter stood in the doorway, his hair wet and pushed back out of his face. He was scowling at her, lips pursed tight. On Wendy, the gray T-shirt with the purple fish on the front was too baggy for her to wear out in public. But it clung tightly to Peter's shoulders, the fish taut and distorted over his chest. It was hardly long enough to cover his stomach. Then, there was the matter of the gym shorts. While they were technically big enough to fit his legs, they only covered about the top third of his thighs. Clearly he didn't have the same proportions as her.

"How did you even get the shirt *on*?" Wendy asked, voice breaking from suppressed laughter. She clamped her hands tighter over her mouth as her shoulders started to shake.

Red bloomed on Peter's cheeks. He threw his wet towel at her head. "Do you really not have anything bigger than this?" he asked, tugging uncomfortably at the collar of the shirt.

Wendy shook her head, fingertips pressed to her bottom lip. "I'm so sorry, that's all I've got," she told him. Her cheeks hurt from the smile on her face.

"I hope you realize how embarrassing this is," Peter said flatly. He crossed his arms over the sliver of skin that peeked out from below the shirt.

"It's just—" She cleared her throat and tried to regain her

composure. "It's just until the morning," she reminded him. She couldn't help looking him up and down once more.

The giggles started again.

"Stop that!" Peter scolded, trying to sound stern, but now he was starting to laugh, too.

"I'm sorry, I can't help it!" Wendy said before covering her mouth again. She needed to be quiet or else she'd wake up her mother. "Ugh, okay," she said, wiping tears of mirth from the corners of her eyes. "I grabbed some food." She gestured to the assortment on the bed. "Help yourself. I'm going to . . . clean myself up." Uncertainty started to creep up her spine again. Chewing on her bottom lip, she eyed Peter as he plopped down on her bed. He crossed his legs and immediately started opening the Chinese food containers.

Wendy grabbed some pajamas from her drawer and shut herself in the bathroom. She peeled off her clothes, which were sticky with stale sweat.

As she stepped into the shower, there was already a layer of dirt settled in the bottom of the tub. Peter must have been filthier than she'd thought. Wendy turned up the heat as high as she could stand. The water rushed down her body, taking the remnants of the woods along with it. She leaned her forehead against the cool tile and took a deep breath, letting the water wash along her neck and across her parted lips. The rhythmic pounding against her skin was comforting. Her muscles ached and burned, especially across her shoulders. She was thorough in scrubbing herself clean. She shampooed her hair twice. When she was done she stepped out of the water and pulled a dry towel from the rack. She rubbed it through her hair before wrapping it tightly around her body. The knots and tangles in her short hair were stubborn, but the conditioner and some rough handling with a brush smoothed it out.

Wendy dug through the pile of pajamas she had haphazardly grabbed and picked out a nightshirt and cotton shorts. She used the damp towel to wipe the fog from the mirror. She stared at her smudgy reflection, focusing on her exposed legs.

Peter was just on the other side of the door, and they were going to be sleeping in the same room.

Her heart was beating fast, but not the jarring pound in her temples like when she was in the woods. This was a light flutter at the base of her throat. She did her best to swallow it down. *Woman up, Wendy Darling,* she chided herself before stepping into her bedroom.

Peter was on her bed next to an empty container of cold chicken chow mein. He was lying on his side, his cheek pressed against her pillow as he hugged it to him. His nose was tucked into his shoulder, his eyes closed, his lashes splayed against his freckled cheeks. One of his legs was bent and one foot hung off the side of the mattress. The curve of his back was relaxed and languid.

Quietly, Wendy stepped farther into the room. Had he already fallen asleep?

It was so strange to have him there. Peter Pan—*her* Peter—was in her world, in her room, on her bed. The boy she'd daydreamed about as a little girl. A boy who was supposed to be just make-believe, a creation of her mother's imagination, only real in her stories. But he *was* real. A little worse for wear, and older, and he was here, with her.

Careful not to jostle him, Wendy knelt down next to the bed. Her chin rested atop her hands on the edge of the mattress. She would never get this close to him when he was awake. A thrill ran up her spine, like she was taking something she wasn't even supposed to touch.

Warmth bloomed from her chest, where her acorn hung. His back rose and fell slowly with his breaths. That same crease was between his eyebrows, the one that never quite seemed to leave, a mark of the weight he balanced on his shoulders. She lifted her hand, but hesitated and bit her bottom lip. She wanted to feel the softness of his hair, to touch the warmth of his skin. Peter looked how summer felt.

"You have no idea how amazing this feels," Peter mumbled into his shoulder. His eyes opened and the sudden closeness of those astonishing eyes made her spring back.

Tripping over her own feet, Wendy struggled for a moment before popping back upright. "What?" she breathed, her hand hurriedly running through her damp hair.

Peter pushed himself onto his elbow. For a moment, he lay there, looking up at her with a curious tilt of his head. "Your bed," he finally clarified, a small shadow of a smile on his lips.

"Oh, yeah, it's the mattress pad." Wendy's rushed words tumbled out of her mouth. She cleared her throat and took a step back. "You can sleep on the bed, if you want," she offered suddenly. "I don't mind sleeping on the floor."

Waving her off, Peter slid to the edge of the mattress. Wendy took two more steps away.

"No way, you sleep in your own bed," he told her. He went to the floor and sprawled out on the sleeping bag. "That wouldn't be very gallant of me," he pointed out, arching his back and gripping at air as he stretched.

Wendy plucked a pillow from her bed and tossed it at him. "Since when are you gallant?" Wendy asked.

Peter caught it easily. "Your words *wound* me, Wendy Darling," he said with a smirk before tucking the pillow behind his head and flopping onto his back.

Wendy laughed—a nervous, shaky thing. Gathering up the remaining food, she moved it onto the bedside table.

"Aren't you going to eat anything?" Peter asked, peeking at her from the other side of the bed.

"I already scarfed down half the chow mein," she told him. But she did reach out for the orange and peeled it as he devoured the Chinese food. She split it in two and tossed Peter one half, which he easily caught out of the air. Wendy ate the slices and reveled in the sweet, cool juices of the orange.

When she was finished, Wendy crawled into her bed and curled up in a ball on her side, close enough to the edge that she could still see Peter. Her bed smelled like him: grass, honeysuckle, and earth woven into the soft threads of her pillow. She breathed it in. She breathed it out.

Peter tucked his hands behind his head, the motion pulling up the hem of his ill-fitting shirt. He heaved a deep sigh as he closed his eyes.

"Peter?" Wendy said quietly.

He opened one eye and tilted his head to look up at her. "Mm?" he hummed.

She wasn't sure how to phrase her question. "Are you— Do you think the shadow is going to come for you again?" she asked. "Are you any safer here? With me?"

Peter frowned as if he hadn't considered it. "I'm not sure," he confessed with a shrug.

Wendy's fingers brushed against the acorn where it hung at the center of her chest.

"I won't let anything happen to you," Peter added earnestly.

"It's not me I'm worried about," she told him. She needed

to keep Peter safe. If the shadow showed up, would she be able to protect him? The uncertainty did little to soothe her already frayed nerves. "Will you wake me up if anything happens?" she asked.

"You'll be the first to know," Peter told her with a nod.

Wendy reached out and clicked off her fairy lights, plunging the room into darkness. She never slept with them off, but she didn't want Peter to think she was a child who couldn't sleep without a nightlight. Wendy pulled the covers over her. The weight of them felt reassuring, but almost immediately she got too hot. Summer was no time to be hiding under a down comforter. She pushed it off. Wendy closed her eyes and tried to force herself to fall asleep, but her imagination wouldn't let her. She rolled onto her other side. Every noise outside startled her and every shadow in her room seemed to shift.

Every nerve in her body was tense and screaming. She couldn't relax. There was no way she could fall asleep.

Wendy's hand shot out and clicked the fairy lights back on.

Peter was already watching.

"Sorry, I . . . can't," Wendy muttered. Shame sweltered on her skin. She felt like she needed to explain herself to him. "I—"

"It's okay," was all Peter said. His voice was gentle, which only made her feel more pathetic.

Wendy rolled onto her back and tried to will herself to sleep, but her mind wandered to the woods.

The gentle chirping of crickets drifted to her ears. She looked over at Peter. His eyes were closed, arms still tucked lazily behind his head, but his mouth was pressed into a small circle. Delicate cricket chirps flowed past his lips. Wendy blinked slowly, admiring the warm glow of the fairy lights on his skin. The slight dip in his throat. The trail of freckles down his bare arms. Wendy's eyes slid shut. She drifted off with Peter's cricket song and his smell enveloping her, lulling her to sleep with thoughts of Neverland.

CHAPTER 18

Pain

Wendy didn't know how long she had been asleep, or what had woken her up. The fairy lights stood watch over her head and a soft breeze floated in through her window. Everything was dark and silent as it only was in the dead of night. There were no sounds drifting in from outside and no crickets chirping. Wendy rolled onto her side, searching for Peter, but she found only the abandoned sleeping bag and pillow.

Quickly, she sat up and looked around the room. "Peter?" she whispered into the room, but it was empty.

Through the haze of sleep, a thought occurred to her: What if the shadow had taken him? What if it had gotten into her room and did something to Peter while she was asleep? Wendy's fists squeezed her rumpled sheets.

She leapt from bed, ran into the hall, and stopped at the top of the stairs, perched on her tiptoes. Where did he go? Wendy's heart raced and she struggled to form a coherent plan. She was about to run down the stairs, to see if maybe—hopefully—he'd just gone to the kitchen for a drink of water, when she heard a soft noise behind her.

Wendy spun around. She expected the shadow to be

standing there, waiting for her, but the hallway was empty. Just the locked door to her old room. She heard the noise again. This time, she could tell it was coming from behind the door. Again, she glanced around. The sound of her own breathing felt deafening in the quiet hallway.

Slowly, she stepped closer. Anticipation tingled in her fingers, like she was breaking a sacred, unspoken rule. Carefully, she leaned her ear against the door.

There were voices coming from the other side. The quiet murmurings from the woods. The same whispers that had followed her when she was chasing Alex, the same ones she heard coming from the tree. They were on the other side of the door, whispering to her. They grew louder, clearer.

Wendy pressed her ear to the doorjamb. For a long moment, there was only silence. Had she been imagining it? Maybe she was just—

Wendy.

The voice hissed right into her ear with such sudden nearness, Wendy leapt back. Her breath caught in her throat and a thrill ran up her spine. Hope swirled in her chest, dangerous and sharp. Wendy's eyebrows tipped as she pressed her fingers lightly to the cold wood. If she could just open the door, she could hear what the voices were saying, she could understand them.

Her mother's voice floated down the hall. Wendy jumped. She glanced in the direction of her parents' room before turning back to the locked door.

The voices behind the door had gone silent.

Wendy's hand fell back to her side. The hope drained out of her, all the way to her bare toes. Embarrassment flared on her neck. She turned her back to the bedroom door and shook her head at herself. She rubbed her nose on the back of her hand. She really needed to get a grip.

Again, her mother's faint voice tickled her ears.

Wendy crept down the hallway to her parents' room. The door was cracked open and she could clearly hear her mother speaking.

"Are you all right, my darlings?" she gently cooed. Wendy's grip on the doorframe tightened. Her mother was just talking in her sleep again. "You aren't hurt?"

"Of course not, Mommy."

Wendy froze. Her heart lodged in her throat.

She knew that voice. That was her brother Michael, so soft and always on the verge of laughter. She could hear the smile in his voice.

"I would never let anything happen to Michael, you know that." And that was John. His voice was distinct. He always sounded much older than he was, like he was impersonating their father's timbre, always speaking in absolutes. Wendy could picture him pushing his glasses up on his nose by nudging the lower corner with a knuckle.

It was John and Michael. They were just on the other side of the door. They were here, *they had come back.*

Wendy pushed the door open silently, fingers trembling, eyes wide.

But what she saw didn't make sense.

Her mother lay in bed, her eyes closed. Her brow puckered and her lips were parted. The edges pulled down in a way that made her look like she was in pain.

And there, perched on the dresser next to her mother's side, was Peter.

He sat cross-legged, looking down at Mrs. Darling with

his hands in his lap. The moonlight coming in the window glanced off the side of his face in silvery silhouette. His head was bowed, as if in prayer, and his eyelids drooped. The shadows caught the heaviness of his brow, painting the circles under his eyes an even darker shade of blue. His thumb massaged the center of his palm.

"Are you frightened?" Mrs. Darling said.

Peter's lips parted, his tongue wet his bottom lip, and John's voice flowed out. "Not at all. Try not to worry about us," he said.

"Yes, we've got each other." Peter spoke with Michael's voice. "We're safe."

Safe.

Wendy felt as though the world had disappeared beneath her feet. She couldn't understand what she was seeing. Her fingers dug into the wall to balance herself.

Her mother's face began to relax. "I miss you both so much . . ."

"We miss you, too, Mommy," Peter said in Michael's voice.

"We think about you all the time," he added in John's.

A small smile began to form on Mrs. Darling's lips. "I love you so much, my sweet boys . . ." She rolled onto her side and pulled her pillow close.

Peter sat there silently for a moment. There was something about the way he looked at her mother that made Wendy ache. He shouldered her grief like it was his own. Propping his elbows on his knees, Peter buried his face in his hands, pushing his fingers through his hair. He looked so small. Young and exhausted.

Wendy stepped carefully into the room. "Peter?" she whispered.

Startled, he looked up. The moonlight gave his surprised face a ghostly pallor. Streaks glistened on his cheeks. Peter jumped down from the dresser, quickly wiping the heel of his hand across his eyes.

For a long moment, Wendy didn't know what to say. She couldn't make sense of what she had just seen, or maybe she just didn't want to. Hope had been ripped from her so quickly, she was still reeling. "What are you doing?" Wendy finally asked, wrapping her arms tightly around her middle.

Peter lowered his head. He flicked a glance back at Mrs. Darling before meeting Wendy's confused stare. His shoulders rolled in an uncertain shrug. "Trying to help," he said. His voice was low and hollow. Resigned.

Wendy's brow furrowed and she gave a small, confused shake of her head.

He stepped closer and spoke quietly, so as to not wake up her mother. "I . . . after I brought you back, sometimes I would come and check on you. You know, to make sure my shadow hadn't found you . . ." He rubbed the back of his neck. If the light were on, would she see him blushing? "One night, I heard your mom talking in her sleep. I thought . . . I thought that if I could speak to her with their voices, try to reassure her, she wouldn't be in so much pain?" His brilliant blue eyes searched hers.

Wendy thought back to when she had first come back home, after Peter left her in the woods and she had been released from the hospital. She remembered how she'd thought she heard her mother talking to her brothers. She'd felt that same rush in her stomach, the desperate sense of relief.

"That was you?" she asked.

Peter's eyes fell to the floor and he nodded. His mouth

twisted into a grimace and a crease formed between his eyebrows. Everything about his posture looked like he was bracing himself.

Wendy pressed her fingers to her lips. Even then, Peter had been trying to look out for her, and her mother. He was always trying to take care of people, to ease their suffering and bring them happiness, whatever way he could.

"How do you manage it?" Wendy asked with a small shake of her head. "How do you take all of that on yourself?" She stepped closer, closing the space between them.

Peter stilled. "My magic used to make it easier," he told her, still looking at the floor. "It takes more of a toll now . . ."

"If you're busy taking care of everyone else, who takes care of you?" Wendy asked.

Peter finally looked up at her, surprised.

She didn't think he had an answer.

Wendy reached out, lightly touching the skin just below the corner of his jaw.

A sigh smoothed out the tense lines in his face. He tilted his head, pressing his cheek into her palm, his skin soft and warm.

How many times had he gone through this? How many people had he helped? What terrible things had he witnessed? What had he sacrificed to protect others?

Wendy motioned for him to follow her. She led him back into her room and closed the door with a quiet click behind them. Wendy sat on her bed but Peter went back to his sleeping bag on the floor.

"Do you have a choice?" she asked. Her voice seemed loud in the dimly lit room.

"No—but it's not a burden," he told her as he lay out,

clasping his hands on his ribs and staring up at the ceiling. "I don't expect you to understand. There's some things that just don't have a cut-and-dried explanation." He paused to consider his words. "It's what I exist for," he said after some thought. "I'll do whatever I need to stop my shadow and save those kids, to keep other kids safe."

Wendy didn't know what to say. Peter took care of people, from the way he interacted with Alex at the hospital or Cassidy across the street, to soothing her mother with John and Michael's voices in her sleep. He found lost children, took away their fear, and gave them a home in Neverland.

Peter rolled onto his side, hands twisting the pillow under his head.

What was it like to be him? To prioritize everyone else's happiness, to bring other people joy, even if it meant suffering himself?

Wendy rolled over and inched to the edge of her mattress. She couldn't see him, but she reached a hand down and felt his shoulder. She brushed her fingertips along his arm until they found his hand. Her fingers hooked around his and she gave them a gentle squeeze.

For a moment she lay there, holding her breath. Then Peter tightened his hand around hers. The acorn around her neck pulsed bright.

When she woke up the next morning, her hand was empty.

Her sleeping bag was rolled up tight, but the straps were put on the wrong way, making it lopsided. This was clearly the handiwork of Peter, so she didn't worry about where he was. He probably just woke up early and—judging by the fact that no parent had barged in demanding what she was doing with a boy in the house—snuck out without her mother or father seeing.

On her way down to the kitchen, she saw that the door to her parents' room was closed. When she got downstairs, Mrs. Darling stood at the stove cooking eggs.

On the counter sat a stack of toast, a bottle of orange juice, and a bowl of fruit. Wendy's jaw went slack.

"You're cooking breakfast?" This was a rare thing that only happened on birthdays, and even then, it was Wendy who did the cooking. Usually, breakfast consisted of cereal or a granola bar.

Mrs. Darling looked at her from over her shoulder. "Good morning," she said with a smile. An actual smile, not one of those fake ones she usually forced. "I woke up and decided that eggs and toast sounded like a good idea. They were supposed to be fried eggs." She frowned down at the pan. "But I broke the yolks, so I sort of just"—she twirled the spatula—"turned them into scrambled eggs."

Wendy crossed the kitchen and openly stared at her mother. Her hair was down. Wendy never saw her mother with her hair down. It was always in a knot at the top of her head, even after she had just taken a shower. But here it was, down! It was a warm, light brown that pooled in loose ringlets to the middle of her back.

"Are you feeling okay?" Wendy asked, a small laugh escaping her.

"I feel fine," Mrs. Darling said. She gave Wendy another smile at she stirred the eggs again. "I feel really good, actually. I slept so well last night. I hardly remember what a good night's sleep feels like."

Peter.

Wendy snatched a piece of toast and took a huge bite. With a big yawn, Wendy slumped into a chair at the small dining table and watched her mother as she cooked. How strange it was to see her like this, so conventional and domestic. It was unsettling, but more . . . surprising, even a bit nice. There was a weird buzz in Wendy's head that she couldn't quite define, something like a rush of excitement and a soothing warmth.

Wendy shook her head and took another large bite of toast. Her mother cooking breakfast really shouldn't make her feel so *sentimental*, but here she was, looking away to ease the squeezing feeling in her chest.

Unfortunately, the television was the closest point of distraction. And, again, the news was on. The same pictures of Benjamin Lane, Ashley Ford, Alex Forestay, and now Joel and Matthew Davies were grouped together over footage of volunteers and officers trekking through the woods.

The large bite of toast in her mouth was dry and stuck in Wendy's throat as she tried to swallow. She stared at the images, letting them wash her with guilt. She needed to do something. She needed to get them back. It wasn't just her brothers who were relying on her. If Wendy failed, there were dozens of people whose lives would be destroyed. Not just the missing kids, but their friends and especially their families. Wendy would not have wished the unrelenting suffering and gradual destruction of losing a loved one—of not knowing what became of them, helpless to get them back—on her worst enemy.

She didn't want others to go through what had been done to her family. It was because of Wendy that her family had been pulled apart, that her parents had lost their sons and been haunted by it for the past several years. She wouldn't be the reason that loss and suffering spread to others. She would fix what had happened. She would find her brothers, and the other missing children, and she would bring them back. Failure was not an option.

The television screen went black. Wendy blinked up at her mother as she set the remote on the table, and then a plate of burned eggs in front of Wendy. Her eyes stung as she watched her mother sit in the chair beside her. The small, sad smile had returned.

With effort, she swallowed down the toast, but it did little to relieve the tightness in her throat. "I just wish I could help—I wish I could remember." The words were strained, toppling from Wendy's mouth before she could think better of it.

The smallest flinch crossed her mother's delicate features.

Wendy swallowed hard again. "If I could *remember* what happened, I could help, we could find John and Michael—" Her voice wouldn't let her continue as the tremor in her chest stirred.

Wendy's mother let out a gentle sigh, a soft melodic sound, like the start of a lullaby. "Oh, darling," she said, her eyebrows tipped with worry.

Wendy sucked in her lips between her teeth. How ridiculous was she? To be ruining a good morning with an outburst like that? Heat flared in her cheeks. She was embarrassed to be acting like this in front of her mother, who probably thought Wendy was on the verge of another mental breakdown. It wasn't fair of her to be even more of a burden with everything else that was going on.

"The mind is a complicated thing," Mrs. Darling said, considering her words as she spoke. "Sometimes it acts on its own, and quite often it controls us against our will. And I think, sometimes . . ." she said as she reached out and tucked a bit of Wendy's short hair behind her ear. The light brush of her cold fingertips against Wendy's cheek was fleeting but electric. "It takes us away, maybe not when we want it, but when we need it."

Wendy thought of her mother sleeping, of the dreams and nightmares her mind used to pull her through at night. Of what happened in her subconscious that made her talk in her sleep, and then of Peter, coaxing her through the worst of it. How her mother's pained expression had relaxed into one of peace.

Wendy sniffled noisily as she dragged the back of her hand across her nose.

Her mother's hands had retreated back to her lap. "You should eat before it gets cold," she told Wendy after a long pause.

Taking a large bite of burned eggs was the only response Wendy could come up with. It was bitter, but not terrible. She wouldn't mind eating a bit of charred food every meal if her mother made it.

"Your father got home just a couple of hours ago," Mrs. Darling continued. "He's upstairs sleeping, so let's try not to wake him up while we're cleaning."

"Cleaning?" Wendy repeated through a mouthful of food.

"Yes, cleaning. You don't have any plans today, right?"

"Uhh," Wendy stalled. She couldn't think of an excuse fast enough that didn't involve Peter.

"Good, then you're free to help," Mrs. Darling said, plopping a mound of scrambled eggs onto a plate for herself. "You can start with the laundry while I clean up the kitchen, and then we can both work on the living room."

Wendy sat down heavily at the table. "Greeeat," she muttered. Since when did her mother care about cleaning? Usually it was Wendy who picked up around the house. Sure, not a lot of chores had gotten done lately, but she had a good reason for it. Of course, *now* her mother wanted to get involved.

Meeting up with Peter would have to wait until she'd cleaned enough to satisfy her mother or Mrs. Darling went to work. Wendy looked down at her hand. Waiting to be able to see him again was not going to be fun. She had a feeling the day was going to drag on.

And drag on it did.

When she went to throw a load of laundry in the washing machine, she saw that Peter's clothes were gone. She checked the dryer and it was also empty. Well, at least he wasn't out walking around in her shirt and gym shorts that didn't fit him, but did that mean he'd left in wet clothes?

Wendy tossed out all the old magazines her mom had brought home from work to read, put abandoned mugs in the dishwasher, and wiped down the top of the TV and entertainment unit.

"Could you clean out the garbage from your father's study?" Mrs. Darling asked as she washed her hands clean of dust in the kitchen sink.

Wendy glanced at the closed door. "Uh . . ." Really? She wanted Wendy to go into the study? "Sure," Wendy said hesitantly. She got a garbage bag and paused at the door. She had never been explicitly forbidden from going inside, but it was always off limits, another unspoken rule of the house. It was her father's cave, where he'd go to hibernate away from his family and the real world with a bottle of scotch.

Wendy pushed the door open and stepped inside. It was a lot cleaner than she'd expected. Two of the walls were painted emerald green and the others were completely filled with shelves of books, but not the good kind of books that Wendy and her mother liked to read. They were old, tattered things with peeling covers, or newer paperbacks about accounting. There was even a particularly archaic set of encyclopedias. Wendy was pretty certain they didn't make those anymore.

A brown leather armchair sat in one corner of the room with a reading lamp perched on an end table next to it. Set in the back of the room was a heavy-looking wooden desk. There were opened letters, a couple stacks of paper, and a scotch decanter set on the corner. The decanter only had about two inches of amber liquid left in it.

Wendy crossed the room to the trash basket tucked under the desk. There were only a couple of empty beer bottles inside.

She emptied them into the large garbage bag in her hand. When she went to pluck a lone beer bottle from the desk, she noticed a small wooden tray filled with loose change, a letter opener, and a half-empty pack of gum. However, what caught her attention was a key, or rather the keychain attached to it. It was a circular piece of dark leather with *#1 Dad* sloppily burned into it. Wendy recognized it as the keychain she, John, and Michael had made for their father when they were away at summer camp one year. Since Father's Day had happened while they were away, they decided to make him a keychain in woodshop. They picked out a piece of leather and Wendy used a wood-burning pen to brand *#1 Dad* into it with the help of an instructor.

Wendy stared at the key. What did it open? It wasn't the house key—it was too small—and it wasn't his office key—that one he kept attached to his work badge.

The only other door with a lock was her old room.

Wendy picked up the key and turned it over in her hand. Maybe this was it?

"What are you doing in here?"

Wendy jumped and looked up to see her father standing in the doorway.

"Dad, hi!" She tucked the key into her pocket and snatched the beer bottle off the desk. Wendy turned to face him. "Nothing, Mom just asked me to take out your trash," she told him, trying to sound as nonchalant as possible.

Mr. Darling squinted at her for a moment. He looked tired. His eyes were bloodshot and his bushy hair was matted down on one side. A tall, army green thermos was in his hand. Wendy thought he was going to say something more, but all he did was grunt, cross to the armchair, and pick up the jacket draped over the back.

"Where are you going?" Wendy asked, following him back into the living room, garbage bag in tow.

"I'm heading back out with the search party," Mr. Darling told her gruffly.

"Oh, okay," she said. If that meant he would be out all night again, it would be easier for her and Peter to sneak around. "I saw the hunting shack on the news," Wendy said, testing the murky waters of her father's mood. "Did they find anything?"

Mr. Darling made another grunting noise. "Just some clothes and food. Looked like someone had been hiding out. There was still wood burning in the stove," he told her, not making eye contact as he spoke. "Doubt those sorry excuses for detectives will find anything useful," he growled. "It'll be up to us to bring them back home."

Wendy knew her father disliked the police even more than she did. They were supposed to find his missing boys, and they had let him down. No wonder he didn't trust them to be any use now.

"I'll be back late again," Mr. Darling continued. "Lock up tonight."

She nodded. "I will."

He stared at her for a moment. It felt like he was trying to decide whether or not to say something. Wendy was trying to guess what when he reached out and gave her a side hug, awkwardly patting her on the shoulder with his big hand. The weight of it felt foreign. Before Wendy could register what was happening, he turned and left through the front door.

Wendy stood there, frozen in place. He hadn't tried to hug her in . . . she didn't even know how long. The missing kids, being thrown into the same situation Wendy had lived through five years ago, had clearly gotten to him.

She shook the strange feeling from her shoulders.

After she took out the garbage, her mother had her hose down the two lounge chairs in the backyard, dry them off, and put the cushions on them. Mrs. Darling had decided that today was a good day to lie out in the sun and read for a bit, and that they deserved a break after all the hard work they had done around the house. Wendy threw together some peanut butter and honey sandwiches for lunch.

The key hung heavy in Wendy's pocket. She urged the afternoon to go by faster so she could find Peter.

While her mom easily settled in with a book, Wendy's eyes couldn't stay on the page. They kept wandering over to the woods. As it grew later in the day, Wendy began to worry about Peter. He hadn't been gone for this long before. Did something happen? Was he okay? Every time she thought about her hand in his last night, something in her chest fluttered. Was he avoiding her?

When the daylight started to wane, they headed inside. Mrs. Darling threw together a quick dinner of sliced chicken breast and salad, a late dinner since she would be working through the night, but Wendy couldn't even eat half the food on her plate. In just a little while, the day would be over and it would be nighttime. She and Peter had lost their window of opportunity to go into the woods. And where was he?

"Don't forget to lock the back door," Mrs. Darling reminded Wendy as she gathered up her purse for work.

"I *know*," Wendy groaned. She sat at the kitchen table, pushing her salad around with her fork.

"And make sure to—"

Knock knock.

Mrs. Darling frowned and looked at the door. Wendy put her fork down and sat up straight. Judging by the look on her mom's face, they weren't expecting anyone.

The last thing she needed was for Detectives James and Rowan to show up unannounced and start asking more questions.

Mrs. Darling crossed the living room and opened the door.

Her face lit up. "Barry, what a surprise!" she greeted him, but then her voice immediately became concerned. "Oh, what happened to you?"

Wendy rushed to the door. Peter stood on the porch, smiling sheepishly. In the orange light of sunset, Wendy was relieved to see he didn't have *new* injuries, just the lingering ones from the day before. The cut on his lip was starting to heal, but it was still a bit puffy.

"Hi, Mrs. Darling," Peter said. His blue eyes slid to Wendy. "I was playing some pickup basketball with some guys the other day," he lied. "Things got a bit rough, but it's nothing, really."

"Come in, let's have a look at it," she said with a sigh.

Mrs. Darling walked into the kitchen and Wendy looked at Peter. If he had a tail, it would've been tucked between his legs.

Wendy stepped close, her fingers knotting into the hem of his shirt. "What are you doing here?" she hissed, frantically searching his face for why on earth he would show up at her house when her mother was still home.

"I couldn't wait any longer—I wanted to see you," Peter whispered back. The earnest but apprehensive look on his face sent a rush from her navel to the tips of her toes.

"Here," Mrs. Darling said, handing a bag of frozen peas to Wendy. "Take a seat, Barry," she told Peter as she gestured to the kitchen table.

Peter sat down obediently. Mrs. Darling eyed the fading bruises and carefully examined the cut on his lip through her glasses. "Hmm, at least it's healing properly," she told Peter. "But you boys need to be careful—you could've lost a tooth." She gave him a disapproving look. Peter sank in his seat. "Keep the peas on it for twenty minutes. That will bring down the swelling," Mrs. Darling said, waving Wendy over.

Wendy tossed him the bag of peas. He easily caught it.

"I didn't know you were coming over, Barry," Mrs. Darling said as she glanced at Wendy, eyebrows raised.

"Uh, yeah," Wendy said. "I meant to ask you earlier if it was okay, but I sort of forgot. We were just going to watch a movie in the living room."

Her mother gave her a dubious look, but she retrieved her purse from the counter. "Well, all right," Mrs. Darling said. "If it gets too late, Barry," she said, looking back at Peter, "I want you to call your parents and have them pick you up, okay?" She tied her hair up into a knot. "I don't want you walking home alone."

Peter nodded. "I will, Mrs. Darling."

She gave him a soft smile, then turned to Wendy. "Stay in the living room, no going upstairs," she said with a pointed look.

Wendy blushed furiously. "*Mom.*" She did not appreciate her mother's amused expression.

"Have a good night, you two," Mrs. Darling said before walking out the front door and locking it behind her.

Now that they were alone, Wendy turned on Peter.

Both of his hands went up in defense, one still holding the bag of peas. "I tried to wait for you!" he said. "But you never came outside!" The look on Peter's face, jutted lip and all, was petulant at best.

"It—it's fine," Wendy stammered, hands smoothing out the front of her shirt as she did her best impression of someone who wasn't frazzled. "I couldn't get away—I was talking to my mom and then she made me help her clean the house." She waved a hand through the air in frustration.

"We're running out of time," Peter said, gingerly pressing the frozen peas to his lip.

Wendy pushed her hands through her hair. "I know, I know."

"I'm nearly out of magic," he said, examining his hand. "Without it, I don't know how we'll stop my shadow."

Wendy chewed on her bottom lip. Indeed, he seemed even more exhausted than he had last night. His eyelids drooped and his skin had a faint pallor to it.

"How will we know if it's all gone?" Wendy asked.

"I don't know, exactly, but I'm sure it'll be obvious," he said gravely.

Fear reached its way up her throat and clawed at her tongue. What would happen to Peter when his magic ran out?

Would he just disappear in a wisp of smoke? Crumble into a pile of ash? Or drop dead at her feet? The very thought made her head swim.

"How do we weaken something that feeds off fear?" Wendy said aloud.

Peter shrugged miserably.

That was the real question, the problem they needed a solution to. What could they do? What was the next step? Where could they look for answers?

Wendy remembered the key in her pocket.

"Last night, before I found you in my parents' room," Wendy began suddenly. Peter looked confused at the sudden jump in conversation. "I was in the hallway, and I swear I heard voices coming from my old room," she told him. "They were the same whispering voices I heard when I was trying to find Alex in the woods, when I dreamed about the tree, *and* when we were standing right in front of it. The door's been locked for ages, but"—Wendy dug the key out of her pocket and held it out for Peter to see—"I found this on my dad's desk today. I'm almost positive it unlocks the door."

Peter examined the key carefully. "So, you want to go check it out?" he guessed.

Wendy nodded. "The voices have to mean something, and there has to be a reason I can hear them in that room," she told him. He looked uneasy. "It doesn't hurt to poke around, right?" she pressed. "Maybe it'll help jog my memory for something useful." Her hand pressed to the acorn where it hid under the neck of her shirt.

"It's the only idea we've got," he agreed, after a moment, even though he looked like he wanted to argue it further.

Wendy tugged on his arm. "Let's go."

CHAPTER 19

Growing Up

As they stood at the door, everything was silent. There were no whispers, no murmurings, just a pull in her chest that urged her to go inside. Wendy took the key and slid it into the lock. Suddenly, the idea of going into her old room overwhelmed her. Until now, the locked door had stood like an entrance to a tomb. What if she couldn't handle it? What if she was met with a flood of memories? What if the ache for her missing brothers hurt too much?

She looked at Peter and, as if sensing her distress, he moved, lightly pressing his shoulder against hers, and gave a small nod. Wendy turned the key in the lock and pushed the door open.

At first, she could hardly see anything. The only illumination came from the moonlight that streamed through the large bay window on the opposite wall. Wendy blindly moved her hand along the wall until she found the switch. With a flick of her finger, strings of fairy lights lining the four corners of the ceiling illuminated the room. Her father had rigged them up when Wendy was born.

She slowly stepped into the room, drinking it all in. Peter

hung back, leaning against the doorframe, giving her space but watching intently.

John's and Michael's beds were set against the left wall while Wendy's was pushed up against the right. They each had their own dressers and a large bookshelf took up room next to the bay window.

It didn't feel like a preserved monument to her brothers. In fact, everything looked exactly how she remembered it, but with more dust. It was like John and Michael had just walked out a minute earlier. There was an opened box of colored pencils on the small table in the corner. Michael's backpack was slumped with its contents spilling out in a corner by his bed. A book was laid open on John's. Even the comforter on Wendy's old bed was pulled back, probably from when she had woken up screaming the first and last time her parents tried to have her sleep in it after being found in the woods.

Wendy let out a soft laugh. "It's like they never left," she said quietly into the room.

Peter stepped inside and looked around, then over at her old bed. "Pink floral, huh?" he said, lifting an eyebrow. The corner of his lips twitched, threatening to curl into a grin.

"I had a very different aesthetic when I was little," Wendy told him firmly as she followed him inside. "I wonder how they'll change it when they come back," she mused, trailing her fingertips along the edge of the blanket on her old bed. Peter's eyes shifted to the floor.

She turned to the bay window.

The seat below had a soft pad and storage underneath. Wendy knew it was filled with more books.

"That was my favorite spot in the whole house," she said, nodding to the blue-and-white-checkered seat. "I used to sit there and tell John and Michael stories before bed."

"I know," Peter said with a tired grin. "I spent a lot of nights listening to them just outside the window."

"Yeah, that's still creepy," she told him, throwing a smile over her shoulder as she walked over to Michael's bed. A small teddy bear sat slumped against the pillows. "I almost forgot about this little guy," she said. She picked it up and brushed the dust off the top of its head. "Peter, this is Fuzzy Wuzzy," she said, holding it up.

Peter gave a half bow and removed an invisible hat in greeting. "'Tis a pleasure, my good sir."

Wendy let out a small laugh and shook her head at him. She hadn't felt this close to her brothers in years. It was like they were in the room with her. She wanted to soak it all in. She couldn't even imagine how perfect it was going to be to have them home.

Wendy walked over and sat on the window seat. "Michael was in love with this thing," she said, placing the bear in her lap and moving its lumpy arms. "He took it with him everywhere. He did this weird thing where he chewed on the nose all the time, right? He did it so much that one time, when we were playing in the backyard, it popped off." She pressed a finger to the bare space where the button nose should have been. "He was in hysterics, completely inconsolable. We must've looked for it for more than an hour, but we couldn't find it."

Peter slid to sit next to her. He tucked his hands into his pockets. "All because of a nose?" he asked with an amused look on his face.

"It was very traumatic." Wendy nodded with a grin, bumping her shoulder against Peter's. "I had to come up with a story about how Fuzzy Wuzzy had lost his nose in a daring lion taming–related incident," she told him. "God, he made me tell that story at least a dozen times. Michael was always more sensitive. Then you had John, who acted like a little old man, even at ten."

"Yeah, what's all that stuff by his bed?" Peter asked, nodding toward it.

There was a collage of magazine, newspaper, and online articles printed out and tacked to the wall. "Oh, *that*," Wendy said. "John was fascinated by things that scientists and archaeologists found at the bottom of the ocean. Shipwrecks, evidence of underwater cities, stuff like that," she explained. "Whenever he found those stories, he would cut or print them out and then hang them up on the wall. He wants to be an underwater archaeologist when he grows up—or he used to, anyway. I have no idea if that's still true." Wendy frowned. It was strange to consider that her brothers had grown and changed enough that maybe she had no idea what they were like now.

"When you were little, what did you want to be when you grew up?" Peter asked. His tone was quiet, eyes locked onto Wendy's with his head tipped curiously to the side. He sucked on the puffy cut on his lip.

"A nurse, like my mom," Wendy said with a shrug. "I think most kids want to be like their parents when they grow up. And a nurse was a far more interesting option than a banker," she added with a crinkle of her nose.

"And what about now?"

"Hmm," Wendy hummed to herself, absentmindedly rubbing the bear's ear between her fingers. She thought of all the forms and pamphlets back in her room. Of the academic roadmap she'd made for a nursing degree. Of the unfinished one for premed. "I don't think I know yet," she confessed. "Maybe a doctor?" A thrill ran up her spine. It was the first time she'd said it out loud. "But I haven't decided. That's what college is for, right?"

Peter's expression fell and he busied himself with examining his palm.

"What about you?" Wendy asked, trying to bring him back.

"Me?" Peter said, furrowing his brow. He let out a small laugh that lacked any humor.

"Yeah, did you ever have dreams about growing up?" she persisted.

Peter shook his head. "No, I can't grow up—or I wasn't *supposed* to, anyway," he said, looking down at himself.

"But everyone thinks about possible futures for themselves," she said. "There wasn't anything you wanted to be? Other than just yourself?"

"No, I never had that feeling," he told her. "I was Peter Pan, the boy who never had to grow up. I got to live in Neverland and anything I could think up, I could become. A pirate, an explorer, a scuba diver," he listed, staring out the window. "Growing up meant responsibilities: school, jobs, getting old and eventually dying—"

"But you had all those lost kids to look after," Wendy pointed out. "That's a big responsibility, isn't it?"

"Yes, but it's still fun," he countered. He chewed on the inside of his cheek, thinking. "In Neverland, I could do whatever I wanted. I was free."

"But were you, Peter?" Wendy heard herself ask.

He paused and then shook his head, not understanding.

"You could do whatever you wanted, play whatever make-believe games you could come up with, but lost kids were always coming and going—you said so yourself," Wendy said. "And it was always just make-believe. Didn't you ever want something . . ." She tried to find the right words. "Real? You never felt like you were missing . . . something?"

Peter's celestial eyes locked on hers. "Not until I met you."

There was a low rush in the pit of Wendy's stomach. It was so sudden, so simply put, that she wasn't sure she had heard him right.

He watched her carefully.

Wendy shook her head, trying to think clearly.

"You . . . what?" she asked.

Peter took a deep breath. "I was fine with what I was, what it was my job to do," he told her, watching her intently. "Your mom was the first person I met who wasn't a lost kid. She was the first person who became my friend, who didn't live in Neverland with me. We would have pretend sword fights in her backyard, she would tell me stories, and I told her what it was like in Neverland. But, just like everyone else in your world, she had to grow up."

This was the most Wendy had heard about Peter and her mom. "So you couldn't visit her anymore?"

Peter nodded. "I had mostly forgotten about her after a while, too," he said. "Your mom remembered me, but she forgot that I was real. When I decided to look for her again on a whim, I found you, sitting in this window." He looked like he was struggling to find his words. The tips of his ears were tinged red, but he didn't look away, so neither did Wendy. "When I heard you telling my stories, I felt like I *had* to meet you. I wanted you to see me, to see that I was real," Peter said.

He spoke with a rushed urgency, like he was trying to explain himself.

"When my shadow first went missing, I thought it was punishment for letting myself get—get distracted by you, because I was trying to get close to you. I *wanted* to," he added insistently. Wendy's eyes momentarily snagged on his hand as it reached toward hers, then hesitated. "Then when you found me struggling with my shadow, you acted like it was completely normal, and you were the one who was able to reattach it, to sew it back on."

"But how?" Wendy interjected.

Peter shook his head. "I don't know. I thought maybe you had your own magic? There was something different about you. You *felt* different to me. Important." He cast her a sidelong glance. "Special."

Wendy's hands gripped the teddy bear in her lap tightly. Her heart fluttered in her chest.

"Then you started telling my stories less," Peter continued. He spoke faster, his words tumbling from his lips. "I could see that you were growing up, that you were going to move into your own room, become a teenager, and forget about me. When John and Michael were—" Peter let out a frustrated noise and started again. "When I found the three of you in the woods, you begged me to bring you along to Neverland, and I wanted to. I didn't want you to grow up and forget about me, too. It—" He gave her an uncertain look. "It hurt to think about."

Wendy could hardly understand him. She felt dizzy. "What are you saying?" She felt out of breath.

"You were the oldest kid ever to come to Neverland, Wendy," Peter told her. His fingers finally pressed to the inside of her wrist, heavy and warm. "It's meant for children. I think that's why I started losing my magic and Neverland began falling apart. It's my fault all of this happened . . ." His face was twisted.

"But you didn't know that would happen," Wendy said. Her body was acutely aware of him—where his hand was on hers, the way his body was angled toward her, how she was close enough to feel his body heat. The acorn pressed against the center of her chest. It felt hot.

"I went against the rules," Peter told her. "My job is to look after lost kids. I'm not supposed to interact with the others. I could watch, I could listen in when you told stories, but I wasn't supposed to approach." He paused and wetted his lips. "And then everything went wrong," he said, shaking his head. "I don't want you to hate me." He spoke slowly, deliberately.

Wendy's brows furrowed. She didn't understand what he meant, but she couldn't think through the heady fog. Wendy didn't remember leaning in, or Peter moving closer. Their shoulders pressed against each other. Peter's startling blue eyes were wide. His cheeks flushed. His fingers brushed against hers. Wendy's heart fluttered in her chest.

At first, she thought she was trembling, but it was Peter.

"You're shaking," Wendy said.

Peter's throat bobbed as he swallowed, giving a barely perceptible nod of his head.

"I thought you weren't afraid of anything?" Wendy heard herself say. She was lightheaded and breathless.

"I'm terrified," he said quietly. His starry eyes held hers and she couldn't look away. She didn't want to.

"Of what?" Wendy asked.

Peter's words brushed against her lips. "Losing you."

Wendy leaned in closer and placed a hand in the center of his chest. She could feel his heartbeat thudding against her fingertips. His palm pressed against her cheek. Her head swam as she drowned in the smell of humid jungles and salty oceans.

The acorn around her neck burned bright in the small space left between them. It gleamed in his eyes.

"Can I stay with you?" Peter whispered, ghosting over her lips.

Wendy balled the front of his shirt in her hands, pulling him to her.

There was a moment of lips pressed to lips, the taste of honeysuckle, and an unbearable lightness that made her feel like she would float away if she didn't hold on to him.

But then the window burst open, an exploding backdraft of darkness that tore them apart and threw Wendy to the ground.

CHAPTER 20

Truth

The tiny bulbs lining the room popped and burst, snuffing out the lights. The window clattered and swung violently on its hinges. Wendy tried to push herself up, but pain splintered through her head. A groan sounded at the back of her throat and the room beneath her swayed.

Peter let out a cry that snapped her out of her daze. He lay splayed on the floor a few feet away from her. His eyes were squeezed shut in a grimace. His entire body writhed in pain, fingers dragging against the floor. His back arched unnaturally. The muscles in his neck bulged and strained under his skin. His usually warm hair was dark with sweat and plastered to his forehead. His breaths sawed in and out, mixed with guttural cries.

"Peter!" Wendy got herself up and tried to run to him, but her feet wouldn't move. Her body weight pitched her forward. Her feet were caught in something like sticky black tar. She tried to tug them free, but they wouldn't budge.

High-pitched laughter filled the room and cut into her head, setting her teeth on edge. She clamped her hands over her ears.

Lounging on the window seat was the shadow. It leaned

back comfortably and smiled its jagged grin. "That was almost too easy!" it said before laughing again. With a flick of its wrist, thick black strands bound Peter's arms and legs, jerking him up. Peter cried out as he hung suspended in mid-air.

Wendy tried to lunge forward again, to get to Peter, only to fall back to her knees. "What are you doing to him?!" she demanded, her lips peeling back in a snarl. "*Let him go!*"

The shadow turned to Wendy. Its fingertips, thin and pale like bones, pressed together and drummed rhythmically. "I should really be thanking you," it said to her, its lips quirking into an angular smile. Its mouth looked like it had been carved into its face with a serrated knife.

Her face screwed up in anger and confusion.

"Wendy," Peter groaned through agonized gasps, his lips pale white. Sweat beaded his forehead. "*Run.*"

She shook her head fiercely. Fear dragged its claws over her skin, but there was no way she was leaving his side. She wouldn't let the shadow take him. "What are you talking about?" Wendy asked, turning back to it.

"Isn't it obvious?" the shadow said with a puzzled look. "Our dear Peter Pan has kissed his magic away!" It smiled fondly at Peter, pressing a skeletal hand affectionately to his heart. Peter strained against his bindings.

Wendy's heart leapt into her throat. She could see the color draining from Peter's face. Not like when someone became suddenly ill and their skin tinged green, but like his face was fading to the color of ash. Dark bruises blossomed under his eyes. Even the warm auburn of his hair started to fade. From the corner of his contorted mouth, pixie dust trickled down the side of his face. It dripped to the floor like liquid gold.

Wendy frantically tugged against the binds holding her

feet. "Peter!" she shouted. He was slipping away from her. His eyelids drooped and his head lolled to the side.

"And it's all because of you, Wendy," the shadow crooned. It stood and walked over to Peter. It dragged a finger along his cheek, smearing the liquid light between its bony fingers.

Peter's face contorted in pain, a low groan sounding from deep in his chest.

"Don't touch him!" Wendy spat.

The shadow turned to her and wagged a disapproving finger. "Now, now, there's no need for impoliteness," it gently scolded her before holding its hands out at its sides. "I'm trying to *thank* you!"

The muscles in Wendy's face twitched. She didn't care what the shadow was or what it could do to her. All she wanted was to get it away from Peter.

And rip that smile off its face.

"What are you talking about?"

"*Feelings*, Wendy," it said. Wendy's resolve wavered for a moment, but she steeled herself, refusing to let it distract her. "From the very first time he saw you, he felt something for you. Something that kept luring him away from his responsibilities, from Neverland. It's you, Wendy, who has brought the great Peter Pan to his knees." The shadow began to walk in a slow circle around her, his black eyes hungry.

The hairs on the back of her neck prickled.

"I could see what was happening, of course, though he was far too oblivious," it drawled. "With each visit to hear you tell those silly stories about him, I could feel him growing weaker. It was thanks to you, Wendy, and his feelings for you, that I grew more powerful.

"You see, Peter Pan is the embodiment of all things good, and light, and joyous." It spoke with a disgusted sneer. "Peter never had reason for a bad thought or worry. His existence was simple—take care of the lost children and bring them happiness. That was all that was required of him! He never had reason to want to leave Neverland, to abandon his duty, his sole purpose of being, until he met you." Thunderous laughter rolled through the room. "But the very first time he laid eyes on you, I could feel it." The shadow's hands clenched into fists.

"It was disgusting really, how he couldn't stop thinking about you, but it wore on his resolve, and I could feel him waver. I even nearly succeeded once! Dear Peter couldn't help himself. I took the chance to escape, while he snuck off to see you, his heart aching with the need."

It was a memory that had been lost for so long. How she'd awoken to Peter in her room, upset and wrestling with his shadow. How she'd helped him sew it back on. That was the reason Peter thought she could put an end to it now.

How wrong they both had been.

"Alas, I was premature, I'll admit, but not this time. I waited and let the feelings fester. The more he thought about you, the more he missed you and ached with longing, the stronger I became. And then finally, my opportunity came! Peter wanted to keep you, and he broke the rules. He brought you to Neverland, but you were no lost child, Wendy, not like your brothers."

Wendy glowered at the shadow, her face pinching in confusion. She still didn't understand. She looked at Peter, but he was barely conscious, his breaths coming sharp and shallow. His blue eyes tried to find hers, but they kept losing focus.

The shadow floated across the room in long, languid steps. It stooped over Wendy and clutched her chin with its sharp fingers. She tried to wrench herself free of its grip, but it was cold and strong as iron. The air around it drained the warmth from her skin, tickling the hair on her arms.

"*Don't touch her.*" The breathless growl was Peter's. Teeth clenched tight, he struggled against his restraints, shoulders lurching as his arms pulled and flexed, trying to break free. But it was no use.

The shadow kept all of its focus sharp on Wendy, but it closed its hand into a fist. The black ropes wrapped tighter around Peter, biting into his skin. An anguished cry ripped from his throat.

"*Stop!*" Wendy shouted in the shadow's face. "Let him go!" She hated the panic and pleading in her voice, but how much longer would Peter be able to stand this torture?

Slowly, a triumphant smile stretched across the shadow's lips, splitting its twisted face in half. "I know Peter's deepest, darkest secrets," it said, its low voice reverberating through Wendy's bones. "Because I *am* those secrets. I am the consummation of his fears."

It released Wendy's chin. Her cheeks burned from where its sharp nails had bitten into her skin.

"His fears were about losing you. He was afraid of what you might think of him. That you would hate him and never want to see him again if you knew the truth."

She couldn't trust what it was saying. Everything it did, it did with purpose, to gain the upper hand. Wendy could see that now, and she wouldn't let it consume her, even when she felt the panic coursing through her veins. "What *truth?*" she spat, but it continued on as if it hadn't heard her.

"His fear gave me strength, and *finally*, I was able to escape the confines of our bond. But"—it turned back to Wendy—"as long as Peter had his magic, he posed a risk. It was a simple plan, and he fell for it so easily." The shadow laughed. "To further weaken his resolve, I just had to lead him back to you, and Peter did the rest. He missed you when you were gone."

Wendy's throat was tight. She was terrified, but the words sent her stomach tumbling.

"It left him heartbroken, really. He *wanted* to choose you, Wendy. All I had to do was present him with the opportunity." The shadow tutted disapprovingly. "So, I led him here, dropped him right in front of you for you to find. Peter's weakness for you was his undoing."

Wendy choked on her own breath. The guilt was crushing. The sticky blackness oozed up Wendy's legs and climbed up her arms. Her brothers, the other missing children, and Peter, ensnared and in pain—it was all because of her.

"Don't get me wrong, the fear of those children has given me plenty of strength, as well. And I admit, your fear and guilt are especially"—it inhaled a deep, rattling breath—"delicious. You're such easy prey. All I have to do is lure you into these woods and it just pours from you. The scars of trauma are just so mouthwatering.

"But it's Peter I've been after. He chose you, and, by doing so, he has abandoned the lost children and has been stripped of his magic. So, lost children they will remain."

Peter's eyes bulged and glistened, frantic and scared. "*No,*" he groaned, fighting his restraints with renewed vigor. "I need to go back—I need to help them!" The words rushed from Peter's lips as he struggled, muttering as if to himself.

The shadow laughed.

Wendy could feel herself sinking deeper into the tarlike blackness, as if it were pulling her through the floor. Wendy's entire body trembled, her breaths ragged and tasting of salt. Sticky tendrils snaked across her thighs and up her arms. Tension swelled, pushing against her ribs, expanding like a balloon. It ached and burned. It felt like it would break at any moment.

"Where are the children you took?" Wendy demanded, refusing to give in to the shaking creature in her chest. "Bring them back!" She tried to wrench herself free but only sank deeper into the oozing blackness.

The shadow threw its head back. Screeching laughter filled the room. "They were merely pawns to get to you, Wendy! Haven't you put it together yet? Haven't you remembered? Hasn't he told you?" it asked, peering at her through narrowed eyes. Its face—Peter's face, but cruel and dark and distorted—held sick glee in every sharp angle.

She heard its words, but they didn't fit together in her head. She couldn't make sense of it or of the plummeting sensation in her gut, as if it knew before she did. Wendy wanted to rage and scream. "Bring my brothers back!" Her voice quaked and broke.

"Oh, Wendy." Its grin was cruel, its chuckle amused. "I don't have your brothers. I never did."

Wendy froze. *What?* She shook her head. The shadow was lying, of course it was lying. It wanted her to be frightened. It was trying to mess with her head. Wendy looked at Peter for answers, but he didn't meet her gaze. His attention was locked on the shadow. The muscles in his jaw bulged.

The shadow leaned in close. It smiled as if reading her mind. Its breath reeked of decaying leaves and the thick must of wet dirt. "Lost children are the souls of children who have lost their way. Peter is their guide."

"Guide?" Wendy repeated. Confusion and panic ripped through her body. She felt dizzy. She couldn't breathe. She shook so violently, she was nearly convulsing. It was like her body knew what was coming but her brain couldn't keep up.

"It's his job to ease their suffering, to help them become unafraid so they can pass on."

Her breath became sharp and frantic. Wendy shook her head. "Peter, what is it talking about?" she asked.

But the look on Peter's face . . .

This was just a nightmare. She wanted it to stop. She wanted to wake up in her bed and for this not to be real. She thrashed against the tendrils as they gripped her tighter.

"Wendy—" Peter voice was pleading and weak.

"No, don't," she said feebly, shaking her head. Wendy tugged, and the tendrils stretched taut as she tried to stand, tried to run away. They purred and flooded over her skin, excited and hungry. As Wendy struggled to her feet, they tightened around her torso and clawed toward her neck.

"You have to understand—" Peter pressed.

"*Don't.*" Wendy's stomach gave a nauseated twist. No. No no no.

"I—" A black gag twisted around his mouth, silencing Peter with a choke. He fought against his restraints with renewed vigor. His back arched and the muscles in his arms strained. His eyes sparked, frantic and rimmed with red.

"Allow me to help explain," the shadow said. "After all, *I've* been completely honest with you since we've met," it pointed out with a lift of its eyebrows. "Peter guides the souls of dead children to the afterlife. When they've died in a particularly horrible way"—the shadow made an exaggerated cringe—"he takes them to Neverland." It was talking so plainly, so simply. Loss fell on her like a heavy weight, threatening to pull her to the floor. "It's like a sort of limbo, really. Where dead kids go and come to terms with what happened to them, and then they can cross over."

The shadow leaned forward, catching Wendy's chin in its

icy grip. It inhaled deeply and its eyelids fluttered, savoring the fear as it poured from her. It spoke slowly and deliberately, savoring each word as it hit her. "Which is exactly what he did with your brothers. When he saw you next to their bodies, *begging* him to let you go with your brothers, he caved in. But live girls don't belong in Neverland, Wendy," it said.

"Your brothers have been stuck in Neverland ever since, unable to move on, too worried about *you*." It released her chin and gave her a gentle pat on the cheek. "So, here we find ourselves. Peter, without his magic, and you, without your brothers as they spend the rest of eternity stuck between this world and the next." It steepled its fingers together and looked back and forth between the two, simply beside itself with glee.

No, this wasn't possible. It couldn't be true. Peter wouldn't lie to her. He'd told her they were trapped, that he and Wendy only needed to defeat the shadow and they would be released. Her eyes searched out Peter's for answers. "Is it true, Peter?" she asked. Her voice broke. Her vision blurred. "Are my brothers dead?"

The shadow snapped its fingers and the gag around Peter's mouth disappeared. He gulped down air. He could barely meet her gaze. His face was racked with guilt, his eyes glassy. It was impossible to tell where the pain in his voice came from. "I'm so sorry, Wendy."

The words hit her like a final blow, knocking her to her knees. She couldn't stand, she couldn't think, she couldn't breathe. The ache in her chest was catastrophic, like being ripped in half. The hole gaped, and all of her grief spilled forth with uncontrollable force. The shadows swelled over her bowed shoulders. "How could you?"

"You have to understand, I needed your help to save those

kids—to protect them," he pleaded, the words tumbling from his lips. "You were the only one who could help me, you—"

With another snap of its fingers, the shadow returned the gag to Peter's mouth. "And there you have it," it announced triumphantly.

Tears flowed freely down her cheeks.

They're dead.

The words repeated themselves in her head, over and over. The shadows cascaded around her like a blanket of oil. She could feel them reaching up her neck. "The missing children?" Wendy managed to choke out the question through her grief. Were they all dead, too?

"Oh, no," the shadow said dismissively as it examined its long fingernails. "They're still alive, but not for long." That terrible smile cut across its face. "Now that I have what I want, with no Peter to stand in my way, there's no need for them anymore." It sighed wistfully. "It will be *delicious*," it purred. "While your suffering is also quite delectable," the shadow's voice whispered in her ear, "I'm afraid Peter and I have some other matters to attend to. Good-bye, Wendy Darling."

She couldn't move, but she didn't need to look up to know that Peter and his shadow were gone. Wendy lay curled up on her side. The feel of the rough carpet against her cheek told her the shadows had vanished with them. She remained on the floor and wept, heavy sobs shaking her body. Her fingers dug into the carpet, trying to ground herself while everything around her spun out of control.

Her brothers were gone. John and Michael were dead. She would never see them again. There was no hope for their return. And she had seen their bodies. She had been next to them when Peter found them.

What had happened? Why couldn't she remember?

Tears spilled across the bridge of her nose, trickling across her cheek.

A part of her must have always known, even if it was her subconscious. Whenever she got close to the truth, a part of her always pulled away. Was that what her mother had meant? She didn't remember because her mind had made her forget? Her body was trying to protect her by hiding the memory away?

She couldn't keep hiding.

With a shaky hand, Wendy gripped the acorn around her neck, pressing it into her palm. She squeezed her eyes shut. She needed to remember.

Wendy was in a different place and time. She was in the woods, but surrounded by a haze. She was running through the trees, searching.

"John, Michael!" Wendy could hear the words of her younger self from her own mouth. "Where are you?"

"Over here!" John answered back.

Branches slapped lightly against her palms as she pushed them out of the way. Up ahead, she should hear her brothers' voices. She entered a clearing to find John and Michael, exactly as she remembered them. They chased each other around the base of the old, pale tree, which was still gnarled and gaunt as it loomed over her brothers.

Nana, their old St. Bernard, loped around them in circles, her tail swishing, her jowls flopping with thick drool.

Fear rose in Wendy's chest at the sight of the tree, but the forms of Michael and John laughed and ran. Snow crunched under their shoes.

John raised his arms over his head and let out a strange animalistic sound, lumbering back and forth as he stomped after

Michael and Nana. In return, Michael bared his teeth. "I'm not afraid of yooou!" he howled, and Nana joined in.

John began to laugh but then resumed his howling.

He chased Michael around the tree again, Nana fast on his heels.

"Don't leave me behind like that!" Wendy huffed. Nana greeted her with a slobbery, warm lick on her palm. "I couldn't keep up!" Wendy reached down and scratched Nana behind her large, velvety ear. She looked back over her shoulder. "We should head back. I don't know—"

A bang rang out through the trees.

Wendy jumped. Nana recoiled. Michael's small hands clamped over his ears.

John collapsed.

There was a moment of stillness as the echoes of the shot faded.

"John?" Michael stepped toward where John's body lay in a heap.

Nana whined at Wendy's side.

"Wait—" Wendy said, but before she could finish, another bang rang out.

Michael dropped to the ground.

Twelve-year-old Wendy didn't move. Her chest heaved, her breath ragged. Nana whined more urgently, on the verge of a yelp.

Wendy stared at her brothers. "John?" She stepped closer. "Michael?" Neither boy moved or spoke.

John lay on his back, his legs bent at odd angles. Michael was curled up on his side.

Their eyes stared, open but unseeing.

"Stop playing, you guys. This isn't funny," Wendy said as she crept closer to them.

Crouched low, Nana inched ahead, snuffling at the ground. Her paws crunched in the snow. She nosed Michael's limp arm.

Red blossomed on the chest of his shirt.

It spilled from John's neck, pooling and melting through the snow.

A sob caught in Wendy's throat.

Nana crooned, nudging and butting John and Michael, circling and crying. Red caught in her creamy fur.

Wendy stood there, frozen on the spot. Standing in the snow, staring at her fallen brothers, her entire body began to quake.

The sound of feet stomping through the woods made Wendy jump, shaking her from her trance. She looked around frantically before running behind a set of trees standing closely together. She crawled under the large shrubs at their base.

Nana ran frantically back and forth between John and Michael, her tail tucked between her legs.

A man in a bright red plaid flannel jacket stumbled into the clearing. He wore a fur-lined hunter's hat. A rifle was slung over his back. His back was to Wendy, but she could see a beer bottle gripped in his hand.

Nana placed herself square between the man and John and Michael. Sweet Nana, usually so gentle and doting, bared her teeth and growled.

"Nana?" the man asked. His voice was familiar, confused. "'Ey, get outta here," he slurred, kicking up snow at Nana. Nana flinched but refused to move. With snapping jaws, she began to bark fiercely.

"HEY!" the man shouted this time. He stuck his beer bottle in the snow and removed the rifle from his shoulder.

Terror locked up every muscle in Wendy's body.

But he aimed it into the sky and shot off another round. The shell spun through the air and fell to the snow.

Nana recoiled and bolted out of the clearing.

"Dumb dog," the man grumbled, hitching the gun back onto

his shoulder as Nana ran away. "Gonna get yourself shot runnin' 'round like that." With a large hand, he swiped the hat off his head.

Cold shock crashed over Wendy, robbing her of breath.

Mr. Davies wiped the sweat from his brow on the sleeve of his red plaid flannel. "What've we got," he mumbled to himself as he walked up to the old tree.

He stopped suddenly. John's and Michael's bodies lay slumped on the ground before him.

Mr. Davies fell to his knees. "No! No, no, no!" His voice was much clearer now, pitched with horror. He shook John and Michael, but they didn't stir. He muttered to himself as he looked around wildly.

Wendy hunkered lower in her hiding spot, stuffing her hands against her mouth to stifle herself.

Mr. Davies struggled to his feet and, tripping over himself, ran back in the direction he had come from.

When the footsteps faded, Wendy crawled out from her hiding spot and rushed to her brothers. "John, Michael!" She collapsed beside them and shook them as hard as she could. "Wake up!" she pleaded. "Please, wake up!" Wendy doubled over. Her body shook with violent sobs. The cold, hard ground pressed painfully into her knees.

Wendy had never felt so powerless. Saliva pooled in her mouth and she thought she might vomit from the sheer horror of reliving her younger self weeping over the bodies of her dead brothers. She felt the urge to run away, to pull back and refuse to let herself see the rest, but there was more noise in the underbrush.

Peter descended through the trees, swiftly flying down to land a few feet from where Wendy cowered. It was the same version of Peter that she'd seen in her memories of Neverland. A young boy with wild auburn hair, dressed in clothes made of thick leaves.

He saw Wendy crying over the bodies of her brothers and froze. "Wendy?" he said.

Wendy looked up, tears streaming down her face. Recognition struck her in her heart, desperation quick on its heels. "Peter, help, please help!" she begged through sobs.

Peter slowly moved to Wendy's side, his eyes wide and bright. He looked at John and Michael. Gently, he shook his head. "Wendy, I'm so sorry . . ."

"Please, help them, Peter!" she cried.

"I can't, Wendy. I have to take them with me," he said, his expression pained.

Wendy sobbed harder. Her voice cracked. "No, you can't! You can't take John and Michael away!"

The sound of approaching footsteps made her and Peter look up again.

Wendy began to panic. "He's coming back! Please don't leave me here alone. You have to take me with you! Please, Peter!"

Wendy saw the mournful look on Peter's face. He took her hand, and everything plunged into blackness.

Grief was sharp and all-consuming. Wendy lay curled on her side. The image of her brothers lying in the snow, red pooling on white, burned through her mind. They had fallen at the base of the tree. That was why her subconscious kept reminding her, making her hands draw it with such urgency. It was trying to make her remember, and Wendy saw now why she'd fought so hard against it. She had been hiding from it, but she couldn't escape being haunted, and now she feared she never would.

Her brothers had been killed, and it was all her fault.

She was their older sister. She had known they weren't supposed to go off into the woods on their own. If she had said something, if she had made them turn back sooner, none of this would've happened. They would still be alive. She was supposed to take care of them and protect them, but she'd failed. And failing meant losing her brothers and, even worse, destroying her family. If it weren't for her, they'd still be whole.

And now? Not if, but when they found out, they would truly see it was Wendy's fault.

For years, they'd been left not knowing, all because Wendy couldn't face the truth. Had she really been lying to herself this whole time?

Wendy curled up tight. She buried her face in her knees and her fingers in her hair. Her sobs wracked her body, primal and uncontrollable.

She thought of Mr. Davies, drunk and stumbling on John and Michael in his bright red jacket.

Mr. Davies. She could hardly believe it. He'd shot John and Michael. He'd killed them, and all this time, he'd never confessed. It made her sick, thinking of how kind he had been to her growing up—checking in on her, tipping her extra when she watched his sons in order to save up for college. Had he been trying to make up for what he did?

Anger smoldered between Wendy's ribs. He was her father's *friend*. Mr. Davies had allowed her and her parents to suffer. Their mourning had dragged on for five years. He'd not only robbed them of John and Michael, but he'd kept them from knowing the truth and finding closure. It had torn her family apart.

She wasn't the only one who John and Michael had been ripped away from. Her parents had suffered, too, and still did. Wendy hadn't just lost her brothers. She'd lost the soothing touch of her mother rubbing her back when she was sad.

She'd lost her father, firm but gentle, talking her through her worries and nightmares. Now, her mother and father were just ghosts of their previous selves. The Darling home had lost its light and laughter. Wendy's childhood had ended the day she and her brothers went into the woods.

And now, four more families would suffer the way hers had. Four more families would mourn the loss of their children without any answers or explanation. Five more children would be lost, taken and kept by the shadow, terrified and fed off of to give it strength.

Two of them were Mr. Davies's own sons. Wendy wanted to be glad for it—to be comforted that he would be forced to go through what he'd put her family through—but she couldn't manage it. Matthew and Joel were good boys. They didn't deserve to be locked in a nightmare for the rest of their lives for something their father did. As mad as she was, as furious and vengeful as she felt toward Mr. Davies, she couldn't bring herself to wish the suffering she and her parents had gone through on anyone, not even her worst enemy. She knew *all* of the missing children, and she knew their families.

She couldn't stand by and let more families suffer. She wouldn't.

Wendy refused to give up on them, and she refused to give up on Peter.

She pushed herself to a sitting position, hiccups bucking her chest as she dragged her hand across her eyes.

Peter had lied to her, but he was trying to save the lost children in Neverland. It was an even more important job than Wendy had realized. What was it like, to see the suffering of children? To be there to guide the souls of children who'd met such horrific ends? To try to coax them from their fear, to bring them happiness so they could pass through to the other side? Peter was trying to take care of them as best he could. Wendy had just gotten in the way.

No wonder everything on the island had begun to fall apart. Wendy had been the only living girl in Neverland.

And Peter had developed feelings for her.

Wendy's stomach fluttered and she pressed her fingertips to her lips. The memory of the look on Peter's face, so scared and anxious as he leaned in close, flooded warmth through her entire body. She thought of his shining eyes. The way they squinted when his smile claimed his face, wide and unabashed. Wendy thought of his gentleness with Alex, his playfulness with Cassidy, and his steady, unwavering gaze when he talked to Wendy.

She needed to make everything right. She needed to stop the shadow and rescue the children. She needed to save Peter. Without him, the lost kids in Neverland would stay lost. Her brothers would never be able to move on.

Wendy was terrified, but she wouldn't give up. She would not fail John and Michael this time. Struggling to her feet, she stumbled into the bathroom. The sewing kit sat on the edge of the tub where she'd left it when she'd mended her jeans a few days ago. She snatched it up and stuffed it into her pocket.

A deep, steadying breath filled her lungs. She squeezed the acorn around her neck tight in her fist.

No matter what it took, Wendy would put an end to this nightmare. She would fight.

CHAPTER 21

Lost in the Never Woods

Wendy raced through the woods. Jumping over the fence and plunging into the trees had been like running headfirst into a whole new world. A dark one made of gnarled trees, undulating shadows, and the sounds of *things* she couldn't see.

Her heart thudded an erratic rhythm, drums pounding in her veins. Branches groaned and swayed. Gusts of wind dragged cold fingers through her hair. The speed with which she threw herself through the trees was the only thing that kept her feet from tangling in gripping vines or sinking into the ground as it shifted and rolled.

The shadow's magic seeped through the woods and unmade them, contorting them into a nightmare, and it was only growing more powerful with each step. As adrenaline surged in her veins, so did the black shapes in her peripheral vision.

They galloped and screamed, pushing in close, snapping at her heels. They swarmed as if sniffing her out, closing in like hungry beasts. They crowded her as if trying to herd her off course, but Wendy kept running, urging herself to move faster when they got too close.

It was as if the moon and stars had been blown out.

Nothing looked familiar. She couldn't tell where she was or where she was going. She had no idea if she was getting closer, or if the deteriorating woods were twisting in on themselves and running her in circles. She refused to let the movements in the corner of her eyes distract her.

Instinct was the only thing leading Wendy through the woods. They were unrecognizable, but her feet led her between trees, over fallen logs and under low-hanging branches. Her body knew the path like muscle memory, even if her mind didn't.

Every noise slipping between the trees ran over her skin. A rattling inhale brushed the nape of her neck. An unnatural scream of a buck jolted her spine. A cacophony of screaming owls dragged cold nails across her stomach. Wendy's breaths came in heavy pants. Her hair stuck to her lips. Her heart raced. She couldn't turn back. She couldn't stop. She needed to find Peter. She needed to get to the children before it was too late.

Wendy pushed herself forward and burst into a clearing. She skidded to a stop, kicking up dirt and leaves. The string tugging at her chest that had pulled her through the woods vanished, as if suddenly cut.

Looming before her stood the tree. The darkness made it look even more towering. Shadows caught in the crags like deep scars in its graying, fleshy bark.

"Wendy!"

Her chest heaved, a moment of relief like a shot through her body. "Oh my God, I found you." The words were choked as she rushed over.

Benjamin, Ashley, Matthew, Joel, and even little Alex huddled together in some kind of cage. They were a little worse for the wear—with tousled hair, faces smudged with dirt, and grimy clothes—but they were all in one piece and alive.

"Wendy, help!" Ashley cried, cheeks red, tears spilling down her pale face.

"*Please!*" said Benjamin, his voice jumping with a sob as he pulled on the bars.

"Shh, shh, it's okay. I'll get you out of here," Wendy croaked.

Of course, they were not normal bars. Not a normal cage. It was made of the same undulating shadow tendrils that had tried to ensnare her twice. The ones that had wrapped Peter in their binds.

Wendy gripped them in her fists and pulled hard. They had little give and pulsed against her palms like a grotesque heartbeat.

"You have to get us out!" Joel pleaded. Matthew huddled against his older brother's side, his fingers knotted into Joel's shirt as he wailed.

Their voices tumbled over one another, begging and pleading, except for Alex. His entire body, drowning in his large blue hoodie, quaked violently. He reached an arm out for Wendy, his tear-stained cheek pressing against a bar, trying to shove himself through. Wendy caught his tiny hand as it swiped helplessly through the air. It was cold and clammy in her palms.

"It's okay, it's okay," she said over and over, her voice tight and betraying her own fear as she tried to console them. Crouching down, she met Alex's wide brown eyes. "It'll be all right. I'll get you out," she said, cupping Alex's cheek in her hand. He turned his face into her palm. Sobs jerked through his tiny body.

"I'll get you *all* out," she stressed. "I just—I just—"

"We really must stop meeting like this. It's starting to get annoying."

The shadow sprawled out on a thick branch, one leg dangling. Its eyes were narrowed into slits as it stared down at Wendy. All traces of its earlier venomous mirth had vanished.

"Let them go," Wendy demanded, pulling herself away from their prison. Sniffles and whimpers sounded behind her. "I won't let you hurt them."

"*Hurt* them?" Its dark eyebrows furrowed. "I need them alive and *frightened*. It's the mental and emotional suffering I'm after." Its gaze shifted down to the children. With a twirl of its wrist, a shudder of air rolled through the trees. The very corner of its lip peeled back from its teeth. "However, I am growing quite tired of this game of cat and mouse, Wendy." It flicked her a hollow stare. "It's not fun anymore."

"*Wendy*," Ashley squeaked.

"I'm not going anywhere." Wendy took a step closer to the tree and firmly planted her feet on the ground. "Where's Peter?" she said. Her legs shook, but at least her voice sounded steady.

"Peter?" The shadow yawned, bony joints popping as it stretched on the branch. "Oh, he's a bit tied up at the moment." A wicked smile twisted its lips. A long finger pointed somewhere above her head.

Wendy looked up.

Suspended in mid-air was Peter.

Thick, ropy shadows hung from one of the gnarled branches of the great tree. They snaked around his waist, pulling his back in an unnatural arch. More shadows twisted around his arms and legs and up his throat. They pulsed and thrummed, draining him of his light.

Peter's skin was nearly colorless. The rich red and brown of his auburn hair had faded. Now it was ghostly silver, the color of starlight. Thin lines of gold, liquid magic, ran from Peter's nose and the corners of his parted gray lips. He didn't move or speak. His eyes were closed, his deep-purple eyelids barely fluttering. A single drop of gold rolled from his eyelashes and ran into the silvery hair at his temple.

A sharp inhale caught in Wendy's throat. "Peter."

"It's just a matter of time before Peter Pan is no more," the shadow said slowly, as if savoring the taste of each word.

Anger burned inside her. "Why are you doing this?" Wendy snarled.

"Why?" the shadow asked. Its eyes narrowed to black slits. "*Why?*" It was no longer relaxed and enjoying itself. It stood up, its body growing rigid. The ground beneath her feet began to quiver. "Shadows and darkness used to rule over man with fear," it told her. "Then light magic began to take over, like Peter. He was created to be my opposite, to bring joy and laughter," the shadow spat, its lips curling back over its gleaming teeth. "Peter took care of the lost souls of the children that I used to torment!"

Its booming voice thundered deep within her chest. A chill snaked up her bare arms. She heard the frightened cries behind her. Wendy squared her shoulders, firmly placing herself between the children locked in their cage and the shadow perched in the tree.

"He brought them peace, and soon there wasn't enough suffering for me to feed on. I grew weak and was bound to him!" The limbs of the tree shuddered. The shadow rolled its shoulders and popped its neck. It closed its eyes for a moment and took a deep breath. "But all of that will be over soon," it said calmly with a grin. "I will destroy your precious Peter, and nothing will be able to stop me."

With a flick of the shadow's wrist, the black tendrils holding up Peter snapped. His body fell to the ground with a heavy thud. His arms sprawled out on either side of him like broken wings.

"Peter!" Wendy ran and fell to her knees at his side. "Peter, open your eyes, you need to wake up," she said, frantically shaking his shoulder. She pressed her palm to the side of his face. Her thumb grazed the gold trailing from the corners of his mouth. It was warm and sticky against his icy, pale skin.

He was so pale—was he still alive?

Peter groaned, a guttural sound from deep in his chest.

Something between a sob and a sigh of relief burst past Wendy's lips. His chest rose and fell in quick, shallow breaths. "Wendy?" He tried to open his eyes to look at her, but they kept rolling back into his head, unfocused. The cobalt starlight had vanished from them, replaced with nothing but yawning black pupils. His hand, heavy and with little control, fell to the side of her face. His cold fingers pressed into her cheek, his palm on the hammering pulse at her neck. "No," he moaned, thick with grief, catching on a sob. "You have to—you have to get them out of here." Peter's eyes tried to find Benjamin, Ashley, Matthew, Joel, and Alex in their cage. "You have to take care of them." Another shuddering breath. Peter's face crumpled. "I'm sorry, I'm so sorry," he murmured.

Wendy put her hand over his and squeezed it tight. "It'll be okay, you'll be okay," she told him. A hot tear fell from her chin. "You just have to hang on, okay?" She couldn't lose him, she wouldn't. But how could she possibly stop the shadow on her own?

"This is actually quite poetic!" the shadow announced. It smiled, pleased with itself. "You'll be able to watch as I suck dry what's left of Peter, and his last thoughts will be of how he failed to save you," it cooed. Its black, hollow eyes shifted to the children, who shrank back from the bars. "Mmmm." Craning its back, it inhaled deeply through its nose, mouth splitting into a wicked smile as it refocused on the children. "*Delicious.*"

Peter's eyes were wide and pleading. He was too weak to say anything more. His hand chased after Wendy as she pulled away.

With one last look at Peter, Wendy stood and turned to face the shadow. "He doesn't need to save me." She planted her feet, placing herself between Peter and the trapped kids, and the shadow in its tree. Her hands clenched into fists at her sides. "I won't let you take any of them from me," Wendy said, raising her voice.

Small, panicked voices rose behind her.

"Wendy!"

"*Don't!*"

The shadow threw back its head and let out a screeching laugh. "You are *terrified*!" the shadow howled with cruel mirth. Its smile stretched, peeling back over sharp teeth, ear to ear. "I can smell it on you, Wendy Darling. It spills from your eyes and seeps from your skin."

It was right. Her knees shook, her eyes burned and she was drenched in a cold sweat, but she refused to back down. "I won't let you hurt them anymore!" she shouted at the shadow.

A low growl grew in the shadow's throat. "You dare try to stand up to me?" its voice boomed. Shadows swirled and circled the base of the tree.

"You think you're so powerful, but all you do is go around frightening little kids!" Wendy shouted.

"Wendy Darling," the shadow growled. "You can't save any of them, just like you couldn't save your brothers!"

The words shook her to her core, but she remained standing.

"Because of you, they're doomed to wander the in-between, unable to rest or find peace!"

Her brothers' cries filled the air. Wendy tried to find them, but their cries for help swirled with the building shadows, circling her and pressing in.

"Your own mother and father can hardly even look at you!" the shadow shouted. "You are nothing but a reminder of what they lost!"

Dark thoughts invaded Wendy's mind. The closed door to her old room. The muffled sound of her mother crying in the bathroom. The reek of alcohol coming off her father as he slumped over his desk. Wind whipped through her hair, which slapped against her cheeks.

"John and Michael were killed because of you, Wendy Darling." The words struck her like a kick in the gut. Wendy staggered.

Under the haunting voices, Wendy could still hear Ashley's and Benjamin's voices calling to her. Through the swarm of shadows circling her, she could barely make them out. The cage was beginning to fade, the bars quivering and thinning as the shadows were sucked into the smoky vortex around her.

The shadows were converging, forgetting about the trapped kids in order to rain horrors—terrible memories and the cries of John and Michael—down on Wendy. She watched as the kids tugged on the bars. Matthew had nearly gotten himself through, closely followed by Joel.

Good—if the shadows were distracted enough by her, then maybe the kids could run away. The thought gave her a small swell of determination. Wendy's body shook violently, she was hardly able to stay on her feet. She could feel the shadows closing in now. Could feel them pooling at her feet and winding around her legs. Could feel them filling the gaping void in her chest.

"Give up, Wendy." The words echoed through her mind. The shadows clawed at the base of her throat.

Wendy tried to reach out for more happy memories as bad thoughts struck her in a barrage. She thought of the waterfall and the lagoon. She thought of Peter's dimpled smile, the drip of water hanging from the tip of his nose.

She made herself think of breakfasts when she was little. Of her and her brothers plunging their fingers into a bowl of pancake batter as her mother laughed in front of the stove. Of her father chasing them around the backyard on cool autumn days.

The ground quaked beneath her feet. The wind slapped her cheeks and pulled her hair. Wendy curled against it. Terrible screams filled her ears. The shadows vibrated against her skin. They were unrelenting. Through the swarm of darkness, she could see the last remnants of the cage fall away, could just make out the children being freed before everything plunged into darkness.

The images of her murdered brothers cascaded over Wendy. Hot tears spilled down her cheeks. The voices in her head roared.

Gone. Dead. Murdered. Your fault. Your fault. YOUR FAULT.

Wendy tried to hold on to the memory of her brothers lying on their backs—not on the cold snowy ground, but in their backyard on prickly grass as they stared up at the stars on a clear summer night. She held on to the memory of her parents sitting on lawn chairs and drinking lemonade as she and her brothers ran through the sprinklers.

Wendy remembered Michael careening into her chest. She stumbled back a step. She could practically feel it, his tiny body running into hers, his small arms wrapping around her middle. Wendy felt another thump, this time against her back. John, joining in the embrace.

A sob bucked in Wendy's chest. She could remember it. She could practically feel them holding on tight. John's face tucked against her shoulder. Michael's downy hair under her fingertips. The sensations were so real.

Too real.

Wendy opened her eyes.

The shadows continued to swirl and screech, but—

She looked down. Wendy's fingers laced through soft brown curls. A jolt shot through her. *Michael?* His arms were locked tightly around her, his head tucked against her side.

Tears swelled in Wendy's eyes, blurring her vision as her hand cradled the top of his head. From behind, arms encircled her waist, holding on tight.

John? Blindly, Wendy reached back, trying to grip his side.

Electricity ran through her body as she tried to hold on to them, to drag them closer even though their grip on her was so tight, she could hardly take a full breath.

Wendy's hands scrambled for a tighter hold. *They were alive.* Her fingers caught the back of Michael's thick hoodie—

She froze.

His . . . hoodie?

Wendy looked down, squinting against the battering wind.

A blue hoodie that nearly swallowed him whole.

She realized there were more than two of them. Wendy stood surrounded by quaking bodies, encircled by desperate hands and arms. Benjamin, Ashley, and Matthew huddled against Wendy, their backs to the howling shadows.

Joel, not John, braced himself against her back.

It wasn't Michael hugging her, but Alex, terrified and trembling.

The cage had weakened, and they had broken out. They'd escaped, and, instead of running away, they'd run to Wendy. They were trying to protect her.

They were trying to keep her safe.

Before her, the shadow contorted and howled. It swelled and grew.

Wendy was afraid, but she wasn't giving up. Peter had said that in order to stop the shadow, she needed to reattach it to him.

The tree shook as the cruel version of Peter morphed into a mass of twisting shadows and claws.

She'd done it before, she'd do it again.

The shadow sprang forward. A gaping mouth formed at its center, revealing sharp white teeth as long as fingers, protruding in jagged angles.

Arms splintered and lashed out at Wendy, ensnaring her arms and grabbing at the children. But Wendy grabbed back.

She snatched the sticky tendrils, wrenching them from the children and gathering them in her fists. Gritting her teeth, Wendy tugged hard.

The shadow flickered, its distorted face almost looking surprised.

"I'm putting you back where you belong!" Wendy shouted.

The shadow's cavernous mouth opened wide and let out a roar that shook Wendy's bones, but she didn't back down. Quickly, she coiled the ends of the shadow in her hands, reaching and pulling.

Everything shifted. The shadows that had ensnared Wendy were now trying to wrench free of her hold. They jerked Wendy forward, but she refused to let go.

Suddenly, there were more hands. Joel, Matthew, Benjamin, Ashley, even little Alex—they gathered fistfuls of the shadow, trying to help her reel it in.

The wretched creature collapsed on the ground.

"Don't let go!" Wendy shouted. The children scrambled, tugging and pulling as the shadow stretched.

But it was growing weak. It began to shrink and turn sinewy in her hands.

Tendrils reached out for the base of the tree. Claws dragged at the earth, trying to slip between gnarled roots. It was trying to run away.

Wendy threw herself forward and snatched at the retreating shadow. It was melting into a thick taffy. She plunged her fingers into the ooze as it tried to slip away. Wendy looped it around her hand, reeling it in as it let out another screech.

Ashley yelped and all five of them sprang back, giving Wendy room.

She wrestled the shadow to Peter's side. Gradually, it was becoming weaker, fighting against Wendy less and less as it pooled at Peter's feet.

"Peter?" With one hand holding on to the shadow, Wendy dug her other hand into her pocket, pulling out the small sewing kit. "Peter, hold on— It's okay, I've almost got it—" With trembling hands, she pulled out a needle already threaded with white floss.

There wasn't enough time to think, she just had to do it.

Quickly, Wendy pierced the dirty sole of Peter's foot with the needle before looping it through the slippery shadow. She worked as fast as she could, stitching the quickly fading shadow to one foot before starting on the other.

This was going to work. It *had* to work.

When Wendy bit off the end of the thread, Peter still remained motionless. Her own erratic heartbeat thudded in her ears as she waited, looking from Peter's ghostly pale face to the quickly fading shadow.

It continued to weaken, becoming less and less solid until it was truly just a shadow on the dirt.

"*Please, please, please*—" Wendy begged.

The shadow stirred and began to retreat under Peter. It disappeared, leaving nothing but the crooked stitches on the soles of his feet.

"Peter?" She reached for his arm, but he didn't move.

Tears clung to Wendy's lashes. "Peter—*please*," she choked. He needed to make it through this night, too. Wendy needed him to. Not just for the sake of her brothers, trapped back in Neverland, but for her, too.

Cupping his cheeks in her shaky hands, Wendy searched his face for any sign of life.

Peter's skin was so pale, his freckles nothing but specks of ash. His silvery hair framed his face in a cold glow.

Wendy leaned over him. "Peter!" She'd held up her end of the deal. She gripped his shoulders and gave him a rough shake. "Peter Pan, you wake up, *this instant*!" She'd reattached his shadow, now he needed to—"WAKE UP!"

Wendy felt it first: warmth slowly growing under her fingertips. She jolted upright, eyes frantic as she searched for more signs. Slowly, color started to return to Peter's skin. It practically glowed, sun-kissed and radiant in the darkness of the woods. Pink bloomed in his cheeks. The cuts on his lips and the dark circles under his splayed lashes faded away. His hair darkened back to shades of red and brown.

Peter gasped, sucking air back into his lungs. His eyes shot wide open, darting around the clearing before locking onto Wendy's. They danced with their luster of starlike pinpricks in a sea of deep, dreamy blue. "Wendy?" he breathed, reaching a hand for her. "You . . ." He squinted as if trying to decide if she was a dream.

Relief knocked the air out of her.

Peter plucked a twig from her hair. "You look awful," he told her, laughter already bubbling in his throat.

Wendy shoved his face. "You—!"

Peter caught her hand and stood up. He scooped her into his arms and spun her around in the air. Wendy gripped his shoulders, scared that she might fall, but then Peter was kissing her and all she could do was melt into it.

Shaky laughs shook through her tears. She wrapped her arms around his neck, savoring the tightness of his arms around her waist, the warmth of his skin, and the softness of his lips.

Peter leaned his forehead against hers. "Hey, no explosion this time," he said quietly. His wide smile was unabashed and cut deep dimples into his cheeks.

Wendy grinned. "So help me, Peter Pan," she said, gently shaking her head, "if you start this whole thing all over again, I will kill you myself."

He laughed and it sounded like music. "Noted," he said.

They landed on solid ground. When Peter leaned back to look her in the face, it was hard not to chase after him, to burrow back into his warmth.

"You did it!" Peter beamed.

Wendy could only nod and laugh, rubbing her blurry eyes with the heel of her palm.

Peter's head tipped to the side. "But *how*?"

Sniffling, her shoulders bunched up in a shrug. "It tried to take you—"

"Wendy?" The quiet, trembling voice came from behind her.

Alex stood there, knees wobbling under the hem of his hoodie. His fists, knotted into the long sleeves, covered his mouth as he stared up at Wendy with worried brown eyes. Behind him, Matthew and Joel still huddled close, their heads swiveling as they looked around the clearing. Ashley stood erect and tense, the muscles in her throat taut. Off to the side, Benjamin openly gaped at Peter.

"It tried to take you," Wendy repeated, "but we didn't let it."

"Are you all right?" Matthew asked, worry pinching his expression.

Wendy nodded, a relieved laugh escaping her.

Peter stooped down in front of Alex. "Everything is all right!" he said cheerily, placing a hand on the boy's small shoulder. "You were *incredibly* brave," he said, beaming at each of them in turn. "That shadow didn't stand a chance!"

"Is it going to come back?" Ashley asked, her voice tight.

Peter stood, his fists resting on his hips. Automatically, Wendy's eyes went to the ground beneath Peter—but, of course, it was nighttime and they were standing in the middle of the woods. There wasn't enough light to check for his shadow. Wendy's stomach gave an uneasy twist, but Peter's expression was confident.

"After what you did to it?" He waved a hand dismissively. "That shadow is too cowardly to try messing with you again."

The air shifted, the tension easing with relieved sighs and slumping shoulders.

Benjamin, however, still had the same bug-eyed look of astonishment on his face as he stared at Peter.

"Ben—?"

"Are you Peter Pan?" he blurted out.

Wendy froze. She looked at Peter.

"Who?" He glanced around, pointing a finger at himself. "Me?" His head tipped back and he let out a sharp laugh. "Of course not!" Slowly, he lifted off the ground, hovering in mid-air. Hands on his hips, head cocked, and eyebrows raised. "Everyone knows fairy tales aren't real."

Benjamin stumbled back, eyes bulging.

Sounds of shock and amazement went through the group. Their faces lit up with smiles.

Peter threw Wendy a wink. A slow smile curved her lips.

"Hello?" A distant voice rang out, causing everyone to jump. Alex was suddenly latched to Wendy's leg.

Far off, beams of light cut back and forth among the densely crowded trees. Voices bounced around the woods, accompanied by the soft thuds of footfalls and rustling under-brush.

"Is anybody out there?" another voice echoed.

"The search parties," Wendy breathed with a sigh of relief.

Peter landed soundlessly at her side. "I can't let them see me," he told her.

"No—you need to go," she told him, already pressing her hands to his chest.

Peter hesitated, a mixture of emotions flickering across his face.

Wendy felt it, too—the unwillingness to leave his side— but it was going to be a very long and complicated night, and

Peter's involvement would just make matters worse. Wendy gave him another gentle push. "Find me after," Wendy told him firmly, her fingers gripping the front of his shirt.

It took another moment, but Peter sucked his lips between his teeth and gave a curt nod. His T-shirt slipped between her fingers, and he flew off into trees.

The flashlights got brighter, joined by more voices and footsteps.

"We're over here!" Wendy called, waving her arm and squinting into the lights.

CHAPTER 22

Found

It seemed like only minutes before the entire clearing was filled with people. Their vehicles couldn't make it all the way in because of the dense trees, but they pulled up to the nearest logging road. Paramedics and cops swarmed Wendy and the children, asking questions and checking to be sure they were all right.

Wendy was worried they'd say something about Peter. She kept getting distracted from what the medic was asking her, cutting glances over to the kids being questioned by the cops. But every snippet of conversation she caught was distinctly absent of Peter. They exchanged looks and caught glances from one another between the cops and paramedics. They were all nervous, maybe even a little scared, but under that Wendy could feel the pulse of excitement and triumph. She felt it in her own veins and caught a glimpse of it in the smiles that flickered over their faces.

Even Alex was exceptionally brave, although he refused to let go of Wendy's leg. He was just a tiny form practically swallowed up by a blanket, but Wendy could see the longing in his large eyes. The same look as when she'd seen him holding the origami shark at the hospital.

One by one, their parents arrived, and they were loaded into cars to be taken to the hospital and further assessed.

Matthew and Joel spoke urgently to their mom about monsters as they were loaded into a police car. Ashley put on a brave face, but she was nearly silent, her whole body trembling as she reunited with her parents. Benjamin had a grin plastered across his face, which did little to soothe his mom. She kept touching his face, convinced he had a fever and was delirious.

Alex remained attached to Wendy until his father came trudging through the woods. Alex's father was a giant. He scooped up his crying son in his large arms, gently rocking Alex back and forth. From sheer exhaustion, Alex fell asleep with his head against his father's broad chest while Mr. Forestay spoke with an officer.

Wendy heaved a large sigh. The children were safe, and that was the important part. Even if they did tell the police what really happened, she knew no one would believe their stories.

The paramedics led Wendy away from the clearing and to one of the ambulances on the logging road.

Detective James wasted little time jumping right into his questions. It grated on her already raw nerves.

"So, you were taking out the trash," Detective James repeated, reading over his scratchy notes on a bright yellow pad. He wore a sleek black windbreaker with the sheriff department's seal on the back. Detective Rowan stood to the side in a matching jacket, speaking to one of the crime-scene investigators. "You saw someone in the woods behind your house, and just decided to follow him instead of calling the police?" He raised his scarred eyebrow critically.

"Yes," Wendy said curtly with a nod. "Ouch!" She jerked

her elbow away from Dallas the Paramedic as he dabbed at a cut.

"And then you heard the kids crying for help," he went on.

"Like I said, I lost track of the guy, but I just followed their voices," Wendy explained. She sounded confident. At least, she thought she did. She was getting better at this lying thing.

"And you didn't think to call anyone for help?"

"There's no reception all the way out here," Wendy told him, which was true.

Detective James hummed, his eyes roving over his notes again. "And you just found them in the clearing?"

"They were lost, obviously."

"And the kidnapper ran off?"

Wendy shrugged. "It's dark in the middle of the woods at night. I couldn't keep track of him." She'd heard Benjamin, Ashley, Joel, and Matthew give a similar story. Alex had only given nods and shakes of his head. They couldn't see their kidnapper properly. Joel said they'd been forced to wear blindfolds, to which the others quickly agreed. It was a flawed explanation, but the Astoria police officers seemed too relieved that the children had all been found safe and sound to start poking holes in their stories yet.

Except for Detective James.

He clicked his pen. "How did you get so banged up?"

"Running through the woods," Wendy told him, wincing as Dallas moved to a cut on her temple. "I fell a few times. It was dark, and I was scared."

Detective James observed her. Wendy sat there, staring back, afraid to move or blink under his watchful gaze.

"*Wendy!*" Her father's voice boomed in the distance, echoing off the trees. She started so hard, she nearly fell off the back of the ambulance. "*Where's my daughter?*"

Wendy jumped down. "Dad?" she called, trying to look between the people standing around, squinting in the bright headlights of the cars.

Mr. Darling came barreling into view, pushing people out of his way. "Wendy!" Mr. Darling took her by the shoulders, practically lifting her off the ground. Dallas quickly moved out of the way. "Are you all right?" he demanded, his wide eyes showing the whites as he looked her over. His hands clasped the sides of her head, her arms, her hands, taking inventory. "Are you hurt? What happened?" He stood over her protectively and everyone backed up to give them space.

"Dad, it's okay, I'm fine," she said, giving his arm a squeeze.

In her father's wake, Wendy saw Donald Davies jog up, looking pale and frazzled. His eyes darted around to all the cops and detectives.

Instinctively, Wendy shrank closer to her father.

Detective Rowan's attention swept to Wendy. She looked at Wendy, then over to Mr. Davies before her gaze settled back on Wendy. Almost imperceptibly, Detective Rowan shifted closer. Her hand moved to rest casually on her duty belt.

"Where's Matthew and Joel?" Mr. Davies asked, sweat glistening on his forehead.

"They're with your wife en route to the hospital," Detective James told him.

"I came as soon as they called me," Mr. Darling said. "We were on the other side of the woods, looking for the kids—but you found them?" His words spilled over one another. "I told you to stay inside when your mother and I weren't home!" he barked angrily, but Wendy could feel the way his hands trembled.

"I know. I'm sorry," Wendy said.

"Mr. Darling." Detective James stepped forward. "We—"

"I know where John and Michael are, Dad," Wendy said quietly. All eyes swung to her.

Her father froze, and she rushed on before he could get his hopes too high.

"They're buried under the big tree in the clearing," Wendy told him. Maybe if she said it softly, it would hurt a little less.

Mr. Darling's hands dropped to his sides. He stumbled back a step as if she had slapped him. His breaths sawed in and out.

She glanced at Detectives James. "I remembered," she told him, "when I saw the tree."

Detective James cut a look at Detective Rowan. Immediately, she called over two CSI agents and murmured an order. They headed for the clearing, but Detective Rowan stayed where she was.

Wendy's words hung in the air for a moment. Everyone was quiet.

Mr. Darling was rattled, but not surprised. Maybe he already knew and had just been waiting five years for someone to confirm it. He opened his eyes again.

Mr. Darling turned to Detective James. His face tried to pinch into the angry expression Wendy had grown to know well, but his chin wobbled and his eyes glistened. "What happened to them? Who did it? Was it the man who took the other kids?" he demanded, his voice thick.

"It was Mr. Davies."

All the eyes that had been glued to Wendy swung over to Mr. Davies.

Wendy braced herself, expecting him to immediately deny it, to argue and push back. Maybe he would even start shouting about his innocence.

Instead, Mr. Davies took on a sickly pallor. His eyes fell to the ground. He bent forward and buried his face in his hands.

"What?" Wendy's father was the first to break the silence, his attention bouncing between Wendy and his friend. His face scrunched up, sharp lines of confusion digging into his brow.

"Are you sure?" Detective James asked carefully, stony and serious. Detective Rowan silently slipped behind Mr. Davies. Wendy nodded, her fingers twisting into the hem of her shirt. "How do you know that, Wendy?"

Her hand found the acorn tied around her neck. "I remembered." The gunshots echoing through the snowy woods. Her brothers crumpling to the ground. Splotches of red on white snow. The glint of the rifle. Mr. Davies's signature red plaid. They were seared into her memory now, not soon to be forgotten. Probably never. A new set of nightmares to relive over and over.

Wendy wished Peter were by her side.

"She's telling the truth," Mr. Davies almost moaned, dropping his hands from his face. His eyebrows gathered in, his mouth twisted and miserable. "It was me." His eyes darted nervously among Mr. Darling, Wendy, and Detective James.

Wendy saw Detective James's hand go to his waist. Her father didn't move a muscle.

Mr. Davies swallowed hard. "I did it—it-it was an accident," he stammered. "I was hunting out of season—I had been drinking—I thought they were deer!" He spoke so fast Wendy could barely keep up. Mr. Davies buried his hands in his hair. "I panicked! I got a shovel from my truck and I—I—" He let out a groan like a wounded animal. "I wanted to confess," he said pleadingly to Mr. Darling. Wendy's father continued to stare. Deep red blotches bloomed on his cheeks. "But I had my two little boys at home, and my wife—"

Wendy felt no sympathy for Mr. Davies. She wasn't fooled by his words. He had thought only of himself. By not coming clean, he'd let her family suffer for years. Because he kept his secret to save his own skin, she and her parents had gone through years of mourning with no closure. He hadn't just taken John and Michael, he'd tortured her family. He'd let it happen. He'd watched as they'd borne the weight of losing John and Michael, and fell apart under it.

Saliva flooded Wendy's mouth like she was about to vomit.

Detective James stepped forward. "Did you kidnap Wendy and the rest of those kids?" he asked. His eyes were sharp, his expression severe.

"No! No, that wasn't me!" Mr. Davies said. Panic rose steadily in his voice. "I never laid a hand on Wendy or those kids! When she went missing, I didn't know what to think! I started second guessing myself. I thought maybe I had killed her, too, but I hadn't seen her body," he tried to explain.

Wendy flinched. The way he said it was so cavalier.

"I thought the police would find them for sure, that it was just a matter of time before they figured out it was me—but they didn't. Then those kids started going missing, and Joel and Matthew were taken—" Mr. Davies shook his head roughly. "I killed your sons, but I didn't touch those kids, you have to believe me," he begged Mr. Darling. Frantically, he turned to Wendy and took a step forward, his hands clasped together. "I'm so sorry, Wendy—I—"

Wendy recoiled.

Mr. Darling snapped out of his daze.

"*Don't you DARE come anywhere near my daughter!*" Mr. Darling snarled, his lips pulling back, baring his teeth. "*You killed my boys!*" It was a guttural roar. Spittle collected at the corners of his mustache. "*I swear to God, I'll—*"

Wendy's father surged forward, nostrils flaring, the tendons in his neck corded. Mr. Davies shrank back and his arms shot up to shield himself. Around them, police officers converged on Mr. Davies and blocked her father's path to him.

Wendy leapt forward and grabbed her dad's arm, trying to pull him back. "Dad, don't!"

Mr. Darling froze, but he didn't take his eyes off the cowering man in front of him. His barrel chest heaved up and down. Wendy held on to her father as tightly as she could, but it was like a child holding back a charging bull. "He's telling the truth. Mr. Davies didn't take the kids," Wendy said to Detective James.

"How do you know that?" Detective James asked, keeping his attention on Wendy's dad and Mr. Davies.

"The man who took me was the same person who was keeping the kids hostage in the woods," she said. She didn't know why she was coming to the aid of Mr. Davies, but it was true: He hadn't done it. Wendy was determined to be the bigger person. There was enough pain and hurt to go around for one night. "When I followed the man earlier tonight and saw his face, I remembered him," she lied. "It was the same man that had taken me from the woods."

"You know what the kidnapper looks like?" Detective James asked.

Wendy nodded.

He turned to Mr. Davies. "Donald Davies, turn around slowly and put your hands on your head," he told him. Mr. Davies gave Wendy one last mournful look before he did as he was told. Detective Rowan put him in handcuffs and dragged him to one of the cop cars.

Wendy knew she would have to give a description of some man she would have to make up. Give more statements, answer more questions. But, right now, she just wanted to get out of the woods.

Mr. Darling didn't move. He remained glaring at Mr. Davies's retreating back.

"Dad," Wendy said gently, tugging on his arm.

He turned to her, and Wendy could see pain, loss, and rage warring in his face. It glistened in his eyes.

"Can we go home now?" she asked in a small voice. "Please?"

Mr. Darling rubbed his nose on the back of his fist. With a stiff nod, he hooked his arm over her shoulders, holding her close to his side as they walked to his car down the road.

When Wendy and her father walked through the front door, her mother was sitting on the couch, her phone held up to her ear. She jumped and turned to them, the phone sliding from her hand. Mrs. Darling's brown hair was a rumpled mess. She was still wearing her work scrubs and her eyes were red, the delicate skin around them puffy. Seeing Wendy, she drew a shuddering sigh, her fingers pressing to the base of her throat.

Behind her, the television was on. The screen showed the crowded logging road in the middle of the woods, the camera panning across ambulances, police cars, and yellow tape. There, front and center, were John's and Michael's school pictures. The same ones the news had used when they'd first gone missing.

This time, the marquee read: BODIES FOUND.

Mrs. Darling's voice quaked when she spoke. "They called me." She blinked and tears spilled down her cheeks. "They think it might be John and Michael?"

Wendy walked past her father to where her mother sat on the couch. Steeling herself, Wendy tried to work up the courage to speak. Her hands opened and closed into fists at her sides. Her palms were slick with sweat. Her parents deserved some sort of explanation, something to make up for or ease the pain, but she didn't know what to say.

Her mother stared up at her, confusion and worry denting her brow.

With determination, Wendy sucked in a deep breath, but it rattled in her lungs and tightened her chest. She felt her eyes prickle, felt the burn in her throat. "I—" Her face crumpled. An uncontrollable sob choked her.

"I'm so sorry," Wendy blurted. Fracturing sobs overcame her. "It's all my f-fault, I'm sorry—I'm so sorry!" The words repeated over and over until they slurred together into nothing. Her body trembled and her chest bucked with cries as she wrapped her arms tightly around her middle.

The sheer shock on her mother's face softened.

Mrs. Darling's gentle hands pulled Wendy to her. Her knees sank into the couch and Mrs. Darling gathered her close. Wendy's body went rigid at first. She didn't know the last time her mother had touched her like this, couldn't even remember how it felt. But Mrs. Darling tucked the top of Wendy's head under her chin and wrapped her arms around her. Her hand rubbed her back in long, slow strokes. She hummed softly into Wendy's ear and everything in Wendy released.

She collapsed against her mom, clutching Mrs. Darling as she cried into her shoulder. Spit and tears soaked into the green scrubs.

"I'm so sorry," Wendy choked out. "It's my fault— I was supposed to be watching them— I was there—" Grief squeezed her like a vice. "I saw it happen— I couldn't remember— I couldn't— It's because of me we aren't a family anymore—"

"Shh, my darling," her mom said quietly into her ear. Her voice was somber and edged with pain, but tender nonetheless. She held Wendy close, continuing to rub her back as she stroked her hair with the other hand. "This is not your fault. None of this is your fault."

Relief and sorrow crashed through Wendy. She curled up against her mom. She had put so much energy and care into not letting herself cry for fear of never stopping. But now, the anguished cries shuddered through her body, and she let them.

"I'm so sorry, Wendy . . ."

Wendy wanted to argue, to say that her mom had no reason to be sorry, *she* was the one to blame for John's and Michael's deaths.

"We were trying to protect you, but we let you down," Mrs. Darling said. Wendy could only shake her head. She felt the sigh lift her mom's chest. "We let our own mourning distract us from taking care of you. You are *so* brave, Wendy Darling." Her mom gave her a small squeeze.

Mrs. Darling leaned back. Wendy felt her hands, cool against her flushed skin, cup her cheeks. Wendy hiccupped as she blinked through tears. She felt the weight on the couch shift. Her dad lowered himself next to them. One of his heavy hands settled on her back.

"You've been haunted by this for *so long*," her mom told her, thumbs sweeping away her tears. Mrs. Darling's smile was small but hopeful. "I want you to live, Wendy, not just endure."

It was more than Wendy could take, so she let herself give

in to it. She huddled against her mom, who continued to rub her back. Her dad's steady hand didn't leave.

"You found them, Wendy," her mom murmured against the top of her head. "They're safe."

They stayed there for a long while, Wendy pressed between her mom and dad, letting them hold her close. She felt like she was teetering on the edge of a black pit that threatened to swallow her whole, but every time she felt as though she was about to fall in headfirst, she closed her eyes and remembered John and Michael.

Wendy appreciated her parents' comfort, but after a while, it started to feel suffocating. She was overheated and thirsty. Her lips tasted like salt. She needed some space, some fresh air, and some sleep.

She gently untangled herself from her parents' arms and got up off the couch. "I'm going to go to sleep," she said through sniffles, wiping at her runny nose. "In my old room."

Her mom and dad exchanged looks.

"I'm okay," Wendy told them, and this time it wasn't a lie. She inhaled a deep breath and managed a small smile. "Really."

Her dad finally nodded and her mom gave her hand a small squeeze before Wendy went upstairs.

The unlocked door swung open easily. Wendy crept over to the bay window and crawled onto the bench. The sky was turning a periwinkle blue, creeping toward sunrise. Wendy leaned back against the wall and closed her eyes. She hooked her thumb around the leather cord around her neck and squeezed the acorn in her palm.

A cool breeze rolled in from the woods, carrying with it the smell of honeysuckle. A warm and tentative hand cupped her cheek. Wendy sighed and a smile curled her mouth. When she opened her eyes, Peter sat next to her, his legs dangling out the window. The first ray of sun washed over his skin. His shadow spilled across the bedroom floor next to Wendy's.

"Are you okay?" he asked. Every bit of his brilliance had returned, but that worried line between his brows was still there.

"Yeah," Wendy said. She paused and then shook her head. "I mean no, not really, but yes, I will be," she corrected herself. She sat up and hugged her knees to her chest.

Peter's thumb brushed the corner of her lips before his hand dropped to his side. "And your parents?"

"About the same, I'd say." She leaned closer. "Did you see what happened?"

Peter nodded. He watched her, eyes thoughtful and full of stars.

Wendy looked up into his face, trying to drink him in and memorize every inch of him. The upward curve of his nose. The faint point to his ears. The swirl of his auburn hair. The splash of freckles across his cheeks. She knew their time was running out, that he would have to leave and go back to Neverland. She desperately wanted to savor him for every last moment.

Wendy reached out and brushed her thumb against the crease in Peter's brow. His blue eyes blinked slowly. "When's all of this going to go back to normal?" she asked, bumping her knee against his arm.

Peter gave her a small grin. "Soon," he said. "I'm sure I'll go back to my normal shape and size when I get to Neverland."

Wendy shifted to lean against him. "I wish I could remember it," Wendy said. "Neverland, I mean. I still have that whole chunk of my memory missing. I wish I could remember what it was like, being there with my brothers . . ."

"Maybe you'll start getting the memories back now," Peter said with a small lift of his shoulders. "Maybe now that you've unlocked them, more will follow. Good ones. Happy ones."

"Maybe."

"Or . . ." Peter's grin quirked to a mischievous angle. He leaned in conspiratorially. "You could just come back with me to Neverland."

With that glint in his eye, it was hard for her to tell if he was being serious. Against all logic, hope jumped in her chest. "I could stay with you?"

"You could stay with me," he repeated.

"And I could see my brothers again?"

"Yes."

Wendy dragged her teeth over her bottom lip. Of course, it was too good to be true, or that simple. "But then they wouldn't be able to move on, would they?"

Peter held her gaze, but his smile lessened. "No."

Wendy nodded. "And neither would I . . ." It was a wonderful idea. Running away to Neverland with Peter. Being able to see her brothers again. Having no responsibilities. No real world to have to deal with. But it also meant giving up so much. Wendy let out a small laugh. "With my luck, we'd just kick-start this whole nightmare all over again," she told him.

Peter laughed and bumped his shoulder into hers. "Yeah, I guess that wouldn't be good."

"Well, you could just stay here and grow up," she said, heart fluttering. "With me."

Peter's smile was soft and sweet. Just for her.

She knew the answer before he could say it.

"I can't. I need to go back and take care of the lost kids. I want to," he corrected himself. "To look after them."

Wendy nodded.

"Growing up sounds awful anyway," Peter said casually, with a dismissive wave of his hand. He looked out over the backyard toward the woods. His eyes shone especially bright and the tip of his nose turned pink. "Though . . ." His head tipped and he looked at Wendy from the corner of his eye. "Maybe not so awful if it were with you."

Wendy laughed and wiped tears from her eyes with the heel of her hand. "Will you tell John and Michael when you see them?" she asked. "That I love them and think about them all the time?"

"I will."

With a shaky nod, Wendy threw herself against him and wrapped her arms tightly around him. Peter squeezed her against him. She laid her ear against his chest. His heartbeat thrummed, fast but steady. Wendy tried to ignore the dread weighing on her.

"You have to leave now, don't you," she mumbled against his shoulder. It wasn't a question. She leaned back to peer up at him.

Peter nodded. His hair tickled her forehead as he stared sadly into her eyes.

She wanted to tell him that she didn't think she could handle saying good-bye. That the thought of never seeing him again terrified her. That she needed him, that she wanted to keep him, but she couldn't talk past the lump in her throat.

Peter smiled. He cupped Wendy's cheeks in his hands. Her eyes closed. His kiss was soft. His lips tasted sweet as honeysuckle.

"I will never forget you," he whispered against her lips.

When she opened her eyes, he was gone.

Wendy wrapped her arms tightly around herself. The cool breeze drifting in from the woods tickled her skin.

It seemed impossible for things to go back to normal after a day like today. She knew there would be more questions in the morning. She would have to explain to Jordan what had happened, or as much as she could, anyway. They would probably argue some more, but it was more important for Wendy to explain herself and to keep Jordan as her best friend than to be "right" or the winner of the conversation.

There would be moving on after this. The summer would be over soon, and she would be starting college. A new life and a new path.

Wendy gazed up at the stars, and the stars gazed back.

Epilogue

"**U***gh!*" Jordan dramatically threw her hands into the air and collapsed back onto the grass. "*Why* did I let you talk me into taking this class?" she demanded, shouting at the sky.

"I didn't make you do anything," Wendy told her, chuckling as she neatly tucked her organic chemistry textbook into her backpack. She and Jordan had a tradition of eating lunch on the sprawling lawn between classes when the weather was nice. "We're taking the class because it's required for premed." Wendy fixed her with a stern look, her eyebrow cocked at a critical angle. "Remember?"

Jordan muttered darkly under her breath.

Their first year of college had passed by in a blur. Wendy and Jordan had been placed in the health sciences dorm, right down the hall from each other. It had only taken Wendy one week of classes before she'd gone to the registrar's office and signed up for premed. Jordan had whooped and hollered behind her as she filled out the paperwork at the front desk. It was embarrassing and wonderful.

It was mind-blowing, the difference a year could make.

The university had a great clinic onsite, and her student health insurance included counseling sessions. She'd been seeing the same psychologist all school year, twice a week, and she was slowly learning how to work through her anxiety disorder. After getting her memories back, Wendy had experienced a whole new set of challenges. Nightmares, flashbacks, and insomnia. She got a prescription to ease her anxiety and help her sleep, but some days were worse than others. It was hard. Sometimes it felt impossible, but she had help. She had her parents, she had Jordan, and she had her goals to focus on and pull her through. She was going to graduate with her bachelor's degree, go on to med school, and become a doctor. A pediatrician, specifically.

"I gotta head to my next class," Jordan grumped, stuffing papers haphazardly into her bag. She stretched her hands up over her head, fingers reaching toward the sunshine. "Are we still on to swim laps tomorrow morning?"

Wendy nodded. "Definitely." They'd both made it onto the swim team, but, coming from a small high school in an equally small town, they were far behind the varsity swimmers. It was nice, though, having a reason to really push herself. Not to mention, getting a good swim session in made it easier for her to sleep at night.

"Good." Jordan's teeth shone in a grin as she pulled Wendy into a bear hug. She'd been doing that a lot lately, ever since the night Wendy had found the kids in the woods. When Jordan had showed up to her house the morning after, there wasn't even a discussion of who owed who an apology, or who was sorry for what. Jordan just crushed Wendy against her in a spine-popping hug before barraging her incessantly with questions.

Wendy avoided the ones about Barry and what had happened to him. The occasional poorly done police sketch of Peter still caught her off guard around town when she visited her parents, hanging in a window or half torn from a lamppost. They were still looking for him, as he was the only one who had gone missing and hadn't returned, but active searches had stopped long ago. Most people shrugged him off as just a vagabond who had passed through town.

Jordan tugged on a lock of Wendy's hair as she pulled back. "You're getting awfully shaggy, girl," she said as she stood up.

Wendy smoothed her hands through her hair. "Yeah, I'm thinking about growing it out," she said with a shrug. It was already starting to brush her shoulders.

Jordan nodded. "New look—I love it!" she sang with enthusiasm. Wendy laughed and Jordan beamed. "I'll stop by after class!" she called with a wave as she headed back toward the brick buildings. "I need to show you how to make ramen in your coffee maker!"

"That's gross!" Wendy scolded.

"It's delicious!"

Wendy rolled her eyes but couldn't help chuckling. When Jordan disappeared from sight, Wendy flopped onto her back. She reached her hands above her head and tangled her fingers in the grass. This was her favorite spot on campus, where rosebushes lined the lawn.

Back home, she and her mom had picked out and planted two rosebushes in the backyard as a sort of memorial to John and Michael. John's were white and Michael's were bright yellow. Mrs. Darling spent a lot of time talking to the roses while pruning their leaves. Last time she was home, Wendy had even caught her dad doing it a couple of times when he thought no one was watching.

She watched the roses sway gently in the breeze and thought about Peter. She did that often. When things were quiet, her mind always seemed to drift to him. She'd had a handful of dreams about him, but when she woke up, she was only left with fleeting glimpses of starry eyes and a toothy smile. Many times she'd wished she had a picture of him, or something more substantial than her drawings to remember him by, other than the acorn that she still wore around her neck every day.

Wendy sighed. It nestled into the center of her chest reassuringly. The longing ache came back as it always did when she thought of him. Wendy closed her eyes and did her best to conjure up an image of him grinning. She thought about the small chip in his front tooth and the way the corners of his eyes crinkled. Wendy smiled as a breeze picked up, causing the grass to dance against her skin. The wind brushed against her cheeks, smelling sweet as honeysuckle. Under the rustling of leaves, Wendy could've sworn she heard the soft chirping of crickets.

Wendy's breath caught in her throat. She opened her eyes.

Acknowledgments

Lost in the Never Woods has been seven years in the making, during which I've grown, regressed, and changed. Throughout those years, many people helped this story grow, and, in kind, helped me grow. I owe thanks to so many of you.

Shelby Gagnon: You and your family took me in during one of the darkest times of my life. You introduced me to Astoria one weekend in spring, and I've been in love with those woods ever since. Without you, this story wouldn't exist.

To Kathryn Reiss, for being my guide throughout undergraduate and grad school at Mills. I decided to pursue writing when I was a high school junior and sat in on your Young Adult writing course. Without you, I wouldn't be the writer I am today.

To Marisa Handler, whose mentoring made Wendy's story come to life in beautiful and poignant ways. You were a grounding force when everything seemed impossible to reach.

To Ellen McAmis and Mackenzie Bronaugh, who staged a ridiculous intervention when they saw me struggling, but mostly for your unwavering love and loyalty. Thanks for all the belly laughs and tight hugs.

To Adwoa Gyimah-Brempong: Without you, I would never have survived grad school. You are amazing.

To Elizabeth Stelle and Tanya Lisle, my amazing writing partners. Thank you for encouraging me to continue writing and being with me through every twist and turn of getting this book published. You two are the real heroes.

To all my writing buddies at H.O.W.—Genny, Maggie, Manasi, Mary—some of the most talented writers I know, who created a community where I could improve my writing, explore distant places, and experience magic.

Super special thanks to Alison Morrison, one of my biggest supporters who freaked out with me when I got the official email during a very serious meeting. You have talked me down from several ledges, and I'm sure there are plenty more to come. Thank you for being the best Mom-ager I could ask for.

To Holly West, my phenomenal editor who helped take my story and spin it into gold. I still can't believe I found someone to work with who understands my stories and characters so fully—sometimes even better than I do. Working with you has been one of the best things to ever happen to me and my writing.

To Emily Settle, one of the best cheerleaders who happily shares in my freaking out when I message her with random thoughts and ideas. I hear you're the one who first found *Lost in the Never Woods* and shared it with the rest of the team, and for that I am forever grateful.

There's so many folks at Mac Kids who touched this story and made it shine. Perry Minella and Melanie Sanders for taking my words and making them decipherable—you two are the real MVPs. Raymond Colón for taking my story and turning it into an actual book I get to hold. Rich Deas and Mike Burroughs for creating such a beautiful cover and making a lifelong dream come true.

I also want to thank the other Swoon Reads team members, Kat Brzozowksi, Lauren Scobell, and Jean Feiwel. It takes a village, and you three have been in my corner this entire journey.

To the entire Swoon Squad, I love and appreciate each and every one of you. I am incredibly lucky to be part of such a supportive, talented, and kind group of people. You all are like my second family. A special shout-out to Prerna Pickett and Olivia Hinebaugh, who came to my rescue in my time of need. A huge thanks to Caitlin Lochner, who saved me in the eleventh hour.

And last, but certainly not least, my family. Without you, I would be lost.

heck out more books
hosen for publication
y readers like you.

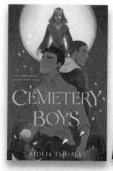

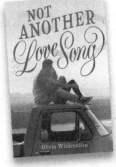

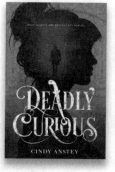